Bestowed
By
Love And Splendour

Bestowed
By
Love And Splendour

Gina Iafrate

Published by Gina Iafrate
Hollywood FL

Publisher: Gina Iafrate

ISBN:978-7752407-3-0
ISBN:978-1-77524-07-2-3

Cover Design: Gina Iafrate

Back Cover Design: Gina Iafrate

Originally published in the USA by Gina Iafrate
Hollywood FL

In Gratitude

This novel is dedicated to my husband, Mario, for his love, kindness, and support; for booking our travel excursion to the marvellous island of Sardinia where my inspiration for this book took place.

My young Architect grandson, Martin Trivieri, for information I needed regarding studying for his profession.

Drs. Bruce and Joanne Lennox, for assisting me on some of my research on the medical references.

"*Bestowed By Love And Splendour* by Gina Iafrate tells the story of a mother and wife who, just like many others, put her life on hold for her family. This is the story of many women who wake up later in life and realize that they lost themselves into marriage and motherhood. Valeria's story is even more touching because at the end of the day all her sacrifice and support was rewarded with bitterness and abuse."

"Through *Bestowed By Love And Splendour*, Gina Iafrate is telling all women in this position that it is never too late to start chasing those dreams you abandoned. To all the women in toxic and abusive relationships, I pray that you will one day find the strength to break free and find true love."

Faridah Nassozi for Readers' Favorite

CONTENTS

Chapter	Page
1 The Arrival	1
2 Tormented by Recalls	5
3 Wishing an Escape	17
4 Consumed by Guilt	23
5 A Cloud on Her Journey	29
6 Lucio's Reminiscing	39
7 The Tour Continues	43
8 Back in Niagara	47
9 Tricks of the Mind	49
10 Amazing Cagliari	57
11 Boris' Search for Contentment	61
12 Alcohol Bliss	65
13 Nature's True Beauty	71
14 Caught in Chaos	79
15 The News	85
16 The Halted Journey	89

17 Valeria Return Home   95

18 Lucio Back in Gloom   101

19 Valeria's World   107

20 Mr. Patty's Dilemma   117

21 Across the Ocean   121

22 Decision by Obligation   129

23 Valeria's Dilemma   135

24 A Resolution   141

25 Sardinia   149

26 Splendour in the Clouds   155

27 Teamwork   161

28 Overseas   165

29 The Shadows   169

30 The Meeting   175

31 At the Riverside   183

32 The Tour Resumes   187

33 Moving Forward   193

34 Florence and Susan   199

35 An Awakened Heart   203

36 Two Souls Brought Together   209

37 The Celebration   215

38 Alghero, Sardinia   221

39 Love Reigns   227

40 The Revelation   233

41 The Last Celebration   241

42 Buried Secrets   249

43 Country Invitation   255

44 Lucio's New Dreams   263

45 Niagara River   267

46 Secret Life   273

47 The New Horizon   279

48 Boris in Action   287

49 New Discoveries   295

50 The Countryside   301

51 The Meeting   305

52 Revelation   309

53 Loan Sharks   317

54 The Discovery   323

55 Lucio's Voyage   329

56 Brazil   333

57 The Ongoing Investigation   341

58 To Canada   349

59 Awaited Encounters   355

60 Life's Surprises   363

61 Love Conquers All   367

Chapter One

The Arrival

The helicopter landed smoothly on the helipad of the island of Sardinia when the pilot Ector, with his heavy German accent, in cheerful tones announced, "Here we are, Mrs. Abrosky."

The announcement jolted Valeria back to the present. Her troubled mind had drifted her thoughts back to Niagara, to the unpleasantness that now clouded her being once more. She glanced at her watch in disbelief.

"Oh, my! That was fast," she exclaimed.

"A one-hour flight from Rome, Signora." Ector grinned widely.

"That was fast! Thank you." She got up and curiously glanced out the window. The sun was as lustrous as the clear blue sky, luminously tying brilliance to the land. She quickly reached for her sun glasses as she needed protection from the glare of this land.

"I see two gentlemen waiting; probably my party," she said, animated, after observing and turning to Ector.

"Oh! Yes, I see."

"The shorter one is the Mayor of the city. I am not sure who the other is." He responded promptly as he picked up her luggage.

"Please, allow me," gesturing for her to exit before him.

"Thank you."

As they walked towards the terminal, Valeria noticed the men were approaching her, smiling.

"Welcome to our island, Mrs. Abrosky," greeted John Minerva, with a welcoming grin on his face, offering his hand to her in a hand shake.

"My pleasure, Mr. Minerva," Valeria replied.

He was a stout fellow, with broad shoulders, and thick eyebrows that overpowered his sunken grey eyes. His bronze tan accentuated his white teeth. She guessed, a man in his fifties.

As he spoke, the twang in his accent resonated the island's tone. Smiling, he nodded, turning towards his friend. He put a hand on his shoulder and proceeded to introduce his companion.

"This is our ambassador and consigliere, Lucio Alvani, my assistant."

"Welcome to Sardinia, Signora Abrosky." Alvani bowed, extending his hand.

She reciprocated kindly while admiring his features. He appeared older than the Mayor. A tall fellow with salt and pepper hair brushed back. His pear-shaped face included a playful dimple on his chin.

"My pleasure, Mr. Alvani," Valeria responded, gazing at his big brown eyes.

He turned to Ector, "Thank you, Signore, allow me to take the baggage from here on."

He took the luggage from Ector and together they walked towards the waiting limo. In no time they were whisked away to the Grand Hotel at the city center of Alghero.

A few polite inquiries about her flight were made; Valeria responded casually. She had been warned by her husband that the men here were skeptical about a married woman travelling alone. *But of course, according to Boris, nothing was ever right in life for a woman. How can anything be considered wrong when I am working to bring pleasure and knowledge to people's lives here and across the ocean.*

"Mrs. Abrosky, here you are. Your new domain for the month." He startled her away from her deep thoughts.

Before departing, with a serious look on his face he suggested, "Mrs. Abrosky, take a good rest. We will see you in the morning. Our honorable Mr. Alvani here will pick you up and be at your service," he said turning to his colleague. "After breakfast, we will go over the details of your assignment. You can check in with your office from the City Hall, and then take a tour of the city. Mr. Alvani will accompany you. *Va bene?* Okay?"

With a forced gracious smile, she responded, "Thank you, Signori, see you in the morning then."

***

After the long flight, Valeria was happy to have finally reached her destination, and was looking forward to some rest, if only her sudden mixed feelings would stop playing havoc on her conscience.

Once she entered the luxurious hotel, the inlaid marble from the floor to the wall pillars and trimmings stole her attention. There was a sudden cool and welcoming sensation in the air. The soft lighting from the crystal chandeliers emitted a calm soothing effect.

She opened the door to her room; the beauty of the decor enveloped her to no end. Immediately struck by it's size, "Oh! My God!" she exclaimed, while embracing herself. "This is spectacular, spacious, bright, and inviting!" Her eyes spotted a marvellous, shiny cherry desk on the opposite wall. She strolled across and slid her hand over its surface. *Is it real?*

A leather chair stood ready and inviting. She turned to look at the king size bed, which dazzled with inviting pillows over a heavy damask comforter. As her eyesight glanced over the walls, the continuity of glamour gleamed with a sparkle of soft gold paisley prints. A fresh breeze from the open window was gently blowing the sheers, reaching, caressing her flushed cheeks. Her eyes darted back and forth in awe. *I feel blessed to experience all this beauty.* A subtle energy force vibrated up and down her spine, boosting her tired body. Then a cloud of sadness appeared, floating over her head as if to obscure any happiness that might surface in her life.

A jolt in her conscience hit her like a piercing spade through her chest, close to her heart. "Oh! I must call Boris! she reminded herself. Reluctantly, she dialled her husband's number; the answering machine came on. She took a deep breath, relieved. She did not feel like talking to him just yet. "Hello, Boris! All is well. I am at the hotel. I arrived safely. Sorry I missed you. I will call you back in the morning! Bye for now," she forced herself to add her "love you," with a sigh of relief and mixed feelings.

She dropped herself on the king size bed, totally exhausted. Her eyes were dry and felt sandy from lack of sleep. The overnight flight from Toronto to Rome made her totally sleepless. Now she felt beat and badly needed to rest.

But Valeria tossed and turned; her brain would not shut down. The torment of her husband, Boris played in her mind; she rationed and justified her thoughts. *Here I can work in peace,* she thought. *I have actually gotten away from him!* But the flashbacks kept haunting her, forcing her to revisit the life she temporarily left behind.

Chapter Two

Tormented By Recalls

The picturesque landscaped home had been custom built along the Niagara river, and sat on one acre of land. Boris and Valeria Abrosky had hired an architect from Beverly Hills, California who was famous for designing distinctive and unique homes. Their land extended all the way to the ridge, sloping back overlooking the Niagara river, and the U.S. coast. The view was unobstructed and sitting in their backyard the roar of the river flowing was music to the ears; very relaxing and soothing. Here Mr. and Mrs. Boris Abrosky resided with their three children. Valeria Russo Abrosky had considered herself a very lucky woman in many ways. She was married to a workaholic husband and was blessed with three children: Rosy, Rino, and Danny. Other than slight disagreements with her husband, life wasn't all that bad. But now many years later, the air with Boris around had become suffocating. He was continuously barking, making her life unbearable and difficult. *Please God, help me to tune this out!* His voice was loud and clear, playing a disturbing tone in her ears like a broken record.

"You are at that computer again? That darn computer…" He would snarl, swearing and loudly bitching, banging his fist on the table. Lately, with the verbal abuse she saw heightened rage, the rage included punches and slapping around. Her body would be severely bruised; the black eyes she would conceal with makeup, and the swellings were treated with ice packs.

Valeria had been suffering silently since her husband retired. Everyone thought Boris was a wonderful man. How could she ruin the image he built for himself; who would believe her! After many years of marriage, who could imagine that her life would turn into a nightmare. The now empty nest, and Boris' recent retirement, had precipitated hell on earth for both of them. He was walking around brooding like a loaded black cloud ready for a major downpour. This had been his resolution now, for most days. She walked on eggshells around him, careful not to cause the thunder to explode into lightning. Their three children were all away and busy with their education and their own interests. They kept in touch regularly by phone and emails. How could she complain about their father? They respected and admired him as the CEO he was, in and out of the home when they were growing up. "A darn good worker and provider," was how grandmother used to praise him. "Mother! Yes! He is a good provider. I agree."

At this time in their lives, only she noticed how he had changed. Boris was a heavy set, tall fellow, with wide shoulders, and wore an impressive air of authority. His dark eyes complimented his complexion. In his own egotistic way, he loved his family, though work and high achievement were his priority. He had been chosen fresh out of university by the auto industry due to his high achievements, graduating with honours. His superiors recognized his high performance and rewarded him with promotions, and in no time, he had moved into a management position. Boris' soul became inebriated by success; with every step he moved higher like an alcoholic. With every promotion, he returned home with a big grin on his face.

"Valeria, I did it again!" He would announce, happy as a lark. "I have to get to the highest position. A CEO you will soon see and be ever so proud of your husband."

His self-praise of fame and glory was his main focus. To have power and control over his peers gave him the greatest satisfaction. Valeria as his wife should have been happy for him. Shaking her head, she would think, *this man is totally obsessed. He wants me to follow him and assist him in his needs, to his convenience, and always be present to jump to his demands.* She had raised his children practically alone, while he travelled to and from his important meetings and conferences. Taking care of the household chores and the demands of raising children kept her busy and her days were full. By the end of each day she would drop exhausted into her bed. As the years flew by, she had a rude awakening when she found herself with much time on her hands. Her husband was often away, and their grown children were also away pursuing their dreams.

Sometime before, after booking a Christmas getaway for the family with World Travel Agency, the owner, Mr. Patty, had informed her he was short of help.

He had asked her if she could fill in a few hours a week while a staff member was on maternity leave. He knew Valeria had experience in the field from her younger days. The job was meant to be temporary. The girl she was covering for eventually did not return, and soon Valeria discovered she was enjoying this new turn in her life. Much to her surprise, her hours increased, and she soon began to outperform herself.

Once Boris was engrossed with his own work, her job wasn't an issue or threat to him. But from that famous day when he was called into the boardroom meeting and given a notice with the date to prepare for his retirement, and his boss announced the company would host a retirement party for him, Boris became a different person. That would have been great for anybody else, but an absolute no-no for Boris Abrosky. After receiving the news, his heart began beating erratically, as if almost jumping out of his chest. Boris tried to control his emotions. He would excuse himself and pretend to have a conference call from China. Later he retired to his private office, closed the door, sat at his desk staring, in a daze, at all the awards of merits and trophies sitting on his book shelf; a reflection of his remarkable success. He crossed his arms and leaned on his elaborate walnut desk, put his head down and broke down sobbing like a baby.

My life is over.

He cried for hours, until his eyes had no more tears to shed. *I am not going home*, he muttered to himself at the end of the day. In low spirits, he drove around trying to calm himself. It was the month of July; the sun was still beaming in the sky and it was scorching hot. He wore a pair of dark sun glasses. He spotted a bar on the outskirts of town, parked, and walked in. He ordered and quickly guzzled down a few shots of vodka until his brain dulled and his anxiety subsided. Since this change in his life, only God could now help him.

***

Valeria on the other hand, was glorifying her career. Rosy, her daughter was happy for her. Many times, she had expressed her admiration and would say to her friends, "My mom, with her new interest is a new woman; vibrant, motivated, and accomplished." She was close to her mother and came to visit for weekends, alone, or at times inviting along some of her classmates and occasionally, a boyfriend. She was a good daughter. The boys were more like Boris, and like him, they were dedicated to accomplishing their achievements with hardly time for anything or anyone else. Valeria suffered silently. She didn't like to talk about the unpleasantness in her home with anyone. She also spared her children much, especially Rosy. At work where she escaped, her deep misery showed in her sorrowful face, especially since the tyrant husband had retired. The escape that work provided had become like her saviour. The walls in her home often closed in on her, suppressing even her breathing. Being out, meeting people, doing research, and exploring glamour holiday places made her come alive. The actual placement of her clients around the world was fascinating and enchanting to her. Their expressed pleasure and gratitude fulfilled her to no end.

At this stage in her life, Boris had become a big problem. Through her kind nature, she justified his behaviour. *Perhaps he is not able to cope with retirement.* Sometimes she truly felt sorry for him. When he worked at his prominent position, it certainly filled his needs. He would come home tired, dropping his briefcase on the front console, to swiftly get out of his stiff suit and tie, into comfy lounge clothing. With a big smile on his face he would walk into the kitchen. The aroma of freshly made tomato salsa for pasta and rolled veal *bracioli* filled the air. After removing the lids to check what was cooking, he would often grab her in a hug and kiss her passionately.

"How is my favourite girl? Honey, it's good to be home!" He would grin, delightfully fulfilled. No one could deny he was a man to be admired. He was always impeccably groomed with his Armani suits and designer shirts and ties, and always ready to please others if they requested his assistance. This gained him much admiration and respect from the people he interacted with daily who looked up to him. Always ready and charming, he easily won everyone over. He was the pillar at their church, going to communion every Sunday, and a good supporter of charitable causes. Now he had turned taciturn, brooding, cross, menacing, resenting even his own shadow.

She was the only one that was aware of these new changes, a new side to the real Boris; a process two years in the making. She had found him crying at times, deeply demoralized, depressed. Her offers to help or her suggestions irritated him more, especially if she suggested he sees a counsellor or the doctor.

"Look Val, I am not crazy and there is nothing wrong with me. I just feel like the rug has been pulled from under my feet. I almost have no reason to live."

"How can you speak such stupidities, Boris! You have me. I need you, the children need you. Our home needs you. Stop the nonsense and see what to do with yourself!" She couldn't push his buttons too much before he would turn violent on her.

He always apologized and hated himself after his rage spurts.

Of late she had become his punching bag.

"Valeria, please forgive me, I can't help myself; I feel useless. I have become nothing; no one needs me anymore, not even you," he would sadly express.

"Boris, stop feeling sorry for yourself. You should be grateful for what you have. Why don't you do some voluntary work, pass on your knowledge. Eh!" Valeria would reason with him trying not to lose her patience. On some serene days he would be meek. His eyes pleaded for forgiveness and looked pitiful, with a sorrowful face like a beaten old dog.

He often made Valeria feel guilty for keeping a job; he felt she should devote herself to him and him only. Lately, she had been getting up at five in the morning trying to finish her assignments before going to work. This allowed her more free time on evenings for Boris. Since his shifting moods, she had been sacrificing much to avoid the pressure from him, and her boss too. Mr. Patty had also become difficult lately, as if she needed that. Yes, he was the president of the travel agency. There were expectations to be met; lately with the online bookings things were a bit more difficult. The pressure was on, more than ever. Cruise bookings and bus tours were also their speciality. It took a lot of research to locate, accommodate, and properly fulfil the demands of their many customers. The double pressure and stress for Valeria was highly accumulating, especially with Boris' difficulties. Mr. Patty had been more demanding, needing revenue to pay to the company franchise World Holidays. He always set a high sales projection, and the tension vibrated onto the staff. Regardless of the demands and obstacles, Valeria did not want to give up her work, especially when Boris acted up. Putting up with his bad moods all day was difficult and challenging; work was a good outlet for her.

"Boris, please! You know I need to finish this research for my clients! Be patient, I have a deadline for this couple's honeymoon trip."

"I don't give a damn about your clients' deadline! I want to be served breakfast! There is no smell of coffee or no sign of cooking in this kitchen. All I see is my wife in la-la land with that damn computer."

Valeria would immediately stop what she was doing to attend to her husband, even if she was under pressure to complete her task at hand. Although she was passionate about her career as a travel agent, she tried to serve her husband like a dutiful wife. Therefore, lately she had chosen to work from home, to be there to accommodate him. But it wasn't working out; the situation was getting too tense. Valeria possessed a brilliant mind. She moved swiftly with her slender built and her mop of long blond hair covering her shoulders. Regardless of the inner turmoil, once on her job, her brown eyes shined, and her infectious smile was enhanced by her plump lips. Her colleagues liked and admired her. The customers sought her out. Boris with his harshness was always putting her down, trying to crush her intelligence.

"Your stupid place there, working on such a small percentage as if trying to make ends meet; it beats me." He would walk around the kitchen in the morning while she prepared his breakfast, talking away continuously, always belittling her and trivializing her passion for her job. Since he retired he wanted his meals on time, and his wife to be at his disposal as always. *Why had the auto company forced him to retire?* The stamina to work was still evident in his physique. The void created had sent him illogical. Valeria knew it did not sit well with him. He missed the power he enjoyed as the big chief who was always in command. She knew her husband was used to big board meetings, giving orders, and closing big deals, and this enhanced his manhood. In the past he would come home all excited. Sometimes he would take her in his confidence, especially when he returned from his China trips. He would relate to her the meetings, the different strategies they would put into play, how the executives would listen without blinking an eye, how it took a lot of careful explanation and honesty to deliver what they wanted. Then the deal would be closed. In retrospection he would narrate that his previously difficult clients would eventually shake hands on the huge deal, with a big grin on their faces.

"Let them declare victory by the small break we give them. We gain by winning them over, gaining their full confidence."

Boris travelled extensively when he worked. Valeria occasionally accompanied him on conventions, and she would be at his side, helping with client promotion. Since she started to work at the travel agency, she didn't mind remaining behind while he travelled. With him away, she could concentrate on her own interest. Her work was rewarding for her. Now, since his retirement, she found his methods had totally changed; his manner of dictatorship had turned him into a more arrogant man, especially towards her. Without his work, Boris seemed to hit rock bottom. He had no other hobbies or interests. Whenever Valeria tried to pacify him, it didn't work. When he slipped into his somber mood, his days became dark. He was unpredictable and could explode at any time. She would often think, *he seems jealous that I still have a career and he doesn't.*

She had just celebrated her fifty-seventh birthday and her husband, ten years her senior, had now been forced to forget his daily high work expectations. Since his retirement, his life had changed and he was in denial. He was acting as if he was much older than sixty-seven and getting nastier with each passing day. He moved about the house with a long face looking for opportunities to start arguments. Oh yes, he was more than ready to explode at every opportunity, regardless of whose fault it was. *Why can't he accept this new life and find a new interest?* Valeria would often rationalize. And to make matters worse, he was now constantly whining about old age and the aches and pains that came along with it.

"Valeria, I need you to pay attention to me! You don't feel what I feel; you are heartless and have no sympathy," he would say, often blaming Valeria for his newly acquired insecurities. His behaviour was shattering her nerves. She would swallow hard while patiently trying to soothe him.

"Dear, dear, calm down! I will get to you soon," she would plead while clicking away at her computer, wishing him quiet.

Oh, how he stood in her way! One morning before she had left for work, as she entered the kitchen, there he was, sitting at the table waiting to be served, with fork and spoon in his hands like a spoilt child. She took one look at him and could not believe her eyes. *Oh my God, how has he become this way?* At times, she was fearful.

In all the years they had been married, he was old fashioned and still believed that the man ruled. But she had never seen him this bad.

Boris was an only child. His parents obeyed his every demand and he always got his way. Valeria had recognized his personality flaw since they were dating, but she chose to ignore it and hoped he would change once they were married. His father had been the same; Boris modelled himself after him in many ways.

His parents had immigrated to Canada from St. Petersburg, Russia. His mother had been a nurturer, always willing to please, and that is how he expected his wife to be. When he was absorbed in his demanding job, he did not bother her as much. Although Valeria had been somewhat contented in the marriage, her resentment was building up lately, faster than she noticed, especially since the physical violence began. When her mother was alive, and Valeria would disclose her feelings about her marriage and her husband's misgivings, mother was quick to reprimand her on the contrary.

"Valeria, my dear, why do you complain? He is a hard worker and a good provider. He is a good father to the children; what more do you want?"

If Mom could see his behaviour now, I am sure she would no longer condone it.

"Valeria, you don't realize how good you have it. Be thankful and count your blessings. When he wants his food, give him his food! Besides, isn't food the way to a man's heart?"

Valeria would shake her head and go along with what was expected of her. *I guess mother was right. After all, I am married to him!* He had been the only one she had ever dated; her father had been extremely strict with his old-fashion custom. He did not approve of his daughter dating different men. They were Italian immigrants; Valeria was born in Canada. Her older sister Maria was born in the old country. She had married an Italian fellow and moved to Toronto. The rules were set by her father. To be a good girl she found herself married to Boris, who had a good job, and was a hard worker. *That is what you need!* This was what her Dad had dictated to her. Her mother and father had passed on now. She had no one to talk to anymore in spite of their old-fashioned demands.

A couple of mornings ago, Boris got up earlier than usual. She was still in bed sleeping when she was awakened by a terrible racket coming from the kitchen. She threw the covers off and forced herself out of bed to go check and see what was happening. She peeked outside through the window, it was pitch black out there. *What time is it?* She muttered to herself. *It's still so early, why is he up?* She glanced at the clock; it said four thirty in the morning. "God almighty, what is he doing down there?" She made her way down the stairs, only to find her husband halfway up a ladder with a pail in his hand.

"Boris what on earth are you doing up there! What has gotten into you at this hour!"

He had a rag, a hammer, and a pail in his hand. In a flash the wet rag landed right on top of her head. She tried to cover her face with her arm, just as the same wet cloth splattered dirty water all over her face.

"Can't you see the roof is leaking and the rain has not relented all night? The ceiling is ready to collapse and you sleep without a care in the world." He shook his arm down at her, retorting, and grandly accusing her.

She shook her head from side to side, befuddled. With the back of her hand, she wiped away the dirty water as it streamed down her face. She snapped back at him. "It's because of your negligence and lack of interest in our house over the past two years, and before that, your job!" A lot of the repairs around the house had been ignored. "The roof is certainly not my department."

The skies had opened up during the night. The rain had been relentlessly pounding on the shingles. He had placed buckets wherever there were leaks. A strong wind had picked up, furiously blowing from the lakeshore which made matters worse.

Boris was not one to take things lightly. Valeria swallowed hard as she didn't know what to do. "I guess I better start to mop up the excess water." Leaks from the ceiling were damaging the wall plaster, expanding in areas everywhere. She took a deep sigh, hoping the buckets Boris had placed all over would take care of the leaks and soon the storm would settle down. It had never been this bad. Once most of the water was mopped dry, she turned around and announced, "I am going back to bed, and when you are done you can come too."

"Go! Go! If you were a good wife you would put some coffee on! Never mind, I will do it myself!"

"Boris, it's five in the morning, but if you want coffee I will make coffee." She walked across to the stove to get the coffee pot going.

His somber mood matched the cloudy menacing sky out there. After she poured his coffee he took one sip and got up from his chair, infuriated. Valeria was startled. She thought a bolt of lightning had hit him. He slammed the mug down, spilling the dark coffee over the white table cloth and the chair where he was sitting. He turned to her in a mad fury and started to slap her about. "All I asked for was a cup of coffee, and what I get from my wife is coloured water! Is this coffee? Tell me!"

Valeria, ducking from his flying back hand striking her left and right, darted here and there in the kitchen putting her arms around her face trying to block the blows. Then like the furious wind blowing outdoor, he grabbed his car keys and headed for the front door. "Going out for a good cup of coffee," he shouted back, slamming the door behind him.

Her flushed cheeks now bore wail marks. The tears streamed, reflecting her deep pain. Her legs buckled and down she went on the floor like a shrivelled old broken tree branch. She cried out aloud in total despair. *I must get away from him!* Sadness sank deep into her soul, and her heart felt shattered.

She didn't know how long she lay there on the floor; her eyes staring into emptiness. "There has to be a solution," she muttered to herself. Later she forced herself up and made her way to the bedroom.

I need to work out a plan.

Chapter Three

Wishing an Escape

The rain had relented, and the wind subsided. The sunrays began peering through the scattered clouds claiming its place in the almost clear blue sky. After all the night rain, the air was now crisp and clear. Valeria, in her solemn despair sat on the chair beside her bed watching the morning resolve itself. As her limp body fought for her mind not to slip into the abyss of sorrow, she put her palms together and implored, "God Almighty, please guide me and tell me what to do?" Today in this sombre mood, she could not think straight. She thought to herself, *I must run away somewhere as far as I could, either on foot or by car, and get lost some place else where he would not be able to reach me. I just cannot continue to live with this strange husband of mine.*

She had no one to confide in; her sister wasn't particularly close to her. Maria had four children and a husband to worry about, she did not need more problems. *The children! But why worry the children?* She continued muttering to herself. *I need to do something, anything!*

***

After nursing her sore face with icepacks, she felt disheveled, with a low morale. She forced herself to tidy the kitchen. There she glanced the computer where it sat idly waiting with her unfinished work. She shook her head. *My focus this morning was to get some work accomplished; now it was futile.* A sensation of

17

cold and hot flashes zipped up and down her spine. *The pest will soon return,* she thought. She got up from the chair, disoriented, heading for somewhere, anywhere, when the shrill ring of the telephone startled her. Reluctantly she picked up the receiver though she was in no mood to talk to anyone. She feared her raw, out of control emotions would give her away. She had been crying a lot lately and her tears resumed spontaneously.

"Hello," she answered in a long drawn out and tired voice.

"Valeria!"

"Yes?"

"It's Mr. Patty, good morning! How are you?" Her supervisor asked in a peachy tone.

"Oh, good morning, Mr. Patty," she tried to sound more lively and pleasant. Lately he had become the source of her second main irritation.

"Valeria, I have some good news! I have a request for a tourist promotion on a historical place in Sardinia, starting from the city of Alghero and carrying through the entire island."

"Oh! I have heard of Sardinia," she heard her voice change tone. "I read an article in the travel magazine the other night. They are running a campaign to heavily promote tourism there."

He was animated.

"I feel you are the perfect selection for this assignment, Valeria. Would you take it? Unfortunately, I was not given much notice. I need to know by tomorrow, otherwise they will contact some other agent in the U.S. The Mayor personally contacted me this morning. They will provide us with an office at the City Hall, and of course, assistance with an escort at your disposal, and hotel accommodation. Our office will bear the cost of your flight."

Valeria's heart wanted to leap out of her body. *Where did this come from? Is it the universe out there gifting me?* There was nothing she would like more than to go on this work trip, to get away, and get lost for a while. *Was this the answer? Did God send me this opportunity, to take me away from this horrible situation to the other side of the world, to that heavenly island I have always admired from magazines? I always imagined myself sitting close to the Mediterranean Sea.*

The girls at work had been talking much about this new destination. They were always looking for new packages to offer their clients. All these thoughts rushed through her confused mind in a chaotic manner. Then her brain began working in reverse gear, against her dreams, driven by her loyalty, duty, and demand as Boris' wife. *My husband will go berserk!* Another shiver flushed through her body. She held her breath for a moment. *I need to think fast.* She put the phone down, speaker on, while bringing both her hands up to ruffle her hair, thinking. *My brain needs to rationalize here!*

"Mrs. Valeria Abrosky, are you there?" asked Mr. Patty, loudly and impatient.

"Mr. Patty, yes! Yes, I am here! Can I let you know tomorrow? I just want to relay the information to my husband."

"I guess."

She sensed his annoyance. Most people would jump to this kind of request; she should have. *Why the hesitation? Is it not what I needed, a chance to get away from him?* The fumed thoughts rushed through her head.

"Please get back to me as soon as you can, otherwise I would need to select someone else." His tone had switched from excited to almost threatening.

"I understand. I will call first thing in the morning."

She put the phone down and began daydreaming of the marvellous island she had always admired. She pictured the scattered islands around Sardinia and all she had read, but never visited. A muscle twitch tugged at her sore face, reminding her of the bruises. Trying to deny the pain, she thought of Boris, and her hope of any happiness started to dissolve. *He will never go for this. Am I crazy to get excited? If only mom was here.* She needed badly to talk with someone about this new turn of events. *I guess I will have to call Rosy, who else?* The boys are of a different mindset. She forced herself into a better mood and picked up the phone once more, this time to dial her daughter's number.

"Rosy, how are you dear?" She had promptly picked up.

"Mom, I am fine. I have been up all night completing an assignment. What's up? You sound down."

"Oh, actually I have some good news. Guess what? Mr. Patty wants me to cover a tourist promotion tour in Sardinia!" She wasn't going to bother Rosy with her low morale.

"Mom, that is great! What an opportunity! When are you leaving?" Her voice echoed with excitement.

"Leaving? I am not sure. Did you forget about your father? You know how he is. He will never agree to it."

"Mom, forget about Dad! Just go for it! Never mind him. It's time you stood your ground! Just tell him you are going, and that is that!"

Rosy knew how difficult her father had been; she had observed him the few times she had returned home to visit. She was certainly not sympathetic to his role as father, or husband.

Her mother never complained to her. She would cringe at how he spoke to his wife with selfish demands. She hated to admit to herself, and her mother, that it was not pleasant to be around him. His huge ego had been crushed lately, and his behaviour was ridiculous and nasty towards her also. *Mom, poor mom,* she thought. He orders her around as if she is his slave. Now that he was retired the ugliness was pouring out of him. He had been embarrassing and obnoxious when she visited the last time with some of her friends, not to mention her boyfriend. She had decided to reduce her visits, just to avoid him. Her brothers didn't go home too often so they couldn't tune in to the happenings. They were self-centered like him. Their sports came first, and they were obsessed with their fitness regime at the club. Their string of endless girlfriends, also contributed in keeping them distracted from what was going on at home. She observed that her brothers modelled their father.

"Mom, don't question it! You deserve it. It's such a wonderful opportunity; please don't chance losing it."

"I know dear! I really would like to go," responded Valeria.

"Never mind waiting for tomorrow morning mom, call back Mr. Patty now, and tell him you accept his proposal."

"Oh, Rosy! You make it sound so easy!"

"Of course, it is easy! You do what your heart desires; just go for it Mom!"

Rosy was young and of today's world. She was right; she had observed her mother over some time and always suspected her suffering under the tyranny of her father. She also noted it was getting worse with time. She did not approve of a passive woman being submissive and playing martyr. Deep down she felt sorrow for her mom. Many times, she watched her mother being victimized by the big CEO jefe, her father. Oh yes, he had even tried to control her. He would want to know who she dated, and what she was doing with her life. With her strong personality, she was driven to act contrary to his commands.

Valeria felt encouraged, but how was she going to swing it! Fighting her fears, and despite her weakness, she picked up the phone and called Mr. Patty.

"Mr. Patty? This is Valeria. I accept the assignment! Please get back to me with all details, and also, go ahead and book my flight."

Forcing herself to be brave and determined, a burst of energy surged through her body. She was not to care what Boris would say or do. It was well overdue for her to live her life the way she wanted. She nodded her head in agreement just to assert herself. *Mother would probably not approve. Sorry mom, I need to do what I have to do before I destroy myself!*

Two weeks later, there she was! After she had flown into Rome from Toronto, a connecting private helicopter had picked her up. They landed on the jewelled island of Sardinia. Just before the landing while surfacing the sea, her eyes became magnetized to the lushness on the many shaped small islands that had emerged through centuries from the Mediterranean Sea.

"Oh yes, Mrs. Abrosky, this place is the paradise named Sardinia," continued boasting Ector.

"I shall see if it is what I have been told." *The hell with Boris and his tantrums,* she thought. *God knows I need to be away from him,* she tried to reassure herself.

Chapter Four

Consumed by Guilt

Now Valeria was in her hotel room, finally alone. Her eyes were getting heavier, and she was slowly drifting away with exhaustion. The unpleasant memories kept churning to torment her. Her body finally succumbed, sending her into deep sleep, dreaming about what tomorrow may bring.

A knock on the door startled her. She looked around her new surrounding feeling disoriented for a minute. She didn't know where she was. Her body felt battered. She stretched out and took a deep breath trying hard to clear the grogginess, hoping whoever was there would go away. When a heavier knock persisted, she immediately sat up and gathered her thoughts. "Oh! My God! I must have overslept!"

She jumped out of bed and slipped into her robe. Wobbling in her footsteps, she opened the door forcing her eyes open, and there stood Signor Lucio Alvani.

"Good morning, Mrs. Abrosky," nodded Alvani with a warm smile.

"Mr. Alvani! Good morning!" responded Valeria, embarrassed. "*Scusatemi!* I must have slept in. What time is it?"

"Not to worry. Actually, it has to do with your time change. If you ask me, we should have let you rest for today. Please, take your time. I will wait for you downstairs in the lobby."

"I am sorry, I will get ready quickly."

She noticed Alvani was in a suit and tie attire. These Sardinians here seemed to dress on the formal side, making her conscious of her own dress code. She tried to put herself together, the best she could in a frantic hurry.

In no time she was downstairs, wearing a flowing blue sundress complimented by a casual linen top, and a white hat to shade her from the beaming sun. Smiling gracefully, she joined Mr. Alvani.

"*Mi dispiace,* sorry, apologies for the tardiness."

"*Ma per carita,* no problem," he responded.

Once her body got into motion, energy seemed to flow back through Valeria's tired legs. She made a mental note to have no more thoughts of Boris. She was going to apply herself to do an excellent job working with these gentle people. Mr. Patty expected only the best from her. The footing on the cobblestones was hard; she tried vigorously to keep up the pace with her chaperone. She sensed when Alvani would occasionally turn towards her in scrutiny, gazing with a keen eye as if trying to figure out her thoughts.

"Mrs. Abrosky, *tutto bene*? All is well?" This was their favourite phrase.

"Oh yes, all is well, thank you."

"Compliments! If you permit me to say so, Signora, you look splendidly appropriate, beautiful like our island!"

"Thank you, but in what way, may I ask?"

"There is only love and splendour here, all offered by nature."

"I can't help notice you are wearing our island colours: blue, white, and yellow. We have lots of sunshine here, and the most beautiful sites. The many shades of blue of our sea are all around us. There are marvellous cliffs, and red rocks that form our famous caves, lush greenery on the hills, and rocky terrain all around. You will soon discover it all when you tour this heavenly place."

"Mr. Alvani, I cannot wait. I will be here for one month; a long time it seems. I should be able to cover the entire island. Wouldn't you say?"

"All I can say to you is that most people that come here don't want to leave." His forehead creased as he spoke, almost as if he was warning her.

Valeria listened attentively. "Is that so? Well! I will let you know." She thought to herself, *you could be right! If you knew the hell I live with, I may not want to go back!*

They pulled up in front of a renaissance building that stood four floors tall. White stucco, ornate Roman columns; it was a masterpiece of antique architecture to admire. They noticed Mr. Minerva smiling and waving, waiting for them. After the greetings, the aroma of delicious coffee trailed to her nostrils. Valeria's stomach began to growl; she was starved. Her cravings were soon appeased by a lovely spread of tastefully prepared food: crispy bacon and eggs, with delicious crusty breads, green and black olives were mixed in, an array of sharp cheeses, fresh orange juice, and a selection of fragrant coffees.

Afterwards, a young photographer, Enzo Artini, arrived in an Alfa Romeo. The Mayor introduced Enzo who smiled eagerly with her.

"Enzo will be your chauffeur. He has been assigned to drive you and Mr. Alvani to the different destinations, Mrs. Abrosky."

"Oh! How delightful," she said, admiring the young man's enthusiasm.

Enzo was a tall and slim young fellow who had a smart peppiness about him. A camera hung off his shoulder. He spoke English with a pleasurable accent to Valeria's ears. His black hair accentuated his cheekbones that seem to pop out of his olive skin. His hazel brown eyes matched the islander look.

***

The tour commenced punctually, but slowly. Lucio meticulously and eagerly explained the history of each place they visited, from the main attractions of the city of Alghero, to the port and the country side.

"Alghero is a medieval city famous for its port; the main entrance for travellers by sea to enter Sardinia from the main land. The Piazza Civica is a must see, with it's palaces such as the Town Hall and Palazzo d'Albis, The Cathedral and its Gothic construction. Santa Maria in Gothic construction, with it's aisles lined with opulent columns. We must make our way to the Ramparts, to indulge in the panoramic cliff top view of Capo Caccia. I will be explaining to you as we go along. You will soon discover, Mrs. Abrosky, the history and beauty here are endless," continued Lucio Alvani.

Valeria followed in awe, taking pictures with the help of Enzo, and jotting down notes as fast as she could, marvelling at the architecture from centuries past that she never imagined. There was a lot of history here to attract tourists. She slowed her steps for a moment placing a hand on Lucio's arm, intending to focus his attention,

"Look at those octagonal domes, look at the secular columns, so precisely carved and installed, it's amazing. I don't know where to look first," Valeria expressed, shaking her head in amazement.

"The old section of the city sits on a promontory elevated from the sea, jutting out onto the Mediterranean. Then we have the Porto Ferro beach with its mantle of red sand. As we drive towards the interior of Alghero, not too far from the sea, Baratz Lake welcomes us with its amazingly natural formation, the one and only in Sardinia." Mr. Alvani proudly explained as they stepped out of the car, while Enzo kept snapping photos for Valeria to add to her collection.

A week had fast gone by. Valeria had been hard at work, visiting sites and interviewing the locals. She had heard of the longevity of the inhabitants of this island; now she could actually speak with some of these folks and hear their stories firsthand. They were usually gathered in piazzas or would just be sitting on the ledge of the platforms off the streets or on bamboo chairs, canes in their hands. The older people gathered in conversation about the town's events, or the latest gossip. Valeria approached to interview an older gentleman.

"How are you, Signore?" She asked, speaking in her broken Italian. She knew they would take no offence here; they were truly wise with age. "How young are you, sir?"

The toothless man managed to pull off a grin, and responded, "One hundred and five, Miss."

"Have you ever travelled abroad or to the mainland?"

"No, this is my island. I have always been here. I am happy here. I will die here. My mother lived until one hundred and seven on this same island. I took care of her," he proudly explained.

***

As the days passed, Valeria was becoming more and more intrigued by these folks, their food, custom, their island. The bays were breathtaking. Sardinia revealed itself as a jewel sitting in the Mediterranean. The scattered archipelago in varying sizes popped up here and there in an amazing display of nature; the major ones accessible by boat. With each passing day she was slowly falling in love with her surroundings.

On Monday, Lucio Alvani suggested they take a drive to an area in La Costa Smeralda where it would be quieter because of the feast in Porto Cervo, another location which attracted lots of visitors and locals, allowing Enzo to take more unobstructed photos of the place.

"As for you, Valeria, you will be able to take notes in the area, undisturbed," suggested Lucio.

By now they were on a first name basis. The day had been fruitful for both Valeria and Enzo. Valeria had a chance to interview a few people visiting from San Francisco. They were originally Sardinians but lived abroad. They had migrated in the early fifties, and the nostalgia and the love in their hearts for this place kept them returning each year.

***

The Mayor was pleased with Valeria's work and reports. Mr. Patty was praising her regularly. She had e-mailed him pictures, interviews, and notes with history of the places she visited. She shared the culture, their delicious recipes of seafood, cheeses, meats, and Sardinian offerings. Her discoveries never ceased to amaze her. She was so impressed and anxiously looked forward to the exploration of the next day.

It was a beautiful Friday morning. To her surprise only Enzo had showed up to meet her.

Chapter Five

A Cloud on Her Journey

"Signora Abrosky, Mr. Alvani had a family emergency today; he would not be joining us. I will do my best to guide you and take pictures as well."

"Oh!" responded Valeria, disappointed. "Nothing serious I hope?"

"His wife is quite ill, but I will leave it for him to explain."

Valeria did not press any further; it was not like her. After all she really didn't know these people intimately.

"Sorry to hear that," she responded politely.

Valeria noticed Enzo was not behaving efficiently today. *He must also have personal plans,* she gathered. He fretted all day. He announced early in the morning that he was anxious to finish the day early.

He winked at her with a smirk on his face, "A big date tonight, Signora,"

She smiled back, "Oh, good for you. She sure is a lucky girl."

"On the contrary, I am the lucky guy. I have been pursuing her for a while. Finally, she accepted. You know Signora the girls here are quite reserved."

"I see!" Her brows frowned as she looked at him puzzled. "Thanks for filling me in Enzo. I sure wish you luck tonight."

It was nice of Enzo to take her in his confidence, she thought. She wondered how her boys felt about their quest for girls. The girls in their path used to call at the house always, flocking around like spring birds in heat. *And they sure didn't have to chase hard in their pursuits.* Valeria was deep in thought. *So much for my experience; another lesson learned in this part of the world.*

As a result, Valeria found herself back at the hotel by two that afternoon. She didn't mind. *A chance to catch up on phone calls and notes.* She had mentally forced the last unpleasant episode of her personal life out of her mind, and as a dutiful wife she called Boris every night; unfortunately, and with much sadness, their conversations usually ending in arguments.

"I want you to come home," he kept on demanding.

Tonight, she would try to talk to him calmly and ask him to come and join her here. Convincing herself that maybe if he visited this island and was among these pleasant folks, it could rub off on him and his mood would change. The placidity here was contagious. These folk's habits were catchy, and it would do them both a world of good, if he could only try and give himself a chance for betterment. But how could he when he believed there was absolutely nothing wrong with him. Would he agree to come? It remained to be seen. Deep down in her heart she knew she could not take on or live with his crazy moods anymore.

She had made herself comfortable for the night and was about to pick up the phone when it rang in her hand.

"Hello, Valeria?" A cheerful voice called out.

"Yes?" She recognized the voice; "Lucio!"

"It's Lucio. Excuse me, *non disturbo*? Sorry I was unable to escort you today," he paused, "I thought of calling you to make up for my absence. I would like to take you to dinner tonight, that is if I am not imposing." He waited anxiously for her answer.

Valeria hesitated, she liked the simple life there. She imagined strolling through the avenues by the cafes, taking in the music and laughter that filled the air, the friendly people, happiness all around, rejoicing on the piazzas, and she thought, *why not? I am here by myself, and it is early.*

"That would be nice. I can update you on my day's discoveries. I'd love to have dinner with you, Lucio."

"Great! I will pick you up at seven," was his animated response.

Valeria put the receiver down and stared at the phone for a moment. Did she really want to call Boris? It would be a forced effort on her part as she knew how he was good at depleting her. She walked away from the phone to check her wardrobe to find a suitable outfit for the evening, one that would blend with the town. To her surprise, the phone rang again, and Boris was on the other end.

"Hello, Dear, I was about to call you. I just got deviated for a while."

"How was your day? I miss you here. It's no fun being alone."

"Boris, it's your choice. I wish you would come. You would love this island."

"What would I do there all day while you are busy working!"

"There is so much to see and do. You could go along with me and take notes, and your own pictures, or sit by the beach, the pool, read, go fishing. I am telling you, there are a lot of activities once you are willing to participate."

"Valeria, are you trying to turn me into a sissy, or a woman? That for me is a waste of time. I need to be productive. How many times do I have to tell you that?" His voice escalating by each second into a crescendo. By now she knew when to back off and let him indulge in his distorted opinionated reasoning.

"Ok Dear, if you change your mind and decide to come, the hotel room here is really lovely, and I would love to share the king size bed with you."

"You wrap up what you are doing as soon as you can. I prefer my wife here, at home, in my own bed. I had enough of hotel rooms in my life."

"I will call you tomorrow night, Dear, have a good night. I have to go now."

"Hold on, are you…, why are you rushing me off like this?"

"I need to get ready to meet my host and take more notes. I have an obligation to Mr. Patty."

"Who cares about Mr. Patty! You are my wife and you should care only to make me happy."

"Ok Boris, good night."

She hung up the phone quite disheartened but before the discussion could get out of hand. Now she was glad she accepted to go out with Lucio; the night air might clear her head. Boris always succeeded in making it heavy and stuffy with his selfishness.

***

It was May. The sun was still luminous, peeking in and out of the fluffy white clouds, as she stepped out with Lucio at her side. The bright blue sky seemed to blend in and embrace the island surrounded by its own blue sea. Valeria's poor spirit paused and allowed itself to be slowly engulfed by the spectacular beauty out there.

She forced herself to totally erase the somber mood created earlier in her room. She had taken her note book and gold pen along to make sure she noted every new sight and idea, as her personal assignment.

She had greeted Lucio with a big smile. In comfortable shoes, she stood ready to take in as much as she could to report back to her base office. She turned to her host, "Lucio, I feel a bit of guilt. I don't want to pry, but Enzo mentioned your wife not being well. I hope I am not taking you away from your family. May I ask, how is she?"

"Thanks for asking. My wife Chiara is as well as can be expected. I wish there was something more I could do to help her," he responded with a sad expression, looking downward while slowly shaking his head from side to side.

Valeria sensed that it was not a pleasant matter, and when he didn't proceed further, she changed the subject without further questions. Lucio, with a raw smile, gently touched her arm and turned her attention to the easterly direction towards the shore.

"Valeria, let me show you something spectacular." He now wore a different expression as he gently put a hand on her arm to guide her.

"We must take a walk along the seaside; a favourite selection for tourists and locals, *la passeggiata*, the evening stroll."

"I am under your guidance. You know better. This is your island," she responded, looking up at him and smiling.

"We will look at the sunset before we go to dinner; I am sure you will enjoy it. Make sure your camera is ready."

As soon as they reached the avenue and stopped by the low walled shore of the beach, Valeria's eyes suddenly popped wide open. The waves seemed to caress the sand, soft music resonated in the air, people were strolling about, different languages could be heard. The coffee shops were well attended. An aroma of fresh baked sweets, coffee, chocolate, and gelato, teased your taste buds and infused the air. She couldn't help wonder how many espresso coffees these people were indulging in a day.

Lucio asked permission to hold her by the arm. The piazza along the sea was crowded and they didn't want to lose each other; after all he was her guide and he felt a sense of responsibility.

He pulled her into a less invaded spot, and here he encouraged Valeria to feast her eyes.

"Valeria, there goes the sun, look at it carefully."

The sun in a huge luminous yellow ball slowly seemed to be swallowed by the sea, or magically disappeared. Valeria was totally captured and mesmerized by the magnetic special effects that the delightful sunset presented. With this distraction she totally forgot about her camera around her neck.

"Oh my! Lucio! I have never seen or experienced anything as spectacular as this before. The sun seems to drawn itself right into the Mediterranean Sea, making you want to reach out and stop it from happening. Oh, how foolish of me, I became totally hypnotized by the visual climax, I never took pictures for Mr. Patty and my clients!" She exclaimed in dismay.

He squeezed her arm reassuringly, "Valeria, I didn't have the heart to take you out of your spell; not to worry, we can catch it again. We have a lot of sunsets like that here; this spectacular scenery is repeated often during this time of the year."

"Oh, thank you for putting yourself out and treating me to this marvellous experience."

She looked at him pitifully, her eyebrows furrowed as some guilt pangs rose in her chest. She thought: *He is a married man, and it is Friday night.* He probably was being duty bound out of his dedication to promote his island for the love of his people, but to be here with her at this off hour! Almost as if he sensed her scrutiny, with a gracious smile, he reassured her, "It is my duty and my pleasure, Signora Valeria. Now that the sun has left us, I suggest we make our way to one of the cafes for an aperitif which will surely stimulate your appetite."

Valeria smiled in agreement. She could not get over the Sardinian people. They had a big lunch in the middle of the afternoon and at night, a light supper followed by the customary amaro, a bitter-sweet liqueur. She needed to get accustomed to their way of eating.

But right now, her stomach craved real food; she was hungry. The aperitif was the last thing she needed to satisfy her hunger. She could have handled a nice plate of antipasto, followed by pasta, and the rest of what her mother used to serve the hungry troop.

The coffee bar Lucio chose was crowded with people, as most were at that time of evening. Soft music resonated in the background and the soft lighting created a romantic atmosphere. Lucio must have been a regular, she noted, as he was greeted cordially by the attendant. "Lucio! Good evening!" was heard coming from a cheerful hostess wearing an impeccable black and white uniform and a glitzy bowtie.

"Good evening, Signora Carla," he said as he extended a hand shake.

He turned to Valeria to introduce her, "La Signora Abrosky from Canada; she is touring our island for a tourist promotion."

"Piacere, Signora, my pleasure, benvenuto, welcome," the hostess greeted. "What can I offer you?" she asked, gazing back and forth at the two standing before her.

"Un amaro di Carciofi? Va bene?" asked Lucio.

Valeria hated the stuff, but out of politeness she gracefully replied, "Fine."

"The usual for me too, Carla. A bitter pre-digestive."

After that Lucio suggested they make their way to the square. The piazza was illuminated by delightful glittering star-like shaped lights in blues. The air was comfortably warm with groups of people or couples seen everywhere. The atmosphere resonated with their laughter, and animated conversations could be overheard. The city of Alghero was alive. When they crossed the arches of the circular avenue, Lucio said, "This is my favourite restaurant. My wife used to love this place. The food is fresh, and the place is authentic; they only buy from local farmers. Not fancy, but quaint and friendly."

Valeria was going along with him, as long as they would soon eat. She had nothing all day. She was still on Canadian time and custom.

"The fish here is magnificent, light, and fluffy. Once you finish your meal, you will feel satisfied, without any regret."

"Great! That is what I am looking for, as I am not used to eating supper this late."

Valeria had made up her mind to experience whatever was here, and to live like the islanders. Her gaze was on Lucio, in wonder. She would catch him crossing one hand over his head pushing back a few strands of hair in a nervous gesture. She would have liked to get into his thoughts as at those times he seemed distant; his brows knitting with obvious worry.

The restaurant was not too fancy but acceptable. The blue flowered table cloth and napkins on the tables were an extension of the lovely blue waters that caressed the nearby seashores. The walls were lined up with a collection of different paintings of the islands. One was in red tones, of the famous caves she had not yet visited. With great admiration she closely examined each of them. These folks here were calm and collective, moving in a slow, relaxed pace. The contrast in comparison to North America was also something to be noted. Hosts would take the time to chat and appreciate their clients' patronage through sincere interest and admiration. The humility was felt by the guests. Their waiter, Madali, aimed to serve them to no end by pleasantly fulfilling all Lucio's requests. They were elegantly served fish with risotto and grilled vegetables, and delicious crusty bread with fluffy creamy butter, rolled in a fine herb mixture. Valeria tried to eat with her best manners since by this time she had an insatiable hunger.

"Lucio, this place is lovely, and the people are so courteous; no wonder your wife loves it here."

"Used to! No more." He scratched his ear uncomfortably, rubbed the side of his face as if soothing himself. He was definitely avoiding something. She sensed he did not want to disclose much or continue talking about his wife.

"Oh, please forgive me. I should not ask."

She perceived his pain as he lowered his gaze to fidget with his napkin. In a whisper he painfully disclosed, "My Chiara is a seriously sick!" He tried hard to hide his face and control the tears welling in his eyes. The waiter once more approached their table to be at their service, just in time to change the mood that was building up.

A catchy dark cloud was creeping its way over them. Valeria's thoughts were taking her back home, slipping in and out of what Boris must be doing. He was the heavy weight that darkened her soul. Anger promptly surfaced to flush her cheeks whenever she gave mental attention to her husband. Boris could certainly be here with her and not miss out on life. She was fighting with her own feelings, trying to justify her trip away from him. He was not only denying himself great golden years of retirement but resenting her for adventuring and fulfilling her job demands.

She shook her head to return to the present. *I cannot help or change him. I cannot afford to keep making myself miserable worrying about him.*

The evening flew by quickly as she was absorbed in the beauty of the avenues at night. The city felt safe. Everyone acknowledged you as a habit, whether they knew you or not.

Lucio, being such a perfect gentleman, walked her back to the hotel promising to see her in the morning. "I will see you tomorrow." He again apologised for his absence during the day. With both his hands he grabbed hold of her hand, looked at her intently, and after a few seconds turned and departed silently. No words. She thought she noticed a faint smile.

Valeria walked into her splendid room, deep in thought, unconsciously comparing the two men now occupying her mind. *This Lucio fellow seems mysterious, placid, kind, and definitely in some sort of sorrow. My husband is a roaring lion and a bulldog all in one, always growling and barking at me. His violent behaviour needs to stop, especially after what I have seen lately. God help me with these men! Or, is something wrong with me? Then there's Mr. Patty! All he wants are successful trips, money, and closed sales. He is unforgiving if I lose a booking; then it will be all my fault.* "You couldn't close that sale, eh!" He would comment soberly whenever a potential customer would walk out the office.

She kicked off her shoes and dropped her exhausted body on the inviting leather swivel chair. Reaching for her blue pen, she grabbed her notebook and recorded the day's happenings. The stunning aspect of the evening was the sunset and she had not taken pictures, that would get her in trouble. She could already hear Mr. Patty's annoyed questioning, "Where are the pictures?"

She would surely have to ask Lucio to take her back to experience the phenomenal sunset. She wrote until her vision blurred into sleep. When she glanced at her watch it was past midnight. Her husband was certainly out of reach now due to the time difference. She crossed her arms across her chest, drawing them around her body in a hug and took a long deep breath. Then she changed into her silk nightgown and crawled under the satin sheets and crisp soft covers. Her tired body sunk deeper into the bed and she soon sailed away into dream land, wishing for tomorrow when another day of splendour awaited her on this amazing island.

Chapter Six

Lucio Reminisces

Sadness hit Lucio as he entered the lobby of his residence. In fatigued motion he took the steps to the second floor. Once he reached the front door of his apartment, he hesitated before placing the key in the key hole. He took a deep breath and held his eyes shut for a few minutes envisioning his lovely Chiara, vivacious and mobile, greeting him at the door, jumping up at him, enthusiastically locking her arms around his neck, showering him with love and affection.

The door opened slowly with a squeak; there was silence. A dim light down the hallway welcomed him. Many times in the last few years he had been wishing and dreaming, allowing himself to think that the situation was only temporary. He compared it to the occasional darkness in the blue sky. Once those heavy clouds subside after the down pour, serenity would return with the sunshine and a rainbow. But his wishful thinking had not yet materialized. "Yeah! Keep hoping for a miracle," he muttered to himself dishearteningly. Now that he had returned home, shadows of malady and sickness reigned in the rooms everywhere.

They had picked this place a few years after their marriage, across from the beach, with an infinite view of the sea. "Darling I love this place," Chiara declared as she glided through the roomy entranceway, and *soggiorno*, living room, leading to an entire glass wall overlooking the archipelago. The infinity of the crystalline sea, with sail boats and ferries filled with locals and tourists perfected the picture. All excited by the endless shore stretching along the coast she would point out, "Darling, darling, look in the distance, there is the mainland with it's artistic shape!"

Lucio had to agree. The different shades of the blue water were indeed breathtaking. She moved from room to room completely ecstatic. She had locked his neck in a strong embrace, kissing him, taking his breath away. "Lucio, my love, you must get me this place. I absolutely love it. I will decorate it in shades of the sea. Once I am finished, you would not be able to wait to come home after a day of work," she had said, continuing to smother him with wet kisses, like a child imploring to have her favourite toy.

"Ma, si! Yes! Chiara, I will see what I can do, my darling." He lovingly responded holding his gaze on her big brown eyes.

Lucio's wishes had been no other than to please his beloved Chiara, but that was years ago. Tonight, with tenderness and pity in his eyes, slouched shoulders and head down, he went directly to the bedroom where his wife lay day and night for the last ten years, but now, since the past six months, worse than ever. She was in a deep sleep with the aid of medications. He gently kissed her forehead, ran his fingers over her once plump and lovely lips, caressed her flushed cheeks, and then quietly and slowly left the room. *If I could only cure her and make her regain her well-being, I would be the happiest man on this island,* he thought in despair. His wife's illness had made his life sad and unbearable. He glanced at his watch; it was ten. Nurse Rosaria was not around. *Maybe she is in her room, or probably gone to sleep.* The house felt eerie and quiet, with the exceptional interruption of the sound of hard breathing coming from Chiara's bedroom; her lungs had become stressed lately.

He walked slowly to the far wing of the house to seek refuge in his library. He needed to jot down some notes for the excursion tomorrow, but his concentration was poor. With both thumbs he massaged his temples in a circular motion, trying to alleviate the pressure building as he felt a headache coming on. He walked away from his desk to the big window overlooking the sea. The sky had lost its lustre by now; the scattered stars were falling off.

The moon hid behind some nebulous formation, jeopardizing its glowing effect on earth. Lucio stood there pensive, sorrow slithered into his heart. He glanced out into the ocean. The extension of the Mediterranean was darker tonight than he had ever seen. The abyss of darkness out there mirrored the turmoil within his own soul.

No part of this house felt comfortable anymore. Not even the sanctuary Chiara had created for him at this side of the library where before, he would often find peace. With his eyes full of tears, he made his way to the spare bedroom which he had been occupying for the last five years. It is because of this the counsellor had suggested some voluntary community work. Dr. Vallardi had said to him, "It will benefit others, and most of all, the distraction will ease your troubled soul."

Tomorrow night he would visit Dr. Vallardi. He would pour his sorrowful feelings to him, hoping with his help a solution would surface to alleviate his misery. And of course, for his work tomorrow guiding Valeria, he would have to be in good spirits. *The lovely Canadian lady that I highly respect, deserves the best tour and opportunity to gather her information on the island.*

Chapter Seven

The Tour Continues

Valeria was up early and excitedly prepared herself for another day of adventure and discovery. She made her way to the lobby where many tourists were seen mingling and animatedly chatting and enjoying a traditional morning treat of savoiardi dolce, ladyfingers, and either espresso, cappuccino, or another coffee of choice. Here, they indulge in sweets in the morning, something she found a bit strange.

Close to the exit she spotted Enzo and Lucio waiting, ready to pick her up for another day of exploration.

"Buongiorno! Today we will drive to La Maddalena, Mrs. Abrosky," announced Enzo with a big grin on his face.

"A real treat, Valeria; I see you are wearing comfy shoes. The place is rocky, but in an amazing setting combined with nature. You will soon see," continued Lucio.

Valeria's entire face lit up with enthusiasm. "You are my guide! I will be glad to follow you gentlemen. How lucky of me! I have a narrator and a chauffeur! I am in great company!" She turned to Lucio glowing in readiness.

With an infectious smile and a sparkle of delight in her big brown eyes she put an arm on Enzo's shoulder and complimented him, "You are an excellent driver, and you sure know the territory well."

"Thank you, Signora, it is for the love of my land."

Off the three went. They drove along the coast. In the distance, the bright blue sky seemed to touch the sea, and with the glowing sun reflecting on the sea, the various tones of blue shimmered like turquoise gems. The yellow glow from the sunrays created a spectacular colour formation of nature on the various rocks, and on the multi-coloured flower blossoms. Once they made their first stop, Valeria was in awe as she stepped out. A pleasant breeze was blowing her loose blonde hair away from her face as if to make sure her sight was unobscured, to totally observe what was in front of her. Wide eyed, and like a child, she let out a squeal of joy.

"Rocky soil in many shapes and colours! Red terrain all right. Oh! My God! Look at the variety of flowers! This is mesmerizing, magical, and they grow so healthy in this rocky soil." Her joyous energy was passed on to Lucio and Enzo, as they also felt the genuine pleasure in her discoveries.

"Lucio, you must tell me about these beautiful flowers, and you Enzo, please take as many pictures as you can while I jot down notes from my own interpretation to my boss."

Valeria felt amazingly invigorated by the sight of this place of sheer natural beauty that must have surfaced from the sea at some time. The sea breeze softly caressed her rosy cheeks, and her eyes danced from side to side to take in as much as she could. She carefully scaled the rocks, hopping from one place to the next. Lucio, taken in by her enthusiasm, followed right behind her. Suddenly she lost her balance by stepping on a slimy moss-covered stone. As she tripped, he instinctively grabbed her torso with both hands to steady her, and she turned around reaching for him to break the fall and regain her footing. Lucio's gaze rested on her big brown eyes, and a shiver of pleasurable energy zipped up and down his spine.

It had been a long time since he had touched and looked at a beautiful healthy woman this close. He had never given himself permission. His beloved Chiara, how devoted he was to her! The sickness had been tearing her away from him from a long time ago. Her once healthy and lovely body had gradually lost all vivacity. He had become consumed with caring for her in her unhealthy condition.

Now, he caught himself staring at Valeria, then suddenly embarrassed he said, "Valeria, you need to be cautious; the rocks are covered with silt from the sea. They are slippery. We don't want you to hurt yourself now!" As he said that, Valeria embarrassingly apologized.

"Sorry, how clumsy of me."

In the sudden move to correct herself, another rock made her loose another footing, and she lost her balance. Lucio was right there to save her again, by nearly falling over himself. As their bodies touched, electrified, their eyes locked in a double gaze; both felt confused and exalted at the same time. For Valeria, to find herself in Lucio's protective arms, gave her a strange sense of reassurance. It had been some years now that she had only experienced menace from her husband who was supposed to be her protector. Lucio, in his unfortunate situation was also starving for affection.

Enzo, a little distance away on the other hand, was busy taking pictures. Since Lucio was chaperone, he felt free to roam about to catch the best shots with his professional camera. Lucio's mixed feelings had caused him embarrassment; his blood had rushed to his face causing him to blush. Touching Valeria by accident had triggered both danger and pleasure.

Enzo soon made his way to them, blabbering away. "Eh! Wait till you see these shots," happy to show off his fantastic pictures, totally oblivious of the confusion his co-worker was enduring.

"Mrs. Abrosky! Look! These are amazingly fantastic! Look! I captured the birds flying across the sky with the combination of the sea, the flowers, and the rocks." He was so proud of himself. "I am eager to deliver the best for this place. Promoting tourism has

become my main interest lately, especially since the natives have decided to share their island."

Valeria and Lucio turned to him perplexed. After eyeing one another and a bit shaken, in a state of embarrassment, and with prolonged mixed emotions, they barely acknowledged his comment in the background. They did not really hear what he was saying. Enzo frowned, somewhat disappointed at their lack of enthusiasm. The young man had no suspicion those two souls were both deeply lost in their own sorrowful secrets. They were living under false pretenses of portraying outward happiness, when only misery reigned in their troubled hearts.

Chapter Eight

Back in Niagara

Boris opened his blood shot eyes; the room was dark and gloomy. It was a rainy morning again. "Gee! It must be still early," he mumbled as he snuggled further into his bed, pulling the covers over himself trying to ease the tension on his temples. The excruciating heaviness in his head was rendering him helpless, as if someone had hammered his skull with a hard-pointy rock.

When he heard the grandfather clock from downstairs methodically bang nine strokes, "Ohhh!" He moaned in pain. At the sudden revelation of the time, off went his covers as he forced himself to crawl out of bed. The hangover from the night before was evident. With a heavy head and sluggish body, he was having a tough time steadying himself. He could hear the rain gently hitting the roof top, in a pleasant and relaxing manner. It almost encouraged him to get back under the covers and pull them over his head, with the hope of making the world around him go away. His footing didn't feel steady.

In his confusion, he realized he needed to check on the roof leaks. Although there was no wind at this time, he thought to check just the same. The last storm had caused chaos driving him to mistreat Valeria, and maybe if he had been able to control himself, she would have been here with him now. Now he found himself all alone in this house, and to soothe himself had resorted to vodka, Tim Hortons for coffee, and a lousy breakfast on mornings. Later in the day after lunch, he would have a few more shots of vodka at a dark dingy bar at the other side of town, selected because it is where he wouldn't run into some of those old saints he knew from the church. They would be quick to condemn him for sitting at a bar which had become his pastime, waiting until the day turned to dusk. The bartender was a Latino guy who was tipped well to keep his mouth shut, "You don't see, and you don't tell." Boris would wink at him and tell him stories of his working days, half slurring; his brain dulled by alcohol.

His loneliness was frantically growing with each sun down. Oh, how he now hated to go home. The alcohol shots created a vagueness of his existence. For a few nights he had not made it to bed until dawn. He felt abandoned by his children, his wife, and the entire world.

Those blokes at Tim Hortons! He had tried to strike up conversation with strangers. *They're so dumb and boring. They don't know their ass from their elbow! What a waste of time to even talk to them! Little do they know I used to be dealing with big brains, and closing big deals, and travelling all over the world! They look at me as if I am one of them. They have no idea who Boris Abrosky used to be!* He would drive himself into a pathetic state, heightening his own misery. Once he was back home, he would walk around the house sipping a cup of strong Arabian coffee he made for himself, hoping the caffeine would clear his head.

It would be five o'clock in Sardinia. Would Valeria be back in her hotel room? He questioned himself. He would order her to come home, he thought. *Enough is enough! She was on her third week now! She and her senseless work for Mr. Patty. The hell with Patty! She is my wife, and I should come first for her! I need her at home with me!*

"I will place a call and give her a piece of my mind. My father used to say, 'My way or the highway, son. Don't let anyone push you around'." He was asserting himself talking out aloud to the empty walls of his home. It was now eleven o'clock. He would call at one o'clock, his time. *Valeria better be back at her hotel,* he rehearsed in his mind.

She will have to hear me out!

Chapter Nine

Tricks of the Mind

Back in Sardinia, Enzo pulled up in front of the hotel to drop off Valeria. Lucio promptly stepped out of the car in his gallant manner to help her out. Extending his hand, he said, "To a better day tomorrow, Valeria. We shall choose a less rocky terrain for you," referring to her slipping on the rocks.

"Oh! Ma, si! Today was fine!" Her head nodded in denial, as she stood there waving them goodbye. She glanced at her watch; it was after six. The sun was still high in the sky, far from sunset. With hesitant footsteps she ventured into the lobby, not having the desire to go up and lock herself in the solitude of her room. Having been exposed to the fresh and sunny air by the sea all day, she felt a bit dehydrated. She deviated to the restaurant. There she thought, *I will sit and have a drink, then go over my notes.* She wasn't hungry as yet. Slowly her body clock was getting used to eating at a later hour, just like the locals.

Once the hostess saw her approaching, to her amazement she heard her order, "Gin and tonic please, with lots of ice and a double twist of lemon." It was her favourite drink since years back when she would go on business trips with Boris. Usually, alcoholic drinks were not her choice. But right now, she felt the need for one. Once her drink arrived, she took big draws through the straw. Her brain started to feel the dull relaxing effect of the gin. She stared at her notes; the concentration or the desire to recap wasn't there. She found herself revisiting the incident earlier in the afternoon; the innocent touch of Lucio and his lingering gaze.

49

"What is the matter with me? I am a married woman! And he is a married man!" She silently scolded herself. She soon retreated to her room and called Boris. Life wasn't fair, she thought. Here she was alone, and so was her husband. She wondered about his wellbeing, even if he had been extremely difficult the past couple of years.

***

At the same time back in Niagara, Boris had been impatiently dialling her room number, only to be redirected to the main desk to a stranger's voice instructing him to leave a message. He had been pacing the floor not knowing what to do with himself. "She needs to come home!" He was talking to himself. He thought to reach out and call his daughter, Rosy. Since Valeria had left, his kids had not called or showed up for a visit. He was feeling resentful towards them, driving himself deeper and deeper into negative thinking.

This Friday night was turning into a nightmarish experience. It was deadly quiet around the house. Occasionally he would hear the ice from the fridge release into the ice box, along with the motor recharge and the fan from the furnace. Only loneliness followed him, accompanied by boredom, like a black layer of tar that seemed to push his existence into the depth of an abyss. He dialled the boys, no answer. He dialled Rosy, her answering machine came across brief, loud and clear. "Please leave a message. I will call you back." Boris muttered the 'F' word to himself and slammed down the receiver without bothering to leave a message. "The hell with all of them.   They are all busy! My kids, my wife; all I am doing is talking to strangers and answering machines, or myself." He made his way to the family room, shoulders drooped and head hanging low. The old lazy-boy leather chair had been bought for him since his retirement; his present. His eyes fell on it. Suddenly his mother's words echoed in his ears, "If you want a man to turn old, sit him on a lazy-boy and in no time, he is finished." That is what she used to say. When he had offered to buy one for his father on Fathers Day, she had strongly protested.

"Who cares? The sooner the better! I have nothing to live for anyway!" He turned on the TV and dropped his body on the old man's lazy-boy chair. He pushed the side button and his legs soon lay outstretched in front of him. He put in motion the rest of the mechanism, swivelling and rocking himself. His eyelids began to droop, bringing him into a state where he automatically shut the world out.

***

Valeria was just about ready to gather her things and go up to her room when a bunch of gregarious young people were directed to sit right beside her. They were harmoniously speaking in English. She couldn't help noticing and admiring the group. They were tourists no doubt, which stirred her interest even more. She discreetly glanced at them, listening and enjoying the chit-chat as they were in hearing range. After all, it was her job to observe, listen, and take in as much as she can.

There were three girls and a young man. Once the waitress brought them their drinks, they happily cheered, "To Sardinia, and our wonderful vacation!" Two of the girls burst into loud laughter that turned heads around them. One with shoulder length blonde hair turned to Valeria with an encouraging smile, "Sorry, please excuse us, are we too loud for you? We just arrived last night and we are celebrating my birthday. My friends here are a noisy bunch," she said with a big smile. One could tell they were in harmony with each other and having a great time.

Valeria waved her hand in denial, "No problem, don't mind me. You are entitled. You are on vacation!"

"I notice you speak perfect English. Where are you from?"

"Niagara Peninsula, and you?"

"Really? Toronto! Oh, my goodness!"

The blonde was friendly, chatty, and amicably receptive. She got up and made her way to Valeria extending her hand to introduce herself.

"I am Lidia Morana."

"Nice to meet you. Valeria Abrosky!"

She pointed out her friends. "The one with the blue eyes is my sister Maria, then Rita, our cousin, and our friend, Bruno, stuck with us three girls. We feel sorry for him, but ah, he is so lucky!" They all laughed in wholesome fun and continued to chat about usual tourist things.

Valeria couldn't help sensing the good energy among these young people. They were so natural and free. Since her arrival her full attention was given to the exploration of places of interest for Mr. Patty. She had not interacted with anyone other than Lucio and Enzo. She was totally immersed in her duties. She couldn't help but enjoy looking at these young people who were from her side of the world. Lidia, being the friendliest of them all, asked, "Mrs. Abrosky, are you alone? Would you like to join us for a drink? Come on, I am celebrating my thirtieth!"

"Congratulations! Happy Birthday!"

She pulled her chair over, Bruno ordered her another drink and here she was in the lobby of her hotel, enjoying the great company of these lovely and joyful young people.

***

Once Lucio returned home, A reminder note was set on the table. "Lucio, you are to see Dr. Vallardi tonight; no deviation please." He hurriedly grabbed a quick bite. Two nurses were part of their home, looking after Chiara. Vittoria and Rosaria, they were on shift work. Vittoria a mature lady in her fifties, a Sardinian, professional and dedicated to her caring. Rosaria, the older hired nurse was on duty at the house tonight. She was a chubby lady in her sixties, with short curly salt and pepper hair, and wore an impeccable and starched uniform. A serious but caring smile governed her lips; she was five feet tall with an amazingly sharp brain. Rosaria had set everything on the table for him. She kept a diary for both Alvanis. A certified nurse that came from the main land of Torino, she loved Sardinia for its clean unpolluted air. She was known to crack the whip with her operational rules. He didn't particularly like to visit the doctor on a Friday night, but Rosaria had insisted. "Mr. Alvani, you must. Your weekends are bleak. By talking to him you will cope better," she would say to him with a serious look of concern.

They both seemed to have taken the family health matters into their own hands in a motherly fashion. After many years of them working there, Lucio, just did as was ordered. Both nurses devotedly rotated night and day to care for Chiara. It was not an easy task. Lucio felt duty bound towards them. They had been hired by his wife fifteen years ago. He must vouch that they were excellent employees.

At seven o'clock Lucio walked into Dr. Vallardi's office, psyching himself up to get his mixed-up feelings out in the open. He lay on the couch massaging his shoulders to relieve the tension that often settled right across his shoulder muscles. Tonight, he wanted to ask questions and he wanted answers. Dr. Vallardi was in the habit of listening and nodding. Lucio never knew the doctor's reactions to his disclosures.

He was going to mention Valeria to him. Since he started to work on this new interesting subject of tour promotion, it had given him a new lease on life. Valeria, with her own enthusiasm had empowered him to see, to do, and to discover. When he was out there with his new friend and Enzo, his life seemed meaningful. To his surprise, his work distracted him enough, transporting him to another pleasant world. "Doctor, please tell me how I can let that pleasantness that I feel during the day flow through me in continuity after I return home?"

"Lucio, it is up to you to stay in the mood, focus on the moment, rehearse the day's events, hold on to it, and rejoice in it. Shut out the negativity that wants to enter your mind. Meditate until calmness takes over your entire being. Do you know how to do it?"

"I am not sure what I know at this point."

"Would you like to try it for a few minutes?" The doctor asked.

"Yes. Why not?"

Dr. Vallardi began guiding Lucio in meditation. He put on some soft background music. "Sit upright and inhale and exhale deeply and slowly. Let your feet touch the ground. Close your eyes. Place your hands on your knees. Slowly relax each part of your body, beginning at the toes and ending at your crown. Once your body lets go of all the tension, silently and slowly repeat your personal mantra. Transport yourself to an imaginary place where beautiful white light glows from within you. Enjoy this experience for as long as you wish! Stay there until peacefulness abounds. Once you immerse your total being in this way and make it a daily practice, you will be sure to regain control of yourself."

After about ten silent minutes, Lucio came out of the meditation.

"Dr. Vallardi, when deep sadness hits me like a bulldozer, I feel crushed, tumbled and rolled over like a discarded and ruined object. Often in my dreams, this uncontrollable tsunami takes over my body and has its way with me. These horrific feelings usually begin while I stand by and check on my wife and persist for what seems like forever."

"Acceptance will ease the burden. We need to accept things that we cannot change to move on in life. I remember saying this to you many times before." His tone was strict. *How long have I been seeing this patient now? A few years?* The doctor remained calm and shook his head slightly. *He is not applying my advice.*

Lucio, in his own despair was trying but for him, it was easier said than done. He loved his precious Chiara immensely. Desolated, he walked out of the office towards his car, at the end of the session. With a heavy heart, instead of going home, he decided to drive towards the beach in the opposite direction of the city. There was always life there; maybe from the water. The moon and a stellar constellation were shining explosively tonight and reflected on the water. Lucio parked his car and decided to practice what Dr. Vallardi had preached many times over.

"God, please dear Lord, help me accept the things that I cannot change," he prayed, repeating the words over and over.

He sat on a bench and closed his eyes. *Despite the ugliness of my situation, there had to be hope on the horizon for me.* He felt as if he had been suffering an eternity.

After his meditation, in his calmness he sat there, admiring the illuminated moon reflecting on the surface of the ocean. *What a lovely evening for lovers,* he thought. He let out a huge sigh then got up and made his way back to his car and started the engine. He drove around in circles for a while feeling numb, or maybe calm; he was not sure.

Chiara would be sound asleep at this time. She would not be missing him. She could not. For six months now, her body and her brain had been totally wasted; it was impossible for his existence to have meaning for her.

He needed to accept things as they were, his subconscious self-reminded him. He switched on the radio and heard the announcer say, "Folks, we are closing our program tonight with this last song by the great Elvis Presley. Tune in tomorrow night, same station, same time. Then the earth-shaking voice of the legend came on, "Are you lonesome tonight…" It was midnight.

Elvis helped him to shove his sad thoughts aside and Lucio felt himself smiling, while envisioning Valeria waiting for them in the morning for another day of rewarding work and adventure. Conquering his loneliness, he headed home.

Chapter Ten

Amazing Cagliari

Valeria was waiting in the lobby. She wore a yellow dress teamed up with a flowing white scarf and sandals to match. She was holding a light cream hat at her side; it was trimmed with ornate orangey ribbon that secured a yellow orchid. A perfect vogue picture. She didn't have to wait long as Enzo and Lucio arrived right on time. As usual, Lucio displayed polished manners to escort her to the waiting car and opened her door to see her well seated before closing it.

Today they were to do some driving along the coast until they reached the provincial capital city of Cagliari, as Lucio had advised her before they parted yesterday afternoon.

"Thank you! Good morning," she greeted Enzo who promptly acknowledged her. She had noticed Lucio was meticulously well groomed, and a radiant glow was apparent on his face. Yesterday she had caught him pensive and distracted at times. She had wondered if the cause was the rocky site they visited, or maybe his own family affairs. She would never invade another's privacy, so she let it go. Her role here was strictly business. The accidental slip yesterday was what it was, an accident. She would make sure the next time to enquire in advance and wear the correct shoes for certain excursions.

"Another glorious day in paradise, Valeria; wouldn't you say?" He said cheerful once the tour started.

"Yes! Of course. Every day since I have arrived has been

splendid!"

"Today you will love Cagliari. It has a lot to offer and so much to see. The city overlooks the Gulf of The Angels. We will start our walk from the Port to via Rome. You will get to see the many arcades and palaces in Gothic design. We will also visit the Cathedral of Santa Maria; the side chapels are master pieces of architecture. We can also visit the Archeological Museum, a sure eye opener. We should save the Roman amphitheater for last; it is the highlight of Sardinia that no tourist should miss." Lucio explained it all with much pride and animation. She had no doubt he loved his country and was taking much pride in his work on this project.

"I am ready! Once I can make my notes and Enzo gives me the best pictures! It is important we capture it all," she said smiling back at him.

"You will love Cagliari! The piazzas are full of nonstop action from early morning to late night," Enzo added.

"It looks like we have a good plan on our agenda. Tell me, do these people ever sleep?"

"Oh, they manage well. Everything in life is well apportioned. They know how to live here; therefore, most of them live longer. Their attitude adds years to their life."

Valeria listened attentively, careful to correctly report her findings. Then she asked, "Lucio, don't you think their longevity is related to the clean air they breathe here, the food they eat, the abundance of fresh fish, the unpolluted water, and the crystal-clear water of the sea in which they swim?"

It took Lucio a few minutes to respond as it seemed his thoughts were temporarily shifted to another planet.

"Yes, for the majority of the inhabitants of the island." He held his breath for a moment. "They are blessed with an unpolluted island, and their low-keyed lifestyle."

His thoughts had gone again to his Chiara. *No, I must not, or this glorious day will be wasted.*

Valeria sensed the shifting of his attention, with his eyes flashing from vagueness back to the present.

There is a mysterious distraction hovering over my new friend. Whatever it is, may his soul find peace.

Chapter Eleven

Boris' Search for Contentment

It was nine in the morning when Boris rolled over on the sofa, stretching his aching body. He had never made it to bed. His pants were in a mess of wrinkles, his shirt crumpled, the tie hanging around his neck, as if strangling him. He yanked the tie off swearing, "The hell with this *struzzine*, tie around my neck; that's what my wife calls it. Who in the hell am I trying to impress with a tie, those bozos at Tim Hortons, or the bar tender at Gibby's?"

His head felt heavy and the pressure on his temples had not eased from the night before. He staggered around the room then made his way to the kitchen to get some coffee going. He checked his watch. *No time to call anyone now. Rosy would be in class and Valeria on her mission.* He resigned himself to having no other choice than to wait for tonight again. *I will try again.*

His morale was slowly sinking lower, taking him into a deep depression. The drive he once possessed was totally gone. The thick flowing blood he always felt filtering through his veins seemed to be draining, rendering him helpless more and more as the days went by. He did not bother taking his blood pressure medication these days. Valeria usually had it out for him with his breakfast routine. Since she left there was no routine. He missed her, but most of all he missed going to the office and being the chief in command with his subordinates bowing to him with respect. The adrenaline rushes he enjoyed from exceeding his monthly quota, and always outdoing himself and his colleagues each month, translated into pure power and he basked in it twenty-four hours a day. Now he was unemployed, and alone. *What a letdown! Later I will call Rosy again, maybe she will come home for the weekend,* he muttered to himself. He knew Rosy wouldn't look forward to coming home especially since her mother was away.

Boris had always tried to control her and would turn up his nose at the guys she dated. In the recent past when she visited on weekends, they often clashed with heated arguments due to the young man she was bringing to visit.

"Dad, is there anybody you like to see your daughter date? You seem to find fault with everyone that walks through the door," she would say to him, walking away infuriated and then avoiding him as much as she could. Rosy couldn't wait to go to university, especially to get away from her father. She got along with her mom better. She felt her mom was more understanding. But at times she resented her mother for not standing up to her father and defending herself more. The battles were endless. It he wasn't on her case, it would be her mother on the receiving end of her father's fury. Her brothers had it pretty good, Rosy figured. But with his daughter he was an angry controller. The way she dressed, the curfews he imposed, wanting her back home by midnight, frustrated her to no end.

"I am nineteen, for heaven's sake! I should be able to return home whenever I feel like it!" She would rebel. And his scrutiny of all her male friends had become an embarrassment, both to her and her friends.

"What does he do? Does he go to school? What is he studying? Where does he live, and who are his parents?" The grilling he would put them through! She wondered how anybody would want to take her out. She had a strikingly attractive body, was blessed with a busty contour, and had with a stylish gait. The boys in high school were always attracted to her. With her popularity, she didn't lack being asked out. The jealousy was evident from her classmates and she had many requests for the prom. She felt privileged to be able to pick and choose her dates while her poor classmates would not be as lucky. Her father was a pain, and some of the boys would be afraid to pursue her by calling again due to his intimidation. Rosy would roll her eyes when her father walked around her friends with an air of superiority. His belittling demeanour drove her insane.

And Mom, my poor mom! How does she put up with him? She certainly didn't like the way he demanded to be served by her mother, and how he aimed to control her every move. "Mom where is your backbone? You should be doing only what you want to!" She would often scold her mother especially after an argument with her father.

Valeria was always accommodating. Coming from the old school of obedience and the rules implemented by her old-fashioned upbringing, she had to honour her marriage vows, and her husband.

Rosy was happy when the time came to go away to university. For her it was the perfect escape from her father's dictatorship which she totally resented. Lately Rosy had been dating a young Latino fellow from the U.S. His name was Pablo Alvaro and they studied architecture together at the University of Ottawa. They were in the same classes, often studied together and helped each other with assignments. Pablo was humble, attentive, intelligent, and handsome. This gentle young man had a beautiful accent, and a sweet demeanour, and had totally captured Rosy's heart. He was so opposite to her father and she admired his gentle personality. He was tall and slim with thick black hair and wore a military style haircut. An infectious smile dominated his lips, and his big dark sparkling eyes glazed over her in mutual adoration.

She was reluctant to take him home and introduce him to her family yet, especially her dad. Lately they had been inseparable. Her comfort zone with Pablo was such that she did not want it disturbed by Boris Abrosky.

Rosy rushed into her residence to grab some items to work on a presentation before meeting Pablo. The flashing light on the answering machine caught her attention. She pushed the play button and there was her dad's voice, "Rosy! Where are you? Give me a call! I need to talk to you!" This was followed by a second, and a third message. She checked her watch; she was running late to meet her friend at the library to study. She quickly dialled her dad's number, no answer. *Oh well, I will call him later.* Then she ran out the door.

Boris had dialled Valeria's number and was once more asked to leave a message. "The hell with all of them." Lightening seemed to have struck his brain. He walked to the liquor cabinet and grabbed a bottle of vodka. He brought it up to his lips in a rage, gobbled the liquid until he filled himself to capacity. His eyes only saw shadows of darkness swaying in the dead silence of his home. He yanked the car keys from the holder; with a wobbly body and shaky hands he managed to turn on the engine, and off he went. The car swayed on the roadway as he drove.

Chapter Twelve
Alcohol Bliss

Under the influence of alcohol Boris was on an unusual adrenaline high. He felt the road was all his and the black Lincoln was at his command. He swerved from side to side, inviting disaster to occur any minute. The quiet neighbourhood was totally deserted that morning. A chill in the air and the gloomy sky must have discouraged the usual early walkers, not that Boris was aware of anything or anyone. He was definitely in a world of his own. Mrs. Jennings, the neighbourhood eavesdropper from across the street, as Boris had nicknamed her, had keenly observed as he pulled out of his driveway that morning.

Valeria is away; I wonder what that old goat is up to! Mrs. Jennings wondered. She had been watching his comings and goings. She was a widow in her eighties, lonely and bored and confined to her home. Her window was her connection to the outdoor world, especially when the weather wasn't too promising. She didn't particularly fancy her neighbour, Boris. She thought he was a boor because he never smiled or greeted her, or anyone else. A few times she had heard his raised voice at his wife, ordering her around when they were occasionally outdoors tending to the lawn and flowers.

Her eyesight was compromised with macular degeneration. When she stretched her neck to follow the car's direction as it went further down the street, it seemed to her that he was swaying from side to side. She wondered if it was her vision playing tricks on her, or this crazy neighbour of hers doing strange stunts going down the street. *Oh, my, my! Let me call Susan down the street and see if she can see him go by.* Dragging her feet, she busily aimed for her phone. Susan, a divorcee, bored like Mrs. Jennings, answered on the first ring, "Hello!"

"Susan, it's me, Nora! Good morning! Are you on your cordless? Could you please do me a favour and walk to your front window? The boor from across the street just left his house driving and I believe he is as drunk as a skunk. I watched him drive down the street with the car swaying from side to side. Look and see if you can spot him. I tell you! His poor wife! How does she put up with him, I will never know!"

Holding her phone, Susan who was just as nosy, couldn't wait to peep out. She quickly walked to the window, wide eyed and ready to investigate. Anxiously she said, "Nora, Nora!" and took a deep breath, "He has stopped right across the street!" She stretched her torso to take a better look. Then curiosity made her go and open her front door. She stepped out onto her porch while holding Nora is suspense on the phone. "He's slammed against his steering wheel!"

"What? Are you serious?"

"Would I say that if I wasn't staring at his car right across from my house?"

"Susan, I bet any money he is drunk first thing in the morning!"

Susan shook her head and didn't know what to make of Nora's comment. She was known to exaggerate about things. It was strange seeing the retired executive of years gone by, hunched over his steering wheel almost in front of her doorway.

"Susan, if I were you I would go and check on him. Please, for my poor friend, for Valeria's sake, before someone calls the police and he gets into trouble, or he gets going again and kills someone."

"Nora, I will grab a sweater and go out and check him out. I will call you back."

"Good, I am glad I called you! I am dying to know what's up with him!"

Mrs. Jennings put the phone down and sat waiting anxiously for her friend to report back to her. Thanks to Boris, there was some action taking place in her life today starting first thing in the morning. Shaking her head, she thought, *That poor wife of his! What he puts her through! Good for her that she got away a bit. If I was as young as her I would never come back!*

Every now and then Valeria would take Mrs. Jennings into her confidence, not having anyone else to confide in. The old woman had become her sounding board. Whenever Valeria missed her own mother, in her distress she would turn to her for comfort. Troubled by her anger towards her husband, she didn't realize that by relating to the old lady she had developed a strong resentment towards Boris.

Susan walked across the street slowly making her way to the car, while looking around to see if any of the neighbours were around or peeking through their curtains. As she approached the car, Boris came into full view, slumped over the steering wheel. She was not sure if he was asleep or passed out. The car motor was not running. She looked closer through the window and wondered what she should do. She tried the door and it opened without difficulty.

"Mr. Abrosky," she called out, "Are you ok?" She didn't know if she should touch him or shake him, or anything. No response. Susan decided to put her hands on his shoulders and gently shake him.

"Uhh, huhh. Where am I?" He asked, lifting his head, feeling disoriented.

"Mr. Abrosky, are you all right?"

He shook himself and tried to clear his head. "Where am I? What are you doing here?"

She shrugged her shoulders embarrassingly, then quickly said, "You tell me what is going on!" His breath stunk of alcohol. Anyone standing near to him would have to turn away to avoid his horrible breath. Susan decided he was definitely drunk.

Not aware of what he was doing, Boris got out of the car and found he could hardly stand up. Susan was beside herself, not knowing what to do or how to handle the situation.

"Mr. Abrosky, that is my house over there," she pointed across the street.

"Why don't you come in, and I will try to see what we can do to make you feel better?"

Realizing he was in no condition to walk on his own, she put an arm around his waist and asked him to put his arm across her shoulders and she escorted him towards her front door.

After dragging him to the sofa in her living room, she made him lay down and made him comfortable by covering him with a blanket. Under two minutes he was knocked out again. The loud snoring felt as if it was shaking the room.

She thought now that she had him settled, she needed to go check for the keys in the car and see whatever else was going on. That is when she realized the car was empty of fuel and the engine had gone dead. *Oh, my God*! She muttered to herself while brushing a hand through her hair. She rushed back to check on her new patient. *Oh! I need to call Nora.* She dialled the number and Nora promptly picked up and began bombarding her with questions.

"Nora! Yes! He is drunk, and totally stretched out on my sofa, dead to the world! His car ran out of gas. Maybe that was a good thing."

"I could tell things were not right, even with my blurred vision. Good Lord! What are you going to do with him?"

"Wait until he wakes up, get him sober, then guide him back to his house!"

"Well Susan, don't go getting any ideas with him now! He is no fun to be with!"

"What do you mean, Nora!"

Nora Jennings laughed out loud. "You know what I mean! Don't go getting fresh with him, ok silly! You always tell me how you are starving for love. He is certainly not one to be desired."

"Oh Nora, for heaven's sake! The man is stone drunk, and half dead; who would want him with that stinky breath? I'll keep you posted! I must go now, bye. Call you again later."

The spunky old lady laughed at herself while shaking her head. *Oh, Susan, Susan! Too bad I am getting old!* She was known to be feisty and flirty in her days. Nora Jennings had not lost her wit with age. She had much spunk all her young life, and even later with a husband that adored her. She had fun teasing and enticing men. It had been a game for her, she would laugh at how the men fell for her kibitz, as she called it, and would now laugh about it with pride and a sense of accomplishment.

No doubt, Lady Jennings in her younger years was, and to date still a very attractive woman. She was of medium height, with capturing blue eyes, shoulder length brown hair, and a well-shaped body. Her charming personality and panache still attracted admirers.

Her friend, Susan, from up the street did not possess Nora's qualities. Her interest in the drunk on the sofa was totally innocent. She took one look at him, covered him to make him cozy, then left to resume her chores in the kitchen. No sooner, a knock on the door startled her. She hesitated, puzzled, then made her way to go check. *Who on earth would be at my door so early in the morning? Today sure seems a day of events.*

She opened the door and found yet another surprise. She was

suddenly face to face with a police officer who, with a stern look on his face, questioned her about the car parked across the street.

"Miss, that car there is illegally parked near a fire hydrant. Your next-door neighbour told me it belongs to a visitor of yours?"

With a pitiful expression on her face, she tried to respond calmly, "Sorry, Officer, it seems my neighbour fell ill. I helped him to come into my place and he is now resting. He will move the car as soon as he can."

The officer listened and nodded. As he was ready to go off his shift, and was tired, he felt a bit merciful to let things go, but he warned her saying, "Madam, the car needs to be moved at once. I will be off duty shortly, but my colleague will soon be on duty and the car will be towed away! Your visitor will face a fine of three hundred dollars!"

With a sorrowful look on her face she begged him, "Please, Officer, give me a chance to look into it. I'll see what I can do because he is not well right now! At the moment , he is in deep sleep."

"You have been warned, ma'am!"

"Yes Sir, thank you. I will soon act upon it."

Her body shivered as she watched the officer walk away. He must have been as beat as Boris was, and ready to call it a day. How was she going to move the darn car without gas? She paused for a moment to regain her train of thought, then took a deep breath to clear her lungs. *So much for my peaceful morning!*

She was quietly closing the front door when an odd growling sound came out of her sleeping guest. She turned her head in time to see Boris roll off the sofa onto the floor. Froth was bubbling out of his mouth.

"Oh my God! What is happening to him now?" She cautiously walked towards him, shocked and totally alarmed at the scene right before her eyes.

Chapter Thirteen

Nature's True Beauty

Before departing, Lucio had enthusiastically given her a preview of the day's agenda, saying in his gentle tone, "Valeria, tomorrow we will visit the countryside. We will travel to the farmland deep into the center of the island. Enzo will drive to a certain area with our car, but in order to experience the real adventure in the country, we will hop onto a jeep with another driver that knows the area, and of course our fellow here, Enzo, will come along with his camera. I know it's not his favourite place, eh Enzo!" He remarked then turned to Valeria, winking mischievously, "Our young fellow here prefers to be by the seashore where he can admire the young girls in their bikinis!"

Valeria didn't know what to make of it and simply responded, "Oh Enzo, I sympathize with you, I hope the trip won't be too boring for you."

"On the contrary, I can't wait for the shepherds' treat! Maybe we will buy some of their specialty cheeses."

"I will tell you no more, Valeria, ok!" Lucio retorted, winking at her again.

Enzo responded, "It will be a lovely surprise! We will leave the rest untold and for you to discover. But I can assure you it would be interesting for all of us. We would be out in the country all day," he said, shrugging his shoulders and making a funny face.

"Woh, Enzo! Should I be elated, or worried. You make it sound mysterious?" She questioned him, smiling, thinking to herself, *maybe Lucio is right; he probably prefers the sandy beaches with the girls in bikinis.*

"You will see!" He said as he gently patted her shoulder in a kind gesture. The people here were touchy with expressions. Valeria attributed it to the warm culture of the island.

As scheduled for the next morning, bright and early, Lucio Alvani and Enzo were at the front door of the hotel, right on time to pick up Mrs. Abrosky. With a big smile, she was more than ready to hop into the front seat, all set with her note book and camera hanging from her neck, feeling joyful and empowered. She greeted them cheerfully.

"Good morning, fellows! I must say, on this journey, in your company and with your guidance on this splendid island, I feel that since I arrived here I have been living a magical dream! To be surrounded by the turquoise blue sea and the splendid sun that transforms the island into the most amazing colours, I am left totally mesmerized."

She had a tough time sleeping last night and couldn't wait for today's excursion. From the conversation last evening, she knew today was going to be a totally unique experience.

After a long and treacherous drive into the country, in both hilly and flat terrain, and reddish dust flying around, they finally arrived at a flat extension of land where about a dozen shepherds waited for them. An older fellow with a wide straw hat that covered half his face stepped forward to greet them. After respectfully removing his hat, he humbly approached them with a half-smile. Then with a serious look in his eyes, he introduced himself, "I am Nando Celeste. Welcome!" He spoke while extending his hand first to Lucio.

"*Molto piacere*, my pleasure. Thank you," Lucio reacted quickly, introducing himself and his party.

The rest of the men had stopped whatever they were involved with, and respectfully lined up with shy smiles, each dutifully following the other to nod and offer a handshake. After that they excused themselves and quickly returned to their work.

Nando remained to chat, explaining, "My men and I are putting the finishing touch to the mid-morning snack, and will be all ready when you return."

"*Grazie molto*, thank you! A treat for all of us, especially for Mrs. Valeria. It's her first time in Sardinia. *Vi ringrazia,* she thanks you," said Lucio.

Valeria listened, puzzled, but smiling. Enzo had made his way to join the shepherds who were now back to work, busy like bees, sweeping with cane brooms and clearing the area, and setting up a large picnic table with tree branches. Valeria assumed Nando must have been the fellow in command as he was busy talking to Lucio.

"*Consigliere*, Counsellor Alvani, the jeep with it's driver is waiting for you by the main trail up there." He pointed up to where the vehicle stood, surrounded by black pigs, goats, and other animals, all peacefully roaming together and feeding on wispy dry weeds and all of nature's bounty. Nando waved to the driver of the jeep indicating their readiness, and with his new visitors, proceeded in that direction. After they were comfortably accommodated in the jeep, he leaned over and said, "Have a good journey on this part of the island. We will see you back in a couple of hours."

Off they went to begin their adventure through this central part of Sardinia, away from the blue waters and sandy rocky beaches.

The adventure began with admiring the countryside. It was quite a change from sightseeing the bustling cities, buildings, cathedrals, and Gothic structures. Here, another calm, serene, world existed, with trees in varying colourful foliage. This part of the world certainly seemed to belong to the animals, totally untethered and roaming about freely.

They stepped out of the jeep ever so often and walked around, guided by the driver, Alfonso. He was well-spoken and dressed in country clothes; a reddish checkered shirt and heavier dark grey pants. He had a vast knowledge of the history of the earliest settlers. The shepherds were the remainder of indigenous people from centuries ago. He also pointed out some of the historic *nuraghic* structures, now listed as world heritage sites. They looked like stone bee-hive structures scattered in the distance. Alfonso said sadly, thousands were destroyed over the years. They represented churches, ovens, and wells of the early civilization. The information on the wells made Valeria curious. She heard Alfonso say they were of interest to many because of their unique formation, representing the female reproductive organs. The water in the well represented the womb, the mother; the people then worshipped the female form. *This is the most interesting part of the sites here.* She smiled wickedly as she tried to make eye contact with Lucio.

Valeria's heart rejoiced in the natural serenity she was experiencing. She thought, *it would be nice to be lost in here for a while, just with nature and the animals, and the wide blue cloudless sky. No demands.*

Suddenly her mind became troubled by thoughts of Boris. Lately, she had managed to put him out of her mind, forced denial. Lucky for her, the driver's voice brought her back to the present. After checking his watch, he announced, "I think it's time for us to return to the base. I am sure the fellows would have our snack all set up and ready."

It was mid-morning, but that was their custom; a treat for the visiting tourist. Valeria didn't question it. Enzo and Lucio were all smiles and more than happy to go back for whatever treat awaited them. They probably knew what to expect, but it was all a new experience for her.

Lucio noticed his lady friend's reluctance and saw the look of worry on her face. He leaned over to Valeria, touched her hand and said, "Valeria, wait and see, you are in for a real treat! This is the best of the best you will ever experience." His touch she needed.

The slight thought of Boris had disturbed her mood and suddenly placed a damper on her enjoyment of the remarkable surroundings.

She looked at him puzzled. She wasn't hungry yet. What could these shepherds offer in the middle of nowhere; she had not noticed any structure, or restaurant of any kind. Politely she smiled back saying, "Lucio, I am willing to experience and discover anything new; this is why I was sent here."

Once the jeep took them back to the base, Valeria was wide-eyed observing a picnic table with platters of a variety of cheeses, prosciutto, salami, soppressata, with gourmet breads nicely set up in baskets, covered with beautifully embroidered napkins awaiting them. Bottles of Merlot were set on the table, ready to be poured and served. The men couldn't wait to indulge in the food and wine.

Nando announced, "This is with the compliments of our local shepherds. Everything is homemade, and naturally grown and prepared. The shepherds are mighty proud of their products, their territory, and whatever they can offer the tourist making their way out here to explore their land, and to see the animals."

Valeria was more than happy to join in, just as her friends were. To her surprise, her taste buds relished the freshness of the variety of goat cheeses, sheep cheeses, and the array of cured meats. It was no comparison to anything she ever tasted before. The wine went down well even though it was mid-morning, and it complimented the food perfectly. After their delightful indulgence, they hopped back onto the jeep to continue further along the journey. The driver, Alfonso announced, "Dinner will be ready for us before sunset when we would have completed the tour."

Valeria thought she had eaten enough food to last her until the next day. Enzo and Lucio cheerfully chuckled, and Lucio said, "Oh! Their charcoal roasted pig is the best! I can't wait!" They were all in a good, relaxed mood now, fully satisfied. With much joy and laughter, they continued to drive along the rest of the tour, and Valeria learnt and discovered much more to take back to her boss.

Valeria's mood had also changed after the wine drinking. She felt heavenly again. *Thank God! I am glad to be totally removed, in another world far away from home, and in great company.* Here she was, lost in the middle of a countryside, where no one could reach her to disturb her peace.

They were going to explore some more nuraghi. They seemed to take pride in showing these structures. There were wells deeply dug into the ground and accessible by carefully taking all the rugged stone stairs going down. To her surprise, with the walking and fresh air, she felt light and agile, ready to eat again by the end of the day. The sun was going down as they made their way back. This time Alfonso took them to another location where a large rectangular white building was their place of reception for the roast pig dinner. It was a rustic country style restaurant with a lovely large patio. A bar was set up with fresh juices and other fresh drinks your heart could desire.

The smell of roasted meat was enticing. There were men and women busy with the task at hand. Others arrived in groups; tourists like Valeria. Before she realized it, the place was full and appeared more popular than she had anticipated. The hostesses were wearing island-style long peasant multi-coloured skirts with matching antic tops, and their heads covered with yellow flowered, blue and pink scarves. They were gracious and courteous, serving and pleasing everyone by their gentle nature. The exquisite meal ended with liqueur, coffee, and desserts which were served outdoors, under the reddish and blue sky that was bathed by the colours of the setting sun. To top it off, a group of dancers appeared on the platform dressed in traditional Sardinian costumes to entertain them with their folkloric singing, *cantu a chiterra*, and dancing, to special music from their flute-like instruments, *launeddas*. The evening ended in perfect harmony.

When they headed back, the men continued singing folkloric

songs. They tried to teach Valeria some ancient Sardinian words. Although she couldn't quite get the words, the tune from the launeddas instruments echoed pleasantly in her head. She arrived at her hotel in high spirits. Another lovely day had passed on this island, full of discovery and splendour.

The phone had been ringing in the hotel room all afternoon, only to be re-directed to the service desk to leave a message. It was Mrs. Nora Jennings who was desperately trying to get a hold of her. She had managed to get the number from the receptionist at the travel agency after attempting to get in touch with Rosy to no avail.

I must get in touch with her. "Please, Valeria, answer your bloody phone!" Mrs. Jennings was getting more and more desperate by the minute.

***

Smiling to herself, Valeria was making her way to the elevator to go to her room when the desk clerk called out, "Mrs. Abrosky, we have a message for you. Someone has been trying to get in touch with you urgently. Here is the number!" He handed her a piece of paper with a name and phone number. She glanced at the paper in her hand and muttered to herself, "Mrs. Jennings! Why her? What would she be calling for?" She brought a hand up to brush her hair back, hoping to also clear the sudden blur in her eyes. *It would be the middle of the night in Niagara now. I would have to wait until morning to make the call.*

Chapter Fourteen

Caught in Chaos

Shaking like a leaf, Susan's mind was spinning. Her entire body had been taken over by shock and fear. She was moving around in a disoriented manner not knowing which direction to go or turn. She brought her hand up to her forehead is dismay. This turn of events and confusion was just too much for her.

"Oh, my God! Is this guy dying right in my own living room?"

She gave out a scream of exasperation as she turned and stared at him. He was there on the floor, his body stiffening and turning blue by the seconds. Then a guiding light sparkled and zipped through her brain. She ran to her kitchen counter, grabbed the phone, and shaking hysterically, called 911. A female voice tried to calm her to make out what she was saying and get her address. She managed to get her name.

"Susan, help is on its way, an ambulance has been dispatched, the paramedics will be at your door any minute. I will remain on the line until help arrives. Everything will be fine, take a deep breath, hold, and exhale, try to calm down."

As she had said this, the sirens were soon heard right outside her door. The well-equipped paramedics quickly entered with their medical apparatus and gurney to diligently work on the patient. One fellow began taking Boris' vitals while the other moved swiftly at cleaning and clearing his mouth. Immediately the older one started chest compression, massaging steadily with the heel of his right palm and the left over for steadiness. Susan just looked on stupefied. Boris gasped, and the paramedic took his pulse again. They looked at each other and the younger of the two, who seemed well in control and knowledgeable, said to his companion, "There is a faint pulse, no time to waste; let's get him on fast, there is a slim chance."

Susan stood at a short distance away, stunned. She wasn't too courageous a person. Her self-esteem had decreased more after her husband had walked out on her. She looked on at the men; they were prompt and resolute and knew exactly what they were doing. At the same time, she wished them out of her house, including Mr. Abrosky who had surfaced this morning, invading her peace. While the paramedics were taking him away, one of them turned to her and said, "Mrs. Butler, you can ride in the ambulance with him. Please follow us."

In a zombie-like state she followed, dazed. Once outside there was more action going on. The fire department was there, and Boris' car was being taken away on a tow truck. The ambulance quickly whisked away, siren blaring. Susan was sitting beside Boris' stretcher, half out of her mind, going along with instructions. At one point she closed her eyes and wished this nightmare would go away. Once at the hospital, Boris was taken to the emergency room where a trauma specialist who was paged in advance waited. Registration and paper work would be taken care of afterwards. Susan stood there as if she was the next of kin; the nurse assumed she was the wife. A cardiologist came out asking for her while pulling his blue cap off. He introduced himself.

"Mrs. Butler, I am doctor Johnson, your husband has suffered a heart attack. There is some damage to his heart, but he will survive. As in similar cases, there is a chance that a secondary attack could follow. For now, he is stabilized in intensive care and we are observing him closely."

Finally, it dawned on Susan she should speak up. "Doctor, I am a neighbour, he is not my husband. I helped him into my house after his car shut down in front of my house when he ran out of gas. I found him slumped over his steering wheel. I believe he was drunk.”

“In that case, is there someone I can call?”

“I am afraid not at this time. His wife is in Europe on business and their three children are all at college. As soon as I get home, I would try my best to contact them all.”

“Ok. Sure. His blood alcohol level was high and combined with obesity it is not difficult to figure out what precipitated the heart attack. Ha and his family ought to be thankful you intervened otherwise he wouldn’t be here with us.”

“Thanks, Doctor. I should leave now. I must notify the family as soon as possible!”

Another blaring siren was heard getting closer just as the doctor’s pager buzzed. He quickly scribbled a note on a paper as he was almost half-way out the door, handed it to her and said, “Thank you. Please have the family call me. I would be happy to answer their questions. He is not out of danger and will remain in intensive care.”

After the doctor left, a nurse with a caring smile came to talk with her. She kindly assured, “I am taking care of your husband, Mrs. Butler. He is resting comfortably right now. I suggest you go down to the cafeteria and get yourself a coffee or something to eat. Later, you may be able to see him.”

Susan got a hold of herself and told the nurse what she had previously recounted to the doctor. “I must call my friend before anything. His family members are all away at this time. I am his neighbour.”

“Well he is one lucky man, I tell you! To have a caring neighbour such as you! For now, go look after yourself. You need some time out; you have been through an ordeal.”

The first thing Susan wanted to do now was place a phone call to Nora Jennings. She had to pass on the news and inform her of the turn of events, and how the old woman set her up. But she reflected, *didn't the doctor say that if I had not intervened, the man would not still be alive?* She found a telephone, fed it some quarters and dialled Nora's number. In no time she picked up.

"Hello."

"Hello, Nora? It's me, Susan!"

"Susan! It's about time you called! What on earth have you been up to with him? Did you take him to bed, or tried to keep him all to yourself all morning? You had me in suspense all day here, waiting to hear from you. There had been some action going on up and down the street. I saw fire trucks and two police cars go by. No sign of Mr. Big Shot returning home, so I thought, today Susan is getting her fill!"

"Nora! Nora! You have such a dirty mind! Do you know where I am calling from right now? The hospital! You'd never guess what I got myself into, and all because I listened to you!"

Nora replied, "What! Wait, give me a minute. Let me adjust this darn hearing aid. I cannot make out exactly what you are saying."

"Nora, can you hear me now? Nora!" *She is still fooling around with those plugs in her ears. I thought she was all set with the latest ones she had picked up from the guy that had flirted with her when she was advising him on tricks to play with the girls. Oh, Nora, Nora, why do I bother with you!* Finally, her voice came back on the receiver louder than ever, erupting her ear drum.

"SUSAN, ARE YOU THERE!"

"Yes, can you hear me now?"

"Yes. Sorry. These darn things! They work one day and they are a nuisance the next, as if I have not paid enough for them. Tell me now, what on earth are you doing at the hospital?"

"What I am doing here? Your Mr. Boris suffered a heart attack! He scared the heck out of me! He has pulled through but is now in intensive care. Don't ask! You need to call his wife and children. I want to go back home, and I rather be alone than put up with all the craziness that I have endured since this morning. Your bright idea to check on Mr. Abrosky! He was drunk and ended up having a cardiac arrest, and right in my living room! The police came to my door to enquire as his car was left in the wrong place. The ambulance! His car was towed away; it ran out of gas! Don't ask! My nerves are out of control! And on top of everything else they assumed I was his wife, until I explained to the doctor and the nurse; the hospital needed to know. They want us to contact his family now. You get a hold of his wife, his daughter, and whoever you know; tell them to come and assume their responsibilities. Nora, the only good thing out of this shamus is I was told that if I had not been there he would have died."

"Oh, good heavens! And here I was, thinking you were in bed with him!"

"Nora, you have one-track mind; sex, sex, and sex! Please lighten up! You got a job on your hands. As much as I am concerned about his wellbeing, I am done here! Find his wife and his daughter!"

"Of course! I will! As soon as I hang up with you. If you would like to stop by, I would treat you to a stiff drink; that might relax you!"

"I am not sure. I am so tired, Nora. You cannot imagine! You need to get busy; please get in touch with them as soon as you can!"

Susan felt lighter now. A big weight had been lifted off her chest by disclosing everything to Nora. She hoped the Abrosky family would soon get the news, and the sooner the better. The poor fellow would be better off with his own family looking after him. No, her decision was not to stop at Nora's. The experience had been more than she could take for one day. Later, she would call to enquire if she got in touch with Mrs. Abrosky, or any of the children.

Nora Jennings wasted no time calling Rosy's residence but got no answer; she left a message. Next, she called the travel agency, and once she was given the hotel number, she kept calling for Valeria, but she was totally out of reach way over in that country. Having to leave repeated messages unnerved her, but what else could she do now but sit patiently and wait for a reply.

The sun went down, night fell, yet there was no phone call from Rosy or Valeria nor did anyone return to Niagara. In the morning she would have to try to reach the boys.

***

Meanwhile, back in Sardinia, Valeria walked into her room holding the newspaper. Her phone message system continuously flashed a red light indicating some messages. Curiously, she picked up the receiver and dialled to retrieve them. "Mrs. Abrosky, this is the Niagara General Hospital. We are trying to get a hold of you. This is our number for you to call back, or we will try to contact you again."

The beautiful day with nature, the animals, the tasty food and wine, music, her lovely friends, all became a blur and seemed a dream. A chill zipped up and down her spine. *Please my dear God, keep my family safe.* An uneasiness had suddenly taken over her body. I guess I could call the hospital now. Since it is the middle of the night I'll leave Mrs. Jennings for the morning. She began to pace her room back and forth, in total panic.

Chapter Fifteen

The News

Against her will, Valeria forced herself to pick up the phone and dial the number for the hospital. She needed to know; her anxiety was just too much to bear since her worst fears inundated her being. *Has something drastic happened to Rosy? The boys? And Boris? Who knows what he must have been up to!* She had not talked to him in the last couple of days.

"Niagara General," a female voice promptly responded at the other end.

"It's Mrs. Abrosky. I got a message the hospital has been trying to reach me. I am out of the country currently. I am returning your call; sorry I could not call earlier, I have been working outdoors all day."

"One moment Mrs. Abrosky; I need to transfer you to the cardiac department."

Cardiac? Her head went fuzzy and she felt faint. The few minutes she was placed on hold seemed like an eternity as she impatiently held on to the phone with her shaky hand. Finally, another female voice came on, "Cardiac Department."

"It's Mrs. Valeria Abrosky, I got a message to call the hospital? I am presently out of the country. Can you please tell me what is wrong?"

"Mrs. Abrosky, I am the hospital's head nurse, and yes, Dr. Johnson has been trying to get in touch with you or your family. Mr. Boris Abrosky is in intensive care, but he is stable and resting

85

well. Dr. Johnson would call you in the morning. I am the nurse on duty tonight. You would need to speak to the doctor in charge. I am sure he would like to speak to you too and answer any questions that you may have."

"I see," she replied, confused. After a short pause she said, "He's my husband! What has happened to him? Is he going to be ok?"

"Mrs. Abrosky, I am sorry, only the doctor can give you details. I am only the nurse and not at liberty to discuss the patient."

The seriousness of the matter finally registered on her, and before slowly putting down the receiver, she said, "Bye, thank you." *It's Boris! What has happened to him!*

She had a long and restless night. How could she sleep while waiting and hoping the doctor's call would soon come? Night fell upon her combined with the darkness of her worry. The unknown was frightening. With her head in a fog and a mist of tears in her eyes, she moved around her room like a zombie. *What do I do now?* She reasoned with herself. She flung open the closet door and pulled out her suitcases. With anxious strides she began pulling down her clothing from the hangers, shoving them randomly into the cases. *Who cares what happens to these clothes; my life is now doomed!* Before long all her belongings were packed, and she was ready to go.

She called Air Canada and booked her return flight. She would arrive into Toronto at five the next evening.

"Hector! I need to call Hector to get me to Rome!" Since the people here engaged in strolling the night until late hours, she didn't hesitate to dial his number. To her luck, Hector answered promptly. "Hector, I need you to get me back to Fiumicino as soon as possible! I must fly back home tomorrow."

"Mrs. Abrosky, may I ask, has something drastic happened here? Why do you need to leave?"

"I am needed at home. I cannot begin to explain. All I know is I must get back at once! My family needs me right now!"

"Mrs. Abrosky, I will make the arrangements at once and send someone to pick you up. I will also get ready to leave."

She replaced the receiver. Her body slumped down on the chair and she put her head down and allowed the tears to freely stream down her cheeks.

"Oh, Boris! Boris, what will be next with you!"

After the relief from a good cry, she walked to the mirror. Her eyes were red and swollen, her mood at the lowest.

"I cannot afford to disappear just like that! What about my agenda here? Lucio and Enzo are scheduled to pick me up in the morning! They would not find me!"

She glanced at her watch. It was past ten; four in the morning in Niagara. There was no turning back now, regardless of the phone call she awaited from the doctor; when it would come. Boris was in intensive care in the cardiac wing. It did not sound good, and with his obesity and food addiction over the past couple of years, she had no doubt he was heading towards serious health issues.

I must get to him as soon as I can. But Lucio, Enzo, and the Mayor? They need to be notified.

She didn't have his home number, and his office was now closed. She grabbed a pen and paper and started to write a note; she would leave it at the front desk. It wasn't her style to disappear in such an abrupt manner.

So much for exploring La Maddalena tomorrow, as Lucio had said to her before they last parted. She would be flying home instead, back to her nightmare with Boris, and at this point, the unknown.

Chapter Sixteen

The Halted Journey

Lately, Lucio couldn't wait to start the day. He knew the sites of his island well and it gave him immense pleasure to proudly narrate its history and recommend places to anyone interested. This morning especially, he got up bright and early and after a quick breakfast proceeded to check in on his beloved, Chiara. He kissed her forehead when his new mantra took over, *remember to accept*. He didn't linger there too long as he would often do and feel sorry for both of them. With quick strides, he walked out the door.

Another splendid day awaited him and Enzo. The sunrays were bright and radiating a lovely warmth and the clear blue sky inspired the soul.

Cheerfully, Lucio greeted Enzo and playfully slapped a hand on his shoulder, "Are you ready my friend? Lately, I must confess, I am looking forward to starting the day. Today is going to be special! La Maddalena is my favourite place. I can't wait to see the look on our Canadian friend's face when she sees the elevated mansions in their various structures overlooking the islands. The lush greenery, the huge rocks that had surfaced from underneath the sea and now lay scattered in an array of shapes is an exhilarating view for all to enjoy. I have them all underlined here in this map, along with the names of famous Americans that live in some of the impressive residences."

"Lucio, you are good at narration! I am convinced they couldn't have picked a better person to do this promotion."

"Oh, my friend, I couldn't have done it alone! You are also enthusiastic about all the picturesque sceneries; I can tell. And you have been taking such great pictures! Not to mention how la signora, Valeria, is mesmerized with our Sardinia. She is different, and she cares. One can tell that she truly enjoys her work with a full heart."

"You are right, Lucio, she is encouraging. This is why I want to give her only the best of my work."

They pulled up in front of the hotel. *Strange,* thought Lucio with a frown; *the lovely lady is not waiting in her usual spot.* They waited for a brief time, but no Valeria to be seen. Lucio decided to step out of the car as he turned to Enzo, "Maybe all that walking and riding in the country, the fresh air from yesterday, and the wine and food must have been too much for her! She may be a little late. Wait here; I will go and check with the concierge." As he walked towards the entrance a strange premonition invaded his thoughts. He approached the front desk.

"Good morning Signore. Excuse me. I am Lucio Alvani. Here to pick up Mrs. Abrosky. Would you please ring her room?"

"Oh, Mr. Alvani, Mrs. Abrosky has checked out." He took an envelope from the message rack behind him and handed it to Lucio. "She left this for you."

Lucio's world immediately became blurred. *Why, and how could she do this? This is absurd! We are not yet finished with the project!* "Sir, please tell me; was anything wrong? What time did she check out?"

"I cannot say. I don't know. All I can tell you is she has checked out."

Lucio walked away, back to Enzo waiting in the car; the unopened envelope in his hand. He felt disheartened. He opened the car door, embarrassingly holding back tears. He felt his heart and soul had suddenly been ripped off.

Enzo took one look at him, "Lucio, what's wrong? Is our friend well?"

"Enzo, she has checked out! She is gone! She is not here anymore!" His voice was shaky and his hand trembled while still holding on tightly to the envelope.

"I am surprised! Something urgent must have caused her to do this! What is that you are holding?"

"An envelope; they handed it to me at the front desk."

"So there! Lucio open it; that's your explanation!"

"I don't want an explanation! All I know is she is not here! It's not acceptable!" He responded irritatingly, and oddly for his character, in a high tone.

"Lucio, for heaven's sake, calm down; shit happens! I am as disappointed as you are! I am sure something must have happened; that's why she had to go. Open the darn letter and read it! Then we will both know exactly what is going on!"

Lucio was reluctant but slowly tore the envelope open under Enzo's watch. He did not wish to reason. Then he read,

My dear friends, Lucio and Enzo,

With much sorrow in my heart, I regretfully write this note. I must fly home first thing in the morning. Apparently, there has been a medical emergency with my husband and I must be there for him. It's my duty as a wife. I am so sorry to interrupt our tour at this point.

Thank you for your assistance. You are both wonderful people to work with. My regards to the Mayor; I will leave it to Mr. Patty

to get in touch with him with whatever he decides moving forward.

I wish you both well,

Valeria Abrosky.

Lucio finished reading the letter feeling even worse than when he first started. He turned to Enzo sitting there in the heat and said, "Please make the car cooler; I am boiling here," as he wiped the sweat off his forehead.

"You see Lucio, she had to go. I am sorry too. What else could she do?"

Lucio shook his head, "Enzo, you won't understand! She gave me reason to get going in the morning! She was alive, empowering, and I enjoyed her company. She was here, on our island, sent from heaven for me. I don't want to know or hear about a husband, family, or duty as a wife! For me Valeria was the beautiful Canadian lady in sole existence, without other attachments. I cannot accept that she has more important commitments. I know it is crazy for me to think that, but I can't control my feelings; the renewed life she brought me was stupendous."

"Lucio, I suspect you have fallen in love with her? You are a married man, aren't you?"

"Oh, Enzo! A married dead man! I love my Chiara! She was my life! You know she has been gone for ten years now; alive yes but gone! Gone, Enzo, gone! It began when she was diagnosed with multiple sclerosis which went from bad to worse over the years, and then the early onset of dementia compounded it all for my wife, now she is bedridden. She doesn't know me anymore; she is shrivelling to nothingness from just lying there. I have tried to seek further medical help for her; no one can help her anymore. I have become desperate! I have cried! I have been dealing with depression! I see my therapist regularly to cope! Since Valeria arrived I felt like living again, when before I wanted to die. And now she is also gone!"

"Sorry, Lucio, about your wife I mean. Maybe Valeria might come back; after all we are not finished. But now you know she is married, my friend?"

"Please, don't remind me! I prefer to think of her as free; free like a bird flying around the blue water of our sea."

"Think what makes you feel good, Lucio. Reality is reality." He looked at him with concern.

***

Valeria had checked out at five in the morning. Hector was on time to assist and take her to Fiumicino airport to board her Air Canada flight direct to Toronto.

In a somber mood, she made her way through the crowd. After two attempts to get in touch with Dr. Johnson from the airport's public phone she still didn't know exactly what had happened to Boris, other than he was in intensive care. She didn't want to worry the children. Besides, she had no more liras to drop into the public phones that seemed to gobble her coins; it wasn't as easy to make a phone call as in Canada. Distracted and ready to drop from a sleepless night, she wasn't thinking straight. At this stage, she couldn't wait to collapse in her seat in the plane and fall asleep, making her cruel world temporarily disappear.

Chapter Seventeen

Valeria Returns Home

Valeria tried to move as fast as her fatigued, aching body would let her to exit the airport at Pearson. She knew no one would be there to greet her on her arrival since she had not been in touch with Rosy or the boys. As she looked around, she noticed some travellers being received by dear ones who welcomed them with hugs and kisses, some with flowers. A pang of self-pity and sorrow hit the pit of her stomach. Dragging her suitcases, she made her way to the ground transportation desk, and soon she was on her way to Niagara.

As she opened her front door, to her surprise she heard, "Uh! Hi! Valeria! Thank God you are back home!" Mrs. Jennings, the neighbourhood watchdog called out from her window, shuffling her feet in house slippers, excitedly making her way towards her from across the lawn. Valeria, even though in a hurry, was happy to at least see one human being reaching out to her. She knew Boris disliked Mrs. Jennings, but at least she was the first person to greet her on her return.

"Mrs. Jennings, how are you?" She embraced her like she used to hug her mom with sincere affection from her heart. "Oh! Valeria, darling, I tried to call you many times yesterday! I couldn't get you! You poor thing, you must have heard about your husband."

"Somewhat. I am told he is in the hospital, but I have not been able to reach the doctor. I have to run to the hospital now; as soon

95

as I drop off my luggage."

"Oh! You don't know dear? He suffered cardiac arrest! I was told, but of course you need to go to him. I will run along now. I mustn't keep you."

While walking away she kept looking back and mumbling, "I will talk to you later. I must tell you, I tried to get Rosy but she couldn't be reached either."

She waved her off, rushing along to drop off her stuff. She immediately headed for the hospital, almost holding her breath, not knowing exactly what had happened to her beloved Boris.

Once she reached the cardiac wing, nervous and shaky, she approached the nurse at the desk who seemed absorbed in whatever she was doing and ignoring Valeria.

"Excuse me, I am Mrs. Abrosky; I am here to see my husband. I would like to know what room he is in, and I was wondering when I would be able to talk to Dr. Johnson?"

By now her anxiety level had her totally out of whack. The nurse, cold and removed, came around from her desk and simply said, "He is in room 204 at the end of the hall. I will have to page Dr. Johnson to see if he is still in the hospital, otherwise you will have to try to get in touch with him tomorrow."

She cautiously walked into room 204, and there on the semi-elevated hospital bed lay Boris' lifeless body all hooked up to tubes: intravenous fluids, feeding, and a heart monitor. It was a scary sight. It caused Valeria instant goosebumps. "Oh! My God! What has happened to him?" She kissed his forehead as his face was inaccessible with all the medical apparatus, and gently stroking her fingers through his greasy hair, she tried to talk to him.

"Boris, honey, I am here, can you hear me?" He seemed sedated and completely out of it. He reacted to her touch, half opened his eyes and tried to answer, slurring in a whisper that Valeria hardly understood what he was saying. "I am tired, I have no power," then he closed his eyes. He didn't seem fully aware of her presence or anything much; whether she had returned from her trip, or any other concern. Her husband was just lying there, in a state of weak consciousness. Valeria's panic escalated. *I must meet the doctor at once and find out exactly what is going on with my husband! I need to call Rosy and the boys! This does not look good to me!*

After many attempts at paging Dr. Johnson, he finally arrived.

"Hello, Mrs. Abrosky, I am Dr. Johnson, the physician in charge of your husband. Let's sit here and talk. Your husband has suffered a cardiac arrest which has caused some damage to his brain. He now has a bit of a speech impediment but is resting comfortably. Once he regains some strength, this can be reversed with speech therapy. We will keep him in intensive care for two more days merely as a precaution. The good news is, there is no reason why we should not see a full recovery, but with time. It would be difficult for him at first, but with the right care, his determination and family support, he should be well again." He smiled, shook her hand, and started to walk away. Valeria hesitated for a moment then called out, "Doctor, I need some answers! What brought this on, what are the chances of recurrences? I have to call my children! We all need to know!"

"Mrs. Abrosky, once he is discharged for home, a health nurse would be sent to him. She will assist him. She will go over the instructions with you, on how to proceed with him and what diet and exercise is necessary."

Valeria was still confused and not at all satisfied, but before she had a chance to ask more questions, the doctor was out of sight. Pensive and desolate, she walked to the hallway phone and decided it was time to call Rosy, Rino, and Danny. She needed their moral support. Boris looked seriously helpless, regardless of what the doctor had said. She needed to further investigate his condition. She dialled Rosy's number, no answer. *Let me try the boys.* They shared an apartment. She dialled Rino's, and after the third ring he answered.

Valeria let out a sigh of relief, "Rino, it's mom! How are you? Is Danny home with you?"

"No mom, he is out. Where are you calling from? Are you still in Europe? You don't sound right. Is something wrong? When will you be back?" He sensed the melancholy in her voice and knew that something was odd.

"Rino, I am back home. I am calling from the hospital. It's your dad; they tell me he suffered a heart attack! He is in intensive care right now. I arrived home tonight; have you seen or heard from Rosy? Where is she?"

"Mom, I don't know about Rosy. When did this happen. How is dad?"

"He doesn't look good to me, but the doctor says he has a good chance of recuperating."

"Mom don't worry! I will get Danny, and get a hold of Rosy, and we will be there as soon as we can." Rino cared about his father a lot and at once he became seriously concerned.

"Thanks, Rino. I will be waiting for you."

In the meantime, she was ready to drop. With jet lag and not enough sleep, her head felt foggy and her legs as if they would soon buckle under her. She made her way back to Boris' room and collapsed on the chair beside his bed, hoping to remain there in vigil all night. Boris was sleeping soundly while the monitor kept track of his vitals.

The next day the children arrived. Valeria was somewhat relieved. They were all the family she had, and they brought her much comfort. Boris' face lit up on seeing them around his bed; that gave Valeria a boost of hope. She loved her family in spite of the fact that her husband had been difficult over the past few years. But now he looked so pitiful and helpless lying there, and this brought tears to her eyes.

A week passed, and Boris was taken out of the ICU and later discharged from the hospital. Valeria, with the help of the health nurse, assumed her responsibilities as a devoted wife to help care for her husband. Like the doctor had said, it would take time but eventually he would come along.

His speech slurred and he could hardly maneuver his right leg and arm. He faithfully went to therapy three times a week. Valeria felt Boris was now her priority, so she called Mr. Patty and arranged a leave of absence.

"Valeria, I am sorry about your husband. We would like to have you back as soon as you can be available."

"I understand, Mr. Patty, but right now I cannot promise you anything. I will pass on to you all I have gathered so far from my trip to Sardinia. You might have to send someone else to complete the tour."

After she hung up, she turned and looked around her kitchen. The sink was full of dirty dishes, the house was in a disastrous condition as though a storm had passed through when she was away. Boris lay on a movable stretcher in the living room, asleep. The nurse had advised, "He needs to be on the ground floor because he definitely cannot do the stairs right now to access his bedroom."

Valeria patiently embraced her fate. Occasionally she would close her eyes thinking she was in a dream, and she would envision her two lovely friends and the splendour of that faraway island she was forced to abruptly leave behind.

Would I ever see them and that place again? How would I now! A dream; it was only a dream!

Chapter Eighteen

Lucio Back in Gloom

While Valeria indulged in daydreaming, the two dear friends she had abruptly left behind in Sardinia and who had become used to the lovely lady from Canada, especially Lucio, were left disheartened and confused. After her sudden disappearance, they walked into the Mayor's office at the City Hall looking for answers on what to do next. The program needed to be completed.

The tour had been abandoned with Valeria's unforeseen departure. Lucio, shaking his head kept saying repeatedly to Enzo, "Her disappearance was totally unexpected!" Lucio sat across from the Mayor's desk and presented him with her note.

"Look, John, this is all we are left with. Tell me this is just temporary." Deep down he expected him to say something like, "She will have to return to complete the job that she left unfinished." Anxiously waiting for his response, he nervously fidgeted with a piece of paper in his hand with her address, and the phone number of the travel agency. He turned to John Minerva again, handing him the paper he was holding, "John, you are going to place a call to the agency, or would you like me to do it? I would ask for La signora! If I recall correctly, you should have an agreement with that Mr. Patty since the beginning of the project?"

"Yes, Lucio, you are correct; we had an agreement for a period of one month. We had agreed to pay for her airfare, the cost of hiring Enzo, office accommodation for Mrs. Abrosky, and the hotel was also booked for a month. We have incurred some expense, taken from our tourist promotion fund, which we couldn't afford but did anyway because of the anticipated benefits."

"Our funds have been bled into red for a long time now. Here we thought this programme would help us; now we are left with an unfinished job. Mrs. Valeria Abrosky was taking in the excursion deeply, and with genuine interest. I know she would have promoted our island well." Lucio expressed himself in a strong tone of voice. Deep down he knew why, and Enzo also figured out why his friend's thoughts were full of passion. His interest wasn't as much about the unfinished job as it was for the lovely lady's absence from making his days brighter. Enzo thought to himself, *I must admit; she was a joy to have around, and she so loved our island and warmly embraced our culture. I was lucky enough to have met her and even more privileged to have worked with her.*

John Minerva listened intently, and had to agree that his *consigliere,* advisor, Lucio Alvani, was right. He would soon have to place a call to World Travel, Niagara, and discuss with Mr. Patty about exactly where they all stood. Would Mrs. Abrosky return to finish off from where she had left off, or was she going to be replaced by another agent? It was left to be seen. He looked at his watch and said,

"It's too early over there to call now, given the time difference; I would place a call later today. I would surely keep you posted, Consigliere, *Va Bene!* Ok! Let's meet again tomorrow morning." With that he got up, placed a hand on Lucio's shoulder and said, "Let's call it a day! I am sure we will find a solution."

Lucio drove home with an elated morale. He walked into his flat; silence reigned throughout the place, as usual. With the dim nightlight in the hallway, he walked around a bit before making his way to Chiara's room. She was curled up in a fetal position. He bent over and kissed her on the head. He saw no body-reaction, received no response from her. He retreated into the darkness and made his way to his lonely bedroom. He had been taught by his father that boys don't cry. He wasn't hungry, and his stomach felt queasy. Still dressed he slumped onto his single bed, brought an arm up and across his brows, and relaxed with the sensation of his body sinking into the mattress. Before long he drifted off in serenity. The next morning the sun's rays filtered through the window of his room. He took a long stretch to invigorate his blood flow. With some renewed life in him he decided to keep up his spirits. *Maybe today when I go to the City Hall, I would receive news that my new-found friend will be returning soon.* Only hope would keep him going.

***

John Minerva arrived at the office bright and early and anticipated Lucio Alvani's visit any time soon. He did make the call to World Travel before leaving his office the night before and had a long discussion with Mr. Patty about the future of the programme. He made it clear that he had delivered as promised, providing the best cooperation on his side. In return he was reassured that the best employee for the job would be selected and they would all work together diligently, to promote his island.

"Oh yes, Mr. Minerva, we would be able to compile a well packaged tour! With the proper marketing, your hotels would be fully booked in advance, and the island would have buses of tourists in a continued stream for the summer; April to October."

The Mayor had done due diligence, delivering on all his promises with the expectation that his people would benefit from this promotional campaign. Furthermore, he desperately wanted to boost the citizens' pride by giving them the opportunity to show off every aspect of their marvellous island, Sardinia, not omitting the unique archipelago that was equally beautiful and amazing to explore and experience. Sardinia was gifted with its surrounding islands only reachable by boat and cruisers. It was surely a great boost to the island's tourism.

So much was involved. Apart from the gorgeous scenery the islands offered travellers, Sardinia's sportsmen, its ports, fuel consumption, retailers, hotels, restaurants, and businesses at large, all stood to gain much from the expected developments. The Mayor was looking forward to the materialisation of these ideas for his country. Now this agent had abruptly abandoned them, leaving behind no explanation but a brief note. *What kind of professional behaviour is that? What kind of business are they running? We don't carry on business like that ever here! We are genuine people; we stick to our promises. Our word is our honour!*

After the last conversation with Lucio and Enzo, John Minerva became perturbed. *You start something, you bring it to a close,* he thought, shaking his head in confusion. A few hours after they left, he picked up the phone and made a person to person overseas call. "Operator, Mr. Patty at World Travel, Niagara, please." He was going to give this fellow a piece of his mind before he really lost his cool.

In no time Mr. Patty was on the phone. "Good morning Mr. Mayor, Minerva, how are you? My sincere apologies to you, Sir. I should have called you before. Sorry! I have been in total dismay at the sudden interruption of Mrs. Abrosky's trip. I have been waiting to have a meeting with her, to see where we stand, then get back to you."

"Yes, Signor Patty, our programme has been left incomplete, at a standstill! Your lady suddenly departed! All I have is a brief note with no real explanation about the future of the contract. I have not heard from you. My colleagues are left in suspense, and not to mention the funds we put together to support the promotion: donations from our businesses here that they can hardly afford. Furthermore, we had set up a gala evening for the last night, in honour of Mrs. Abrosky. People have bought tickets, caterers have been hired, and musicians have been engaged. We would now have to refund money to the people, plus lose our deposits. I am not sure you realise how much we have sacrificed, Mr. Patty! Pardon my apparent impatience!"

"Believe me, Signor Mayor, I feel badly about the situation too. Apparently, Mrs. Abrosky's husband suffered a massive heart attack. It was a family emergency. She had no choice but to come back and attend to him. I am told he is in pretty bad shape right now. Therefore, I have been patiently waiting to talk to her to see if there is any chance of her completing the tour, or if I would have to recruit a replacement. Please give me a few more days. And again, I am so sorry. I hope you realize this was quite unplanned, but family matters are unpredictable. I am hopeful as I have confidence in Mrs. Abrosky's commitment to her work."

"I am sorry about her husband and I am sad for her; she is a nice lady. I would talk with my *Consigliere,* advisor, and get back to you, or you can get back to me with whatever information you would have. Either way, we need to aim to finish what we have started."

"I completely understand, Sir. I will try to have a meeting with Mrs. Abrosky as soon as she is available, and we would take it from there. Let's hope she would be able to return and there won't be need for a replacement."

At this point John Minerva thought, what was the use to insist on anything; it's better to wait a while and see what will happen. "Mr. Patty, get back to me as soon as you can because as of now, everything is on hold. Ok. Bye for now."

Mr. Patty, mortified, said, "Bye, Signor Minerva, have a good day. I promise to call you as soon as I have an answer from Valeria Abrosky."

Chapter Nineteen

Valeria's World

The health nurse, Florence, could only offer a few hours a day to assist Valeria with her husband's care. Valeria as a good wife, felt dutiful to be there also, to provide for Boris' added comfort. The exercise therapy the nurse was putting him through was painful, but with his wife's encouragement he would endure until the sessions were over. Other than that discomfort, his medication made him relax; he was sleeping a lot and Valeria could not believe how calm he had become. Through his slurred speech he was polite, his demands had diminished and when in need he was reluctant to be his old self and was gentle instead. Valeria's gaze lingered, fixated on this helpless man lying before her, and asked herself, "Was this man the same person I had escaped from; my dictator husband?" She felt sorry for him. Now he was likeable, and a totally different man. Had this dramatic episode changed his personality? Whatever it was, her only hope was that he would soon recover, especially regain his mobility, and leave behind his negative side, then she would love and cherish her new Boris and be happy.

The phone rang, and she ran to pick it up. The nurse was to arrive soon. Her privacy was somewhat invaded. She hurriedly answered, "Hello!"

"Valeria, Mr. Patty here!"

"Oh yes! Hello, Mr. Patty."

No more delays or escape from him now. I owe him explanations and answers. She had been avoiding him, cancelling two appointments to meet due to the situation at hand.

"Valeria, how are you? Tell me first, how your husband is?"

"The best that can be expected. I have a health nurse who works with him well. It will be some time before he is totally rehabilitated."

Mr. Patty was trying to be sympathetic. In his mind his number one interest was the business in Sardinia coming to a halt. And Mr. Minerva needed answers.

He was trying to control his anxiety while listening to her laments. Then he impatiently interrupted, "Valeria, can you come to the office? We need to talk about the unfinished work. I am under pressure here to figure out what to do next. Please, how is tomorrow morning at ten? I appreciate your situation but I also need to move forward."

Valeria didn't know if she could get away. She needed to check with the nurse, and besides, it made her feel guilty to leave her husband. Her mother had always impressed on her what should come first in a woman's life.

Poor Valeria was torn between reality and duty. She knew Mr. Patty was right. If only she could complete her tour of that splendid paradise with Lucio and Enzo. But fate had turned the direction of her ambition for her to return home. After all, she did have a family. Boris was right to complain about her job. He had provided well, he was a hard worker, and their savings account was proof of this. This job was totally for self-reward. Maybe she should have worked harder at helping him get over his sense of inadequacy and worthlessness after he retired. Instead, she chose to build on business rewards for Mr. Patty and his agency. But she was also a good worker and her boss perceived her as his highest achiever as she never lost a sale.

Valeria now slept upstairs, alone in her bedroom, and all these guilty thoughts tormented her. The children had been coming home to visit their dad on the weekend, especially Rino and Danny who had great respect for him. Boris adored his sons. He would often say to his wife, "Eh! Valeria, look at our boys! They are the best; clean cut, high achievers. We are lucky I tell you!"

In the morning she would call Rosy to see if she could come home on Saturday since it would be the nurse's day off. Maybe she would stay with her dad while Valeria goes to meet Mr. Patty. Was he right? Was she too taken with her husband's condition? With her emotions out of whack? She had abandoned Mr. Patty's project, along with her obligation towards everyone concerned.

She would have to impose on Rosy to look after her dad. She could not delay the meeting with Mr. Patty any longer. This was important.

***

It wasn't easy to find Rosy at home. Often, she stayed up until the wee hours of the morning finishing her assignments. She was studying to become an architect and had a heavy workload with presentations that were quite draining and demanding.

Valeria's phone calls again went unanswered. Instead of getting angry she muttered to herself, *on second thought, I must agree with Boris. Our children are hard workers, more like their father.* She didn't give herself too much credit. She could detect subtle traces of her own personality in Rosy, although she was resentful of being told what to do by her father. Her daughter also had that strong side like her father; she often scolded her mother to get on with her life in today's times. She often accused Valeria of being old fashioned like her own mother, not giving any importance to her own self-worth.

To her surprise her phone rang, and there was Rosy enquiring about her father. "Rosy, oh Rosy! I am so glad you called! I have been trying to get a hold of you!"

"Mom, is anything wrong? How is dad?"

"Your dad is coming along fine. Once he improves his speech, he should be well on his way to recovery. He is making daily progress in regaining strength in his arm and leg."

"I am glad! You sure had me scared there for a minute!"

"Rosy, can you come home this weekend? I need to go meet Mr. Patty and I would feel comfortable to leave him knowing you stayed with your father."

"Mom, I have an important presentation tomorrow. I am exhausted right now, but I would be fine to drive home after class. I should be there by seven o'clock tomorrow night. And, of course, I would be glad to look after dad on Saturday morning."

"Thanks, Rosy, you are my saviour. It will be a huge relief for me, once I get to submit my research information and be done with Mr. Patty's nagging."

"Wish me luck with my presentation and see you tomorrow night! Bye, mom! Love you!" Rosy was always in a hurry. Before Valeria could add another word, the call ended.

She smiled with pleasure in her heart. *Rosy is a good daughter.*

She walked into the living room to check on Boris and found him sound asleep. Now she needed to place a phone call to Mr. Patty and set up an appointment with him for Saturday morning. That had been a heavy weight on her mind, apart from the turmoil at home. Determined, she picked up the phone and got on to the agency's receptionist. "Hello Vanda, how are you? It's Valeria! May I please speak to Mr. Patty?"

"Yes, he just walked in. I will connect you."

"Hello! Patty here!"

"Mr. Patty, it's Valeria! How are you? I can be available on Saturday morning at ten. Can we have our meeting then, that is if it's convenient?"

"Valeria, yes! I have been waiting for your call. I will make myself available. The sooner we solve this matter, the better."

"Good! See you on Saturday then! Bye, Mr. Patty."

She let out a sigh of relief and walked to the front door. These days Valeria hadn't been out of the house much. After errands to the drugstore and the food market to purchase the bare necessities, she would rush back home to her duties.

In her preoccupied state she had not noticed Mrs. Jennings across the street, discretely watching as usual from her window. Her old friend was noting her comings and goings, dying to know what was going on with her friend's boor husband. She didn't want to pry or phone. She waited for Valeria to visit her, for when she wanted to talk. She could see his car parked in the garage. Somehow, she missed noticing when the boys had brought it back.

They had paid a fine of three hundred dollars to retrieve the vehicle. No one had told Valeria, or the boys, or Rosy, exactly how everything had happened. Mrs. Jennings couldn't wait to tell Valeria about Susan's episode with her drunken husband, and what the poor girl had endured being stuck with him. They didn't know that thanks to her, he was still alive otherwise he would have been gone.

Mrs. Jennings had much free time on her hands with no family living with her. Her sweet husband had passed away three years ago. Her son was married and living in England and never visited. She would only get a letter from him once in a blue moon. She had given up driving due to her failing vision and hearing. At this time in her life, she had resorted to her backyard and her front window for entertainment. She enjoyed working on the flower beds at the front of her house, being out there inconspicuously, spying on the neighbourhood folks. Lately she had been bored out of her mind. She called Susan after noticing not much happening in her immediate surroundings. The phone rang but no answer from Susan. "I will try again," she said to herself.

At Valeria's home, life wasn't dull. They needed to take Boris for checkups and other appointments. It wasn't an easy task to lift him off the bed to take him to the car. Valeria and the nurse together tried to manage with his limited mobility. Dr. Johnson received them in good humour this morning.

"Mrs. Abrosky, I am pleased with his pulse and blood pressure readings; he is definitely improving. Keep up the excellent work! Eventually he will have a fine recovery."

"Dr. Johnson, I agree with you. He rests quite comfortably. As for his mobility, he has a hard time, and his slurring is a problem for him; I can see how it frustrates him. The nurse only has so much time, and before you know it the day is done. Nurse Florence here is great at what she does. I would like a speech therapist to help him with speaking clearer. He is slurring badly and needs some help."

"They didn't send you a notice for that yet?" He asked surprisingly.

"No one has contacted me in that regard, and I would like something done about it, soon."

The doctor scribbled a referral and handed it to her. "My receptionist will contact you with an appointment as soon as she gets one. I will see you in two weeks?"

He got up to leave for another room with a waiting patient. Valeria was not too pleased with this doctor; he was curt and always in a hurry, like her Rosy. She worried about her husband. He seemed to be making progress with his mobility with nurse Florence's perseverance, but was still left with the problem of his speech.

Her husband had been a dynamic keynote speaker when he stood at podiums and was much in demand to address thousands of people, mainly smart executives from big companies. Boris would then be passing on his knowledge to them on how to succeed in the corporate world. You never heard a peep while he spoke as his audiences would be totally enthralled. Valeria had accompanied him in earlier years, as her mom had encouraged her to go along while she looked after their children.

"Valeria you must support your husband! Accompany him! I will take care of the little ones," she would say. Her parents were extremely proud of their son-in-law. For them he could do no wrong.

Now, here he lay; a handicapped man, unable to get a full sentence through his lips nor move at will.

Valeria felt immensely disturbed after the doctor's visit. After they got home the nurse helped feed Boris and gave him his medications. She slowly closed the door and walked towards the kitchen where Valeria stood doing the dishes. She poked her head in the doorway and whispered, "Mrs. Abrosky, I will return in the morning for the regular scheduled exercises. I have given Mr. Abrosky his medication for the night. He should rest comfortably." She quietly excused herself and left for the night.

Valeria felt the need for some fresh air. The doctors, nurses, the hospital, being out all day, were just too much for her. She stepped out her front door and walked around to check on her shrubbery and hydrangeas that were now in full bloom this time of the year. The colours of blues were her favourite. With Boris' absence, they were a faded colour of pink now. The gardener had not attended to them. Boris had insisted that it was his job now to play around with the miracle of colours by applying acid chemicals to the plants.

"Valeria, my dear, sweetheart," she heard a frail voice calling. As she turned, the voice seemed familiar. It was Mrs. Jennings from across the street, waiting on the side like a bird of prey, and summoning her.

"Mrs. Jennings! So sorry; I had not seen you there!" She exclaimed as she walked towards her neighbour. Valeria gave her an apologetic hug, "Sorry, my head seems to be in the clouds these days. I don't know if I am coming or going. How are you, Mrs. Jennings?"

"I am fine, dear."

Mrs. Jennings tilted her head in a caring expression while taking hold of Valeria's hand. "How are you my dear? How is that husband of yours?"

Valeria felt her eyes blurring with tears but managed to cover it up with a smile. "He is coming along pretty good, considering everything."

Affirming with a nod, Mrs. Jennings responded, "I am glad, dear. Now, should you need any help you know you can count on me. Should you need to talk or anything, I am always here for you."

"Thank you, Mrs. Jennings, I know. You are a good neighbour."

"Your Boris, he is not getting out much. I guess he is not allowed to drive yet?"

"Mrs. Jennings, I know I have not told you. His mobility is not the best right now, but he is coming along great with therapy. My biggest concern is his speech; he can hardly express himself. I got upset with the doctor today. To this date they have not made arrangements for him to see a speech therapist."

"Really? What a shame! Listen, let me know how you are making out. You know my friend Susan, from up the street? She is a special aid teacher. She's retired but qualified for that sort of work. I am sure she can help."

"Good to know. I will wait a couple of days and if I don't hear from the clinic, I would decide what next to do."

"I must go now, I need to check on my husband. Mrs. Jennings, nice seeing you." And she walked back to her home, reflecting on the neighbour's suggestion.

On Friday night, in preparation for her Saturday meeting with

Mr. Patty, she reviewed her notes from the trip, placing all the information in order, pausing at times to admire the picturesque sceneries of that faraway place of perfection and splendour.

Chapter Twenty

Mr. Patty's Dilemma

Mr. Patty cheerfully greeted her at his office, offering genuine support regarding her husband's recent illness. Valeria was relieved at this reception because she had been worried about his reaction to the incomplete work assignment. With the recent turn around of events in her life, she had no time to entertain thoughts about her boss's reaction. He had sounded upset and disillusioned by her sudden return, and she imagined with the situation now pending it must have been distressing for him. To her amazement, this morning he was amiable, and courteous, which was encouraging. With a big smile she spoke.

"Mr. Patty, you are in for a big treat; just wait till you see the amazing pictures I had professionally taken! I promise you they speak for themselves! I cannot begin to tell you of the marvel of the place."

And before Valeria sat down from across his desk, she opened her pouch and removed a file and laid it on the desk in front of her boss. The pictures were all in colour and looked alluring. The accompanying notes against each picture left him deliciously curious. Mr. Patty was wide eyed in total admiration at the master work presented to him.

With a big grin on his face he motioned for Valeria to sit down. "Take a seat, please, Valeria. We have a lot to discuss about this report."

"I am so sorry I had to leave in the manner I did, Mr. Patty, I truly am. I must mention that I was treated royally, besides being guided through the paradise called Sardinia for those three weeks."

"Valeria, you know your tour was not complete. I signed a contract with the Mayor and his assistant, the consigliere. You must return there and finish what you started." As he spoke, he was totally engrossed with the pictures before him; his eyes never moved to her. He was almost talking to her work, not her.

"Mr. Patty," she tilted her head trying to get his attention away from the pictures, for him to look into her eyes, "I am quite unable to return to finish the tour at this time." She put a hand to her chest. "Believe me, there is nothing I would enjoy more than to be there along the shores of those islands, to complete our work with those wonderful people."

"Valeria, you must! You are part of the original agreement, and you had accepted that. I cannot disappoint those people! I won't! I need to fulfill my contract with them."

"Mr. Patty, I don't think you understand! My husband is gravely ill. I cannot leave him under any circumstances."

"Valeria, then hire someone to take care of him! Get medical help, two nurses, one for the day and one for the night shift."

"Are you serious? No! I am sorry; I cannot do that! My duty is to be here with my husband and to take care of his wellbeing," she protested.

"Valeria, these people can sue me, and you, and World Travel! You signed a contract, remember? I have a copy if you need to be reminded."

Valeria was more shocked and confused. How on earth was she going to leave the mess, with Boris in such a condition, and return to Sardinia! A shiver took hold of her body. She brushed some stray tendrils off her forehead trying hard to think clearly. *Dear Lord, please help me!*

"Mr. Patty, I really cannot go. Not matter what the consequences!"

"Valeria, before you say no, please think about it. I beg you! I will keep the file you brought me, and by the way, you have done a wonderful job so far, but you must finish what you had started. I honestly can't see anyone replacing you at this point in the contract!"

She felt pressured and violated. Who was she going to talk to about this additional burden? Boris was definitely in no condition to listen to this nonsense about her heading off again to Europe. Valeria thought, *that would be cruel, and insane on my part. How could I?* The temporary relief she had felt with her boss when she first arrived had now vanished, and her brain felt crowded with jumbled thoughts. She noticed Mr. Patty's grin had disappeared. He reminded her of a finicky cat. The strange look on his face seemed insincere. His smiling twitched under his moustache.

Her gut feeling was not good. She had doubts in the past about Mr. Patty but managed to brush them off. Mom would always preach, 'Think positive! Negativity can damage one's own wellbeing.'

The kind souls she worked with in Sardinia were lovely and genuine people; a bit laid back but proud of their homeland. They were sincerely eager to show it to others. Their simplicity was their secret, to live day by day. They struck her as do-gooders, not greedy or harmful, or of a suing nature. The toothless old fellow she had interviewed had gracefully described that their longevity was based on their aim for unity among families.

But she now needed to dedicate her time totally to her husband. She owed it to him and her family. After all, he had worked hard throughout the years to provide for them all. He needed her more than the job did; he needed much help to recuperate, and there was no way she was going to be ordered by Mr. Patty to abandon her family obligations and resume work to suit him, to benefit his company.

A sadness began settling deep in the core of her heart. She kept her thoughts about Mr. Patty to herself. Politely she shook his hand, forced a big smile and left his office promising to be in touch within a few days.

After Valeria left, in the privacy of his office, Mr. Patty became fully concentrated going over the pictures and the notes she left him. He was amazed and admitted to himself, *Valeria's work is quite professional!* Feeling proud, he patted himself in thought. The astute businessman he was, he got up from his desk and paced about holding her report close to him, thinking hard of a plot to come up with to rekindle Valeria's dedication to the pending project. He knew he had already injected an element of worry into her mind, about the dangers of an unfulfilled contract. He hoped his threat would motivate her to forge ahead, husband or no husband. He had to admit at this point; she was his best employee, without a doubt. He only needed to convince her to get back to Sardinia. If she still refused, he would highlight the small print on the contract. Once she realizes the importance of her commitment and how much she stands to lose, he was sure she would reconsider.

Chapter Twenty One

Across the Ocean

Since Valeria's departure, Lucio had lost his newly found zest for life. Depression seemed to vehemently seep from his brain into his soul. This morning was no different. His motivation to get up and go was nonexistent; his enthusiasm was lost. In a gloomy mood, he lingered around the apartment, resentful and irritated. Nurse Vittoria had arrived earlier than usual that morning, unknown to him, to invade his territory. She was to take care of Chiara whose condition had lately taken a turn for the worse, which added to his suffering. Vittoria wanted to support him as much as she could because of the advanced state of his wife's illness. She was nervous and chatty.

"Signor Lucio," she started as she took a seat beside him in the kitchen where he had been staring at his breakfast with no appetite. "I summoned Dr. Rainer yesterday, to come and check on Chiara's condition. I think we should increase the medication to make her more comfortable. She has been restless lately; I can tell from her eyes that she is suffering immensely. But of course, I am only the nurse. The doctor will be here sometime this afternoon; would you be here when he comes?" Lucio's eyes blinked to clear the tears. He took a deep breath to suppress his growing grief, placed both hands on his head in despair and half crying he responded, "How can life be so cruel, Vittoria? My beautiful wife is wasting away, and my hands are tied! I would give my life to make her better, but her condition is now beyond my control."

"Lucio, I wish you would stop torturing yourself! Don't you

121

know we are all at God's mercy? All I wish to suggest is to relieve some of her pain."

"Vittoria, yes, I want to be here when the doctor comes. I want to know what is going on with my poor Chiara as she cannot tell me herself! How sad is that!"

"Lucio, please don't go there or you will make yourself more distressed. I have noticed how unhappy you have been lately. I don't like to see you like this. My suggestion is for you to go out this morning; leave the house. The doctor will stop by at the end of the day so there is no reason for you to stay. I don't want to see you moping about the apartment."

He listened and accepted that Vittoria did make sense. That was what he had been doing since his guided tour project with Valeria came to a sudden halt, and she had to suddenly leave. He felt sad for everything that was taking place around him.

"Come on, Lucio; don't waste another minute," the nurse encouraged.

Lucio, like a wounded puppy, got up and mumbled through the tears, "Vittoria you are right. I seem to have regained my stamina there for a while. But I must admit, lately I feel as if I am falling deeper and deeper into a bottomless well, and it is so dark and frightening in there."

In an encouraging tone she replied, "We don't want that, do we? You have always been a smart man. The Mayor needs you, the citizens of Alghero need you. Go to your office and spread your knowledge. We all know how much you care about your work and our country."

After listening to her words, he admitted to himself she made sense. Still in his somber mood, he forced himself to get groomed and decided to step out. Everyone seemed to want to engage in conversation today, including the doorman at his building. "Good morning, Consigliere," he greeted cheerfully.

Lucio responded in an annoyed tone, slowly pausing to complain. "Tell me; what's so good about this morning? The sun is hiding behind the clouds, a chilly wind is blowing from the sea, the sky is ready for a downpour. The heavy air is blocking the sun from delivering its splendour onto our exquisite island. And good morning, you say?"

"Consigliere, let's not be so pessimistic; lighten up." Are you not happy today?"

In an unusual nasty tone, he remarked, "Oh! I'd hate to tell you!" Then he sighed. "I am starting to hate this place and everything about it, including myself."

In alarm, the doorman responded, "Oh man! What is wrong with you? Change your mood. You know after the rain, we are always blessed with a beautiful rainbow!"

The confused doorman shook his head and thought to himself, *when a person is in a miserable mood, no one can get him to see beauty in anything.*

The doorman stood there all day, six days a week. He observed people closely, and from their expressions he could tell who was happy and who was troubled. *The Consigliere doesn't look happy these days; I can tell.* He lowered his head. *I know he has a sick wife; I hope he finds peace.*

Lucio had made his way to the City Hall with the intention of talking to Mr. Minerva. He glanced at his watch; it was early. He thought, *just because I rushed out of the house this morning doesn't mean others are in the same mood.* Pensively, he made his way down the hall when he passed by the office that Valeria used to occupy. He slowly opened the door expecting a miracle; to somehow see her charming face and infectious smile. The office was empty. He walked away to get to his own office while talking to himself, "Today a decision has to be made! I must turn the page and move ahead."

He had left his door ajar when a knock made him look up, and there stood Mr. Minerva. *"Permesso? May I?"*

Delighted to see him, he stood up and smiled.

"Please do, John!" He walked towards him feeling encouraged and extending a hand. "Welcome. I was hoping to see you today. How nice of you to stop in at my office!"

"Lucio, I was hoping to see you too. We need to address the unfinished matter with World Travel."

"That is why I am here earlier than usual. We need to decide what to do, John." A sudden burst of enthusiasm invigorated him, and it felt good.

***

On the other side of the ocean, in a different time zone, Valeria had also got up early having tossed and turned all night, troubled by her meeting with Mr. Patty. She couldn't sleep. She quietly tiptoed to her small home office trying not to wake up Boris or disturb him in any way. She could hear him snoring and felt reassured. *He is sound asleep.* Rosy was a heavy sleeper; she didn't have to worry about disturbing her. She opened the filing cabinet and retrieved her file. She had to admit to herself that when Mr. Patty had first called with the business idea, she was in a distracted mood due to her husband's ongoing irrational behaviour. And Rosy had encouraged her to take up the business offer as a timely distraction. *How stupid of me; I never anticipated trouble of any kind. It was just a job assignment for heaven's sake! I must admit, my desperation to get away erased any questioning or reasoning. But I was happy there. Now this turn of events with Boris! What am I to do now?*

She took out the contract and began reading the fine print, something she had neglected to examine before signing it blindly that day in her euphoric state. There it was at the bottom in fine print that one almost needed a magnifying glass to read. The conditions were clearly spelled out. *Should World Travel not abide by, or fail to complete or deliver the contract's agreement... To reimburse all expense incurred by the municipal office of the city..., holding the officers free and clear of any wrong doing... The same applies should the city and their officers not comply with the said agreement.*

Then she found another agreement with her signature regarding her indebtedness to World Travel. *Should I fail to deliver and act upon my duties and obligations...* It was all there in black and white. She must admit, her life in the recent past had been a nightmare, turning her intelligence into that of an illiterate.

There was money involved here. Nothing came free in life; she ought to know better. What a light headed dumb blond had she turned into! She thought Mr. Patty had taken advantage of her state of despair. He was a fox to not clearly explain to her, the consequence should she not fulfill her duties. But why blame him? At that time, she was ready to go into the fires of hell, once she could get away from Boris.

Now that she knew the facts, she was mortified. She put the papers down. This was serious. Later she would discuss it with Rosy and also her boys; she felt trapped in this crucial situation. *What am I to do?* Finally, at nine o'clock the nurse arrived. Rosy emerged half asleep from her bedroom. Valeria needed to get out of the house to have some privacy with her daughter. She suggested to Rosy that the two of them go out for breakfast.

"Rosy, we need to talk!" She whispered close to her ear.

"Mom, you sound mysterious! What is wrong?"

"I will tell you at the restaurant! I need help to make a decision." And she walked away, impatient to chat privately with her daughter.

Chapter Twenty Two

Decision by Obligation

Lucio was more anxious than the Mayor to get to the main subject of interest. He gestured for John Minerva to take a seat. *"Si accomodi,* John! Please make yourself comfortable."

"Thank you," said the Mayor. Lucio crossed his legs and sat back in a serious but relaxed mood. "Lucio, you will be glad to know that I have already placed a call to World Travel. I talked to Mr. Patty; he is aware of the unfinished aspect of the job. All he asked of me is a few days extension. I must be fair; we must give him a chance to sort things out. We were all pleased with Mrs. Abrosky's genuine interest and true love and passion during our promotion. I don't condone the manner in which she departed. But Mr. Patty promised to make it up to us, and he has apologized profusely."

"I understand, John. How long can we wait? We don't know at this point if we should pursue the other promo offered to us from New York or wait to complete this one. Enzo is in limbo, careful not to commit himself to another job. By the way John, he expects to be paid for the time he has invested so far."

"I understand. I am sure we have to recompense him somehow. I promise you I will give them one final call and then we will move forward accordingly." The Mayor got up, feeling the urgency to get back to his office to take care of further pending demands of his job. Before departing, he saluted Lucio, shook his hand and placed the free hand on his shoulder in an assuring manner, indicating he will deliver his promise.

After the Mayor had left, Lucio sat at his desk, desolate once more, asking himself, *why does my life feel so empty right now? While Chiara is at her worst, Valeria came into my life and revived me, brightening my days, and now she has disappeared.* He looked at his watch; it was early afternoon. Vittoria has said the doctor would visit by the end of the day. Chiara had become a helpless woman, unable to do anything for herself. What could the doctor promise? He picked up the phone and dialled Enzo's number. Enzo was unemployed these days and he answered on the first ring.

"Enzo, how are you doing? Lucio here; I wanted to pass on to you that John promised we will have an answer in a couple of days. A decision has to be made, and soon."

"Lucio, I don't know about you, but while waiting I have kept myself amused by watching girls in their bikinis at the beach. You should join me my friend; it will do you good."

It brought a smile to Lucio's face, "Enzo, you are funny. Wait till you get to my age."

"What do you mean? Eh, Consigliere; the heart never ages. Tell me!" He chuckled, "Did you tell the Mayor that the Canadian lady had such an effect on you, to stir your blood right where it should be and bring you back in full swing?"

Lucio couldn't help himself from breaking into a hearty laughter, "Enzo, Enzo, you are incredible! I enjoyed the Canadian lady's company, but only innocently. I am a married man and she is a married woman too."

"Lucio, please, we are talking here man to man, don't give me the bullshit of married-man reasoning. I have seen how absorbed you became with her. I also noticed how upset you were since she left."

"Enzo, please, of course I was; I didn't expect her to leave! Weren't you too?"

"No, I was not, but I know you were! I don't think you remember the things you said; the look on your face when you walked out of the hotel that morning, holding on to the note she left."

"Enzo, that was a normal reaction on my part."

"Signor Lucio, normal, eh! Normal, my foot! You didn't fool me! Maybe even you don't realise it! Believe me, married or not married, you got the hots for her! You are infatuated with her!"

"Enzo, I love my wife! As a matter of fact, I must end this conversation as I have to go meet the doctor."

"Didn't I hear you say, you were a married dead man? Or did I make it up? You were furious when Valeria left; I heard you say it out aloud."

Lucio shook his head. *Oh, my goodness!* "Enzo, I have been upset about everything in my life. Now I must go. I will call you in a day or two."

"Ok! Bye. Cheer up my friend; better days are coming!"

The call ended. Lucio remained there, replaying Enzo's conversation in his head. He had to admit since Valeria left his life had become unbearable. The fact that Chiara had taken a turn for the worst also contributed to his misery. He felt confused and messed up. He loved his wife; how could he be infatuated with the Canadian lady like Enzo was suggesting?

He walked out of his office and headed for home. He admitted to himself it was not something he was looking forward to. Then there's that darn doorman who would be standing there to bug him with his senseless comments. It was still early for the doctor's arrival. He turned his car around and headed towards the beach. He took a long walk along the seashore, deep in his own thoughts, reflecting on his life. *Yes, I hate to go home to what awaits me.*

***

It was nine o'clock in the morning on the other side of the ocean in Niagara. Valeria and Rosy had walked into the Victorian restaurant for pancakes and coffee. They were escorted to a window table overlooking the Falls. It was a bright sunny day. The Niagara river seemed to flow at a calm pace, until it reached the catastrophic drop of the falls. The sky above without a cloud, presented itself as a mantle of true blue. This serenity transmitted a calm sensation to Valeria's soul. The place was almost empty and the quietness restful. The waitress filled their cups with coffee and glasses with water, then took their order. Pancakes layered with mango and syrup. This was Valeria's favourite place and the waitress knew her order by heart.

Rosy anxiously crossed her arms and asked, "Ok, Mom, what is troubling you now!"

Valeria pulled the agency contract from her purse and handed it to her daughter. Rosy was a fast reader and gave it a quick glance, placed it down on the table then sternly looked across at her mom. "Mom, I respect you for being a devoted wife and good mother, but you know when you make a commitment, you should diligently act upon it and deliver your best. You shouldn't leave things unfinished!"

Valeria was ready to protest. Rosy put her hand up, "Mom, stop right there! I know exactly what you are going to say." She rolled her eyes and tilted her head and said with a smirk, "Mother, Mr. Patty is right! You must finish what you started!"

Valeria's expression turned into an alarmed one. "Rosy! I am surprised at you. I need to know if the agency has the right to a monetary claim from me. You know I cannot go back right now… your father…"

"Mom! Mom, please, don't give me that! Dad is doing great. It is a matter of time and recuperation with him. He has a nurse taking care of him, and you have been researching additional private therapy. You always insist on babysitting him! Go finish what you started. Your boss is right, Mom! Should Dad need me or the guys, we would be there for him. I will come home on weekends while you are away; if it will make you feel any better."

Valeria listened, shocked. How could Rosy be saying this! Her place right now was beside Boris. "Rosy, you are not serious? There is no way I would leave at this point in time."

"Ok, Mom, then you would have to face the consequences. Besides, do you feel good about yourself having left those people hanging, and Mr. Patty flustered? And you worry about your duty?"

Valeria felt confused. She would have to discuss this with Boris and get his approval. He seemed in a mild mood now, maybe he would give her his blessings.

"Rosy, I need to take it up further with your father."

While she was reflecting on how simple and practical everything was for today's young people, the waitress arrived with their delicious breakfast. Rosy wished that her mom, with the soothing feeling of the warm food in her stomach, would rationalize better.

Valeria was now more concerned than ever. When they returned home, Boris was seated comfortably looking at the sports channel, and no one was expected to disturb him.

Rosy announced she wanted to go visit a friend. The nurse had left early since it was Sunday; she had only come to give Boris his medication and physio.

Valeria, immersed in her own thoughts, decided to go outdoors and take a walk around the house while racking her brain on how to handle the dilemma at hand. When she heard her name being called, she looked around and there was her friend, Mrs. Jennings, siting with company on her front porch. She was waving at her to come over. Valeria was not in the mood for chatting, but on second thought she decided not to be rude. "Eh! Why not!" she mumbled as she walked across to her neighbour.

Mrs. Jennings greeted her cheerfully, "Valeria, you have met Susan before, haven't you?"

"Yes, I have; a long time ago if I recall correctly," she said as she tried to place the face

"How are you?"

"Great, thank you. And you?"

Mrs. Jennings grabbed another chair, quickly trying to accommodate Valeria, and delighted to have more company.

Susan had been briefed by Nora Jennings on Boris' condition, so she politely asked, "How is your husband doing?"

"He is coming along pretty good, thank you. He is slowly regaining his strength. His speech still needs much improvement."

Mrs. Jennings quickly jumped in. "Eh! Susan, maybe you could help him with that? You are qualified!"

Valeria's ears perked up on hearing this. The response from the clinic had been slow, unsatisfying, and that was her main concern since everything else seemed to be working out well. She turned towards Susan with much interest and asked, "Are you a nurse, Susan?"

There was some distance between their homes and Valeria didn't know the people around the neighbourhood too well.

"No, I am a retired teacher, but I specialised in therapy for children with speech impediments."

"That's interesting. My husband had a stroke that has left him with some problematic speech. It took time for the doctor and the clinic to send someone. He has finally started therapy once a week, but I don't think it's enough."

"I agree. I taught children on a daily basis; it's the only way to measure improvement. For an adult, I think it should be at least three times a week, if not daily."

Mrs. Jennings was all ears and tried hard not to interrupt. She couldn't wait to tell Valeria about her husband's episode that got him in trouble. But she couldn't, at least not now. She knew eventually it would come out, either from her or Susan herself. She sincerely admired Valeria but felt that husband of hers did not deserve his wife's devoted attention. According to Mrs. Jennings, the man could love no one else but himself. It was too bad he was now sick. As far as she was concerned, he had brought it all upon himself.

Valeria listened to Susan while her brain was calculating. Boris had been an intelligent man, with lots of practice he could be back in shape sooner than expected. Then she thought, they had a pretty hefty bank account, so why not hire someone at her expense and speed up the recovery process. She turned to Susan with renewed hope.

"Susan, would you be interested in taking my husband's case as a challenge? I am not pleased with the little help he presently receives, and I believe my husband deserves much better."

Susan didn't know how to respond. The drunk she had assisted into her home was no one to be proud of, but who was she to judge.

"Let me think about it. I am retired now but I must admit, I do have some time to spare."

"Please, I will give you my phone number. You let me know or, I can get back in touch with you," said Valeria, desperately wishing for her to oblige.

Mrs. Jennings had slipped away to fetch some cold drinks. In no time she emerged carrying a tray of three glasses of orange juice, spiked with a little vodka to give her guests some zest.

"Cheers! To better days, Valeria! Let's drink to the entire episode; for it to soon be behind you, my darling!"

The three women smiled and raised their glasses. Cheers!

***

Early Monday morning Mr. Patty anxiously arrived at his office. Today he was going to give Valeria an ultimatum, and then he would phone John Minerva, and action would be taken accordingly.

Chapter Twenty Three
Valeria's Dilemma

Valeria had returned from Mrs. Jennings in a pretty good mood. She wasn't used to drinking, but she must admit to herself the drink lifted her spirits. She walked over to Boris and gently leaned over to embrace him and place her lips teasingly against his ears, working her way to his lips. He pulled her back with his good arm, staring at her, and half stuttering he forced himself to speak.

"V-V-ale-ria, what's gotten in-t-t-you?" He thought, *she hasn't shown much interest in me in a long time.* He smelled the alcohol on her breath. *Is it the effects of alcohol? It is pleasant though; I like it.*

The sound of a blaring horn in urgent repetition came from their driveway. Valeria let go of her husband and ran to the front door. There was Rino and Danny stepping out of their car, in their usual boyish animated manner, goofing around and laughing.

"What a surprise! The wind from the north must have blown you two this way," she joked; a big smile on her face. With quick steps, she ran and embraced her sons.

"Mom, what do you mean! You know we wanted to come home for dad!"

"I am delighted to see you boys, truly I am! Rosy is in town too! This is going to be like old times once again," she beamed.

"Yes mom, we know!"

As they entered the house, the pleasure on their father's face was also evident as Boris forced himself to stand up with the help

135

of his cane and greet them. His eyes widened in admiration, beaming as his sons approached and embraced him. He felt frustrated with his slurring and the limitedness of his physical movement. His slowness in expressing his words was unacceptable to him and annoyed him greatly. The more he forced himself to speak, the less it was for others to understand him.

Rosy arrived shortly after, all smiles seeing her brothers. She didn't let on to her parents that she had been the one to call her brothers, urging them to come home. "Forget the girlfriends and come and spend family time with mom and dad," she had demanded of them. Being the oldest sibling, her brothers looked up to her.

Since it was now difficult for Boris to go out and be comfortably accommodated at restaurants, Rosy took charge and announced, "We are having a feast tonight! Chinese food! Mom, you will relax tonight! The boys and I would set the table and also clean up afterwards." Valeria moved over to Boris, put an arm around him and whispered, "Aren't we blessed with our beautiful children, dear?"

Having her She was going to help her husband get better, as if her life depended on it.

They all sat around the table, including Boris who had been assisted by the boys. After they had feasted, Rosy served ice cream with fresh strawberries, and espresso coffee. She thought this was as good as any time to bring up the discussion of her mother's dilemma. Rosy was sensible, intelligent, and mature for her age. She opened up the discussion in a debated manner between her and the boys, bringing in her father too.

"Rino, Danny, especially you Dad, Mom has found herself in a situation. We all know that she had an overseas job assignment. She had abandoned everything to come back because she was concerned about you dad, without even knowing what had happened to you. Now guys, an unfinished job is an unfinished job. World Travel is asking Mom to finish what she had contracted to, and so are the people in Europe, and rightfully so. Money has been invested by both parties, but more than that, when you open a circle, you are also responsible for closing it. An unclosed circle is unprofessional and unacceptable. Someone else taking over from you to close it, could never achieve the intended results. Having said that, I think Mom needs to go back and close her circle. How do you guys feel about that?"

Rino was the first to put his hand up. "Rosy, Mom, what about Dad? Who, or what is more important?"

Rosy quickly intervened. "Before you go any further, be informed that I volunteered to cover for mom on weekends. While she is away, I will be filling in until she returns."

Danny said, "If you cover for mom, we can take turns. I have no objection."

Boris remained wide eyed. He pointed at himself putting a hand on his chest while trying to speak. "M-e, I don-t kn-ow. Rosy, fi-ne." He had no voice to fight back.

Rosy shot a stern look to her mother. Valeria, in a serious tone said, "Look here my dears, I have no intention of leaving your father right now, and I don't care what is involved. My interest is to have him well again, especially his speech."

Boris patted her arm gently, expressing approval of his wife's commitment. Rosy noticed it. "Dad, you have been an executive most of your life. Of all people, you should understand! We would be here for you. It should only be a matter of two weeks at the most. Eh, Mom? What's the big deal here! And as for you mom, you make everybody happy, always placing yourself last. You don't disappoint anyone! You always aim to please!"

Valeria wasn't listening or paying much attention to what was being discussed. She was thinking she would talk to Mr. Patty on Monday. He could send whoever he wished to fulfil the rest of the contract. If she had to reimburse him with costs, so be it!

The family discussion ended inconclusively. The boys soon left to return to their summer jobs. Rosy remained behind with no intention to leave until her mother had come to her senses.

***

Mr. Patty picked up the phone and dialled Valeria's number.

"Hello, Valeria. It's Mr. Patty! Today is Monday. As we have discussed, I need to get back word to the people in Sardinia. I need to know your decision." He held his breath and waited for a positive answer.

"Oh, Mr. Patty! No, I have none. I had my children here on the weekend and we did discuss it somewhat. I really feel if you have someone to replace me, you should go ahead and do so."

"Valeria, I wish you would reconsider. I will remind you that if I am forced to send someone else, you will have to reimburse a portion of the expenses incurred on your part. As you can appreciate, we will have to absorb the expenses that have already been disbursed. Think about it!"

His tone was stern. She held the phone away from her ear and felt resentment for Mr. Patty. He was slimy and always after making money. She hated to give in to him or allow him the satisfaction of feeling he intimidated her. Controlling her anger and choosing her words carefully, she replied, "Let me get back to you by Wednesday. I need more time."

"Valeria! I am sorry! A few weeks have already gone by. I need to know! Call me back by late afternoon. I need to call Sardinia! Those people are waiting on word from me!"

"Sorry, I can't right now; I need to have more time to come up with a plan. I will call you back on Wednesday."

"Valeria, I am warning you! Remember that!"

138

Totally upset, he hung up the phone. Now he was in deep thought, shaking his head and swearing out loud as he tried to release his anger.

***

At the Abrosky's residence, Valeria walked over to Boris, feeling extremely disturbed. She was looking for comfort. Unfortunately, his personality had changed incredibly since his episode. He was in no condition to offer any emotional support to his wife. Furthermore, he had never agreed with her involvement with that idiot, Patty, as he would refer to him. Valeria reflected. *Maybe Boris had been right all along.* She was being consumed with resentment for Patty as she felt her boss wasn't appreciating her personal family situation. Furthermore, she thought he had no right to pressure her in this manner.

Rosy bounced in at the right time as her mother's emotions were getting the better of her. Her raw nerves left her imploding, and the dam in her was about to burst into a good cry.

"Mom, let's go out for a stroll to the mall and I will treat you to a cappuccino. It will do you good. The nurse is still here with dad."

They were ready to walk out the door when the phone began ringing. Valeria continued walking, ignoring it. She was afraid it was Mr. Patty calling again. She had no desire to talk to him. The nurse picked up, then rushed to catch Valeria as she went through the doorway.

"Mrs. Abrosky, there is a lady on the phone asking for you; it might be important!"

"Hello. Oh yes! Tomorrow? Fine. What time can I come? Good. I will be there." She hung up and scooted out the door were Rosy stood patiently waiting for her.

"Mom, who was that calling? The nurse made it sound urgent."

"The lady I met at Mrs. Jennings', one Susan Butler. She wants us to meet at her house tomorrow morning at ten. I must see her! Actually, she might be able to help your father with his speech as she is an accomplished speech therapist. I am glad she called; I can't wait to chat with her."

Chapter Twenty Four

A Resolution

A good night's sleep had become a rare pleasure for Valeria. Since she had returned from her work trip, she was having a tough time relaxing, and last night was no different. The sun was already rising and daylight filtered into her room. Overcome with sleep deprivation her eyelids were too heavy to stay open and she finally fell asleep.

It was nine o'clock when the doorbell rang. Startled, she jumped out of bed. The once a week speech therapist send by the clinic, was at the door to proceed with her short session. As she rushed downstairs, Rosy's snores could be heard in the hallway. Oh, how she loved to sleep late. Boris' physical health was improving so he could help himself a bit. When she realized the time, she rushed to the kitchen to get coffee and breakfast ready for him. *What a difference now,* she thought; *he cannot holler anymore and make demands like he used to.* She glanced in his direction where he sat waiting, quietly and patiently just as an obedient child.

Later nurse Florence would arrive to take care of his medical needs. Valeria insisted on preparing his breakfast every morning. But this morning she was impatient since she had to get to Susan Butler for ten. The rush was stressing her out. Her fatigued body was not allowing her to move as she would have liked. Just before ten she was fretting, rushing about to quickly leave when Rosy calmly waltzed into the room.

"Sorry mom, I slept in," hating herself as she apologized. Valeria gave her an impatient look since this was one morning she could have used some extra help. Her mood was not at its best as she was sleep deprived and had to rush to meet the neighbour on time.

She flew out the door leaving Rosy to fetch her own breakfast. "Look after your father also," she commanded. Soon after, she was pulling into the driveway of Mrs. Butler's modest brick bungalow.

"Good morning, Mrs. Abrosky," cheered Susan.

"Good Morning!" Valeria tried to sound upbeat to try and change her gloomy mood. "Please, Valeria will do. How are you?"

"As good as can be expected, now that I live alone."

Valeria wanted to turn around and leave. She already had enough to contend with; Mr. Patty, sleepless nights, and all the running around since her return. She certainly could not handle any more laments. She didn't engage much with the neighbours nor saw their goings on. Valeria's house was conveniently set back from the others. The back of her property overlooked the Niagara river which marks the boundary between Canada and the US. Rarely would she sit on her front lawn. She was always fully absorbed in her own affairs. Occasionally she would encounter her friend, Mrs. Nora Jennings, who was nothing short of a riot. Nora couldn't be avoided and at times, Valeria actually enjoyed conversing with her.

Susan was born in Liverpool, England. Valeria hardly knew her. Mrs. Butler wasn't used to addressing people by their first names unless she had their permission. A retired teacher, she was a bit old fashioned in her ways, well mannered, conservatively dressed, her long hair pulled back in a knot with the grey roots untouched, and she didn't wear any make up. She looked older than she probably was. To the observer she appeared a little stiff. On a positive note, Valeria would think, *a down to earth soul; plain and polite, with an English accent.* Like Mrs. Jennings, she lived alone, with a son out in Vancouver and a daughter in Toronto.

Mrs. Jennings had confided in Valeria that her friend up the street had been dumped by her cheating husband, a high-ranking banker whose office was in the city. He eventually moved in with his young secretary.

"Well Valeria, I am telling you, Susan is a nice person. I apologize for saying all this about her husband. Power is no excuse for a man to cheat on his wife. I kept warning her about the girls in the office with their charm, sexy skirts, great bodies, and who flirt especially with older married men." Valeria listened and reflected. She never worried about Boris in that way. He was obsessed with his work but was not interested in anything else, other than his deals and his drive for personal success.

She looked on as Susan fussed with the treats while the smell of coffee filled the room, along with fresh baked muffins placed on two fine china plates, all ready to be served.

"Here we are," said Susan. Valeria was brought back to the present moment when her hostess returned from the kitchen, gesturing to her, "Please Valeria, make yourself comfortable," as she escorted her into the living room. With a soft smile on her lips, she invited her to sit on the same sofa Boris had rolled off on that fateful day. The stains on her carpet were still noticeable. The rug had been shampooed but the stains had left their shadows.

"Let me pour you a cup of coffee and offer you some of my muffins." she said charmingly.

Valeria didn't want to impose, although the smell of fresh baking and the aroma of the coffee did make her feel a bit hungry. She said, "Thank you."

Susan took a seat facing her and politely enquired about her husband. "How is Mr. Abrosky coming along?"

Valeria began narrating about the stroke her husband suffered while she was away, and her knowledge of the entire episode, totally unaware that Susan already knew what had taken place, even better than her, as her forced intervention gave her first-hand knowledge.

Susan hesitated for a bit then spoke up, "I called you on Mrs. Jennings insistence. She has been adamant for me to offer my help. My friend likes you, and she means well. As you know I am a speech therapist; I have helped many people recover from stroke aphasia applying techniques suitable to the patient's unique case, after evaluation by a speech-language pathologist. My interest would be to help your husband regain his speech and become as functional as possible, but it is all entirely up to you and Mr. Boris."

Valeria couldn't help noticing how sincere Susan sounded. She was somewhat shy, reserved, and a matter of fact person; an interesting contrast to Nora Jennings. Valeria listened totally absorbed. Of course, Mrs. Jennings would verify her credentials. Susan picked up a large brown envelope and handed it to her.

"Here is all you would need to know about me; my resume with references."

Susan wasn't sure if Nora had related to the family the episode of Mr. Abrosky and her involvement, of being innocently dragged into it. Since no one had thanked her she suspected that Valeria and her family didn't know what had actually taken place.

She leaned back in her chair and asserted herself, then she took a deep breath and carefully poured it all out. "Valeria, you should be thankful to our friend, Mrs. Jennings, for saving your husband's life. You know, it was early in the morning when she saw him pull out of the driveway and unsteadily head up the street. She called me urgently, insisting I look out my window to see him coming my way. I saw a car stop at a strange angle across from my home, and noticed the driver leaning over the steering wheel. I went out to check on the person; the door wasn't locked. I recognized your husband who looked as if he was either asleep or passed out. The keys were still in the ignition, but the engine was dead. The situation didn't look good. When I called out to him and got no response, I shook him a bit then he turned his head to me with a blank look in his eyes and, sorry to say this, his breath reeked of alcohol. I was surprised he was drunk that early in the morning. I helped him out of the car, and don't ask me how I managed to bring him inside thinking I could help him. I tried to make him comfortable on my sofa and he fell fast asleep, at least I thought he did.

"Soon after, a policeman was at my door enquiring about the badly parked car and demanding to have it removed as it was blocking a fire hydrant. This is Niagara as you know; the patrol cops are quite alert. Luckily, the officer left me with a warning that he was just about to end his shift, but his replacement could soon come by and issue a ticket against the owner of the car.

"When I walked back into the house I almost passed out in shock. I found that your husband had rolled onto the floor into a mess of his own puke. In my confusion, I managed to call 911. The ambulance came and he was taken to the emergency with me riding in the back beside him. They thought I was his wife. When dealing with emergencies, especially a heart condition there is no time for questions or formalities; that is usually attended to afterwards. Later on, I cleared my name and made sure they noted I was a bystander. I came home afterwards to see his car had been towed away. There! Now you have the whole story!"

Susan sighed; she felt relieved! "The funny part is that Nora waited until the next morning for my call, scolded and accused me, in her own thinking, that I was making out with your husband! Can you imagine…?" She laughed nervously.

Valeria was stunned at hearing these details; her thoughts began floating, lost above in the dark clouds. *Leave it to Boris to get himself into shenanigans! He must have brought the cardiac arrest onto himself. God help me!*

Valeria felt both embarrassment and disgust at the same time. "Susan, I am so sorry for all the trouble you went through on our behalf. My children and I owe you a huge apology. We ought to be grateful for your kindness. How can we ever pay you back? Most of all, Boris owes you his life!"

Susan got up, "Let me pour you another cup of coffee. It's decaf but will do you good."

"I think I need a stiff drink to settle my nerves, morning or not," retorted Valeria.

"I do have Baileys! Would you like some in your coffee instead of plain milk?" Susan promptly suggested.

"Yes, thank you!" Valeria promptly acceded. "Now Susan, going back to your speech therapy offer; I would love for you to help. Please apply all your expertise. I am now living with such a sorrowful man that I hardly recognize. He's not the tyrant husband I once knew."

She didn't want to go into details and explain how miserable her life had been in the past years. She wanted to push it behind her. Her pathetic husband needed to regain control of himself, and her focus would be on helping him as much as possible.

Deep down Valeria felt cheated. She took her last sip of coffee and as she stood up, suddenly stronger and more resilient, she asked, "Susan, when can you begin the therapy sessions? The sooner the better for me and my family!"

Susan put up both her hands in front of her as an expression of surrender, "Valeria! Presently, I have lots of time on my hands. Whenever you are ready, just say the word! Anytime is good for me!"

"As I said before, the sooner the better; both for him and for me. I have an important job waiting to be completed!"

Unaware of what she was doing, Valeria walked towards Susan's kitchen, cup and plate in hand, and a sudden flow of determination permeated her body as she stood at the sink. *Mom,*

do what you enjoy in life! Do what YOU want to do! Rosy's words resonated in her head. Now her own thoughts took over, I need to get on with my life! I have never felt fulfilled! It's time I did!

Chapter Twenty Five
Sardinia

The prognosis given by the specialist doctor that examined Chiara had completely devastated Lucio. Accompanied by the nurse, they all walked out of the bedroom; Lucio with a sorrowful expression.

"Mr. Alvani, I am sorry to have to tell it to you like this. I pain for both you and your wife. I wish there was something more we could suggest for her. Unfortunately, there is not. Your wife's internal organs are barely functional. Her body has been reduced to an empty shell."

"Doctor, what do you mean by 'an empty shell'?" Lucio was confused.

"*Coinvolt*, a bottle in form, but empty. I want you to be prepared; it's just a matter of time for her. She has been sick for too many years, and she has suffered immensely and. ..." The doctor paused on seeing tears stream down Lucio's cheeks. Like a broken man, Lucio wailed loudly, echoing through the entire apartment.

He put an arm around Lucio, trying to offer some friendly comfort. It is never easy for a doctor to have to deliver such the death sentence.

The doctor motioned for Lucio to sit down as he joined him on the living room sofa. The attentive nurse was readily offering them each a glass of water. She felt just as sad as Mr. Alvani. It had not been easy for her over the years, to watch the debilitating effects of

MS on Chiara's almost perfect body, reducing her to a useless bundle of nothingness.

The doctor turned to the nurse and said, "It is at a times like this that I dislike my profession; we were taught to control our emotions, but easier said than done. It hits the core of our soul when we cannot further help a patient. Accepting defeat is always tough."

"Doctor, believe me, I know exactly what you are speaking about."

The doctor took a deep breath and leaned forward, continuing to find words to comfort Lucio, "Mr. Alvani, we all know she has been through much, and for too long. Maybe she is hanging on for some reason. Maybe you know, maybe you don't. No one can doubt your devotion as a husband and caregiver, silently enduring your own pain. Keep well, my friend. Take care of yourself. Call if you need me."

After the doctor left, Lucio walked slowly and quietly into his wife's bedroom. He kneeled at the bedside, hugged her shrivelled body and again sobbed. The nurse could hear him from where she sat in the kitchen but decided not to interfere. *It will do him good.*

***

While Lucio was enduring his own torment, sitting and staring blankly through his library window that overlooked the Mediterranean coast; across the Atlantic Ocean in Niagara, Valeria was again unable to sleep. She turned on the light to look at the clock; it was one in the morning. In her nightgown and barefooted, she quietly made her way out of the house towards the end of her back yard. They usually kept the trees nicely clipped, not to obscure the view. Valeria lowered her body to sit on the grass and listened to the night creatures the river attracted. A full moon illuminated the sky tonight, reflecting much lustre on the river. It was peaceful and quiet except for the echoing sound coming from the flowing Niagara river. *The crickets must have gone to sleep by now,* she thought. She got up and walked a little further until she reached the edge of the property, a cliff. She squatted again curling her feet under her body. It was a warm summer morning in June; the calmness in the air brought her much relaxation, and her nerves slowly settled. Since she had returned, everything was so unsettling. The pressure and the demands of life itself left her with rattled nerves. She looked at the gorge down below and wished she could disappear into thin air. That is how she had been feeling over the last few years, and more so lately. She sat there gathering her thoughts that were shifting between duty and desire.

A flashback to the morning before took her to the conversation she had with Susan. Mentally she slowly digested what Susan had disclosed; she shook her head in dismay. Then, stroking her arm for comfort and talking to herself, she said, *I need to sort this mess out! Boris needs to be rehabilitated and Mr. Patty threatens for money reimbursement. The people of Sardinia were kind and genuine; I have left a job unfinished and I have disappointed them. God Almighty! Please tell me what to do and which direction to turn? It's not my style to leave things pending.* She then brought a hand up and brushed her hair back as if the motion would alleviate the stress to her brain and clear her thinking.

One thing for sure, after that chat with Susan, she felt less guilty over her husband's episode. She remembers opening the bottom shelf of their bar unit, and sure enough it would be lined up with empty vodka bottles. He was drunk first thing on mornings. *The way he has been devouring and demanding food lately, what else was there to expect! You cannot help someone that doesn't want to be helped. I think Rosy is right; it's time I do what I need to do. I am fifty-seven years old and life is slowly passing me by.* She remained there staring into the sky where the stars had disappeared, and the luster of a new day was taking place. Her attention returned to the matter at hand and she focused deeper on the thoughts swimming about in her head. It was almost dawn when she tip-toed back into the house and silently entered through the sliding door entrance at the back of the house.

The next morning after she fed Boris, she resorted to the privacy of her bedroom upstairs. She called Mrs. Nora Jennings, "Good morning Mrs. Jennings. How are you?"

"Valeria, so happy to hear from you. How are you, my dear?"

"I am fine, thank you; at least the best I can be at this time. Mrs. Jennings, I visited with Susan yesterday. I want to thank you for your important role in getting speedy assistance to my husband when he had his accident. She told me everything!"

"Oh, Valeria, so now you know! I wanted to be cautious and not infringe on your privacy and decency. I was hoping to talk to you about it at the right time."

"Mrs. Jennings, that's ok. You are a faithful friend! I called to let you know I have decided to hire Susan as Boris' speech therapist. I have devoted nurse Florence looking after him, and Rosy has offered to come home as often as she could while I return to my incomplete project in Sardinia."

"Good for you, my dear! You do need to remove yourself for some time. It would do you a world of good, and you deserve some peace. As for Susan, I can vouch for her. She has been a model teacher and therapist and dedicated to her work. I assure you, Boris will be in good hands!"

"This is encouraging. I am happy. It was a big decision to make. I have not been able to sleep at night from worry."

"Ah, Valeria my darling, you need to live, precious! I wish I was your age. You go, do what you have to, and put yourself first because I know you! Those nuns did a number on you, but never mind. You deserve it, and don't feel guilty about anything!"

Valeria needed that boost from Nora; she was her confidante

and often her second mother. "Thanks, Mrs. Jennings, I shall, and I love you!"

Another call was placed to Susan Butler, and they both agreed she would begin the sessions the following day after breakfast. Since Valeria was taking charge, she did not plan to even ask Boris for his permission; the change would take place whether he liked it or not!

Next, she resolutely dialled World Travel and asked to be connected to Mr. Patty. "Mr. Patty, Valeria here," she spoke assuredly and determined. It was mid-week. "Book my flight for Sardinia! I can leave by next Monday for the latest. Please proceed with the arrangements and inform me accordingly."

"Oh! Mrs. Abrosky! How wonderful! This is the best news of the week! I will work on it right away! I am thrilled you decided to reconsider. It would save me a lot of grief and inconvenience. I spoke to the Mayor yesterday. He told me, we were close to the final stage of the project."

"Sorry, Mr. Patty. I finally made up my mind and would be ready to leave as soon as you provide my travel details."

Rosy was half asleep when her mother went to her bedside. She shook her awake. It was late enough, and Valeria was anxious to announce to her daughter her recent decision. "Rosy, wake up!"

"Mom, what's so urgent?" She opened her eyes to find her mom's face close to hers. "Mom, what has gotten into you?" she questioned.

"What has gotten into ME?" Valeria responded loudly. "You were right! I have decided to go back to Sardinia to resume my work and close off the project."

Rosy circled her arms around her neck, "Mom, good for you! It's about time you really woke up!"

"I will take up on your offer, Rosy! You would be in charge until I come back."

So far, Valeria had acted bravely on the exterior, claiming her rights, but her inner soul still needed some convincing. It is hard to break old habits. *I have an obligation to honour what has been entrusted upon me.*

***

Back in Alghero, Sardinia, the phone rang first thing in the morning at City Hall. Mr. Patty informed John Minerva of the good news that the project will continue. Valeria Abrosky will return!

John promptly instructed his secretary to advise both Enzo Mangorio and Lucio Alvani to prepare for the resumption of the tour with the Canadian agent.

Chapter Twenty Six

Splendour in the Clouds

Once Valeria's plane took off, she became lost in her thoughts. Her resolution was whatever she had struggled with in the past, was going to be pushed to the far corner of her mind until her mission in Sardinia was complete. After connecting from Rome, here she was at the Alghero Airport. Her eyes scanned the crowd for Lucio and Enzo, but they were nowhere to be seen. She was puzzled. *They had always been prompt.* She leaned her tired body against a wall near the exit; her luggage at her side. She waited impatiently, nervously tapping one foot, while bringing up her fingers to rest against her chin as in her signature pose.

Several porters and taxi drivers approached her, offering their services which she refused by nodding them away. After what seemed like an eternity, she spotted Enzo and John Minerva approaching, pushing their way through the crowd. She tried to get their attention as they neared her. When Enzo heard his name call, he turned around and grabbed John's arm and looked in her direction.

"Oh, Mrs. Abrosky, so sorry!" They were both apologetic, and their expressions reflected it. She glanced around for Lucio, but he was not to be seen. John Minerva was agitated as a stranded fly and proceeded with his cordial greetings. Enzo, with a big smile shook her hand, "Welcome back! We have been at a loss without you here, especially Mr. Alvani!"

As they proceeded to exit the airport building, she engaged

them in conversation. With a frown of concern, she asked, "By the way, where is Signor Alvani? I kind of expected to see him here with you, Enzo!"

In a reluctant manner John announced, "Mrs. Abrosky. *Il consigliere*, our counsellor has not been managing too good as his wife passed away this morning."

Valeria brought a hand to her mouth in shock, "Oh my! I am sorry! I was told she wasn't well but never imagined it to be that bad."

In the Sardinian way, John solemnly lowered his gaze while extending an arm of comfort across her back. "Our friend has been through plenty. How he has survived all these years, only God knows."

Enzo spoke while Valeria walked between the two men. He too felt the need to touch her consolingly before his comment, "I felt for him too. Often, I would try to kid around with him, to uplift his spirits; he has been suffering silently for many years."

"What was wrong with her?" Valeria enquired.

"She was sick with MS. It began in her forties, then she went downhill after that with many attacks. And if that wasn't bad enough, dementia also set in. I believe she had been sick for some fifteen years."

"I thought people here lived well over a hundred?"

"I know, but unfortunately not all of us. Mrs. Alvani was originally from South America, Rio De Janeiro. She came here, fell in love with her much adored Lucio, our island and our people, and never left."

Valeria listened. A pang of pain struck her heart for her friend's grief. She recalled sensing his distraction at times. Now she understood why. On deeper reflection, she felt her complaints about Boris couldn't compare to Lucio's suffering.

***

As much as Lucio should have known Chiara's fate, he was devastated by her death. She was too young to have endured what she did. His wife was only fifty-five. None of her family from Rio came for the funeral. She had a brother and a sister, both older and estranged. Lucio was an only child and his parents had passed on. His only relatives were some cousins. They stood by his side and helped Lucio with the funeral arrangements. The two nurses were always faithful assistants. They had been employed for such a long time that they had become part of the family and cared immensely for Lucio's wellbeing. The funeral was well attended. Lucio had been a public figure at the City Hall and had done a lot of good for the citizens and the island, therefore everyone wanted to pay their respects, including the Mayor, Enzo, and Valeria.

People had loved Chiara. She was sweet and friendly and well versed in Italian, Portuguese, and Spanish. She was a kind person when she was well, a supportive wife standing beside her husband at the many charities they patronized. They had no children of their own but Chiara adored children. When her illness struck, they both retreated within themselves. Lucio had been totally devoted to his wife and his work. It had been a very difficult journey for him, coping with his wife's illness. Now it was all over. The next morning after all the visitors had trickled away, he found himself pacing back and forth in his study.

The exotic view of the sea was right in front of him but could not think to enjoy it. The sky was as serene as it could be. The fascinating blues of the water seemed to harmoniously connect with the cloudless blue sky above. Boats were floating by in droves, some full of tourists, some with private owners out for fun. The heavenly scenery outside did not matter; nothing had meaning since the recent developments in his private life. He walked to his desk and sat on his chair, holding his head with both hands asking himself, "Why, why! Why has my Chiara been taken away from me?" He shed the last remaining tears and his body felt drained and limp.

***

After the funeral Valeria felt deeply sad for her friend. She found herself at a questionable point in her project. Who was going to be accompanying her? There was no doubt that Mr. Alvani was in bereavement and needed time to grieve the loss of his life partner. But what was she to do now? Tomorrow she would meet with the Mayor and it would be up to him to decide how they move forward. She walked down to the hotel lobby to get a drink from the bar and heard herself say to the barman, "Gin and tonic, please."

Alcohol! She whispered to herself, then her thoughts suddenly took her to Boris. *His emotions must have hit rock bottom for him to resort to dulling his brain with alcohol. And now, what am I doing?*

In the morning, she was awakened by the bright sunshine filtering through her window. She drew the drapes and inhaled the crisp air that poured in; the sun was in full splendour.

The phone rang; Enzo was on the line.

"Valeria, what time would you like me to pick you up? We wanted you to rest after yesterday's ordeal. The Mayor said he will make himself available when you are ready."

Valeria responded, "Thanks Enzo, how considerate of you both. Please give me an hour then I will meet you downstairs." She couldn't call home as there was a six hours time difference; Canada was behind European time. She decided to leave that task for later when she returned.

They walked into the Mayor's office for their meeting. John Minerva was kind and apologetic, "Mrs. Abrosky, I am so sorry that you arrived here to find a funeral on your first day; I will try to make it up to you. As for the *consigliere,* we need to respect his grief at this time. I cannot pressure him. I would leave it up to him to decide when he wishes to resume work."

"I understand. In the meantime, maybe Enzo and I can continue where we left off? I would like to apologise for leaving the island so abruptly. My husband sustained a cardiac arrest and I panicked when I received the news; I was not thinking too clearly when I hurriedly rushed home."

"No need to apologise; as long as we get this promotion finished. I must warn you, there will be some delay since Lucio is absent. You may have to stay a bit longer than previously planned. Unfortunately, we cannot predict when the good Lord will take us. It is most unfortunate that Mrs. Alvani passed away just as you arrived."

"Please signor Mayor, don't worry. I am sure we can work it out somehow."

Then she reflected on his concern about an extended stay. She had left Niagara hoping to return at a fixed time. How was she going to stay longer with her husband at home in his condition, along with the rest of the turmoil in her life. Again, her mind was playing tricks on her, making her weigh her duty against her desires. *When would I put myself first!* She took a deep breath, willing life to take its course. On second thought, *what will be, will be!*

Chapter Twenty Seven

Teamwork

Back in Niagara at the Abrosky residence all was going well with the three women dedicated to the challenging work of caring for Boris, as assigned to each. Rosy, who diligently handled being in charge, had joined Susan outdoors where she had suggested they move Boris for more pleasant natural surroundings and fresh air.

Rosy said, "Mrs. Butler it is a lovely, sunny day, why don't we help my dad outdoors. You could conduct your session with him in our backyard. It's stuffy in here and it will do him a world of good, with fresh air filling his lungs."

"Oh, yes! That would be wonderful!" she promptly agreed. I love the outdoor myself, and it is a bright summer day. Why not!" Susan responded.

"I will help you guide him to a comfortable spot outside."

With the help of the cane and two escorts, Boris took one step at a time, dragging his weak leg along. With Rosy's coaxing, he finally reached the sofa, very exhausted. He slumped his body onto the padded seat with a huge sigh of relief.

"Ok, Dad, rest for a few minutes, I will get you a drink of water and then you will be ready for your first session."

The backyard was set sprawled high above the river with double sliding doors leading from the house to a natural stone patio that led to a brick oven and fire place area, all encircled by a thirty-six-inch-high circular wall. Valeria had hired a professional decorator to add the finishing touches and meticulously make the

161

place into a cozy getaway haven. It was cleverly designed for private evening relaxation and entertaining families and friends. The fine furnishings from Hauser were in white, blue, and mauve. The same romantic colours were carried through the flowerbeds that adorned the green shrubberies.

This pleasure place had turned into a war zone since Boris' retirement. Rosy knew her parents hardly enjoyed the beauty of their outdoor paradise. She was artistic herself and loved her family home. Therefore, she chose to study architecture; she liked building, creating, and constructing amid the city, and among nature. Nurse Florence had previously attended to Boris giving him his medication, and worked with him on his physio, strengthening his extremities. Her duties were completed for the morning. She promised to return late afternoon to make sure his blood pressure was in check and to administer his second dose of medication for the night. Susan Butler arrived later. She had met Rosy beforehand and she happily introduced her father.

Mr. Abrosky, in his drunken state at the time of the incident and after all that ensued, certainly had no knowledge of Susan's involvement in his recent tragedy. They both had heard of one another, but they were strangers up to that point. Susan was now seeing Mr. Abrosky from a different perspective. She was not here to judge him. Her profession was to help and rehabilitate anyone she can, applying her skills, considering recommendations from the speech-language therapist. She was well prepared to carry through with her own assessment of Boris Abrosky's condition. With Rosy's help and her new patient's cooperation, though he slurred, she managed to complete the necessary forms.

Rosy had resented her dad for most of her life, and she had been rebellious towards him. Now that he was sick, she became overly concerned and sincerely caring, working hard towards getting him well and back on his feet. She realized her father now deserved all the empathy she could offer. Besides, she had promised her mom she would give her total devotion to her father while she finished her work.

Susan was well prepared for the session. She conducted it in a professional and impressive manner. Boris followed her every instruction and cooperated like a young and eager teen.

"I suggest we do one hour today. Should you get tired, Mr. Abrosky, you can put a hand up and we would take a short rest and only resume when you are ready."

Boris would nod in agreement, and this was amazing to Rosy as she hardly knew her father as the cooperative type. He was obeying and paying attention to Susan, even if he was asked to do one exercise over and over. Sweat dripped down the sides of his face from concentration with the vocal exercises, and as he attempted to grasp the words and try to pronounce as instructed.

"Good, Mr. Abrosky, you are doing just fine." From her years of experience, she knew the exact steps to apply with this sixty-seven-year-old patient. Each day she would need to push him just enough to stimulate the areas of his brain affected by the stroke. Timely and consistent exercises would stimulate the nervous system, increase blood flow and oxygen intake, strengthen the muscles, and awaken the stressed areas. The more the patient pushed the better for his recovery.

This, with the right amount of cooperation and determination, would quicken the healing process. With time, unending patience, and trust from all sides, it usually unfolds nicely. She knew she was good at her work. She has a no-fail motto. The greatest setback however, is often at the beginning when the patient cannot find the will to push himself and this can challenge both patient and therapist.

Susan was prepared for the long haul ahead and she knew patience, on both their part, was a great factor in success. Rosy would worriedly interrupt her when she felt her father was pushing too much.

"Mrs. Butler, is this normal? He looks pale, weak, and totally drained. Maybe we can stop for now?"

"It's his first session, he is trying real hard. I must say he is unusually persistent, which is a good thing but can have its dangers. I have to monitor this as we go along. Yes, he is drained."

"I certainly don't want him to experience a relapse of any type!" Rosy expressed with raised eyebrows. "Shouldn't we consult the doctor on this?"

"I always use caution. I was told he was an extremely intelligent man, proud, and with a giant ego. There is no doubt those qualities are still there deep inside him and is fighting to resurface. I would not like to see him lose this level of determination. But it is a clever idea to get the doctor's opinion once you have concerns."

Once the sessions were over, Boris would drop his weak and tired body onto the sofa, completely worn out. When Rosy would see her dad in such a frazzled state, she would usually fetch a light blanket, remove his sandals, tuck in his bare feet, and cover his body. The previous bouts of heat he experienced would turn into shivers. His body endured a shift in temperature at times, from hot to cold, brought on by his weakened state. His dutiful daughter would diary all progress and concerns, often consulting the speech-language therapist with problem areas.

And Boris Abrosky silently prayed for a full recovery.

Chapter Twenty Eight

Overseas

Nora Jennings from across the street was on guard, as usual. She had watched as Susan arrived at the Abrosky's. She was pacing back and forth, from her kitchen window to her front door, and out her front yard. Bored out of her mind she was trying to catch Susan leaving the premises and invite her over. Her nosiness was getting the better of her; she couldn't catch a glimpse of anything although the curtains across the street were drawn. Since the house was recessed, her eyesight seemed more strained. *Oh! How I hate this old body.* But not giving up, she continued sneaking around. *I would like to know how the boor is doing!* She wondered, *Susan is an old English fort living by rules and regulations; her sessions on clients are kept strictly private and confidential. I may not get anything out of her, but no harm in trying.* The snooping Mrs. Jennings snickered. *Maybe Susan will get lucky with him! She has never dated or engaged in any kibitz as I did in my youth, but still has a chance as she is relating well to male patients with her speciality.*

Susan often ended up at Nora's on a Saturday evening. After a drink or two one evening, she confessed to her friend that she was better off easing her frustration with the help of a vibrator. "I don't trust men anymore. I never did! They are all jerks if you ask me!"

It was a snowy Saturday night when out of frustration she burst out with her sexual revelation. She had been confined many evenings sitting at home with no dates, no male companion, abandoned by her children, not to mention her idiotic husband who was taken up with that sleazy secretary of his. He had openly cheated on her right in front of her face. When she would attend business functions with him in the past, it was all conveniently planned by him. He liked to give the impression he is a family man and make himself look good to his clients and peers. He would be gently attentive and cordial to her in public while on the side, he eyed the tramp.

Mrs. Jennings had secretly believed it was her own fault that her friend had no sex appeal, especially as she aged, and her zest had totally disappeared. Her many attempts to get her spruced up were not successful. Nora had resigned herself to accept and leave Susan alone and accept her as she was. *You cannot change people. They are the way they want to be!* She had to admit though, her general appearance, and her cut-and-dry mannerism left much to be desired. They both had British accents and Liverpool knowledge in common, and Nora appreciated this. They would exchange old recipes. Sometimes on Sundays they shared meals together since they both didn't have man friends. Susan would take Nora grocery shopping since she couldn't drive anymore. You would think Susan would adopt some of Nora's flirting, but she always remained aloof. She had been recognized for her work and received many awards in the past. Over the time the local paper published articles and interviews on her outstanding work.

The minute she spotted her friend leave the Abrosky's house, Nora called out to her, waving crazily, motioning with her hand for Susan to come over. Susan waved back while walking hurriedly to her car, shouting across, "Talk to you later Nora. I must go to my next appointment. Sorry, I cannot be late." She then got into her car and sped away. Nora was disappointed. But she knew once Susan returned to the quietness of her home in the evening, she would call her. Only then would Nora could try to squeeze the scoop out of her.

***

Valeria, on the other side of the ocean, had returned to her hotel room from meeting John Minerva and Enzo. It had only been a day of planning. When they would restart their work from where they had left off, was as good question as any! Lucio's absence was definitely felt. They were at a terrific disadvantage until he resumed his work. They could only hope that soon enough he would become emotionally strong and ready to resume working with them. She stood in front of her window, pensive, admiring the Mediterranean Sea. A gentle breeze caressed her warm cheeks like baby fingers touching her. The beauty she beheld beyond was mesmerizing. The scattered vessels out there took tourists island hopping within the archipelago. Life continued at a peaceful pace among the islands. The sun was still high up with its shining golden yellow glow. People on the seashore were basking in the sun, soaking up all the splendour. Suddenly, Valeria felt a pang of sorrow twisting trough her stomach. Here she was alone, surrounded by all this heavenly beauty, and no one to share it with. *What a pity!* She had no desire to adventure out anywhere alone.

She had called Rosy to get the day's report and was assured that everything was well at home. "Mrs. Butler's sessions were coming along terrific, and Dad was cooperating magnificently." Valeria didn't ask to speak to Boris as she knew he would get upset when she could not understand what he had to say.

For an instant, she thought of calling Mr. Alvani to check on his wellbeing. She had been told he was overtaken by grief. Reconsidering, she thought it better to leave well alone. She was not familiar with how the Sardinians handled grief.

Feeling helpless she picked up the phone and ordered room service. Once the food arrived, she picked at it as she had little appetite. The meal came with a glass of merlot which she sipped until she felt relaxed. She closed her eyes and enjoyed the relaxing sensation to her tense body. Her morale wasn't at its best, but soon her body welcomed the arrival of slumber, and she let herself go. There, sitting on the love seat beside her bed she fell into a deep sleep. She didn't know for how long she had drifted away when the phone rang and startled her. By the time she reached for the receiver in her frame of sleep stupor, the ringing has stopped. She realised she was now surrounded by total darkness.

How long did I sleep? She blinked slowly to adjust her eyes to the sparse dim reflection of the moon illuminating her room. As she stood up a creepy sensation trembled right through her spine. A fear of sorts that couldn't be attributed to anything in particular took over her body. It was way late, in the middle of the night; who was she to call now? Some force beyond her control was nagging at her conscience. She paced the room in the dim light with her arms embracing and comforting herself; she was shivering. *How can I stop this uneasiness that has come over me! God, please; you guide me!* She heard herself pray.

Chapter Twenty Nine
The Shadows

While Valeria was trying to control her uneasiness, confined to her hotel room, her friend was also in despair and confined to his home along the coast. Lucio Alvani, in his own misery kept pacing the floor of his study. He wouldn't dare go down the hall because it would mean passing by the empty bedroom where Chiara had been lying bed ridden for the past ten years. This was the first night that he was left totally alone. The two nurses were busy all day packing all of Chiara's belongings. They felt the sooner the better; Lucio had suffered enough all those years. They wanted to remove everything that would remind him of his wife's and his suffering.

He ordered them not to touch the wedding pictures on the wall where they both glowed with love and happiness. He had a stunningly marvellous picture of his wife in his study. He often stood and admired her beauty; young and vibrant, full of life. Her eyes were captivating, capable of hypnotizing any man in the past before she was stricken by the horrible disease that eventually took a huge toll on her. He had felt so luck with his beautiful wife.

Nurse Vittoria and her assistant had always been in charge of the household. They had been hard at work all day.

She called Lucio into the kitchen and asked him to have a seat and joined by the younger nurse she poured tea for all three of them. Vittoria was the oldest and always acted as a mother hen, fussing and protecting her employers. Lucio trusted her and had become dependent on her. She handed him his cup of peppermint tea with honey and fresh lemon. In a regretful tone she spoke, carefully choosing her words. Vittoria knew how much he had suffered in the past; the pain he now endured was clearly piercing his heart.

It was turning dusk outside as the sun eased down into the horizon. "Lucio my dear, we all loved Chiara; she was a remarkable human being. Life can be cruel. I feel your pain. I am concerned about you. There comes a time in life that we have to be resolute. You know she was suffering, and I know you did not want such a life for her. Rejoice in her memories, but soon you would have to pick up the pieces and move on. I also want to tell you our work here is over. We don't want to take your money and stay idle." She gave him a stern look. "It's time you try to release yourself from your suffering. You need to resume your work and find meaning once more in life. It will be hard, Lucio dear, but you must try. You promise me you will do that?"

Lucio's body shivered. Her maternal warmth made him emotional and he broke down crying, he lost control and his raw emotions emerged fully. Vittoria put an arm around his shoulder; she had been taught not to condone sorrow. "Now, now, Lucio; you make life difficult for me. You must get a hold of yourself. Once you continue like this how could I announce to you Lucio, that I also need to move on to help others in need."

He tried to compose himself, sniffing and wiping away his tears. Vittoria had gained a lot of experience through her years of nursing. She understood that most men didn't cope well with the loss of a loved one. Women seemed more resilient.

She continued, "Lucio, from tonight onward you will be here alone, and occupying your own room. No need for me to overnight anymore. You must promise me that you will be fine otherwise I will be forced to stay here and babysit you. Right now, I am urgently needed by another family with a sick member."

Lucio, ashamed of himself, still with his head lowered whispered softly, "I will be fine. I think I need to visit my psychiatrist again; he will help me out. I must get back on those darn pills he prescribed for me. Since he did not renew my prescription, I have been feeling quite depressed, especially lately. I must ask him if I should continue with them for a while again."

"I think you should. But I want you to assure me that I should proceed with my duties elsewhere." She gave him a hug. Then she and her assistant politely excused themselves from the room to go gather their things before leaving. Vittoria decided to check on something she had noticed while packing. In one of the bottom dresser drawers in Chiara's bedroom, she discovered a hidden compartment that she had never noticed before. Once she pulled out the small carved wood drawer, another drawer appeared to be sitting there and in it lay a white box. She opened it and found a photo album. The surface was embroidered in silk and it stayed closed by two flat bows neatly tied together, one was blue and one pink. She undid the bow and carefully lifted the cover. On the first page she found a picture of two infants neatly inserted in a hidden pocket. She turned the next page to find another picture of a girl, maybe five, and a little boy, about seven. More pictures of these two children appeared at different stages of growth. Remarkably, their eyes had the same sparkle as Chiara's. Inscribed behind the first photo in silver ink, in Spanish were the words, *a souvenir of my two beloved children*. Behind another picture, two names were written; Antos Ramos and Cintia Ramos; Ramos was Chiara's maiden name.

Vittoria had safely tucked back the infants' pictures exactly where she found them and replaced the album where it rested all these years. "Oh! My! Dear Lord! Who are these children? Where are they? This is a mystery! What do I do with this album? Chiara had never mentioned children in their discussions, and neither had Lucio. Is Lucio aware of these children?" She muttered to herself.

A brother and a sister had not showed up at the funeral; there had never been mention of children. She had worked with the Alvani family for fifteen years and no one had ever shared any such information with her. In reflection, Vittoria recalled that when Chiara first became sick and was unable to drive, there were a few instances when she had requested to be taken to the post office, adamantly refusing any assistance from Vittoria once they arrived there. Chiara would struggle with her cane, and Vittoria would wait in the car. Afterwards when her sickness advanced, there were no more trips to the post office or anywhere else.

This was not the time to approach or question Lucio about the discovery. Later she would return when Lucio should be in a better state of mind and consider raising the topic with him. She had also seen their wedding album; the photos clearly indicated they were both beaming, radiant, and so much in love. As she thought of it, she decided to retrieve and leave it on Lucio's desk in the study. *I don't think Lucio would want me to discard this album.* She left without looking back promising herself to make all effort to check in on Lucio weekly. He and his wife had become like family to her and she cared a great deal about him, especially now.

***

It was three in the morning. Lucio was having the worst time of his life, awakened by nightmares. He kept dreaming of his beautiful wife; she was at the cemetery, abandoned and alone, calling for his help. The apartment was dead silent. He felt the walls were closing in on him. It was pitch black outside as no moon was to be seen. He grabbed a jacket, put on his shoes, and still in pyjamas he took his car keys and out he went. The nosy security guy was off tonight. Another older one was on duty. He didn't ask questions. *Thank God,* thought Lucio. *I am in no mood to answer questions.* And he aimlessly drove off, with no plan or direction in mind.

Before he realized it, he was on his way out of town, heading towards the cemetery. Like a desperate man, he parked the car and on foot walked among the tombstones searching for his wife's grave. It took a while before he found the fresh turned soil; new growth hardly sprouted. He grievingly threw himself on the mound of earth, and with the deepest sorrow in his heart, he let out a loud wail then passed out.

When the caretaker arrived at dawn he was surprised to see a man lying on a grave, but not shocked as he had seen this happen before. He helped Lucio to get up, and carefully escorted him to the nearby office. He recognized the consigliere and tried to comfort him, offering him some coffee from his thermos. He was certainly in no shape to be driving back home alone.

At nine o'clock the caretaker placed a call to City Hall and asked to speak with the Mayor.

Chapter Thirty

The Meeting

John Minerva entered his office, followed by Enzo and Valeria. The day before, Enzo had dropped in on the Mayor after dropping Valeria off at her hotel in the early afternoon. He had plenty to complain about, gesticulating in typical islander manner, complaining frantically. "Mr. Minerva, we need to decide what to do here. I cannot spend the day driving, taking pictures, and explaining the history of the sites. Plus, I must be honest, I am not fully knowledgeable in the subject matter, it takes a historian, a professor of geography, and an archaeologist, to correctly explain everything about our island. It is not fair to Valeria either, to be coasting, waiting, and chance being misinformed. The signora needs to conduct her work properly."

"I understand, and you are right my friend. I am sorry for your frustration. Since you feel this strongly, let's meet tomorrow morning to decide which direction we are going. We both know there is no one better than Lucio. If Mr. Alvani is still not available, I might have to call the university to ask for someone more qualified for the job. It would take the load off you too."

This was the discussion that morning when the Mayor had called the meeting to decide how to move forward. He ordered his secretary to hold all calls. Just as they sat down to commence their discussion, the intercom began buzzing. It was his secretary pleading with her boss and explaining most apologetically for interrupting. "Your Honour, I am so sorry, there is a gentleman, he is insistent that he speaks with you."

"Who is he?"

"One Tony Dardo; says he is from the cemetery?"

"The cemetery? And how is that urgent? Ok! Put him through."

"Mr. Minerva, I am Tony Dardo, the grave digger and caretaker at the cemetery. I apologise for demanding that your secretary put me through to you. I feel you were the best person to call in this case. I have the consigliere here, Lucio Alvani. I know he works at the City Hall. Isn't he your right-hand man and works closely with you? He is in pretty bad shape, and I think he needs your help. You need to come down here and pick him up. He should be taken to a doctor or the hospital, or wherever! He needs a friend right now, Mr. Mayor!"

"He is where! The cemetery you say?" The Mayor shouted in disbelief.

"Yes! I found him on his wife's grave when I got to work early this morning, a little after five. I have no idea how long he had been out there. He is a mess I tell you; wet, muddy, and shivering. If he had been here all night exposed to the cold mist and the drizzling rain early this morning, he could have caught a cold, or even pneumonia. He is coughing incessantly and almost gasping for breath, wheezing. This man is in a bad way, Mr. Mayor; please hurry!"

Minerva brought a hand up to his temple to press a pressure point. "Oh! Good heavens! We will be right there!" He turned to Enzo and Valeria, "My friends, I believe right now we have a more urgent problem on our hands. Our friend, Alvani, he needs us badly!" And he immediately stood up, "Enzo, you do the driving. We're heading for the cemetery!"

"What? Why?" Enzo asked, frowning in disbelief.

"No time to explain. We must go! Come, Valeria!"

They hurriedly left the office, jumped into Enzo's car and headed towards the cemetery. As they walked into the parlour, what awaited them, and what they could have never been prepared for was a most pathetic sight. Lucio Alvani sat on a chair, dishevelled, like a dirty, homeless man. He was unshaved, his clothes were messy, his hair soaking wet. He was almost unrecognizable. They friends looked to one other, speechless.

Enzo broke the silence, "Nothing else could matter at this time! We need to take care of our consigliere. Lucio, come, give me your hand; hold on to my shoulder for support. We will take care of you. We are your friends!" Enzo held back a tear.

At this point, Valeria didn't know what to think or say; she felt deep concern for this kind gentleman. He seemed embarrassed; he glanced at Valeria with a shy smile then lowered his head again. Valeria was touched. She approached him, and gently put an arm around his shoulders to reassure him.

"Lucio, you poor soul, don't worry. We're all here for you."

The dampness from his jacket felt unpleasant against her skin. *Oh! My God! He is in his pyjamas.* She bit her lips without saying a word. *The anguish this man is suffering! It must have been unbearable; for him to drive to his wife's grave during the night to mourn!* To think that she almost called last night to check up on him. She wondered if her own uneasiness then, was a premonition of his distress. He must have felt all alone, abandoned.

She sighed deeply then suggested, "Lucio let's take this wet jacket off; you will be a bit more comfortable." And she took out a light shawl from her handbag and wrapped it around his shoulders. He smiled in gratitude but kept his head down.

In the meantime, realizing that Lucio needed support more than anyone at that time, Enzo and John Minerva were ready to take over and get the necessary help for their friend. The Mayor had been informed by Mr. Patty of the ordeal Valeria had been through, and what she had left behind. He wondered if with this messy intervention she questioned what she has got herself into; leaving one nightmare at home, to fall into another in Sardinia. If she decided to leave again he couldn't blame her. The city would claim no recourse. Now this misfortune with Lucio running to the cemetery in the middle of night was worrisome.

Valeria remained stunned looking on helplessly at her friend, obviously with a broken heart. Good reliable Enzo took the lead and practically carried Lucio to his car, then instructed Mr. Minerva and Valeria and follow in Lucio's vehicle. He would carry his friend to the emergency and have him checked out.

When they arrived at the hospital, the staff was prompt in examining Lucio. He was recognised by one of the doctors. In no time he had an x-ray, blood works, and the necessary checks. There was some concern about his lungs but after a complete physical, followed by the expertise of one Dr. Ramone, a pulmonologist, Lucio was given clearance and subsequently discharged.

"All he needs is a lot of rest. He can use melatonin to help him sleep; it's a natural preparation with no side effects. He suffers from sleep deprivation. Once his body recharges he should be fine. I am told he just lost his wife. It's everything combined that brought him to a state of breakdown. Grief, and the buildup of prior stresses, can have profound consequences on the mind and body. The exposure to the chilly night air at the cemetery has caused his sniffling and coughing, but don't worry, your friend will be better in a few days. I can see he has great friends!" The doctor offered a supportive smile.

With that the Mayor turned to Enzo and said, "You and Valeria can take him home in his car. I have to attend a ribbon cutting affair and I will check in on you all later."

Once Lucio was taken to the car, John Minerva gently placed a hand on Valeria's shoulder and said, "Sorry, Mrs. Abrosky, you may have to play nurse for the time being until I find a replacement. I will make a couple of phone calls this afternoon and organise something."

Enzo promptly interjected, "That should be no trouble; he had two nurses on his staff before. It would be wise to have one of them stay at the residence at nights, even if for a while."

Valeria at a loss didn't know what to say or do. She followed Enzo and awaited instructions. She was concerned about invading Lucio's privacy.

Once they arrived at the residence, Enzo helped him to shower and get into fresh clothes, with Lucio assisting the best he could. Valeria walked around the place, kind of lost and feeling out of place. There was definitely an odd feeling being in this place where Chiara had lived and died, and whom she had never met. She tried to suppress her uneasy feelings, forcing herself to be useful and focus on the matter at hand. She didn't feel right about it; she felt she didn't belong there.

To make herself useful, she thought some warm tea would soothe Lucio, and even Enzo. They had all been shaken up by the unpredictable event of the morning. Reluctantly she went to the kitchen. With her stomach in knots she didn't feel for anything. After serving the tea to Enzo and Lucio, she walked around the apartment, pensively. She stopped; her eyes caught some lovely portraits of a most stunning woman. It was easy to guess that she was Chiara. The face in the portrait looked vivacious, her eyes were piercing; Valeria felt they seemed to follow her. With quick steps she exited the room and returned to the kitchen to discover that Enzo and Lucio had now moved into the living room. They were sipping their tea, engaged in conversation. Since Lucio had showered, shaved, and changed into fresh clothes, she felt he had regained a bit of the glow in his outlook that she knew. She had admired this man much. *His loss was no doubt a huge blow for him.* He looked pale and tired. Enzo was trying to stimulate his sense of humour, trying to cheer up his friend and lighten the mood around the place. He jokingly said to Lucio, "Eh! Lucio, do you want to join me some evening at La Costa Grande? Maybe you can give me some tips on how to best approach some of those fabulous girls doing the river dance!"

"Enzo, why would you want me, when you are the one with all the charm and youth, my friend?" And a weak smile was seen on his tired face.

"Look Lucio, do us a favour, will you? Recharge your body like the doctor suggested, get some rest, and maybe afterwards I show you and Valeria some surprises I discovered around our island? You should know Valeria has placed her work on hold to wait on you. We have decided we can't complete the tours without you! We desperately need you to come back and help us finish off from where we left off. We don't want some 'Joe guy' fresh out of university to replace you!"

"Yes, Lucio, Enzo is right, but first, please get better! We need you badly; myself especially, desperately. I need to return to my responsibilities in Canada, but…" And she hugged him and spontaneously planted a kiss on his cheek.

"Valeria and I need you. We cannot function without you." Lucio liked hearing Enzo say that. Why was his darn body feeling so drained right now? They were right; he needs to rest and regain his strength. He got up to gather the empty cups to take them to the kitchen when Valeria jumped in. "Excuse me! I will do that, thank you! Why do you think I am here! I was given orders by the Mayor to be your nurse until further notice!" And she playfully winked at him.

Lucio smilingly handed her the cups, with a tickle of pleasure running down his spine. He acknowledged how fortunate he was to have these dear people standing by his side. In his sorrow, a pang of remorse also touched him. Valeria had returned to complete her contract. He must resolve not to fail his three trusted friends as he respected them profoundly.

Valeria on the other hand was fighting with her mixed feelings at the house. She liked Lucio and enjoyed working with him; he was great company. She adored Enzo and respected the Mayor. *God forgive me,* she thought to herself. *I just don't feel right in this apartment and I cannot wait to get out of here.*

Chapter Thirty One
At the Riverside

The locust trees were in full bloom; a white and green ornate mantle draped the infinite extension down and along the gorge from the Abrosky's backyard. A warm and gentle breeze circled the air, blowing across from the east bank of the Niagara river.

The river looked like a still sheet of ice, calmly flowing beneath a serene blue sky. It was ten in the morning. A jet boat loaded with tourists would soon appear, cameras snapping away to capture the beauty of Niagara. Boris enjoyed taking in the scenery. Although they were quite a distance off, the tour guide's voice echoed from down below to reach Boris' ears where he stood high up at the edge of his property. The young tour guide usually carried a megaphone. Boris could see him pointing upwards to his property. His exquisite home was one to be admired. It was the end of June. The blooms of Niagara from spring to summer were now fully resplendent. Boris had always loved this time and season. Often in the past he had said to Valeria that he never wanted to go away at this time of year, and she would agree. *Now she was away chasing rainbows, for what reason!* As he stood there reminiscing, he realized he was feeling much better. Then Susan knocked on the sliding door to get his attention.

"Mr. Abrosky," she called out as she stepped out towards him. "How are you? You are brave to come out here all by yourself!" He forced himself to answer one syllable at the time, as clearly as he could, "Wi-th…m-y…cr-ut-che-s… a-n-d…m-y…c-a-ne."

"Great! Good for you! You are doing just fine. Did you hear yourself?" She smiled enthusiastically, not just for his progress but

183

more for her own satisfaction and achievement. Susan always reinforced the positive. Mrs. Butler was not planning to waste time. Oblivious to the beauty Boris had been admiring, she guided him back to the couch, sat in front of him, ready to get into the therapy session. She was pleased. Boris was super intelligent. She had set a goal for his recovery and it seemed they were both determined to attain it.

The days were quickly rolling by. Rosy was giving her mother daily reports. She sensed that her mother wasn't happy and felt there was no enthusiasm in her voice. Rosy thought she was probably worried sick about the situation she had left at home.

***

Valeria was definitely not too happy in Alghero. The turn of events here had caused her mixed feelings. The guilt of having left home with Boris in his state nagged her. With Lucio's incident and she and Enzo being at a standstill, she was devastated. As much as she felt sorry for Lucio, she thought if he couldn't return to work by the following week she would have to seriously talk with the Mayor. In her best interest, she would put it to him that she needed to return home where she belonged. She spent the day wandering around the area, window shopping, visiting the coffee places and indulging in gelato and espresso. The sugar and caffeine combined worked magic on her nerves, stimulating her to move with more energy when before her system felt it would shut down on her.

To her surprise the Mayor called her early the next morning. Cheerfully he announced, "Mrs. Abrosky, I have good news; our friend Lucio has assured me that he will be returning to his duties in a couple of days."

"This is such good news! Both Enzo and I would be so happy, but would he be well enough?"

"Mrs. Abrosky, why don't you ask him yourself! Actually, I believe some hearty company and kind support could lift his spirits. Nurse Vittoria has taken another case, but she has promised to check in on him on evenings. The other nurse has returned to

Torino, so he is really all alone."

"I'll think about it, John." Valeria twitched her lips in contemplation. She wanted to help her friend but his house with portraits of his wife everywhere, with her piercing eyes, spooked her. She didn't want to tell that to the Mayor. She closed her phone and became lost in her thoughts.

Enzo had passed on Lucio's phone number to her. He asked her to check in on their friend. She could call him, and if he felt up to it, they could have something to eat downstairs and discuss the next steps of the tour. Yes, that is what she would do. She dialed his number, *pronto.* "Hello, Lucio Alvani speaking." She held her breath for a second. *He answers the phone as if he is in his office!*

"Lucio, this is Valeria. How are you?"

"Oh! Valeria, *mi sorprende,* what a surprise! Nice of you to call."

"Enzo insisted on giving me your number, so I can check on you. You must know, we are all concerned about your wellbeing, Lucio!"

"I am sorry, *mi scusa,* Valeria, and I thank you. Please, you, Enzo, and the Mayor, you must forgive me. I should have never done what I did the other night. I must have been taken completely by *un incubo,* a moment of insanity."

"Lucio, only if you are up to it, you can come and join me downstairs in the hotel lobby. We could have something to eat, and since the Mayor has shared the good news that we would be resuming our work, we could discuss it, but only once you are up to it!"

"Thank you, Valeria. Are you sure you want to be bothered with this *disgraziato,* miserable man, like me?"

"Yes, I am sure. You need company, and I do too."

"I will be more than happy to come over. I have to be honest with you, I saw my doctor this morning; he couldn't stress enough the necessity of getting out and being with people. Thank you, thank you!"

He hung up the phone feeling anxious. He had taken his prescription. Sorrow had bored down hard on his heart, but he suddenly became aware that it was beginning to lift. Tonight, he looked forward to having a place to go, and good company to keep.

The streets were always noisy, full of people; he lived in a fully occupied high rise building. His life had been too lonely, his heart empty for so long; he would often feel at a loss since Chiara could not function as a normal person. Their friends and social life had vanished as her sickness advanced, taking over her body and slowly destroying both their lives. Other than his interest at the City Hall, Lucio's world was totally empty. The couple of cousins he had, lived far away and had long distanced themselves. He knew they didn't fancy his wife, since way back when they had first met her.

Lucio had a good rest in the afternoon. He showered and groomed himself, and with positive thoughts towards renewal, he promised himself he would make effort to move forward. He would get back to his duties and give the Mayor, Enzo, and Valeria, his devoted attention.

He arrived at the hotel where Valeria was waiting for him at the same spot where she would be picked up from the previous tours. As soon as he approached, she greeted him with a big smile and a friendly embrace; he badly needed it. Lucio reciprocated with genuine appreciation, glad that the sweet Canadian lady was back in this part of the world, at this time in his life. He promised himself to try and put his sorrow aside and try to make things up to her. Adrenalin began running through his body, invigorating him with hope. Valeria also felt she was doing a good deed by having Lucio in her company; heeding the Mayor's request. That he agreed to meet her, no longer was she dwelling on her own turmoil back home.

Chapter Thirty Two

The Tour Resumes

It was Monday morning. Valeria was happily waiting to be picked up by her two friends to resume their journey. A dark thought invaded her serenity. At once her thoughts darted home to Niagara. Her intention had been to spend a couple of weeks, but now she was on her third. With Mr. Patty, she had no problem; he had been brought up to date with the happenings and he was fine with her extended stay. Sardinia was a highly sought destination point by his clients, so the more informed his agency could be, the better for business. He had promised the Mayor full plane loads of tourists from Canada to visit and boost his country's economy. Valeria's concern was that her family was equally important. If her mother was alive, she would have never heard the end of it.

Enzo started the car and pressed the play button on his CD player. He wanted to welcome Valeria with a pleasant melody to start her morning right. He thought the low background melody of indigenous music would surely set the mood.

"Here we are, my beautiful lady; at your service!" added Lucio, trying his utmost to sound upbeat. Seeing the pleasant Valeria brought extra sunshine to his day.

"Good morning Enzo! Where are we heading today?" asked Valeria. The three of them seemed harmonized with each other.

"It's a surprise. I am driving. Lucio the expert knows his history by heart; he simply turns on a switch in his brain. Are you ready with your tape recorder and note book? We three musketeers would soon have this island rocking!"

"You are such a pleasure to work with Enzo," said Lucio, slapping him lightly on the shoulder.

"I can vouch for that," seconded Valeria.

They drove along the coast. Once more the scenery was magical and the company magnificent. Valeria was loving her surroundings and her friends. It was a bright sunshiny day. The air felt filled with renewed karma; the climate was just perfect for her.

Valeria always took a hat with her to guard her face from the direct sun. Since it was a surprise, who knew were Enzo was going to stop first? She was sitting in the back seat. She leaned over and playfully ran a finger through his hair and asked, "Where are you taking us, Mr. Chauffeur?"

"You really want to know, Valeria; don't you?"

"I am sure Lucio does too. Stop playing games with us!"

"Ok, if you care to know, no surprises then! We are heading for Castelsardo at the east end of the Gulf of Asinara, to the alluring Premontorio. Once there I want to see the look on your face when you see the mesmerizing rock formation. You would admire the panoramic view of the medieval village, and from there we would continue along the Costa Paradiso, Isola Rossa, 'red island', Monte Tinnari, where we can admire the famous Rinaggie beaches where you would enjoy seeing beaches combined with unusual formations of fine rocks and sand. Once we are at Costa Paradiso you will surely enjoy the spectacular colours of the different rocks that naturally surfaced many years ago. If that is not enough, you will see the vegetation surrounding the shore, extending to an area in full bloom: red roses, and fuchsia coloured wild flowers. The area is nothing short of a seductive view to the eyes of any tourist. Lucio you can take over from here since you know where I am heading."

Valeria had been listening and taping. She felt seduced just listening to Enzo's descriptions. Lucio took over, turning to Valeria as he began his speech.

"This tour is intriguing, seems too ravishing for anyone to miss. Along the way we will stop by the state highway going to Olbia, there we would admire the Gallura Valley, a place of amazing geologic formation. At this spot you may become bewitched by the sculpture of these rocks such as: the elephant, the bear, the dinosaur, the birds of prey, and the nest. Afterwards we continue to Emerald Coast, *Costa Smeralda,* another stretch of paradise where the crystal-clear water is uncontaminated and takes on hues of green, and many shades of blue. The indented coastline is stretched for miles, and one cannot miss the alternating reddish and yellowish hues of the granitic rocks. The buildings there are surrounded by artfully maintained gardens, arbors, and natural stone patios where people lounge and enjoy the pleasant climate."

"Indeed, it is enchanting. Sounds like a bit of heaven on earth!"

The tour proved to be spectacular. They got back to the hotel on time to catch the astonishing sunset; another phenomenal sight to behold as it slowly disappears beyond the horizon, to leave behind an aura of reddish pink strokes, softly bathing the sky until twilight. It had been an informative and full day; Valeria was fully engrossed in every detail of what she was shown. She thanked her companions figuring it had been a long day and they were all tired. Anxiously, Valeria was hoping to call home to get an update on everyone's wellbeing. Lucio, the usual gentleman he was, helped her out of the car.

"Ciao, *a domani,* tomorrow," he said as Valeria stood waving them away.

When Enzo dropped Lucio off, he teased lightly, "Consigliere, in case you are not tired, you can join me at the discotheque. Eh!" He wasn't being funny, as he had noticed how Lucio would hold his gaze on Valeria at times during the day. He thought to himself, *I bet on my life he is attracted to her and he doesn't even realize it. Is that what happens when you get old and you are unable to identify your feelings? I can see how he is mixed up right now; lost between grief and love. As long as he doesn't keep running back to his wife's grave!* He watched Lucio until he disappeared into the lobby, then drove away.

Lucio turned the key to his door and was surprised to find the lights on, an aroma of fresh salsa hit his nostrils, stimulating his appetite. He walked into the kitchen and there was good old Vittoria fussing about, stirring a pot of *sugo*, tomato salsa and meat balls. The table was set for two.

"Vittoria, you are back! I am so glad to see you!" He lovingly hugged her as if meeting an old friend after a long time, while controlling his emotions.

"The Mayor called me; I should have known better than to leave you so soon. I am occupied during the day but I will make it my business to check up on you on evenings after work."

"Vittoria, I am so sorry for the trouble. You have been such a devoted nurse, the best caretaker we could have ever found for my Chiara. I will always be grateful to you."

"Lucio my dear, you realise all the care in the world couldn't help that poor girl? She is in a better place now; no more suffering. You better take care of yourself now!"

It felt good to have Vittoria here. He hated being alone on evenings; they were the worse.

Vittoria asked, "If you need me I will sleep over on the sofa, otherwise I will go home after I clean up."

"Ma! No, Vittoria! I am a grown old man! I will be fine. You must go and rest well before work tomorrow. Thank you!"

"As long as you promise not to do anything stupid!" She looked at him sternly, threateningly waving her wooden ladle.

"You can rest assured. I promise!" He smiled shyly at her maternal warmth.

Vittoria was ready to leave but paused and pondered for a while. *The album! Those pictures of the two children in the bottom compartment. Did Lucio know anything about them? Were they a secret between him and his wife? Should I ask him about them? Should I show him the pictures? Who were they, and where are they now?* It bothered her, but she thought now was not the time to bring it up. *In time I would have to.*

She gathered her things from the living room where Lucio had fallen asleep while reading the paper. Without disturbing him, she quietly slipped away.

"Good night, dear Lucio," she whispered as she shut the door.

Chapter Thirty Three

Moving Forward

Valeria walked into her hotel room and dropped her notebook and recorder on her desk. Later she would review her notes before submitting them to World Travel. Tonight, her body felt drained of all its energy. The sunshine, the fresh air from the sea, the concentration on her work, all altogether had taken a toll on her. She wasn't feeling hungry. All she desired was to lie down and enjoy total relaxation. She looked at the time; it was not too late, and the call of duty was nagging her. She picked up the phone and dialled her home number, Rosy was instantly on the line.

"Hello Mom, I knew it would be you! I am preparing supper."

"My dear, Rosy! I just got back to my room and wanted to find out how things were. How is your Dad?"

"Mom, everything is fine! You will be surprised when you come home. Mrs. Butler is fantastic, and Dad is making daily progress. I will let you talk with him now," and she passed the phone on to her father.

"Hello!"

"Boris! How are you dear?"

"G-o-o-d, these wo-m-en give me no r-es-t."

"Boris, it's for your own good. Once you go along with them, all will be well. Nurse Florence and Susan are both seeking your interest."

193

"I kn-o-w, b-ut th-ey m-aa-ke m-e ti-red."

"It will all pay off eventually. Trust me and just do as they say."

"O-k, I w-i-ll." Listening to him, she silently thought, *oh my God*, as she let out a deep sigh. *What a change in him, he sounds almost likeable.* He didn't even ask anything about her, or when she would be back. She didn't know if it was from his difficulty to speak, or because he had lost his tyrannic personality to order her around. Whatever it was, she now liked him better. Her stay in Sardinia was already overdue. She had no idea when she would complete her assignment to home, especially with the unforeseen lost time. She hung up the phone feeling relieved, then slumped her body on the bed to take a short rest. She slept right through the night.

The next morning, they once more headed for the caves. Lucio announced, "Valeria, today we will explore the Blue Marina Grotto at *La Cala della mezzaluna*; another beautiful area with a half moon land structure. The amazing caves in the grotto are intriguing and spectacular, somewhat dark with narrow water streams. The high cliffs there are also of natural geological formation." They took a *vaporetto,* a well-equipped water bus, to sail around the attractions. The calm sea with blue hues extended in front of the boat, making the ride enjoyable. A pleasant breeze blowing from the coastline caressed Valeria's cheeks as they approached the rocky shore and disembarked. Lucio was forever hovering around her with dutiful attentiveness. He held her by the arm to secure her, "Valeria, the air in the grotto is humid; it would be a good idea to wear a sweater. Should you feel claustrophobic, please let me know."

"Lucio, thanks for being so solicitous but I will be fine."

Once inside Valeria was speechless, admiring the incredible formation, and she learnt that at one time monk seals had occupied these caves. The unsteadiness in her footing caused her to reach out for Lucio a few times to stabilize herself; the narrow walkway was challenging. After that tour, she was glad to be back out in the sea and the open blue sky.

Enzo had preferred to remain on board indulging in a cold lemonade. He had been there so many times before, the Grotto had lost its novelty for him.

The days seemed to be going by quickly as they toured many more exciting areas. Then they got to Lucio's pride and joy, "The famous nuraghic wells, temples, and other structures, remnants of an ancient civilization developed between 1900 and 730 BCE. Now it has become the symbol of Sardinia's distinctive history," explained Lucio. "The wells are said to carry deep symbolism for the people of that time." He continued, "The water of the well was seen as the womb of mother earth." Valeria could not help but be more amazed than ever as Lucio freely and proudly explained these things with such love in his heart, as if he was personally responsible for their preservation. She was not into history too much, but her guide was exceptional, and he made her become interested in the history! She decided she must read up on these sights in more details to make an impacting presentation for Mr. Patty, to knock his socks off. They had scaled one well, descending the steep stone stairs that were dug way into the earth, and then they tiringly climbed back up. Valeria's physical fitness was put to the test. She privately thought, *I need to return to the gym as soon as I get back home!*

The way their meals were prepared and the hospitality of the gentle people they met, were only to be experienced. It would touch any heart and awaken the soul to the simplicity of life, yet its profound symbolism.

For some nights, after a long day of exploring when Valeria returned to the hotel she decided on room service as she was too tired to get dressed and go out. It was Friday night and Enzo, with his young blood pumping through his veins, had begged Lucio to end the tour a bit early.

"Consigliere, *su,* come on, I have a hot date tonight. I need to spruce myself up for a special *ragazza,* a young woman. Please, let's wrap it up a bit earlier, can we?" he begged.

Valeria was all smiles; she found Enzo entertaining. He reminded her of her boys. "Lucio, of course we will oblige to Enzo's request. He has been a devoted assistant and an excellent driver. I am very grateful to him, so I say let him have a break this evening!"

Lucio was also pleased with him. "*Ma, si!* Enzo! Why not! We have accomplished much if you ask me!"

"Thanks! Wish me luck! I'll let you know how it went! The girl is American you see; they are not used to late dinners, at eight or nine like the locals here. She wants me to pick her up at seven."

"I understand, Enzo," sympathized Valeria.

Lucio, aware of his loneliness, asked Valeria, "Since it's an early evening, would you care to have dinner with me, Valeria; that is, if you wish?" He asked hesitatingly, unsure of himself.

Enzo overheard him and said encouragingly, "Yes! You two should have dinner together! It's Friday night! You are both alone. And you are friends now, aren't you!"

"Of course. I am delighted to be in Valeria's company," he said as he turned to look at her.

"Platonic, that is! Two lonely people sharing dinner."

"Yes! Valeria, what could be wrong with that?" added Enzo.

She smiled, "You two are funny! But I am not questioning it."

By now, she had been there for a whole month. These two and the Mayor, had become good friends but she was particularly fond of Enzo and Lucio. With her Italian blood, she had easily developed sincere affection towards them.

"Eh! Guys, you forget where I come from? We are known for

our out of control emotions. I genuinely love you both."

"Thanks, Valeria. But who wouldn't love a person like you!" Enzo commented. Lucio nodded in agreement like a true gentleman.

"Ok friends, enough! We are getting too sentimental here! Enzo, you go to your date! Lucio, give me a chance to rest a bit and then freshen up. We will have dinner together like two good friends. Will that be ok?"

Lucio was all smiles, and with Enzo applauding, echoed, "*Va bene!* Great!"

"See! Now we are all happy," chuckled Enzo, as he moved quickly to drop off the two so he could proceed to meet his latest conquest.

Chapter Thirty Four

Florence and Susan

Almost two months had passed since nurse Florence had been caring for Boris. At the beginning, she had some doubts; he seemed very helpless and stayed this way for some time. Slowly he began cooperating and that was encouraging. Therefore, she earnestly devoted herself to working hard to successfully rehabilitate him. Boris would complain at times tempting her to shorten the sessions, but she kept insisting that he should persevere with the aches from the exercises.

"No pain, no gain," she would sternly say to him. The hard work was definitely paying off. Boris was walking further and stronger with each new day with his right arm becoming more flexible. Florence was clever, and Boris was lucky to have her for his care. Between the two professional caregivers and Rosy's watchful eyes, he was kept busy. The minute the session was over he would fall asleep in front of the TV, exhausted. And if that wasn't enough, after supper on the weekend, Rosy wouldn't take no for an answer and would insist on taking him outdoors for a walk around the block. He would lament and look for excuses to use with Rosy as he was pulled through the front door.

"I hate to walk out of our driveway and see that old fox across the street. She seems to be always watching our place while pretending to be pruning and snipping away at her dead geraniums."

"Oh, Dad! Maybe you should be nice and greet her. Mrs. Jennings is a lonely woman."

"Me, be nice, and start chatting with her? The old hag rubs me the wrong way!"

Rosy had observed the neighbour's flowers looked lousy due to her relentless watering. She didn't mention it to her father, didn't want to add fuel to the fire, putting him more against Mrs. Jennings. Boris got into the habit of looking the other way as soon as he would spot her. He didn't want to have to greet her, or God forbid, strike up a conversation with her, which would see no end once it began. Boris, with his sinister sense of humour, would look cross-eyed at the old woman. He had even claimed she flirted with him in the past. *Can you imagine! How could Valeria stand her is beyond me!* He had expressed his opinion to his wife, but against his wishes she still bothered with the woman. Boris didn't know that the feelings were mutual, that Mrs. Jennings didn't particularly care for him either.

Rosy didn't condone his coldness towards the woman. She would tug at his sleeve as soon as they got close to the road for him to acknowledge her, but her father continued to be rude.

"Oh Dad, please be kind! I feel sorry for lonely old people."

"Never you mind! She strikes me as an old whore! I wonder how many escapades she had in the past!"

Rosy rolled her eyes at her father's comments and let it slide. She wondered to herself, how did he get married to her mother since he was overtly unsympathetic towards women.

The following morning Susan arrived more cheerful than usual. Boris was surprised. He thought, *the iceberg around her soul must have been subject to some melting.* But this time he kept his thoughts to himself. When Rosy entered he nodded at her with a smirk on his face. Rosy too, noticed the pleasantness in Susan's behaviour this morning. Since she had started her sessions with

Boris, her visits had been strictly professional, very matter of fact, cold and removed. Today they were in for a surprise.

After she was finished with the session, and with a big smile on her face she said, "Last night one of my former patients and I went for supper at the new casino and it was a delightful experience. We were celebrating her successful recovery. All week she had progressed to finishing her sentences totally uninhibited. After supper, we thought we should try our luck at the machines. We chose the Wheel of Fortune, and after only three tries, it was my turn to spin and suddenly all the lights began flashing, and bells started ringing. To my shocking surprise I had won ten thousand dollars!" As she spoke her eyes gleamed with excitement.

"C-on-gra-tu-la-tions," said Boris, seconded by Rosy.

"I knew something had taken place, from the look on your face this morning. We are happy for you!" said Rosy. Boris tilted his head and nodded in agreement.

Susan was all smiles, "Tonight, Nora and I will go out to celebrate. You know her; your neighbour from across the street!"

Boris made a funny face thinking to himself. *Don't I know her!*

"Boris, as soon as your speech is perfected, we should also celebrate, and it would be my treat!" She turned to Rosy, "Rosy, you may also join us."

"Thanks, but the casino is not my thing. I would tell you what we can do. I will go dancing next door at the Dragonfly while you guys have fun at the casino." She turned to her dad, "Dad, I hope you go with Susan and Mrs. Jennings when the time comes; it will be good for you." She was being funny and making faces at her father.

Boris looked at her cross-eyed. *Has my daughter gone nuts? Me at the casino with Susan, the iceberg! And to top it off, Nora Jennings too, in my company? They are picking the wrong guy!*

Susan attentively resumed her duties. As soon as she was done, her jolly mood returned. She swung an arm around his shoulder and said, "Boris, it's up to you! Whenever you are ready, I am ready!" He didn't respond but was wondering if winning the money had stimulated her brain to make her more human. *It's interesting that her new personality has made her more likeable.*

Chapter Thirty Five

An Awakened Heart

Once back in her hotel room, Valeria's adrenalin rush kicked her into high gear, infiltrating her body with a wonderful tingle. Enzo and Lucio were such good company to be with that they unknowingly empowered her and boosted her confidence. Here she was, after working all day, moving about as happy as a lark. She carefully refreshed her appearance and looked forward to an evening with good company and enjoyable conversation with her friend Lucio.

The sun's rays caught the rayon stones of the bracelet watch on her wrist and sparkled. She squinted and glanced at the expensive piece of jewelry her husband had bought her on one of his business trips in Vienna. He had made sure she knew its value.

Time was slowly ticking away. It was still early. The lobby housed some attractive boutiques. Instead of waiting in her room, Valeria decided to go down and browse through the elegant shops that carried signature items. She thought if she was lucky she may be able to shop for some souvenirs to take home; gifts for Rosy and Boris. That would make up the time until Lucio gets back to her.

Once she stepped out of the elevator, there he was waiting for her, standing along the opposite wall. His eyes immediately lit up on seeing her, and with a warm smile he moved forward to greet her. He extended an arm across her back in a gentlemanly manner while asking, "Valeria, would you prefer one of the restaurants along the coast? We could sit out on the terrace overlooking the sea. Since it's still daylight we may be able to catch the sunset."

"That sounds lovely, but whatever you prefer, Lucio; it's your call. Anything is fine with me."

Valeria wasn't going to dictate or demand anything. She was content with pleasant company tonight, instead of alone in her room, having room service.

They walked into a most charming place called La Gondola. From inside the restaurant, they were led to an outdoor area. While walking through, she observed murals covering the entire walls. The artist that had reproduced the scenes on the walls was most gifted, as one could easily get a sense of being in the centre of the archipelago while walking around and admiring the spectacular artwork. The sea, the different islands, the boats in various shapes and sizes, left Valeria mesmerized. Lucio observed the awe in her expression and said, "The artist manages to transport customers within this spectacular indoor, to the beautiful outdoor. Do you feel the effect?"

"Lucio this is more than spectacular; yet another discovery! You never cease to amaze me! You are clever; no wonder the Mayor wanted no one else to take your place. You are the best!"

"Valeria, I am inspired by your interest. When one recognizes appreciation, you automatically want to give more of yourself. It is you, my dear lady, not my cleverness."

"Ok, Lucio, my friend, you are being humble. I like that too!"

They finished touring the murals just as the hostess approached them. "Signor Alvani, I gather you would like to sit on the terrace?" she asked. He had been a regular in the past so the lady knew his preference.

"Yes, Signora! The usual table." On Lucio's request, they were escorted out to the terrace, close to the balcony railing, suspended over the sea.

The sun was losing its potency. The sky was still luminous, changing into a pinkish glow as the sun slowly descended and turned into a falling yellow ball. The warm breeze from the sea was cool, pleasant, and refreshing. Valeria always kept a shawl with her since she found the later evenings turned a bit chilly. She quickly draped it across her shoulders.

Lucio tried hard to stay calm in his contented state of mind. He considered himself fortunate to be sharing his meal with company. He found Valeria comfortable to be with. They conversed in both English and Italian which was fun for them, switching back and forth. It allowed them to express themselves freely, and pleasurably use different Italian phrases of expressions that sounded like music to her ears. Lucio, from the depth of his heart, wanted to accommodate his friend in the best way possible.

Taking Valeria to La Gondola had been another showing on his part. Intending to switch gears, he enquired, "Valeria, we are finished working for now. You are off duty. No more talk about tours and this island. Tell me about yourself; what do you plan for when you return home?"

"I am spoiled here with you and Enzo. I must confess when I go home, it won't be as pleasurable. My first concern is to check on the wellbeing of my husband. You must have been told he suffered a massive cardiac arrest; it was hard for me to leave him. I cannot believe I actually left the messy situation there to return here. My emotions were raw, something snapped in me to make me leave. I was threatened by my boss, and I was told the Mayor was also pressing from here. So, Valeria Abrosky abandoned everything and headed for Sardinia to finish her work. I am glad I came back! My daughter is on duty, covering for me at home. But I need to get back as soon as I can."

"I am sorry about your husband. But we are glad you came back. Both Enzo and myself were at a loss after you disappeared on us. I must confess, you did leave us in a state of confusion. Enzo can tell you how irritated I became, even furious. I apologize for that." And then he outstretched a hand to reach for hers, saying, "We will miss you when you leave. We have grown fond of you."

With a sad look in his eyes, he said, "Seriously speaking, I am afraid this will be another blow for me. After losing my Chiara, and you reappearing on the horizon, I regained an incentive to work again. I do not wish to disappoint you. You and Enzo have given me a reason to go on in life. I refuse to believe that you are going to soon leave us."

"Lucio," she said, as she accepted his hand, "I am not leaving yet; let's not think about that right now. You and Enzo have become dear friends to me too. Let me hear about you; what do you plan to do? Just know, should you need to talk about Chiara, I am here to listen."

He stared at her with a pitiful expression, "Valeria, what can I tell you? I now look forward to going to work every morning because our lovely Canadian lady makes my day; and I dare say, I also speak for Enzo. Enzo is young and chasing love. I am much older and I have no one. At times, life gets difficult for me and I feel lonely and miserable."

"Lucio, I don't mean to invade your privacy. Your parents, Chiara's, children, sisters, brothers; do you have any family around here or elsewhere? Don't you have any support?"

"Valeria my dear, I was on top of the world when I met my Chiara; we were exuberantly happy together. We shared our dreams for a while. Then she suddenly took ill. I had met her after my parents were both killed in a car accident. They died instantly in a head-on collision while travelling through the mainland in Italy; a transport truck was negotiating a narrow curve going down Mount St. Angelo. That was a huge blow for me. I was devastated by that loss.

I had an older sister who emigrated to South Africa and we kept in touch until she passed away last year. I do have some cousins who live inland. It's not easy for them to come to the city as they are busy working their land. With animals to take care of and a resort to run, they have no time. Every now and then they have invited me to visit; a few times they visited Alghero. For some strange reason, they didn't seem to take to my Chiara. After we visited a few times, they stopped visiting. Their invitations also stopped, and the relationship grew distant."

"What about children; did you have any?"

"No, we didn't; my wife never wanted children and she made me promise her we wouldn't. I was somewhat older than her when we got married so it didn't matter to me. Besides, my Chiara was such a beautiful woman, with the greatest body and mind, and we were so much in love that the contentment of having each other was enough for us. We completed each other." He paused for bit, reflecting, then continued.

"Then, when we were at our happiest and had just moved into our new place, and we thought everything was going well, everything suddenly changed. I had even started working less hours, so I could spend more time with my Chiara; she had a way of making me feel special." He paused and reflected again. Valeria wanted to stop him, didn't want to make him sad, but she decided against it. *Let it all out, my friend!*

"Out of the blue one day, she collapsed in the house. I took her to the hospital and she was diagnosed with a horrible disease that quickly took her from bad to worse, until my precious wife was eventually taken away from me, as you now know."

Valeria listened to him carefully. While looking at him and listening, her thoughts drifted in and out. Lucio seemed to fight back the tears while he talked about personal trials. In his voice and expressions, she detected the deep love for his wife, and most of all in his eyes, as he slipped away at times and stared into space. She couldn't help compare him to Boris. Did he ever feel for her, the way this man felt for his wife! She doubted it! Boris was such an egotistic son-of-a-bitch that she didn't want to think about it.

He would brag about how he had provided well for her and the kids. *Big deal!* His affection was all she craved, but never got. This made her sad. He had also turned into a wife-beater, post retirement. *Then why am I fretting about going back to him when he has never been loving towards me!*

Lucio noticed the distraction in her eyes, and her forehead creased in thought, and he asked, "Valeria, are you ok? Did I say anything wrong?"

"No, Lucio! You are such a good man. I have only known you for a short time, but I already know enough. I know you would never say or do anything wrong to offend anyone. Chiara was such a lucky woman to have you as her husband. You should only think of the good times and cherish the memories you had together. Lucio, you must promise me that after I leave, you would continue your life with the same kindness that you have been gifted."

"Valeria, you sound too serious. Let's not mention your departure. Listen, there is music playing inside. Why don't we move in. We can have a brandy or a martini."

"A very good idea," responded Valeria.

They got up and moved closer to where they could better view two musicians who played delightful melodies. One played an accordion, the other a violin.

Chapter Thirty Six

Two Souls Brought Together

The evening progressed with Valeria and Lucio living in the moment, fully relishing the meal and evening's ambience; two friends genuinely enjoying each other's company. They were two lonely people, each aching to be comforted, not fully aware of the extent their lives lacked it. Deep down, Valeria once more felt torn between desire and duty. Lucio, with his confused emotions, had no idea how he would fill the emptiness in his heart. They parted for the evening, each smiling coyly at the other, not looking forward to the loneliness they would later face.

Valeria entered her luxurious suite where silence reigned. Lucio walked into his apartment, just as torn; no liveliness existed. From a window, he could hear voices echoing outside on the street. He walked to the spare bedroom that he occupied for almost a decade. He had no desire to ever return to the matrimonial bed he shared with Chiara when she was well, and life was happier. It would bring back too many memories.

Chiara was an extraordinary woman when it came to lovemaking, and they both enjoyed countless nights of blissfulness. She knew all the tricks it took to stimulate and satisfy the needs of her lover husband; he didn't need to ask for anything. He sat on his bed reminiscing, holding his head in his hands, pressing his temples with his thumbs, as his mind played games with him. *No, I must not relive it! Her vision, her whispers, her caresses, her moaning; they were enough to drive any man crazy. It was an art for her.*

209

He shuddered slightly as tears streamed down his face. He walked to her portrait, stared at it, trying to appease the temptation the man Lucio was presently feeling. Perhaps admiring her painting would magically fill his heart, and distract from present human desires? He stood there, reliving memories until his legs dragged him back to his own bed.

In the morning, he was awakened by Vittoria's phone call. "Hello Lucio, I am just checking in on you. All is well? I called you last night but got no answer. I wondered if you had gone out or was still at work. Lucio, you know I worry about you!"

"Vittoria, thank you. I appreciate your concern. I am fine, really. No need for you to worry." He tried to clear his tired voice from lack of sleep.

"I am not so sure about that, Lucio!" She detected his lack of alertness. "I will soon stop by one of these evenings and check for myself. I still have my key. How about I surprise you with a home cooked meal?"

"Vittoria, I would love that; please, come anytime! You are sorely missed."

"As long as you look after yourself, Lucio. Go out as much as you can; don't mope around that place by yourself."

"I will. I promise." He hung up. *Vittoria was such a caring and nurturing woman.*

Once he arrived at City Hall, the Mayor informed him that Enzo and Valeria were in the board room. They were exploring various aspects of the tours such as bus companies, bus drivers, and knowledgeable local guides to hire. There were lots of resumes to go over and interviews to be scheduled. Enzo being the Don Juan who frequented the best places on evenings with other young people, could recommend preferred spots. Prices for the land tours needed to be established, tour-boat owners to be selected and contracted since the scattered islands could only be reached by boat. There was a lot of work to cover; legal papers to scrutinize, fill out and submit, rules and regulations to consider, and safety measures to be considered. Valeria wouldn't leave anything to chance. Everything needed to be reviewed and perfected.

Lucio walked in, happy to see them both. He eyed Valeria and greeted everyone with his usual, "Good Morning!" He gently bowed head and said, "Valeria, I am at your service; anything you need, please let me know. Am I late?".

"Not at all. I couldn't sleep so I got here early. Enzo just arrived. He has been making suggestions of some people to hire."

"All his girlfriends, I bet!" he said, smiling and making eyes to his friend.

"Eh Lucio! I would have to take you with me some evenings. I can do the approaching and you do the smooth talking; how is that!"

They all laughed as Enzo excused himself and stepped out. Lucio, still standing, bent close to Valeria's ear and whispered, "Valeria, I enjoyed your company very much last night. Could we have dinner again tonight? I have nothing to go home to. That empty apartment has been driving me insane."

"Lucio, we are both in the same predicament; my lonely room drives me bonkers. It's no fun eating alone either! We can surely share dinner again tonight, my friend."

"Please, don't mention anything to Enzo; he has a way of distorting things."

"Our secret; we keep it to ourselves! *In bocca al lupo!*"

***

While Valeria was trying to research some tourism legalities in Sardinia, back home in Niagara Boris was making great progress, showing off to nurse Florence that he could now walk across the room without his cane. He held his body erect in perfect posture, his snobbish nose turned up, an air of superiority governed his face, satisfaction gleamed in his eyes.

"Nurse! Eh! Take a look! This fellow will be in great shape in no time." He was very proud of his accomplishments.

Susan soon arrived. In a good mood he greeted her, "Good morning! It sure is a good morning. Susan, look at me without the cane!"

"Good for you, Mr. Boris. It's all from your cooperation and effort. Your wife would be proud of you when she returns; and surprised too."

The therapist had been spending more time with him, at his insistence. He was anxious to get his speech clearer. They had turned the sessions into play. Rosy had bought some sticky stars at the craft shop to be used as encouragement when Boris didn't stutter, or when he did well at an exercise. He would be awarded a blue star against the different tasks listed on the sheet of paper stuck to the fridge. Susan was aiming for a red star, the highest achievement per task. Boris loved the challenge; he was all for it. Susan had subtly relaxed her reserved personality; she smiled more, and generally seemed more personable, and this made Boris more comfortable. He thought maybe it was Rosy's influence that was rubbing off on her.

Since that first day when she arrived with a stern look on her face, her hair tied in a knot like an old maid; he wondered how on earth was he going to tolerate her for an hour every day. Now the sessions last two hours, and time seems to pass by quickly. He was determined to regain his speech, even if it killed him. *Me and this old hag would get it done!* At times, he thought Susan and Mrs. Jennings deserved one another; for him, they were two old hags.

He called Rosy over one day, now that he was speaking better, and said to her, "You know I am only concerned that she teaches me to the best of her ability. I need to get back into the world out there and live my life. I cannot stand being cooped up day and night in this house."

"Good, Dad! That is what you need; some great will power! Mom will be so happy when she comes home." She could tell that her father was getting better as he was antsy to get out on his own, and do and see things, just as he used to. This was a good sign.

***

Days rolled into weeks and time was slipping by on both sides of the ocean. Valeria and Lucio got used to sharing their evening meals together, deepening their friendship. A growing gentleness about Lucio continued to impress Valeria. She greatly admired her friend. Once back in her lonely room at the hotel, lost in her thoughts, she wondered how on earth was she going to resume her life in Niagara with her Boris. She had experienced a better world where a woman can be appreciated for being herself. She loved her children and didn't want to break up her family, but her heart had been awfully unfulfilled with Boris. What she needed was love and affection, but it never manifested in her married life.

It was good for her to be occupied in her work. What she had experienced in her personal life, apart from her children, was nothing to look forward to. Tonight, after returning from dinner with Lucio, she walked into her room, opened the bedroom window and sat staring to collect her thoughts. It was late evening and while looking at the beautifully illuminated sky with the moon shining and the stars glittering in clusters, Valeria felt a strange sense of belonging to the island. She should have been happy; in one more week she would go home. Instead, her heart felt empty, and her soul craved more of the kindness and affection she was presently experiencing. Here she sat alone, searching deep into the core of her being.

She took a deep breath and admitted to herself that true love had never touched her heart. Her mother had suppressed her all her living years, and Boris had done even worse. Now at this mature stage in her life, she realized how empty her life had been; love never existed for her. Was she really looking forward to going home? The tears flowed freely from her river of sadness.

Chapter Thirty Seven

The Celebration

Valeria had lost track of time. She was unaware how long she sat there, assessing her life. She dreaded the bleak future that awaited her in Niagara. Unfortunately, the days were rolling by quicker than she wanted. She was not looking forward to her return. As much as she tried to distract herself from the worrying thoughts, the cloud of worry kept hovering over her head. Of late, it was always a mystery of what to expect of Boris. Now that he was sick, she wondered what the future held for him, and her. There was also a fact to consider; the change of personality she had experienced so far. In her confused thoughts, she badly needed to talk to someone. She recalled the words of her professor from psychology class. *We all need someone to disclose our feelings to, to vent our frustrations. Confide in someone you can trust. It can be therapeutic.* Who could she confide in? Lucio? He was grieving. Enzo? He was too young. Mrs. Jennings? Maybe when she gets home. Nora was her only friend. Rosy was sweet and loving towards her. She could not admit to her daughter that there was no love in her heart for her father, and there never was. She had put up a false display of joy and smiles throughout her life; even since her childhood.

The work here in Sardinia was almost complete. In a few days she would be flying back home. Valeria was at her office straightening up the files on her desk when the Mayor knocked on her door and walked in; Lucio and Enzo were on tow and smiling. They greeted her as usual, then John Minerva announced, "Mrs. Abrosky, since you would be leaving us next week, we have planned a dinner for Saturday night. An evening's celebration featuring our cuisine, music, folkloric dancing and singing. This would be in honour of you and all the work you have accomplished promoting our island."

Lucio and Enzo made sad faces. The Mayor continued, "These two gentlemen will assist you to the end. We hope yours will be the first agency to guide Canadian tourists here, and we look forward to the day you would be accompanying them. We await your return. I am sure you would be able to effectively pass on to others, all that you have learned and discovered on our island."

Valeria fought back her stirred emotions. She was speechless and didn't know what to promise these kind people since the future with her Boris remained yet to be known.

"Thank you, Signor Mayor. You all have also been very outstanding in your respective roles. I had to work hard to measure up to your standard." She smiled pleasantly.

***

Valeria was unaware that back home there was also going to be a celebration this coming Saturday night, and totally orchestrated by the quiet and removed Susan Butler. She had telephoned Mrs. Jennings and invited her to accompany her to the buffet dinner at the famous Niagara Falls Casino. Nora had responded all excitedly, then Susan announced, "Nora, Mr. Abrosky and Rosy would be joining us."

Mrs. Jennings almost choked on her saliva at Susan's announcement. "What! The boor will be going with us? He never even says hello to me. How am I going to spend the evening with that mean old grouch?"

"Oh Nora; you will be fine! I will do the driving. Boris has been speaking quite clearly for three days now. I was so excited about my winnings that I blabbed away and promised to treat him to a celebration at the Casino."

Rosy meanwhile, was jumping with joy while she placed three red stars of victory on her father's page on the fridge.

"Since Boris' accomplishment, I announced to Rosy and her father, with great humour, that we would be celebrating on Saturday evening at six o'clock. So, get ready, Nora!" And Susan closed her phone.

When she arrived at the Abroskys, she walked into the living room in the same uplifted mood, jokingly accosting Boris, lightly tapping him on the shoulder. "Ok Boris, are you ready for celebration night?"

He smiled proudly, confident of himself; his main interest was to regain his health and feel normal. Susan's elated feelings lately had been stimulated mainly by the excitement of her casino experience. The act of kindness and sharing had surprised the Abroskys, but they knew she didn't have many friends and this was nicely disguised by her reserved personality.

Rosy had stressed to Boris the importance of going along and not disappointing her. When she mentioned that Mrs. Jennings from across the street was included in the celebration, Boris immediately protested and gave Rosy an earful. When Susan arrived the next morning, he continued with his rant.

"Mrs. Butler, sorry, but this guy is not going anywhere with that nosy parker across the street; over my dead body would I!"

Susan looked at him crossly and sternly pointed a finger at him, her other hand pressed on his shoulder, and said in a higher tone than him, "Listen here, Mr. Abrosky, had it not been for your so called nosy parker who you so adamantly like to condemn, you would be dead by now; you hear me?"

"Why-is-that-may-I-ask?"

"Listen to yourself! You are starting to stutter again because of your wrong accusations!"

She was not going to put up with his nonsense anymore. Her

friend meant well. She would defend Nora.

"You ask me why is that? I will tell you why! Nora was the one who called me to check on you when she saw you leave your driveway early that morning, erratically driving up the street. You were drunk, Boris! Drunk! I came to check on you and there you were, slammed against your steering wheel, passed out drunk as a skunk! The rest is history! She saved your life! You should be grateful to her! Nora Jennings adores your wife and is her true friend. As she tells me you snub her and you insist on being ungrateful? Shame on you, Boris Abrosky! You need to come down from your ivory tower! It's time you show some respect, love, and kindness to others, especially those who genuinely care!"

Boris listened carefully to the lecture thinking, this next old hag really respects her friend, and her defense is to be admired. He realized she was no push over.

"Good for her!" he had heard Valeria say on the speaker phone one evening while Mrs. Jennings was relating the incident of Susan's husband to her. He got home to find his belongings out on the driveway. She had changed the locks to her house and he wasn't allowed in anymore. At the time Boris had hollered at Valeria to put down the phone on Nora and stay away from gossip. Now having been around Susan for some time, he realized she meant business. Susan had said a few times, "You do wrong, and you deserve to suffer the consequences." At times, he wondered about her; he was glad she was not his wife.

Saturday night arrived and the four of them headed for the Casino. Susan's stern talk had taken effect on Boris. Everyone could not help but notice how polite he was towards Nora. Susan thought a miracle had taken place. Everyone was delighted to be out on a Saturday night, especially after some weeks of challenging work. The tall fountain at the main entrance with its cascading levels of water attracted people to sit around, admire, and take photos. They walked the promenade that was alive with tourists, teens hanging about, and some younger children with their parents. The brightly lit rows of trees added an aura of festivity. People strolling and mingling about made the place lively. They browsed the many lovely shops and restaurants.

They settled on a restaurant inside the casino, and the variety of food they feasted on was enjoyable to all. Susan selected a bottle of Pinot Grigio. Boris was allowed one glass considering his medication. Like a good sport, he went along with the three women like an obedient saint. Rosy and Susan had given him no other choice, and to his surprise he didn't seem to mind. Mrs. Jennings was extremely courteous towards him. She smiled and laughed a lot; her praises towards him were relentless. After dinner, Mrs. Butler pulled out four one hundred-dollar bills from her purse, cheerfully handing one to each of them as she said, "What do you say my friends; should we try our luck now?"

They moved to the casino machines, each searching for the right one to insert their hundred-dollar bill, hoping to win big. Boris and Rosy had never played the machines before so they relied on Susan's expert guidance. After a few tries at the levers, they got the hang of it; they all had fun! Every now a then there were some winnings and also some losses. The one hundred dollars seemed to last quite a while. Susan had lost all of hers, but Mrs. Jennings had won some money, though not much. The idea of winning made her excited. Rosy had made arrangements with Pablo who came to town for a brief stay, so she left after a while to have her own fun. Boris had broken even and had to admit to himself he liked being in the crowd, as he had been a recluse for quite a while. He felt good to be out. Here he was with Nora Jennings, and the boring Susan. He now had to admit, once he got to know them, they were both completely different people to his original impression. The evening soon came to a close, with Boris being dropped off at his home by his speech therapist.

He walked into the house without the cane which gave him a euphoric sensation. He practiced his speech aloud, just to hear himself, and he was greatly impressed with what he heard. He now reclaimed his own bed. Once upstairs in his bedroom, he wanted to look at himself in the full-length mirror to reassure himself there was no limping. He realized he had no pain in his arms. He smiled at his reflection, which soon turned into a huge grin. Boris promised himself, from here onward he was going to reclaim his life to the fullest. *Oh Yes! And my Valeria would be coming home soon!*

The next morning, he walked into the kitchen where his daughter was preparing breakfast. With a sense of confidence and assertiveness, he said, "Rosy, your mother will sure be surprised when she sees me; wouldn't you agree?"

Chapter Thirty Eight

Alghero, Sardinia

While Boris was rejoicing and contemplating his new outlook on life, Valeria was in Alghero, also finding herself, enjoying an enchanting sea of dreams and experiences as never before. She had bought herself a beautiful Ralph Lauren evening dress in one of the boutiques in the hotel lobby. The chiffon print with soft blue flowers, highlighted with sparkling sequins, added an interesting effect in movement. A pair of neutral toned high heel shoes perfectly highlighted the colours of the dress. She carefully applied her makeup, using white and blueish eyeshadow that enhanced her eyes and completed the ensemble. Her shoulder length hair was neatly piled up on her head, perfect for evening wear. With jewelry to match, Valeria was all set and ready to be picked up. She was not one to fuss a lot about herself, but tonight she felt compelled to present herself to these people in the best way she could, especially as she was guest of honour. Lucio was punctual to pick her up at the hotel. Dressed in a smashing tuxedo, when she saw him she thought, *mighty presentable for an elegant affair.* After admiring her friend, she was pleased with herself for paying extra attention to how she presented herself for the event. When Lucio saw her, he couldn't believe his eyes; the transformation of his coworker in the day to one in evening attire was unbelievable. He could not hide his admiration with his unusually big smile.

"Valeria! You look splendid; what a beautiful lady you are! *Complimenti!* I am honoured to escort you tonight!"

"Oh Lucio! Come on; you are being cordial. You look elegant yourself."

"Thank you. Apparently, the Mayor has taken the opportunity to invite many visitors from the mainland; our Germany, Austria, American, and Brazilian friends would be attending."

"Oh! It should be an affair to remember then!" She responded.

They walked into the gorgeous reception room at Hotel Nettuno where the event was taking place. The room was spectacular, the décor and architecture were in Roman style with renaissance walls and ceiling trimmings. The marvellous colours of the island had also been tastefully reproduced. As Lucio mentioned, there were many people; guests invited by the Mayor that Valeria had never met before. She noticed some were dressed in formal uniforms; impressive and not without the air of authority. John Minerva immediately walked over to greet Lucio and his guest. Mesmerized, he proudly took Valeria on his arm, and led her about the room to introduce her to the dignitaries; politicians, judges, and some high-ranking visitors from the mainland of Italy and other European countries. Lucio followed behind, also greeting the guests as he knew some of them. Valeria was immensely impressed.

Shortly after, Enzo bounced in with a lovely young girl whom he introduced as Alita Giordana. With his usual sense of humour, he eyed Valeria up and down, smiling, and nodding with a grin of approval. Then he accosted Lucio and with a smirk nudged him, drawing attention to the chief guest. The waitresses wore the ancient Roman toga style dresses in rich shimmery gold and black; white veils were pinned to one shoulder and flowed behind them. They graciously moved about as they served sizzling champagne in tulip-stemmed glasses, along with the tastiest hors d'oeuvres while the guests harmoniously mingled and chatted. One of the dignitaries, Mr. Charran Mihar, who had been earlier introduced to Valeria by the Mayor, made his way across the large room towards her. He was holding two glasses of champagne. He spoke in broken English.

"Mrs. Abrosky, I offer you a glass of Champagne?"

He was an older man with a full head of silvery hair, wearing a crisp black military uniform with medals pinned across his chest. He must have been a high-ranking government military officer.

"Thank you, but I am fine," she responded with a smile.

"I am told you doing grand promotion for this island? My friend, the Mayor, is optimistic of the idea. My family and myself vacation here many years, many summer. We love it!"

"So do I!" she smiled. "Yes, the promotion is a great project, and we at World Travel would be working diligently to bring it to reality," she responded courteously.

Lucio, who was never too far away from her, whispered in her ear, "He is a General from Austria, holidaying at La Maddalena with his family. I am told by the Mayor he is a great supporter of the arts and culture."

On seeing this fellow who seemed somewhat much older at close range, Lucio seemed puzzled. He jogged his memory as he believed he had encountered the General before, perhaps years ago, if his memory served him right. It was when Chiara was well and they enjoyed a healthy social life. In a peculiar way, each man seemed a bit uncomfortable around the other by the encounter. Then a distinct memory took him back to Chiara's reaction when they had met the man at a charity fundraiser, years back. She was visibly uncomfortable about sitting at the same table with him. He was accompanied by his wife, a pleasant, plump woman, and a bit too inquisitive, as he recalled. The man was not too friendly at the time. After the dinner, Chiara had insisted they call it an early night, and they left early.

For some strange reason tonight, the General's presence made Lucio uneasy; he noticed his piercing eyes darted between himself and Valeria. Lucio felt there seemed to be a discomfort of sort that he couldn't pinpoint. Soon after, he politely excused himself.

To his relief, Lucio turned to his lovely Canadian friend, gently placed a hand at her elbow leading her to their assigned seats. He felt proud to escort her. It was a pleasure to be with Valeria, and she deserved his full attention. Dinner followed with the same measure of elegance as the surroundings, topped off with espresso, liqueur, and an assortment of pastries. While guests were still feasting on their desserts, the Mayor called Valeria to the podium after he had announced a few words of praises for her role in the tourism project. Valeria was not one for speeches, and in a few words, she thanked the Mayor and all present. She expressed how her love and admiration for Sardinia and its people had enriched her life. Everyone in the room listened attentively, and when she was done she received a lusty round of applause.

The music and the local folk dancers took to the floor to everyone's admiration and enjoyment. Then the dance floor was open to the guests. Lucio had a desire to dance but wasn't sure if it would be appropriate for him to ask the Mayor's honoured guest for a dance, although he had worked closely with her. She was a married woman, and he a widower, still in mourning. The melodies touched his heart and his longing was getting the better of him. Naughty Enzo with his impish looks, tried to urge Lucio to get up and move while he danced a smooth cha-cha-cha with his young girlfriend. When he remained seated, Enzo walked over to the table and bent close to speak to him.

"Consigliere, you are being *a real strunzo!* Foolish and stupid." He then gently took Valeria by the hand, and gallantly led her to the dance floor where they danced the sultry tango to the appropriate melody. He was an excellent leader, and Valeria followed beautifully. Every now and then Enzo glanced at Lucio with a wicked grin on his face. When he returned her to the table he said, "Signor Alvani, she is all yours." He bent over closer to his friend's ear, "Don't waste the night away." Lucio smiled and turned to admire Valeria and whispered to her. "You and Enzo danced the tango perfectly, like two admirable Argentinians," while thinking, *she is such a beautiful lady!*

Enzo kept his eyes on his friend while showing off his talent on the dance floor. When he noticed Lucio finally got up from his seat, leading Valeria with an arm around her waist, he hugged his partner and kissed her on the neck saying, "Alleluia", and nodding for her to turn and look at his friends. Then she asked him, "Is that the way people act when they become old?"

Enzo promptly responded, "I don't think so! I'll tell you; this ticker of mine will never get old. My friend's heart is functioning well; he is just a bit inhibited. Those two are desperately attracted to one another, resisting what nature has in store for them. Mark my word, the intensity of their desires will soon cause an explosion." With young blood flowing through his veins, Enzo wished the same happiness for his friend.

It had been a long time since Lucio had held a beautiful lady in his arms. He felt wonderfully energized tonight. Everything felt right, all made possible by his charming colleague. Valeria felt oddly relaxed and enjoyed the dances. The delightful evening at the luxurious hotel Nettuno soon came to an end and was enjoyed by everyone.

Enzo tapped Lucio's back before leaving, saying, "I am proud of you, my friend; you have made me happy. And you too, Valeria." Then he winked at Lucio.

When Lucio dropped Valeria off at her hotel, he wished the evening would not end. He turned to Valeria and with a pleading look on his face asked, "Valeria, if you are up to it, can we sit in the lobby and talk? After such a wonderful evening, I am not looking forward to returning to my lonely apartment."

Valeria hesitated for a moment then smiled. "Sure, why not." Lucio's face lit up and he swiftly handed the car keys to the nearby valet. He placed an arm around Valeria's waist and like two souls seeking refuge in one another, they made their way into the lobby. People were still mingling around. They eyed a quiet corner and settled themselves on a cozy love seat. Here they would extend their evening and fill their lonely hearts with good companionship.

Chapter Thirty Nine

Love Reigns

Lucio held his gaze steadily on his beloved friend. Valeria stared right back at him sensing his reluctance and hesitation to speak. She felt touched that he just sat there unable to express his sincere feelings. Valeria's notion was to encourage him. She gently took his hand in hers and asked with a big smile, "Tell me, consigliere; what is your next plan for this island of yours after I leave?"

He let out a big sigh and with much sadness on his face responded in a low voice, "Valeria, at this moment I can't even think; please don't mention your leaving!"

He then leaned his body closer to hers and with a languid look on his face, forced himself to speak in a serious but low tone, eyes cast downward, not daring to look into hers, "Valeria, forgive me for saying this to you; I must confess that my heart will suffer another blow when you leave next week. I am in denial, but I prefer not to think of it. All I can say to you is that you have re-instilled life in me, motivating me to wake up in the morning, all because you would be waiting for me before I begin work for the day. Working with you has given me great pleasure and I have grown much fond of you. Your beautiful presence has alleviated the pain I suffered from losing my dear wife ; a sadness you will never know. Now I fear another loss. How am I going to face the days without you! Should I anticipate another empty and unbearable world?"

Valeria's emotions began escalating out of control by the moment, from listening to his heartful confession. Her soft sobs

227

suddenly broke her silence. Lucio lifted his head to look at her. He was not aware she was crying. Tears were streaming down her cheeks like a broken river dam. She had never before felt wanted, or loved, by anyone, and here was this kind and noble man expressing how much he loved and needed her. The pain she suppressed deep in her soul was being stirred against her will. The tyranny of Boris, her domineering mother, her ruling father; no one ever spoke to her with love and kindness. Her uncontrollable tears were propelled by her inner turmoil; her body now shook from nervousness and embarrassment. He put an arm around her shoulder to comfort her, pulling her closer to him. He held her quietly, gently caressing her arm until she calmed down. Then with one hand he gently turned her face to his, fighting the desire to hold her tighter. Lucio wished everything around them in the lobby would disappear; he desperately fought to ignore the fact that she was a married woman. His desire was to claim his rights because he truly cared for her, but he was such a respectable man, viewed by all as a gentleman; he would not transgress without permission. It was not easy to rationalize. He was fighting with his reasoning, blocking off his desires. One thing was for sure, there was a magnetic force pulling him closer to Valeria, and to make matters worse, he had not held a beautiful woman in his arms in such a long time.

The chemistry between them was definitely one that had been ignored by both of them, driven by respect, duty, and consequences. Lucio's longing was getting the better of him when he decided to ask, "Valeria, my dearest, I have no right to ask you this and I know it may seem a selfish request. I sense that you are as lonely as I am, and not a happy woman. Please don't go! Remain here with me!"

"Oh, dear! Lucio! How convenient that would be! How simple! I am sure you would appreciate whether I am happy or not, that I am married, and there are obligations I must honour. I have a husband and three grown children, all waiting for me at home. I am definitely committed. My life is more complicated than you are aware. Presently I have a sick husband, plus much more than I wish to get into at this time."

In the meantime, the cozy sensation of their bodies touching and being close to one another was electrifying. They both secretly wished the existing burdens would disappear and then they would float away on a cloud, lost within the great universe.

Lucio, in trying to be realistic, gave her a squeeze and asked, "Ok then, Valeria my darling, we must claim a little time to ourselves. Will you remain a little longer just for us to be together? No work, just our own little holiday; to simply enjoy the beaches and the evening strolls with a free spirit. We owe it to ourselves! What do you say?" He wanted to convince her at all cost. "Valeria, there would be no obligations, no papers to fill, no reports to submit to anyone. I think you deserve it. And I would stay with you at all times. I need you and if I am correct, you need me too. We must grant ourselves this small token of precious time together. For some strange reason I believe fate has put us together. I know you are married and I have no right to make these requests. But I implore you, allow me to show you how much I care, and to bring some happiness into your heart, and mine too."

Valeria knew too well what Lucio was saying was reality. He must have been reading her heart. As much as she had been trying to assert herself, her unhappiness must have been obvious. *Was I wearing my heart on my sleeve all this time?* She hated herself for allowing her raw emotions to surface. She took a tissue from her clutch bag and discretely wiped away her tears.

She lifted her head and turned to face her friend. Looking at him straight into his eyes she said, "Lucio, my dear friend, I wish I could remain here, or disappear somewhere into thin air. The last thing I want to do is to go back to the nightmare I left behind, and which still awaits me upon my return. My soul is tormented and my heart is torn. I apologize if my feelings have been evident. I am sorry to burden you with my personal problems. You are right, I am not happy with my husband. My marriage has been a farce. As you stated, yes, I am a married woman, therefore I must go back to where I belong."

"I understand, and I respect you for it. But give yourself a break! Aren't we all entitled to even a little happiness? I loved my wife dearly, but I must confess, I was drawn to you ever since I first met you. You are such an attractive woman and as I got to know you some more through our work, I saw other qualities that make you exceptional. Why should we judge and deny ourselves what life presents to us?"

They remained there sitting close to one another, talking until late into the night. Lucio hated to leave her! He had nothing to go home to. Valeria was in the same predicament. Her empty deluxe hotel room added to her loneliness.

Lucio simply said, "Valeria, I am prepared to stay here all night, just sitting with you."

For a moment, Enzo came to his mind. If only he could have the nerve like him, he would ask Valeria to invite him to her room to spend the night with her. But he was sixty years old, a widower, and out of practice for quite some time; would he still be able to perform? That was another problem. All he could wish for was that his lovely friend would permit him to enjoy a few precious days together with her; something he had no doubt they would treasure for the rest of their lives.

Smiling with himself, and encouraged, Lucio asked again, "Promise me you will consider staying. I will show you the best time ever. It will be our treasured memory to help us move forward in our separate lives, to wherever destiny takes us."

Valeria didn't desire anything more than to give into Lucio's offer and gratify herself with joy that had not touched her life before. Impulsively she turned around and circled her arms around his neck saying, "Lucio, my dear friend, I would place a call in the morning and talk to my daughter to find out how things are at home. Then I will decide. Yes, it would be nice to have a memorable holiday. You are right, up until tonight, it's been too much work."

Lucio leaned over, pulled her closer to him and sealed their lips with the most passionate kiss, leaving Valeria totally breathless and somewhat shy.

Chapter Forty

The Revelation

It was Sunday afternoon in Niagara. Boris, after a short rest, walked proudly around the grounds of his opulent home. The roar of the river below was soothing to his ears. The Maid of the Mist was floating by, offering the once in a lifetime experience to float close to the Niagara Falls. The sky was clear and the sun was shining. "What a splendid day," he said to himself. Rosy slid open the double doors to the patio, calling to him to answer the phone; her mom was on the line.

"Dad, it's mom! Pass her on to me after you've finished, ok!"

"Hello, Valeria! How are you?"

"Great, Boris, but never mind me; tell me about yourself!"

"Oh, Valeria, what are you doing over there? I was just enjoying a most splendid sunshiny day here at the back of the house. What a site, I tell you!"

"Boris, I will be home soon. How is your health coming along? You speak well! I can hear you and I am so pleased. Rosy doesn't want to tell me much, she said it's a surprise for when I return."

"Oh yes! You are going to find a new Boris, Valeria. When are you coming back?"

She hesitated, "Boris, this is what I wanted to discuss with you. My work has just been completed. Now my colleagues have asked me to stay a short time longer for a holiday; a period of rest. Since I arrived, there has been a rigid schedule to follow. What do you say? I have not been able to enjoy these beaches, nor have I had any time for myself." He went quiet. "Boris! Are you there?"

"Yes, I am here. I was counting on you being back in a day or two. You can have a holiday here right in our backyard. You have no idea what you are missing here at home! Niagara is the best tourist attraction at this time of the year and all year round, as far as I am concerned."

"Boris, I know it is, but there is the rest of the world out here also, waiting to be discovered!"

"Do whatever you want! Come home when you feel like it! I am starting to live it up since my accident. It's been no fun for me cooped up in this house. I am lucky to be alive, Florence tells me. And by the way, your friend Susan gave me an earful about your other friend across the street. Now I was told, I have to be nice to her."

"Boris, I am glad; of course, you need to be nice! It's good for you to go out and socialize; that's what it is all about, my dear!"

"As you say..."

Valeria knew that Boris, with his tunnel vision, had only experienced the automotive industry, his deals, and his personal achievements. He needed to step outside the box, explore the rest of the world and the people around him. He was always quick to condemn and judge wrongfully; he needed to work on that to get along in the real world.

"Boris, I will extend my stay, ok! I want to return home renewed and refreshed. Let me talk to Rosy; I need to get her approval also."

Boris, shaking his head, not too pleased, called out to Rosy for her to take over the phone.

"Hello mom!" Rosy answered cheerfully.

"Rosy, I will not go into lengthy details. As I said to your dad, I was asked to stay a bit longer for a short holiday since it's been tedious work up until now. Should I? How are things with you, and your dad's health?"

"Mom, he is doing fantastic. Don't worry about him. I agree you should take a little holiday. After all Mom, when would you have that opportunity again; all work and no play make no fun!" Rosy was always encouraging; such a good daughter. Valeria felt blessed to still have her around.

The decision was hers to make. Beside appeasing Lucio, and the ecstasy he had created in her, she badly needed a rest. After collecting her thoughts, she dialled Lucio's phone number and on the first ring he was on the line.

"*Pronto!* Hello!"

"Lucio, Valeria here; how are you?"

"Valeria, I am so glad you called. How am I? Holding my breath until you tell me that you will stay."

"Granted, my friend, but only for a short time." Lucio's heart became flooded with euphoria, rendering him speechless for a few seconds.

"Valeria, I have learned in life to accept whatever small token of happiness I can get, and to enjoy it to the fullest."

They each held on to their phones, staring into it as if they could see the other. Then Lucio broke the spell and said, "Valeria, my dearest, since our time is limited let's not waste any of it. I am at your command; what would you like to do today?"

"Lucio, you are the expert on this marvellous place! I will leave it totally up to you, my dear. I like to be surprised and spoiled!"

"Then I will pick you up in an hour!"

They both didn't get much sleep the night before, but adrenalin flowed within their bodies. Valeria felt like a teenager on a first date, and Lucio likewise. The sadness that had often taken over his existence had now totally vanished.

His favourite place was the island of Spargi, *L'Isola Di Spargi,* an uninhabited island preserved and forming The National Archipelago Park, referred to as the famous Maddalena, which is made up of seven major islands: La Maddalena, Caprera, Budelli, Santo Stefano, Santa Maria, Spargi, Razzoli, and other smaller islands surrounded by the beautiful clear and transparent sea. They all presented themselves as unique and spectacular offerings with their magnificent beaches. Lucio's personal choice on Spargi was Cala Rossa Corsara, one of the most magical for him. The crystal clear and calm water was great for snorkelling. The special attraction was at sunset when the granite rocks seem to react and change colours, from pink to orange to red. And this is where Lucio was going to take Valeria, to show her some magic.

Valeria wore a big straw hat, a glowing sun dress, and flat white striped sandals. She felt like a tourist at heart, ready for the journey, and was looking forward to indulge in Lucio's companionship. Lucio arrived, comfortably dressed in bright colours, and carrying a picnic basket.

They proceeded to the seashore towards La Maddalena, boarded a small motorboat and headed over to the unspoiled beauty of Cala Rossa Corsara. In this bit of heaven, they found a secluded corner all to themselves surrounded by the amazingly transparent water. The veil of multicolour blues, the beauty of the rocks, and the linear coast with its bays in white crystalline sandy soil, were all a sight to behold. Valeria in awe, lowered herself onto the beach towel Lucio had spread out for her, totally dazzled by the glitters strewn on the water that lay before their eyes. When Lucio nestled in a spot on her towel, he secretly wished this moment and day would last forever. The sun was high and the warmth it offered was soothing. Then Lucio sat upright, took Valeria by the hand and gently pulled her closer to him. Without inhibitions, she responded by surrendered to his caring touch and felt herself melt into his arms. Even with the slightly building heat, his body against hers felt right, so perfect.

They held each other in silence for the longest time, like two human beings thirsty for human touch and tenderness. Lucio eased his body back, still holding her, to look into her eyes. And he finally and freely let it all out, "Valeria, I must tell you; I don't understand how this all happened! I was a grieving man with a broken heart; so depressed, and in despair, then out of the blue you came! You have grown on me in a manner I cannot explain. Working with you has brought me hope, exploring the islands with you has brought new meaning and appreciation to what I used to enjoy, but had temporarily faded. I could only now hope you feel the same and want me as much as I do you. The nagging fact that you belong to another man brings sadness to my heart, but I am grateful to have these few days together. I embrace it as a special gift. I know what I feel and I would not hide it from you. Just know, I appreciate you too much to pressure you. A future together with you remains a mystery, but I am willing to wait. One of my attributes is patience." He smiled warmly and sincerely.

Valeria felt like crying, she was so moved by his words. Instead she leaned in closer and offered her slightly parted lips. Lucio graciously accepted the offering from the gods and indulged her in the most passionate kissing ever. Frozen in the moment, neither of the two could care about anything else but mutual adoration flowing through their veins. It was as if they were on their first date, on prom night; a first kiss.

His body might have been older, but in his heart, he felt young and alive with desires. Valeria felt the same. At this moment, this man was her sole focus. Boris, Rosy, Susan, or Nora, were furthest from her mind. She felt in her heart, this bestowing of love and splendour, this man, Lucio, this island, were all meant to be. And she was going to embrace it all, to fulfil her needs, and the unmet needs of all the women she knew. She had never before felt this loved. They teased and bantered like young lovers, frisked about on the sand, bathed in the glittering blue water, raced to the rocks; hugging and kissing at every chance.

At one point Lucio said laughingly, "Valeria, if only Enzo could see us now! He has been secretly kidding me about you, you know? I am sure he would be pleased for us. He is so observant. The day you left us unexpectedly, he noticed I was upset and he said, "You have it for your Canadian friend and you wouldn't admit it!"

She listened to him then asked with a naughty hint, "Did you, Lucio?"

"Oh, Valeria! I was so confused then. My wife was deadly ill; my emotions were in shambles. I didn't know what or how to think. All I can tell you is I was devastated, for many reasons. I think it was Enzo that pressed the Mayor to take action to bring you back for me, to please me. Enzo is a true friend."

With both hands outstretched, she said, "Well, Lucio, here I am! My life at home is not a rose garden; there have been one mess after another regarding my personal life. God help me when I go back!"

"Valeria, my main wish is for you to remain with me, or to return to me!"

"Lucio, let's enjoy the moment and be thankful for what we have, and for what this blessed place has gifted us."

"Valeria, should you wish to spend some time with me at my place, I can ask Vittoria the nurse to come and cook for us. She has always been like a mother to me. All she wants is my happiness, and I am sure she will bless us."

Valeria had no desire to go back to his place. She could not bring herself to tell him she couldn't shake the piercing eyes in his wife's portrait, that she felt followed, even spooked by her when she was last there. She had no doubt that Vittoria was indeed a caring soul.

"Lucio, I prefer we spend time in my place, if you don't mind; tonight, or any other night."

At his place, the closed bedroom down the hallway had given her the creeps; she felt maybe Chiara's ghost was hiding somewhere in there, ready to pounce on her at any time. *What are you doing here with my husband?* Maybe even strike her with a lightning bolt.

The days passed beautifully with each new one proving to be more blissful than the other. They treasured each second together. They would have breakfast at the popular joints, lunch and dinner at exotic restaurants, Lavazza and Danesi coffees, unique flavours of her favourite espressos, and evening strolls in the piazzas, blending with the locals and tourists until late hours of the night. Lucio would linger his adoring eyes on hers, waiting for Valeria to invite him to her room at the end of their evenings. With Valeria, his virility returned easily and he had no cause to worry about his performance. Everything was right between them. All he wished for was to love Valeria to the fullest. To his amazement, he realized lately he had no need to visit his doctor. He was sure there would be no complaining.

The clock was ticking and time was going by too quickly. The days and nights were glorious. After a couple of days had passed, as he drove back to the hotel, very confidently and almost like an innocent child, Lucio said to her one night,

"Valeria, if you don't mind, I would not be leaving you tonight. I want to stay with you all night tonight and love you the way you should be loved, and have you wake up to me at your side, and you to mine. Please, don't say no!"

Valeria was getting used to the luxurious life and the pampering that came with it. The relaxed atmosphere in Sardinia was growing on her, living each day one by one, with no pressure, no stress. The traumatic memories of Boris were furthest from her thoughts; they all seemed to belong to another lifetime. The usual dark fog in her mind became easily dissolved. For a while she was no longer dwelling in the country she came from across the ocean. She couldn't bring herself to think that in a few days, this wondrous love and splendour of could easily dissolve once she boarded her flight back.

Valeria affectionately hugged Lucio, and without words she placed one arm around his waist and guided him towards the elevator to her third-floor suite. Once there, she turned to him and painfully disclosed, "Lucio, when I first arrived here, I called and begged my husband to come and share my room. I assured him he would enjoy what the island has to offer. He adamantly refused, denying my needs; I should even add, denying my existence. The more I ponder on it, the more I agree that you are right; for some unknown reason fate has brought us together. Why should we deny ourselves the opportunity to enjoy what was meant to be!"

Valeria and Lucio, desperately longing for the fulfilment they both craved for so long, succumbed to the hunger, thirst, and passion that flowed so easily between them.

Chapter Forty One

The Last Celebration

An elite affair was scheduled to take place at the grand ballroom on the northern part of Alghero not far from the seashore, at the magnificent roman style resort, the Argenteria, on the Baratz Lake. It would be one of its kind in Sardinia. Lucio always received a special invitation from the hosts. He thought this spectacular place would be perfect to take Valeria. They serve fresh white salted fish, usually light and delicious, ravioli stuffed with shrimps, the choice of a specially roasted suckling pig, and a wide array of food; a feast to remember. The entertainment afterwards promises to match no other; the music for dancing would be sensationally romantic to touch anyone's heart. Once he related the details of the evening's plan to Valeria, she simply replied with,

"Lucio, it sounds like the promise of an excellent evening that would be worth remembering. I would enjoy anything you plan," and she kissed him passionately. Valeria was not used to extraordinary pleasures, or anyone going to extra measures for her enjoyment. She was grateful and content with anything as long as the two of them were together; it was all that mattered. *After all,* she thought, *the fairytale must come to an end!*

When they arrived at the Argenteria, one of the hostess, after greeting Lucio courteously, escorted them to a secluded table that allowed them privacy. White orchids were set on the table, surrounded by low glowing scented candles in blueish hues. A silver container sat aside chilling a bottle of Asti Spumante champagne. This would be their last evening of celebration

241

together. Valeria was not used to drinking. When the server popped and offered her the fluted champagne glass, she didn't hesitate; she thought it best to dull her brain cells a bit to continue living the dream. Soon they were totally engrossed with each other in their own world, while partaking in all the delicious food. Then they heard the announcer from the stage call attention to all present.

"Signore, and signori, we are honoured to announce that we have a special visitor among us tonight. The honourable, General Charran Mihar." The General stood up and acknowledged the introduction, then was called to the stage to address the guests. Valeria and Lucio held their breath while looking at each other.

"Oh, is he the General we had met at Hotel Nettuno?" asked Valeria.

"Yes, it's him, with his impressive uniform."

"I wonder who he is with tonight?"

The applause for the General brought them back into focus. He said a few words, thanked the patrons and praised the management of the Argenteria, then returned to his table where another gentleman in uniform sat with him.

Soon after, a dancing troupe appeared and took to the floor with a folkloric item. They wore very colourful costumes, and the music attracted everyone's attention. To their surprise, the server approached their table and spoke to Valeria, "The General Mihar wishes to offer you both a complimentary after-dinner drink."

Lucio looked at Valeria as she said, "No thanks, we are both fine," as she nodded towards the General.

Lucio had made a special request for a secluded table but it seemed there was no such luck as total privacy. They were both surprised to find the General at the same place as them on this particular night. The music began playing and they got up to dance to the fine music coming from the five-piece orchestra. A female singer took to the stage and soon infused the air with a seductive cabaret. Lucio held Valeria close to him as if he was afraid to let her go. Valeria felt safe, loved, and protected in his arms, with his warm body against hers. She closed her eyes and leaned her head against his shoulder, wishing the allure would last forever. The completeness that ensued later that evening left them both basking in sweet sadness.

The next day came only too quickly. Lucio insisted on taking the short flight to Rome with Valeria. He remained with her until she caught the connecting flight directly to Toronto. They wanted to grab at every remaining moment, to preserve the togetherness they shared. Tears were shed, then Lucio watched from the outdoor terrace until Valeria's plane disappeared into the sky taking his beloved away. Much anguish sank deep into his heart. The last two weeks spent together were totally justified, he thought. No regrets.

Valeria made the sign of the cross as her plane levelled off. She promised herself to embrace whatever she encountered on her return home. The love and splendour she had experienced this past while would have to suffice for the rest of her life. She felt thankful that she had been granted the wonderful opportunity, though briefly, to taste true love and happiness. *It is better to have loved and leave behind, than not to have known love at all.* She remembered reading this somewhere before.

***

Boris, on Rosy's insistence, had stopped at the flower shop and bought a dozen yellow roses. They were on their way to the airport in Toronto to receive Valeria.

When Valeria spotted them at arrivals, she stalled for a moment, inquisitively frowning, then wide eyed questioned herself, *is that my Boris holding up flowers for me? It is hard to believe; has the lion turned into a lamb?* Sure enough, Boris was all smiles. He handed her the lovely roses and hugged her passionately.

"Welcome back, Valeria! We missed you, Rosy and I. Did you

have a good flight?" Boris sounded like a nervous teen.

"Boris are these roses for me? How nice of you! Thank you." She kissed him. "Let me look at you. Eh! What a difference since I left. You look wonderful! No limping, no slurring; Florence and Susan have done a great job with you! Oh! Boris, I am so happy for you!" She put her arm around his when she noticed Rosy standing close, holding the cane.

She said, "Mom, we brought this just in case. Dad is too proud to use it. He wanted to impress you that he has no need for it." She was happy to see her parents cheerfully together. In the past, she had witnessed some of the shenanigans her father had put their mother through, including his daughter. Dad still didn't approve of her dating that Latino guy. Poor Pablo, he didn't feel comfortable visiting their home. Now Mom was back, she would go back to Ottawa, to prepare for her studies and make up to Pablo for lost time.

Once home, Valeria resumed her role as wife and mother, thankful that Boris seemed to have recuperated well. His personality seemed clearly changed towards the milder side. With regards to her job, she had confidently delivered all her research material to Mr. Patty. He was more than impressed at the details of her note-taking along with all the photographs, maps, tourist brochures, memorabilia and tokens of Sardinia she handed over. He had to admit, she was better than him! For a job well done he rewarded her with a tidy bonus. He asked her should new excursion opportunities come up, would she consider undertaking new assignments, adding she would be well compensated. Valeria shook her head, and sternly expressed,

"No sir! I have decided that my place is now at home with my husband and my family, where I am more needed!" She took a deep breath and added, "Mr. Patty, as much as I enjoy my job, I must say, Sardinia has given me an experience of love and splendour to last a lifetime. I now must put my family first. Although Boris is doing well, his doctor says he is still vulnerable;

his weak heart needs constant monitoring. For now, I can only work two afternoons a week. Sorry, but that is the best I can offer!"

Mr. Patty didn't like her response, especially at the present peak time. World Travel was into heavy marketing, enticing people through mass media to travel the world, and bookings were pouring in by the numbers. For him, Valeria had now earned the position of top promoter; a valuable employee.

Instead she had resumed her housewife duties, cooking the best meals for her husband, and the children when they came home for Sunday dinners. Rosy would invite Pablo to visit, trying hard to get her father to accept him. Valeria's resolution was to be a better and stronger human being. Since she was now back home, she and Rosy agreed that Florence and Susan were no longer needed as before. Florence would occasionally stop by to check on Boris' medication and to monitor his pulse and blood pressure. Life was peaceful. Boris had regained his ability to drive. Drinking a glass of wine was only allowed with his main meal.

Occasionally Valeria's mind would drift away across the ocean like a furious wind blowing cold air. Her determination was to be in control. She would quickly banish the encroaching thoughts, reducing them to a blur, then to disintegrate. Her indulgence had been only a dream, she thought, therefore it should easily vanish into the fluffy clouds and dissolve itself into another world where it belonged, not on her terrestrial planet.

The days passed and the weeks rolled by. Summer was soon over; it was now fall in Niagara. Nature began another of its magical display, showing off the beautiful orange, burnt red, and golden brown colours of the foliage. The days were getting shorter, and daylight was reduced. The sun was often hiding behind the clouds. Boris' calm was slowly turning into restlessness. He had regained some strength, and with his health improved, he now had the stamina and desire to be more active. Valeria was happy for him, and glad to see him go out more often and interact with other people. Often, she accompanied him on some of his outings. She noticed he was turning moody these days, but she was thankful that he wasn't violent towards her anymore.

Valeria as a good wife and would encourage her husband to go out and socialize. "Boris, by all means, join in on some club activities. Busy yourself; it will do you a world of good."

Several times they had all gone together to shows at the casino theatre. Mrs. Jennings and Susan always seemed to have tickets to offer and would gladly join them and they would all have a good time together. Valeria was glad that finally Boris was not turning up his nose at her neighbour and was civil to Susan; contrary to his past behaviour. Valeria was now working only a few hours a week and she stuck to her decision, though Mr. Patty would often call and plead with her to make herself more available. She obliged at times as she was now freer, with Boris on his adventures.

Every now and then her thoughts would casually drift far away. She couldn't always prevent herself from thinking and wondering about her friend on the other side of the world.

Boris' outings had become regular, sometimes stretched to quite late in the evening. He was always ready to share his experiences, chatting away with people he encountered, either at the local coffee shop or the casino. Mrs. Jennings and Susan would often mention how lucky Boris was at the casino. Valeria wasn't too crazy about the casino, therefore didn't pay much attention, or share in their excitement. Boris had graduated from the slot machines to the tables playing poker, and the rush he was experiencing there was almost as great as the deals he had closed when he worked in the automotive industry.

Valeria was glad to see him cheer up and if he was down at times, she would try her best to uplift his spirits. He had made a few new friends and that alone was a big achievement.
"Valeria, I met this Charlie guy today; he is a business man and retired broker. He filled me in on all about investments; interesting

guy. A real character; you should meet him!" Boris said one night to his wife. Unfortunately, she wasn't tuned in, as her mind was playing tricks with her again, with flashbacks of her forsaken friendship. She was nodding in pretense, but not really listening to what her husband was saying. Today when she went to retrieve the mail, to her surprise, among the bills a letter stood out, stamped from Sardinia and addressed to her. She couldn't wait to open it.

When she quickly glanced at it, the return address was that of Enzo Mangorio. She tore it open; there were three hand written pages.

Dear Valeria,

I hope this letter finds you well. I am sure you have resumed your routine Canadian life by now. I can't help but wonder if you miss or think of us sometimes. We do miss you. You left a big void in our surrounding, including our hearts. We miss your laughter, your guidance, your admiration for our island, but most of all your friendship.

I am sorry to tell you that since you left, our consigliere is not the same person anymore. He has refused to guide or conduct tours with other foreign agents. He spends a lot of time at home moping. It would be nice if you give him a call or write him a note of encouragement. Our Mayor has also intervened by calling his nurse and house maid, Vittoria, to check on him. Hopefully I am not burdening you with this letter. My interest is only due to my caring, and I know with your kindness, you care too. Please forgive me if I am imposing on you now that you have returned to the daily demands of your life.

If only you could be here, I am sure you would be a great asset for all of us, including our Mayor. We also realize that our dear Canadian friend has her own duties on the other side of the ocean, with her own family. We are grateful to you for your time, and your friendship, Valeria. Thanks for having given us the opportunity to work and spend time with you on those glorious days which have enriched our lives too. We will never forget you, and likewise we ask that you don't forget us. I can assure you, for Lucio and myself, we will always hold you in a special place in our hearts.

I wish you well Valeria, with your family, and good luck in any new project.

Enzo Mangorio.

Valeria held the letter in her hands and read it twice; she couldn't help but relive the dream of the love she left behind.

Yes, of course! She too would treasure the memories tucked away in a special place in her heart.

Chapter Forty Two

Buried Secrets

As much as Valeria cared for the friends she had left behind, she thought it better to ignore Enzo's request and have no communication with Lucio. Their intimate love affair was tightly sealed in a secret corner of her heart, never to resurface again. The letter would be placed in her Sardinia note file and treated strictly as part of a past job assignment, now completed.

The front door slammed open and Boris walked in, all smiles. He was holding something behind him, and he excitedly kissed her as he said, "Valeria, sit down at the table."

"Boris don't be silly. I am preparing supper right now; I cannot sit down."

"Sit down, I am telling you. I have a surprise for you!"

Valeria thought she had better go along and see what the surprise was. "Close your eyes," he insisted. Valeria closed her eyes, giggling. She liked her new Boris. "Now you can open them," he said, smiling proudly. Valeria gaped, wide eyed, shocked. What lay before her was a table overflowing with hundred and thousand-dollar bills; something she had never seen before.

"Boris, where did you get all this money. Where did it come from? Have you won the lottery?"

"You could say that! I hit the jackpot! I won big at the casino." He lifted her up and hugged her exuberantly.

Valeria didn't want to spoil his high mood, but didn't know

what to make of it. Boris gathered the bills and placed them in a large bag, setting some aside. "There! Go treat yourself with a massage, manicure, pedicure, whatever women do; and buy yourself some new clothes."

"Boris, I don't need anything, and I don't want to spend money foolishly. You do whatever you want with it." Her mother's voice resonated, *Valeria, he is a good provider; what more do you want!* Here she was, so many years later, married to this "good provider."

I had better be contented.

***

While Valeria was reflecting on her life in Niagara, Lucio in Alghero was unable to face his own reality. Simple tasks had become difficult for him; it seemed as if they would easily shatter his touchy emotional state. Since Valeria had left, his morale dropped low, taking him into gloom and doom. He wasn't showing up at the office; he would remain in all day in his pajamas, not eating, and sadly lacking motivation. He felt his life no longer had stimuli nor direction.

Good old Vittoria was now working double shifts, but making it her business to check on him, morning and night, and on her day off. She tried encouraging him to relocate and change his environment. But he was not in the least interested.

The empty master bedroom's door was kept locked. She was tempted to remove the portraits of Chiara and lock them up somewhere, but how could she without Lucio's permission. Then she remembered the hidden compartment at the bottom of the dresser, and the album she had browsed through. Who were those two children? Was Lucio aware of this hiding place, or even what was there? Vittoria felt compelled to bring it up and address it with Lucio.

Today she had an off day from her regular job so she had spare time. Lucio was in his study, absorbed in a book. She decided to go into the abandoned bedroom, to dust and clean, and also check out the mysterious compartment again. As she kneeled to dig up the album and some other papers, she found that the drawer slid out easily. There were some files under the album. With uneasiness, she began pulling them out one by one; each was filled with documents. She didn't feel comfortable invading another person's privacy like this; her conscience nagged her. *Of course, I am invading, and I feel like a thief, but I need to do this for poor Lucio.* That is when she decided to call out to Lucio; she felt he needed to come join her and check out her discovery. Lucio didn't appreciate being disturbed, but not wanting to appear disrespectful, got up against his will and walked towards the bedroom to see what Vittoria wanted as she rarely disturbed him.

When he glanced at the pile of papers on the floor, he became even more confused. He couldn't understand why she was bothering him. He wasn't too enthusiastic or interested in anything in that room. Vittoria, in her wisdom, stressed to him, "Lucio, there could be something important here. If I were you I would go through these items. It has to be done at some point, so why not now?"

He stood and stared at the papers disgustedly, then spoke, "They are probably Chiara's stuff," mimicking her in a disturbed tone.

"If I were you Vittoria, I would do away with it all; clean it all up! I don't need to go through any of Chiara's old mail."

"Lucio, I don't understand you! An intelligent man like you, a Consigliere, the counsellor at City Hall! You don't see the need to attend to your wife's papers? There could be something of importance here. You should go through them before I discard anything. If not now, maybe another time, but don't just discard them!" She couldn't help but wonder about the two pictures of the children; the thought of them haunted her.

"Not now Vittoria, I cannot handle anything right now that would remind me of my wife or make me relive anything. But if you insist, pile everything in a box and store it somewhere in my study. To be honest, I don't care right now; I have absolutely no interest! Why did the good Lord take away my Chiara? Nothing else matters to me now. This is all garbage!" Lucio could never imagine or suspect where fate would take him if he explored the pile of discarded and seemingly meaningless pile of mail, and the contents that Vittoria had piled into the box.

Vittoria, just as perturbed, was not going to insist on anything further with him. She did as she was told and left it at that. She piled everything in the box, placing the album at the top, and shoved it all in the bottom cupboard. The mystery box was then set aside, unexplored. Only known to Chiara who had left it all behind.

Lucio had given her orders to dispose of the bedroom furniture since he had no intention of personally using it. If he could find the strength to appease his soul, he might gain enough courage to move away from this place. It seemed to him that whenever he found someone that touched his heart, they would eventually be taken away from him.

After Vittoria left, he sat there, feeling alone and desolate. He held his head in both hands like a desperate man. *My Chiara is gone forever, but Valeria is very much alive. Would I ever see her again? What is she doing right now? I wonder if she misses me as much as I miss her! Does she even think of me?* Lucio's heart ached with a feverishness that only his lively Canadian friend could cool.

"Oh Valeria, I miss you more than you could ever imagine!" His emotions took over and an uncontrollable sobbing broke through. Her sweet voice echoed within. *It will be only a memory for us to cherish for the rest of our lives. We belong in two different worlds, Lucio my darling.* Valeria did make it clear to him she had a husband and family awaiting her.

Lucio tried to justify his reasoning. *I have no right to claim anything from her. Only God knows how more miserable my life has become, now that she is gone.*

Chapter Forty Three

Country Invitation

Lucio's days passed leaving him in a fog. He would move about like a robot, mechanically attending to only what was necessary, and even that was difficult to accomplish. He forced himself to get out of bed and get dressed, then to go to the office and attend to the necessary meetings with John Minerva. Everything was done with no zest, and to anyone observing, he seemed to be acting against his will. His spirits were lower than ever. He would return home at the end of a daunting day, drained and powerless.

As evening approached with the sun just dropping off to the west, leaving a pinkish yellow glare in the sky, it would mean another day is coming soon and Lucio would not be ready for it, his world was too cloudy; he couldn't see clearly. One evening he opened the door to his apartment and the phone was ringing, breaking the usual silence that welcomed him each time he entered. His heart leapt. *Maybe, just maybe, it would be Valeria? Wishful thinking! No such luck!*

"*Pronto.* Hello. Lucio speaking."

"Lucio, *sono io,* it's me, your cousin, Attilio. How are you doing my friend? We have been thinking of you lately. Sorry, we have not communicated since the funeral. I must tell you that we called a couple of times and didn't get any answer. Lucio, Assunta and I would like you to come out here to the country and stay few days with us here, if you wish We have some guests at our resort; it would be nice if you could join us and spend some time with our family."

255

Lucio stood speechless for a minute, but a shaft of light seemed to suddenly charge his brain. How nice of his cousin and wife to reach out to him! What a kind gesture, especially now that he felt so lonely and abandoned.

Excitedly he responded, "Attilio, so nice to hear from you. How are you? And Assunta? You are inviting me? To be honest, you couldn't have called at a better time. I must confess, lately I have been as miserable as hell! I am definitely going to take you up on your invitation; it may do me a world of good! Getting away from Alghero might be exactly what the doctor would order!"

"I am glad; we want you to come! It would be like old times, and it's also way overdue, cousin! Don't you think?"

Lucio was smiling now, "Yes, like old times. What a shame we have not spent much time together lately."

"Lucio, we can make up for lost time. Assunta and I would be looking forward to your visit. Come whenever you are ready!"

"Great, I will look into it! As soon as I can arrange with the Mayor, I will be there."

Lucio hung up the phone. Now here was something to look forward to. Attilio had been his favourite cousin since childhood. At one time they visited back and forth when their parents were alive. Then everything came to a halt after he met Chiara and began dating her. Lucio resented them for not being warm and loving towards her, especially after announcing their engagement, and worse yet after they got married. He had to let it go as he truly and sorrowfully missed them over the years. *Anyway,* he thought, *he has called to invite me, I appreciate that, and I know I badly need to be around family right now. As he said, we would make up for the past.* He had no trouble taking time off as fall was approaching and there wasn't much activity with work. His friends who looked on helplessly at his grief, were supportive of the idea of taking a break from routine.

Attilio and Assunta lived in the centre of the island where they occupied an extensive acreage. Black pigs roamed about freely with goats, sheep, dogs, chickens, roosters, pigeons, and many other animals. There was a man-made pond where white doves leisurely glided on the calm, still water among the trees with leaves of different colours that surrounded their property. Their place presented an amazing experience of natural living and eating, apart from the beautiful scenery. No doubt most of the bus tours listed a visit to their farm on their itinerary. The highlight was the home cooked meal that was offered; his cousins were renowned throughout Sardinia. Their charming hospitality never failed to entice the usual European visitors, among other tourists.

His cousin, Attilio, portrayed a kind demeanour, always with a smile on his face. He was a man of medium stature, with broad shoulders, chestnut eyes, thick brows, generally, a neat appearance, and he always greeted his guests respectfully and politely. His wife, Assunta, was an ordinary lady, more like a country girl who adored the land, and her animals. She had a passion for homemade cuisine; the results spoke for themselves. The Natural Park was famous, and elite clienteles were known to fly in from near and far to indulge in the natural experience, inclusive of the amazing food and wine. They also offered few secluded cabins at the edge of the property for special guests, and were backed up by another man-made creation, a cascading waterfall. Some guests preferred to visit for the weekend, to enjoy quiet time away from their city life, with no phones or televisions, basking in the pleasures of unspoiled nature in the country.

John Minerva was sympathetic towards Lucio. The permission to leave was unselfishly granted. On the following Saturday afternoon Lucio arrived at The Natural Park elated to meet his cousins and spend some time with people that had once been dear to him.

Assunta and Attilio embraced him joyfully with open arms. Lucio was careful with his emotions and tried to remain composed. He badly needed to re-bond with these dear people. He was sincerely happy to be in their company. Not much later, nieces and nephews arrived with their children to greet their uncle.

Assunta, with a floral apron tied around her waist, still the usual busy bee, soon invited everyone to the dining room, ordering Attilio to serve drinks saying, "Lucio, you must be starving. Come! Sit down! We are going to feast and celebrate your long overdue visit."

In no time the room was bustling with family chatter coming from the adults, children, and grandchildren. This was music to Lucio's ears and his heart rejoiced. What a different atmosphere it was here compared to his lonely home, he thought. He fit right in with the family and was grateful for their warm and caring company. Assunta was a good woman. Surrounded by her grandchildren she always managed to skillfully please everyone around at the same time. She was also concerned that Lucio should be specially looked after, and that Attilio pay close attention to his cousin's well-being.

"Lucio, you need to have a good rest tonight as you must be tired; your room is ready. Tomorrow you and your cousin would take the jeep and go explore the land; you haven't been here for quite some time! There has been much development over the years."

"Sounds good to me, Assunta. It's great to be here! It means so much to me; I am very grateful for your kindness!"

Attilio and Lucio were up at dawn, awakened by the calling of the roosters and the different sounds from the rest of the animals. After a hearty breakfast, off they went. The tour was an eye opener for Lucio and he was mighty proud of his cousins' achievements; the investment of hard work spoke for itself. It was everywhere to see. There was a huge open area with an outdoor oven and fireplace, and a bar to receive and greet their guests. The added private cabins were simple but comfortable, the lush gardens a sight to behold, not to mention the part the animals played; their all-inclusive resort was breathtaking.

Lucio patted Attilio on the shoulder and said, "Cousin, I must hand it to you; this is a marvellous place, and you and Assunta are two incredible people, a perfect team. You have prospered in wealth and have been blessed with a lovely family."

"Hard work, Lucio! But I must agree, we have been fortunate, with our children close by, except Ugo who decided to emigrate and settle in Brazil, all is well. And I must add, we have always had faithful help from our employees."

"As for me, Attilio, I know we lost touch for some years after I got married. After my Chiara got ill, my world took a downward spiral from dealing with her sickness and caring for her until the end. Now I am a lonely old man with no children, and no siblings. You are my only family, but I felt I had lost you."

"Lucio, I owe you a big apology. Assunta and myself were not cordial towards Chiara, and you suffered the consequences. But I must tell you, we felt badly when we heard of her condition. My heart went out to you, my dear cousin. There wasn't much we could do."

"I understand Attilio. Now my Chiara is dead, may I now ask you something?"

"What is it, Lucio?"

"I always felt that you and Assunta never cared for my Chiara, and I am sorry to say this, I felt you even shunned her, as if she was some sort of bad seed. That is how it came across to me. My beautiful Chiara! I had a hard time dealing with it! Sorry, I am at fault too; we just stayed away from each other."

Attilio opened his mouth to respond but paused; he didn't know if he should speak or just let it drop. But Lucio pressed him, "She is dead now, gone forever. Please explain to me why you and Assunta didn't like her?"

"Lucio, I don't know whether certain morals in life matter to you or not. As you know we are devout Catholics. Assunta and I both abide by the ten commandments. This is very important to us. If you never knew…; I don't want to now break your heart, my cousin." He took a deep breath and looked at Lucio straight in the eyes.

"Were you aware that Chiara was a prostitute before you met her? A highly paid escort?"

Lucio couldn't believe what he was hearing. "A prostitute? My Chiara? You must be mistaken! Since the evening we met, the sun, the moon, the world itself, revolved around the one love in her life, and that was me! I knew this! I believed it! And now you say this, cousin?"

"Lucio, I am sure she was a delightful woman. You must know that since before Assunta met you, she would not condone girls with questionable lifestyles. I never wanted to tell you, but you now insist. May she rest in peace."

A surge of memories suddenly zipped through Lucio's mind. The evening he met Chiara, she was standing alone by a column, sipping a drink. It was a reception affair at the museum for the unveiling of a famous sculpture donated by a European dignitary.

He had been invited along with the media. When he noticed her, she had smiled at him, and he approached. If he remembers correctly, she said her date had stood her up. She had flown in from Rio for the event, and was stood up, now alone. He was single, she was extremely attractive; he started talking to her and thought to himself, *whoever stood this woman up must be out of his mind, but hopefully my gain! What a fool! This elegant young woman would not pass by anyone unnoticed, especially in an elite crowd.*

After befriending her, from that evening onward, his body knew nothing but pure ecstasy, and his existence became magical. He had an irresistible gravitation towards this woman. Lucio fell madly in love and Chiara reciprocated by giving all of herself and more. Her lovemaking was an art form he had never experienced before. In his euphoric experiences, Lucio would often thank God for sending him this amazing woman all the way from Brazil, South America. He believed she had come to him thorough *la via dell'amore,* the path of love.

Chapter Forty Four

Lucio's New Dreams

While Attilio continued with the tour, Lucio's mind was elsewhere recollecting the past with his wife. The clues that never registered, the questions that he never cared to have explained. He had been blindly in love with this beautiful creature and nothing else seemed to matter. He glanced at his cousin. *He is the richest man on this island, not so much for his monetary achievements and possessions, but mostly because of his humble peasant wife, Assunta, his children, and the gift of grandchildren.*

Lucio privately assessed his own contribution to life; not much to be proud about, he thought. He was a lonely soul; no children, no wife, and he recently enjoyed another man's wife. Assunta and Attilio would not be proud of him if they knew of his escapade with Valeria. *What on earth was wrong with me! Why couldn't I be decent like my cousins!* All these thoughts were now racing through his mind. He had not gone to church in years; for this he deserved to feel miserable, he thought.

A flashback hit him. He and Chiara had discussed children and she had absolutely refused to entertain the idea. In fact, she made him promise that there would be no children from their union. *She had loved me so much that she was not willing to share me with anyone, not even our own children; she wanted to keep me all to herself. Was I wrong to believe this?*

Lucio was obsessed with her tantalizing body that he had agreed, saying, "Yes my dear, I can understand you would not want to ruin your beautiful figure with pregnancies."

They were contented with each other and life was great until

263

she got gravely ill, then their world fell apart. Attilio continued driving. He felt badly that he shocked Lucio with his honest reply. He noticed it left him preoccupied much of the day, then he asked,

"Lucio, obviously I have upset you by sharing what I know about Chiara; I thought you had known but ignored it, which some men in your situation would do. Nothing is wrong with that, but as you know, Assunta is a different breed of woman, and I am right behind her, giving total support to her beliefs system."

Lucio hesitated for a moment then asked, "Attilio, how did you find out?"

"How did I find out! We keep records of people that stay in our cabins. We have an excellent supervisor, Bruno Mantese, who has been with us for years; a sharp fellow who always keeps an eye on our guests and our property. Assunta and I don't always get to meet everyone; some choose room service when they come here just for a tumble in the hay, a private getaway. We get them from all over; they fly these girls in from far and must pay them good money. Most of the men are executives, even married with families. The way they cleverly disguise the reservations, we cannot control what happens when they turn up. But our Bruno notes everything.

When you introduced Chiara to us, he immediately recognized her; seeing her around as one of the girls who discretely escorted different men. One time, Bruno confided in me one girl's date, a general, had been detained and could not show up; she was going to be paid just the same, he told me. If Bruno was willing to have sex with her, she would have reduced the fee for him; a double pay for her. He told me he had refused her, as he has respect for his wife and children. I believed him. Then some time later, we see her with you! I had Bruno check her out; she had come from Rio De Janeiro, and you are not going to believe this; her own mother was her pimp and there is suspicion that she died from some type of venereal disease. We asked my son, Ugo to investigate her and this was confirmed; Chiara was known as a highly paid escort. She had a sister and a brother who were not close to either her or their mother. So now you know everything. It pains me to be the one to tell you this disturbing news, really. But if it would help you to rationalize and alleviate your sorrow, then the shock is worth it. Assunta has this great belief that if you associate with Satan and hurt other people, eventually he will win you over. Lucio, we are truly sorry for your grief. We hope through our love and support, you would be able to draw a little peace into your life."

By now Lucio was moved. Attilio stopped the jeep and asked him to walk to the end of the path, towards a wooden cross and a low bench for kneeling. He put his arm around his grieving cousin's shoulder and said, "Lucio, as God is my witness, we want to share our happiness with you. You are my uncle's son; we are blood! We don't want you to be alone anymore. You are now sixty; why not retire and move here? You can occupy one of the cabins. Assunta, God bless her, she cooks food to feed an army every day, so you won't have to worry about meals; our home is open to you, my cousin. You are welcome to stay with my family for how long you wish. I encourage you to consider making the move; enjoy this piece of heaven, maybe until the good Lord calls us."

Lucio knelt in prayer followed by Attilio. A soothing calm infused his body; no resentment, no hatred. He made the sign of the cross then stood up. Attilio followed. Lucio then turned and gave him a warm embrace, whispering, "Attilio my dearest cousin, thank you, thank you so much! I would consider your offer as I cannot continue to live an empty life."

When they got back it was past noon; the aroma from Assunta's kitchen stimulated their taste buds. All smiles and wiping her hands on her apron, she ordered Attilio to get the wine.

"You Lucio, amuse these two little brats," referring to her grandchildren, "while I make our plates. Do you like manicotti, Lucio? I made them this morning with fresh ricotta and spinach. I also have cannoli filled with fresh goat cheese, and figs for dessert. Come, sit down; it's feast time!" Lucio assisted the girl child,

Assuntina, into her high chair while the older, Mimmo sat beside him. Assunta said a prayer before starting the meal. "Buon appetito!" she wished them all.

Lucio had forgotten how wonderful family get-togethers were. He decided he needed to change his life around, for the better. He couldn't continue with how his life had turned out; a drastic change was necessary. After the meal while they were having espresso and sambuca, he lifted his glass and said, "Assunta, Attilio, I wish to thank you! I am most grateful we have reconnected. You know you are the only family I have. I will go back to Alghero, take care of a few things, resign from my duties at the City Hall, then work towards moving here as Attilio has so graciously offered. You have offered me hope. Thank you both immensely!" They all lifted their glasses and Assunta said, "Let's drink to that!" The children cheered on along not really understanding what was happening. It made Lucio happy to see everyone around him pleased about his presence.

The time spent at his cousins was delightful. Lucio returned home determined to put his old life behind him. As he entered his apartment, Chiara's portrait welcomed him face to face at the entrance of the hallway. He put down his suitcase and immediately walked to the once special portrait and carefully took it down, next were the rest of her pictures that hung in every room. He vowed to himself, the past or any reminder of it was going to be buried then and there. From now on he was going to adapt himself to a simple and uncomplicated life, just like what he had experienced in the countryside over the last few days. After he removed the portraits, they all stood on the floor facing the wall. He walked into his study and found there was mail placed on his desk by Vittoria. He turned to sit when his eyes fell on the box on the shelf, the same box with Chiara's personal stuff. Vittoria felt it imperative for him to check it out before discarding. Lucio took a second glance and thought, *tomorrow will be another day.* Once he was done with that stuff it was going to be part of his past, behind him, sealed off forever.

That was his thought then. Little did he know, fate always plans differently for us.

Chapter Forty Five

Niagara River

Proud of his winnings, Boris announced to Valeria that he was planning to install an enclosed escalator leading from their backyard to the gorge below. Since she liked hiking to the spot, he felt this would make it easier and safer for her. He was also going to shop for a German Shepherd as an addition to the family. He was glad that Valeria was now also semi-retired. He discussed it all with his wife and she had happily agreed. Valeria was much pleased with Boris since her return from Sardinia. At times she would think of the special friend she left behind, and her heart would ache. She would then take a deep breath, brush the thoughts aside, then refocus.

She walked across to Mrs. Jennings, smiling, to have a girlish chit-chat. Nora Jennings was always hospitable and glad to receive company. When Valeria arrived at her door and rang the bell, the door opened promptly; her neighbour had been peeping from behind her curtains, watching as she approached.

"Valeria, how nice to see you! Please come in!"

"I can't stay long. We are waiting for some tradesmen to arrive and start work in our backyard; you know Boris has ordered an escalator to get down to the river, and he said he would also buy a dog, especially for me. I thought to come over and inform you before the trucks arrive and all the commotion begins."

"Oh my! It's all good news! Boris is ambitious to do these things; he must be feeling well. After all his winnings, I must say he is putting his money to good use! I am glad for you, dear."

"I must admit, Nora, since I returned from my trip, he's been pretty good to me and I think he has finally adjusted to his retirement. Before I went to Europe, God help me, I was losing my mind with him! I dreaded coming back! His stroke, the rehabilitation and the process, had me overwhelmed! But you girls have been a blessing to me and my family. I guess my mom was right; deep down my husband is a good man."

"I am happy for you, Valeria, for the way things have turned around. I must confess, many times I looked on helplessly to see him storming and bullying you out of the house. I didn't like him myself, and I felt for you. Now he is civil to me too! I actually enjoy talking to him. I have come to know there is a kind side to him, after all."

"Thank you; I think so too. I must go now; I will be in touch. We will have tea soon, ok?" She gave her a hug and scooted out the door. Brushing her hair back as if to clear her thoughts, she thought how foolish she was to have almost thrown away her twenty-five-year marriage. The attraction to Lucio, and her giving herself away to him was something she had to live with for the rest of her life. She had never dreamed of being unfaithful to her husband; unfaithfulness didn't sit well with her. But it was all appropriate and irresistible at the time mainly due to her emptiness, she rationalized. She was relieved she found the strength to pull away and return home. Her wish was the need to put a lid on her liaison, and let it remain forever behind her. She vowed to herself if thoughts of Lucio surfaced in her mind, she would work to quickly discard them. With the residual guilt on her conscience, Valeria began to work towards being the kindest wife to Boris, and the best mother to her children, hoping to justify her worth.

Six months later the backyard work had all been completed. Boris came home with a beautiful German Shepherd with black fur at the head and ears, a gleaming white torso, and a shiny black tail. He was an added piece of art to the home. Husband and wife were both excited about having the new family member. Like two children with a new toy, they busied themselves making plans for Chico. They had him checked by the veterinarian, taken him to obedience school, checked out the latest products for healthy pet food, toys, and whatever else that would make Chico happy. Valeria would call her daughter often to update her on the goings on with the pet. Rosy was happy that her parents had found a new and mutual interest, and the renovations at the house were all done. At least the complaining had stopped. She could now focus on her relationship with her boyfriend in Ottawa and not feel pressured to run home every weekend there was a crisis. With school work and other life demands, they too had full lives.

Boris got into the habit of getting dressed early in the morning, either having breakfast at home or out at a coffee shop. He had met some people at the casino with whom he would often exchange greetings, and lately meet for coffee. Charlie Golden had become one of the regulars to chum around with. He was a smart Jewish fellow who now owned a chain of wholesale food supply stores, and always bragged about how good business was and how much profit his company raked in. Boris didn't mind listening to the bragging because this is where he got the opportunity to also boast about his big automotive deals of the past and the money he made for his company. They soon became two peas in a pod. After the cardiac arrest he suffered, Boris came to realize his ego was not as important as it had been before; the near-death experience had changed him. Also, the time spent struggling with rehabilitation was another wake-up call for him. He was happy now to have his cup of coffee, go to the casino, chat with the people around him, then go home for supper where his doting wife would be waiting with Chico.

At times on Valeria's suggestion, he was more than happy to pick up Nora Jennings and Susan Butler, and all three women would accompany him to dinner at the popular buffet, followed by fun at the casino. The girls played the slot machines but Boris had now graduated to the poker table. Some nights he would win, others he would lose.

"Big deal," he would say to his friends and the girls, when comparing their losses and winnings, "a few dollars blown here and there is not going to hurt us at our age, so why worry!"

The next night he would go by himself to find Charlie who was usually playing at one of the tables. He would jokingly slap him over the shoulder and say, "Eh! Charlie! What the heck! Let me have a round also!" Lately it had become a habit of meeting Charlie on afternoons, and they had become pretty good friends. Charlie seemed to be popular around the casino and he knew many important people. The week before, he had proudly introduced his new friend, Boris, to a couple of his buddies, Tommaso Ancone and Vincy Dardo.

"These are high rollers, good players!" Charlie whispered wide-eyed. "They have VIP cards and enjoy all the perks the casino has to offer. They can also share their privileges with deserving friends; I am sure they would invite us sometime once they feel we show real interest in joining them."

Boris didn't want to sound like a misfit, "Eh, I am open for fun and games! Why not!"

"I will tell you," he said shaking his head, "it's fun to watch them play. The money they place as bets is nothing like what you and I would! Compared to them, we are small potatoes, my friend! That Tommaso guy plays nothing but baccarat; there's big money there!"

Boris did observe the two gamblers had an air about themselves; a slick look. Both wore combed wool sports jackets, over distinctive trimmed shirts, and short trimmed haircuts. Tommaso was tall with broad shoulders and heavy set, with severe black eyes looking out over a large hooked nose. He spoke with a strange mixed accent that Boris couldn't figure out.

"What nationality is he?" He asked Charley one day.

"What do you think? Italian from the south!"

Vincy, the younger one, standing beside the giant Tommaso, looked frail with a medium stature. But when he spoke his voice was deep and his speech eloquent. Charlie said, "Those two big-shots fly everywhere to play: Atlantic city, Vegas, Australia, Europe, you name it! They are professional gamblers!"

"You don't say!" Boris didn't really care for them, especially the older fellow. "I don't know about you, Charley, that big guy Tommaso strikes me as ruthless."

"With some people, money goes to their heads; they think it can buy them everything, even power. They don't realize that in the end we all end up in the same place. You know Boris, you and I are sensible down-to-earth people; this is why we get along, buddy!" He jokingly slapped Boris on his shoulder.

"I will say," nodded Boris in agreement.

"I guess I will see you tomorrow then?"

The friends went their merry way. Boris arrived home, took the dog for a walk, even stopping to chat with some of the people in his neighbourhood. He was mighty proud when they would comment on his well-groomed dog. Valeria was still going to the travel agency two days a week, as arranged with Mr. Patty. He had informed her they had six full bus excursions for Sardinia in the spring and summer.

"Thanks to your diligent work, Valeria," he said to her when he called her into his office. "Would you be interested in guiding one of them?"

"No sir, I am done with Sardinia or any other work excursions! I will be more than happy only to do bookings for you, Mr. Patty."

She walked out of the office to her car, turned the ignition and drove home. When she pressed the button on the remote to her iron gates, there was Boris with the dog in the driveway, waiting for her. She sat in the car for a minute watching the new dog play tricks with her husband; her eyes darting across and appreciating the spread of her lovely home. She got out of the car. The dog ran and greeted her, pawing all over the front of her business suit. Boris approached smiling.

The sky was blue, the sparse clouds were dissipating; only serenity existed around them. The front door was open. Valeria's mansion stood as inviting as ever. Boris soon calmed the dog, placed an arm around her neck and led her indoors. Everything felt perfect.

Meanwhile, Valeria recited a silent prayer. *Why was Mr. Patty tempting her like a demon in disguise?*

Chapter Forty Six

Secret Life

At the City Hall that Monday morning, John Minerva was pacing his office, asking Lucio to reconsider his retirement, "John, don't make my decision more difficult than it is." Lucio was pleading. "I need to get away. I consider myself fortunate that Attilio and his wife want me as part of their family. Yes, my work is good here, my mind is distracted by the day's demands, but when I go home to the emptiness, it's heartbreaking for me and slowly threatening my sanity."

"Well Lucio, if that is what you want, what can I say! I accept your resignation. You would be sadly missed by all of us, and the community at large."

Lucio placed a hand on his friend's shoulder, "Sorry John, I will also miss all of you, but I need to do what would serve me best. Thank you for always being a faithful friend."

Back at his place another important task was waiting for him which he dreaded. Melancholically he walked into his study and his eyes fell on the box Vittoria had insisted he checks out. Reluctantly he removed the box from the shelf, set it down on the desk, took a deep breath and patiently began going through the contents. He was not comfortable examining his wife's personal things; it did not feel right.

The album was the first. He started to turn the pages and saw pictures of people that were not known to him. Then a little boy's picture caught his attention. He flipped it and saw something like a scripture quote, written in a foreign language: *Lembranca,* remembrance. That is Portuguese, he muttered to himself; Chiara's first language. He continued to turn the pages. He did not know the people he saw; nothing made sense. Then as he turned to the last page; there well centered was another picture of a baby girl wearing a pink bonnet and wrapped in a pink blanket, another scribble was underneath: *uma lembranca*, a remembrance. He recognized the hand writing as his wife's. He closed the album and shoved it aside. Puzzled, he asked himself, *why had Chiara never shown these pictures to me? What do they mean?* His curiosity deepened and he became motivated to keep on searching. In an unsealed envelope, he found receipts for money drafts drawn from the post office; the payees not known to him. By now he had goosebumps and a strange chill zipped through his body.

"What in heaven's name was my wife involved in, and unknown to me?" He asked himself. Exploring further he found a blue notebook with a white pocket holder. He hesitated. It felt creepy going through this stuff. *Either I abandon this ordeal now, throw everything in the trash chute down the hall, or grin and bear it and keep going to get over with it!* Feeling as if his heart was in his throat, he retrieved two folded papers from the notebook pocket. The first one was a birth certificate of one Rodrigo Fernandez, born July 20, 1978. *Whoever is he?* The other was of one Maria Fernandez, May 11,1981. He folded and replaced them just where they sat all these years. Who was going to answer his questions? His wife was dead; his mother in law was also deceased. Chiara's two siblings were estranged. There were still many papers to go through. He felt he had enough for the night. He got up and left the room. *I will continue in the morning if I feel like it. Maybe Vittoria might come by; she had been close to my wife, just maybe she would be able to help clear up some things.* His thoughts went to Attilio and Assunta and why they decided to keep away, how they had kept their knowledge about Chiara to themselves, not wanting to hurt him.

"My beautiful Chiara; an escort for the elite Don Juans?" He shook his head in disbelief. *Did Vittoria know more and never told?* Had he been so trusting about his wife's past because of being madly in love with her? He had shared everything about himself with her but never asked anything about her past; it was not important to him. Whatever she shared he accepted.

When her sickness took over, his heart became scarred; that was all he focused on, for years. Now, questions darted through his mind without answers. Did he really want to know what the masquerade was all about? What is it that Chiara kept secret all these years? How could she have lived with it?

After a restless night, bright sunshine filled his room and woke him up the next morning; he had slept in.

He rushed out of bed as he was anxious to get out of the apartment; lately he was experiencing bouts of claustrophobia. He couldn't wait to get away from everything that was now turning into a nightmare, with his every breath. To think the same place had once brought him utmost joy.

He dialled Vittoria's number and asked her to meet him for lunch. Vittoria sensed the urgency and said, "Lucio it has to be tonight. I cannot leave my new patient, and you know I hardly take time off for lunch."

"Yes, Vittoria, forgive me. I should have known better; you are dutifully dedicated to your work. See you at six then?"

"That would be fine. I will meet you at the cafeteria, Ortonza. We can grab a bite there." Vittoria felt he needed her, and as tired as she would be at the end of a day's work, she couldn't refuse Lucio.

"Good, Vittoria! Thank you; see you tonight then!" She sensed his anxiety. *Is this about Chiara's box of goodies?*

Lucio walked around in a daze for the entire day. He strolled along the beach wishing the fresh breeze and the mist from the sea could brush away his gloom. He also missed Enzo for his sense of humour; he was now assigned to another job. Valeria would occasionally surface his mind; he couldn't help wondering if she ever thought of him. He longed to see her; he missed everything about her. What a mess his life had turned out to be. He couldn't wait to meet Vittoria who was motherly to him, and who always managed to bring him comfort.

He arrived early at the Ortonza and waited for her. In the meantime, his thoughts remained focused on the images of the two mysterious children. *Who are they really?* She arrived, and he cheerfully greeted her.

"Lucio, you look malnourished!" she exclaimed at first glance. "Are you looking after yourself these days? I worry about you!"

"Vittoria, my dear; life can be so unfair!"

"Now Lucio, I don't want to hear that from you! You are a clever man; be thankful for your blessings!"

"Yes, Vittoria, I want to be, but it's extremely difficult. One thing keeps following another. Right now, all I need is to understand the mysteries of Chiara's life that have been totally unknown to me."

She reached out a hand and gently caressed his arm. "Lucio, Chiara has suffered enough; she is now part of the other world where there is no more pain. Let it be . . . please?"

"Vittoria, I admire your faithfulness. Why did she keep secrets from me? What do you know? Please tell me! The stuff from her box has been haunting me."

"Lucio, please don't do this to yourself; I beg you."

"Vittoria! Aren't you the one that insisted I look into the pile of papers in the box? Can you tell me something that could shed light on my confusion?"

"All I know is that she had a mail box at the post office; I always wondered why, but would never ask. I am an employee and I know my boundaries. When she couldn't drive anymore she would ask me to drive her there. As she got sicker, I assisted her only when she asked. I didn't pry and she never disclosed much. I often found her crying, especially after she would check the mail."

"Did you know my wife was a high-profile escort before we met?"

"Not quite. A couple of times she met a gentleman at the post office; he wore a military uniform. They would exchange something that I couldn't make out or see. As her health worsened and she couldn't go out anymore, nothing followed; as far as I know."

"Great! More mystery! Do you think maybe she was being blackmailed?"

"No! I don't believe so. She used to be happy coming from the post office. She would get back in the car pleased and smiling, especially the times she met the gentleman."

"There are pictures of two children; a girl and a boy. Who are they? There are also birth certificates, from Rio. Now that I think about it, their last name is Fernandez; that was Chiara's mother's maiden name. Were they her mother's children; whose were they, Vittoria?"

"I also saw them, but she never mentioned children to me. Lucio, I am sorry that I insisted you look at the contents. It had to be done. But if it's upsetting you this

much, then don't bother anymore! Chiara is dead; let that stuff be dead also!"

"Easier said than done, Vittoria! It's like opening up a Pandora's box. Now I have turned into a curious old woman."

"Well Lucio, I'll leave it up to you; I cannot help you any further."

"This military fellow that you saw her meet; could you please describe him for me?" Lucio was jogging his memory, searching for clues, but at that moment could not put his finger on any.

Chapter Forty Seven

The New Horizon

Lucio didn't relent on his decision to get to the countryside as soon as possible. He needed to get away badly, and it offered a promise of total peace and relaxation. He was now spending his days in an atmosphere where nature allured him with its many wonders. The amazing animals that grazed peacefully all day, and the border collies that herded them at dusk and guided them to their stalls was a sight to behold. He admired how naturally everything evolved, and how happily people worked. *What a difference from city life!* He thought in disbelief. Later he would join Attilio and Assunta for a sumptuous meal.

Bus tours arrived every day with interesting people from many different countries. Some of their languages were understandable, some foreign. When tourists came to lunch, as they often did, Lucio would volunteer to help with the chores required to entertain them. He enjoyed laying picnic tables with trays of different cheese snacks, filling baskets with homemade crusty breads baked in brick ovens, and bottles of genuine wines. Everything was organic and locally made. At times, he would engage in conversation with the visitors that spoke the language he knew. Each day brought newness; an interesting experience for a city boy. Visitors always expressed praises for the gracious hospitality they received, and the peaceful ambiance the site offered. As promised, Attilio and Assunta had assigned him one of the cabins further down the property close to the lake. The tastefully finished quarters included a kitchenette, dining area, a double door leading into a decent size bedroom with an in-suite. It was well furnished. A love seat, a television he hardly used, and a glass coffee table were added to make his living quarters comfortable. A large window facing the lake added spaciousness. The array of trees contributed to the peaceful ambiance of the lakeside setting. In contrast to his past lonely evenings in the city, Lucio found himself pleasantly tired at the end of the day and began looking forward to night time where he enjoyed undisturbed sleep in his new domain.

The box sitting in his closet kept haunting him; he did not have the heart to leave it behind for the trash. Since he arrived here it remained idle night after night as if waiting for him to continue exploring. He genuinely had no time for it. Every night he found himself way too tired. His body couldn't wait, and he would succumb to the comfort of his bed when his sandy eyes would shut everything out. At dawn Attilio would be at his door, having been awakened by the natural alarm of roosters waking everyone to see the morning sun, and they always appeared to be competing at that hour. For Lucio, it was a pleasure to accompany him each day at the immense countryside for the different tasks. The fresh air, the sun, the scent of the pine trees, all had a healthy effect on him.

I am thoroughly done in at the end of the day. Chiara had not entered his mind lately.

To his surprise, every now and then, Valeria reigned in his thoughts. *She would have loved this place.* He would indulge his memory in replaying their love making over the two wonderful weeks they had allowed themselves. The promise of lasting memories. A forbidden togetherness.

***

While Lucio was getting used to his new life and embracing the healing aspect of country life, Valeria's life was also taking a new turn, full of more surprises than she could ever imagine. Boris had become a different man; he was going out a lot which suited Valeria. He also travelled here and there with his newly found buddies. Charley had become his best friend, and they would meet daily.

"Charley, where to today?" She would hear him on the phone. At times he would return home happy with winnings from poker games, and other times a bit gloomy, but optimistic and cheerful, looking forward to the next day. Valeria had developed the habit of walking her dog, which gave her a chance to meet and chat with some of the neighbours, including Susan and Mrs. Jennings.

"Valeria, we saw Boris at the casino last night playing at the tables. A bunch of fellows were with him; their good luck girls on their arms were not to me missed. Is he winning or losing these days?" Susan had asked.

"Valeria, if I were you, I would accompany him some nights. It's not good, I must admit; I don't like the

look of those girls or those characters he hangs out with," suggested Mrs. Jennings one time.

Mrs. Jennings was really an old fox, as Boris used to refer to her. Valeria was contented, and she knew her husband was definitely not a womanizer but, if he had become one, it could be her ticket to freedom.

Often on weekends, she would go to Ottawa to visit Rosy and spent some time with her and her boyfriend, Pablo. "Rosy, you should come home more often now. Your father has changed; he doesn't judge and look down on people anymore, as he used to."

"Mom, Pablo does not feel comfortable around dad. You know how rude he had been to him. It would take some time to convince him. Eventually he will come around. Mom, he is such a good soul, and he treats me special. I love him for what he is," said Rosy.

"I understand, dear. I must admit he seems a fine young man."

"Ok, Mom, if not for Thanksgiving, maybe Christmas. I'll invite him to visit with me."

"Christmas? That would be nice, but what about his family; won't they resent it?"

"No, Mom, they won't. I cannot promise you anything more right now; give me some time to work on my Pablo." She then quickly changed the subject.

Valeria wanted to know more, but Rosy was always evasive when she enquired about her relationship with the young man. No wonder Boris had been harsh the first time she had brought him home. His questioning, his authoritativeness, his air of superiority manifesting without reservation, scared the young man off. When Valeria intervened, she would get a double barrel response from him. "Eh! Who provides for all of you here? Who is this Pablo that my daughter brings home; he needs to be checked out, and if you ask me, have his brain examined too."

"Boris, stop it! You discourage and alienate Rosy. She needs to bring her friends home, so we get to meet them. Let go of your dictatorship." Valeria didn't blame the poor guy for not wanting to step foot in their home again. Since Boris recuperated from his stroke, Rosy wasn't coming home as much anymore due to her father's prior attitude towards Pablo. She did phone daily; she was a good daughter. Therefore, Valeria's trips to Ottawa became necessary. She also enjoyed visiting the boys. No one could deny she was a good mother. It was important for her to see her children. She was comfortable with her status, but when she searched deep in her heart, the love for her strange husband was not to be found.

A rude awakening was to come. Taken up with her own world she was oblivious of what was taking place around her. Her mother's words continuously resonated in her ears. *You have been well provided for. You must thank your lucky stars.* Although a smart girl, when it came to their financial affairs, Valeria just rode along and enjoyed the benefits. She was removed from the hassle of paying bills. Boris showed off and ordered their banker to provide his wife with a prestige debit card, and three other preferred charge cards; all she had to do was charge anything she wanted. They enjoyed private banking which included special service without asking; everything was arranged for her. Besides, Boris had always told her they were well off financially and set for life. Although they had joint accounts, she never looked at a bank statement, or anything in that department. The mail would be placed on Boris' desk, for him to attend to all such affairs. She shopped for anything she needed without blinking an eye, often denying the fact that her marriage was less than satisfactory.

Her responsibilities were to keep a nice home, love her children, be as good a companion as she can be to Boris, especially now that he was less aggressive. She cooked fantastic meals for her family. Of late, Boris was not coming home in time for supper; she didn't complain. It gave her space, and she had her dog. Now two years later Boris had found a new high to his existence. The two characters Charley had introduced him to, had slowly worked themselves closer to him. Tommaso Ancone and Vincy Dardo were always seen playing at their Baccarat table.

They boasted and bragged about their millions, their possessions, and their winnings. The women hanging around them wore short, short skirts, their boobs practically popped out of their cleavages, and they rubbed against the men like doting playgirls.

"Charley, these guys annoy me! They think they are better and smarter than you and I. I should give them a run for their life," Boris said one day.

"Boris, ignore them; that guy Tommaso has lots to throw away. We are small potatoes compared to him; I am not here to blow my entire fortune."

"Charley, what's the matter with you? They look down at us, even that Vincy guy that hides in Tommaso's shadow," Boris remarked mockingly with a twang of a Russian accent.

"Who cares! Let's get out of here; we are done for tonight," said Charley as he pulled his friend away. Charley was Jewish sensible with his spending.

Reluctantly, Boris walked away, not before he noticed Vincy nudge Tommaso and winked at them with a smirk. Boris' bowels boiled. How he hated those two! *They have no idea the deals I pulled through during my heydays as CEO! Who do they think they are to look down at me!* He was going to show them and pull them down, along with their two dumb blondes always hanging on to them. Charley had told him they had wives at home, a couple of homely women only suited for the kitchen. These two leaches were regulars with them because of their tipping; only after their wallets. Boris' ego had resurfaced stronger than ever. Charley was a sincere friend, now he was worried about him since he became obsessed to match them.

"Charley, I am going to play Baccarat and show them a thing or two. You will see!"

"Boris my friend, you will do no such thing!"

By now Boris had become hopeless gambler; his betting was out of control, going from high to low, and vice versa, like a stubborn child on a Ferris wheel that would not get off.

Charley's pleadings fell on deaf ears. When he tried harder to save his friend, stubborn Boris would snarl at him like a vicious animal. Tommaso and Vincy would cheer him on, and the women gently rubbed his back. He was addicted to betting but could not see it. When his financial advisor called to enquire about certain unusual movements with the accounts, he was mean and defensive to him.

"Mind your own business, you don't know how much I am worth! So, lay off! I have a pile of money that you can't even begin to imagine!"

When his liquid funds dropped low and the banker blocked his accounts, Boris went crazy and started to borrow money. Tommaso offered him money for a couple of rounds. He won and gave him back the money, then he continued, and sure enough he couldn't wait for the next day to arrive. Now Tommaso had him where he wanted. He had influenced Boris to play for higher and higher stakes. Whenever Boris won he patted him strongly on the shoulder boosting his sense of importance, just like what he felt when he worked his job.

Time passed, and Boris became deeply addicted to the casino, the baccarat tables, and the girls. When his funds depleted for the night, like a sick man he borrowed from anyone that would lend him. With the two honchos boasting, he only wanted to play tables paying big money, but he was also losing big money. When despair set in, Charley had abandoned him after failing many times to prevent his friend from drowning, with his new hobby. Tommaso became his new best friend and Boris Abrosky turned into a desperate monster.

Chapter Forty Eight

Boris in Action

Boris would come home with a dark look on his face at times. Valeria would stare at him puzzled. Often, she would question, "Boris, where have you been; you don't look too happy! Your friend Charley called for you; I thought you were with him."

"Valeria, I don't have to account to you or Charley for my every footstep or my whereabouts. I go wherever I very well please. I thought Charley had guts; he is nothing but a sissy. Tommaso Ancone has balls; he is not afraid of playing and losing big money. That Jewish fool counts the pennies too much. I rather stick with real men, like Tommaso. He has that Vincy guy wrapped around his finger, and he is the watchdog protecting him, and also me."

Valeria knew not to argue with him. She learned a long time ago to let him roll with his own definition of reasoning. *Boris always knows what Boris wants!* But she could not help wonder as time passed that Boris was spending more and more time out of the house. She heard him mumble something about the savings account drying up, but she was not sure what she heard and didn't want to receive another insult; she let it go. She was confident her home was mortgage free. *Let him be!* In the meantime, Boris thought he still had access to quick loans, a convenience to his persistent gambling, always hoping to recover past losses.

He continued to patronize all the casinos in the area, making trips to Toronto, Montreal, and Vegas, encouraged by his new friends Tommaso and Vincy, who, unknown to Boris, were as sneaky as bird catchers. Valeria was beginning to get worried. She was making a small purchase at the local pharmacy when her credit card was rejected; she thought it must be a glitch. Then the next day her debit card was declined.

"Boris, what on earth is going on? Are you slowly blowing our security away? I am unable to buy things, and it is causing me embarrassment! Are you a full-fledged gambler now, Boris? Please tell me what's happening; you need to talk to me! I hope you are not throwing away everything from your years of hard work, and us in the process, Boris!"

"Hush! Hush, Valeria! I always have things under control! Have you forgotten that?" I did not tell you anything because I always conquer. In a few days it will all be fine!"

"Boris, I am scared!"

"Trust me! Tommaso will give me a loan and I will win everything back! You just wait and see!"

"Boris, you are frightening me! Who is this Tommaso person? You have gone stupid on me and I don't like it one bit!"

"Valeria, watch your mouth; don't push me, woman!" He looked at her angrily, as if ready to slap her about. There was no doubt in her mind; the old Boris was back!

Valeria had never made it her business to go to the bank but she decided now was the time. She called for an appointment as she needed quick answers. When she sat down in the financial manager's office, she almost fainted after he provided the requested information. Their finances were in a shocking state, almost beyond repair, to her understanding.

"Mrs. Abrosky, you had ten million dollars in your joint account, secured in GICs, bonds, and low risk investments. I am afraid to have to tell you that your husband, Mr. Abrosky, has been slowly and frequently cashing in on some of these funds. Our records on file show he was called regularly when we noticed the sudden withdrawal pattern in the accounts, as we are obligated to with long standing customers. This sudden depletion made us suspect fraud. But when we questioned him, his reaction was abusive and defensive, and he admitted responsibility. He rebelled vehemently. We could do nothing more; after all, it's his money!"

"Oh! My God! I feel faint. May I please have some water!" She gasped for breath. She felt she was choking. The young manager quickly brought a glass of water then stooped next to her chair to make sure she was well. Valeria's thought her legs wouldn't hold her weight. The poor manager had never experienced something like this before. He asked Valeria if he should call 911. She sipped the water, took some deep breaths and assured him she would be fine.

By the time she got home, Boris was nowhere to be found, and he would not answer his mobile. She desperately needed to speak with him. *Was this all a horrible nightmare?*

When she saw the headlights of his car flash across the living room where she sat in anguish all day, she immediately rushed out the front door. Hysterically and through her sobbing, she began blurting out everything she discovered, asking questions, talking to herself, confused, almost ranting like a mad woman. She thought she heard a different voice speaking through her. Boris just stood there, unfazed, scornfully eyeing her and as if she needed a slap to finish her rant.

Then as cool as a cucumber, in his most sarcastic tone, he responded, "You, Valeria, never made it your business to take care of our finances. You never wrote a cheque in your life, you never paid a household bill. You are one ignorant woman! Because you are so ignorant, you don't even know how much our house is worth. For your information, woman, it is safe, and in the clear! Did you know that! Our property is worth a fortune; I can remortgage it or sell it if I want, and we would still have a pile of money at our disposal. Why this reaction from you? Don't forget, I worked hard for my money!"

"Your money, Boris? Oh, how low can you get! And I thought you had changed for the better. I wanted to believe in you! You have hurt me so much!" She sobbed uncontrollably.

"Get a hold of yourself, Valeria! All will be well again. Why all this drama! Haven't I always provided for my family?"

"You have, but right now that provider has gone crazy, consumed by gambler's greed!"

"Since our kids are on their own, we can now easily downsize. Have you ever thought of that?" She stood listening to his reasoning; she was beyond stunned.

"Boris, you have gone crazy on us. I might not be a mathematician but I got news for you. I love my home and I have no intention of downsizing at this time. Why would I want to remortgage my house to get money? We should have enough cash at this stage in our lives! It is all gone, Boris! All gone! You have gambled away all our comfort money!" At this point she was screaming at him, from the top of her lungs.

Valeria immediately decided she had enough! Hit by an inner force, she advanced towards him in disgust. "I need to get away from here, and especially from you, Boris! I am taking the train tomorrow to go stay with Rosy for a while. You sort out our financial affairs. When I return, things better be in order. I plan to have weddings here for my children, and celebrate baptisms, communions, and confirmations with our grandchildren. Your so called, ignorant wife has also lived and sacrificed much for her family. For your own good, you had better make sure my wishes come to fruition, or I warn you, I will never come back!" She marched into the house with her head held up high, both arms up in surrender, and slammed the front door in his face.

Boris sat at the kitchen table staring into space. He heard his wife shuffling about the house. She had rushed upstairs to her bedroom, picked up some toiletries, a nightgown, some other items, and went directly to the guest room.

He remained pensive. Tomorrow he would humble himself and call his old Jewish friend, Charley and ask for a loan. *All I need is one good win, secure it back into our account, and never walk into that casino again. Valeria is right! I have hurt her and my family.* This was his good intention. He let out a deep sigh. Boris knew he was in deep trouble but would never admit it to his family.

He wearily dragged himself upstairs to find his bed empty; his wife was not in it. He swore under his breath. "Darn woman! Acting up as if I don't have enough to contend with! I feel so tired; if I suffer another stroke I won't care." He resigned himself to get to bed alone.

Valeria awoke bright and early the next morning, and standing by her resolution, packed and left for Ottawa. A note was left for Boris on the kitchen table. She had underlined her requests to get their finances back in order; only then would she return. Boris was desolate. He picked up the note. He spoke to himself, "Yes, I need to do something. The bills are in arrears, our current account is in the red, our savings are all gone, investments cashed in and blown away by my gambling. What have I done? Oh…, what have I done!"

He slumped himself into a chair, leaned forward on his elbows, cradling his head in both hands. A loud drawn out wail, like an injured wolf, was heard coming from the house. When Boris came to, he didn't know for how long he sat there; he felt drained. His eyes were bloodshot. A knock on the front door startled him. The dog began barking loudly while racing up and down from Boris' chair to the door. Through the side glass strip, he saw a person in uniform. As he opened the door, an identification badge was shown to him; he noticed a gas company truck parked in his driveway.

"Good morning, Sir, I am from the gas company. I must advise you, after all bills, notices, and calls have gone unanswered, based on company policy I must now disconnect your gas."

"What! Is this a joke or something? You cannot do that!"

"Sorry, Sir, I am only following instructions. Here is the order, it is a legal document." He showed it to Boris.

"Look, do you know who I am? I am Boris Abrosky, former CEO of the largest automotive company in the region!"

"Sir, that means nothing to me; I have an order. The office sends out warnings and reminders to customers in arrears; apparently they were all ignored in this case."

"My payments are done automatically by the bank; you are mistaken. Here is my card; I am in private banking."

"So much for private banking! Mr. Abrosky, Sir, this is the last resort. I am sure my office knows what they are doing."

Boris' blood pressure went sky high, his vision blurred, and he felt sick to his stomach. "Wait a minute; please call your office to get a hold on the order. I will get some money right away and pay off the arrears." Now, Boris was begging. The fellow listened then called his office, talked to his supervisor, and after much negotiation, a day extension was granted. Boris made a huge sigh of relief, and as soon as the young man left, he didn't stop making calls, trying to see who would lend him money to immediately pay his bills. He dialled Charley's number; his message service said he was out of town. *God, who else! Old lady Jennings? That was a ridiculous thought! Susan is a divorcee; not much money there.* He was thinking hard, desperately pacing the house. He went out to check his car; the gas tank was half full. He would go directly to the casino; by now Tommaso and Vincy would be there. *They must help me!*

And sure enough, he found them at their regular table! "Eh! Buddy, you are early. You caught our fever! What will you be betting today?" Tommaso mocked.

"Tommaso, you have to help me! I need some cash immediately! My wife is out of town and I cannot get any of my money; it's all tied up. Can you please give me some cash?"

"Eh! We are friends, no? How much you need? All you have to do is ask; Vincy here handles my money. Cut him a cheque, Vincy. Boris, what do you prefer, cash or cheque?"

"Oh! Thanks, Tommaso pal! I appreciate it! Cash will do!" Boris' desperation could not hide.

"How much?"

"A couple hundred thousand should do!" Boris was trembling.

He turned to his assistant, winked at him while he opened his attaché case. Then in large heaps, the money was instantly handed to Boris. Happy as a lark, he said, "Guys, thank you! I will be back soon. I need to get to the bank quickly to deposit this money."

Elated, and like a renewed big shot, he walked into the bank and asked to see Mathew, his personal banker. "Here is two hundred thousand dollars; I told you that you didn't know how much I am worth! Here is the deposit, and you make sure your assistant remits the outstanding payments for our utilities, unlocks our accounts, and reinstates all our credit cards!"

"Mr. Abrosky, we appreciate your business, but I have to inform you that you no longer qualify for private banking."

"Why not?"

"Mr. Abrosky, a balance of one million dollars must be maintained. I am afraid you no longer fall in that category. Please proceed to the teller's counter."

Boris felt like bashing him in, he became enraged and embarrassed, but managed to control himself. "Do you have any idea how much my property is worth, young man?"

"Mr. Abrosky, your millions are not presently cash investments with our bank. Your financial status has changed. We are guided by our computer reports and they are correct; we have audited them!"

"Never mind, never mind." He pointed a finger at him and threatened, "You better make sure those utility payments are taken care of." With that, he walked out of the bank, proud of himself. *I am going to show all those fools who they were dealing with.* He had kept back five thousand dollars, then proceeded to rejoin his new friends, Tommaso and Vincy back at the casino.

Chapter Forty Nine

New Discoveries

Valeria's morale had reached the lowest of low. She had never before felt so distraught. Reluctantly, she poured her concerns to Rosy. As much as she hated to burden her daughter, she needed to talk confidentially with someone she trusted. She was ashamed to face her close friend and neighbour, Nora. She did not realize the time had suddenly come to make a decision regarding her marriage and her life. She was disheartened, at her wits end.

She sat Rosy down and with a serious look in her eyes started. "Rosy, it has not been easy living with your father's changing moods and behaviour. You children were my greatest concern while you were growing up. I didn't want a broken home for you and the boys. We lived within good means but I ignored my heart as it bled at times. But now at this stage in our lives, our security is being greatly threatened by your father's crazy behaviour, his gambling. Rosy, I told him I might not return unless our affairs are back in order."

Poor Rosy, with a sad look on her face, listened attentively to her mother. The details her mother shared left her spellbound. They had always lived a country club lifestyle; how could this be happening to her parents? At that point she could not share with her mother that her landlord informed her the rent cheques had bounced, and from now on he would only accept cash. She got herself a part-time job and Pablo had bailed her out with his meagre savings.

"Mom, I am sure Dad will work something out; he is a wise man!" She responded with a faint smile, unconvinced.

"Rosy, it's not a matter of being smart! He is addicted! He is a very sick man! He won't listen to me; he is too self-opinionated. When I pressure him, he reacts with violence. Hopefully by leaving him alone might make him come to his senses. Our savings are gone, Rosy!" Valeria said this with a trembling voice and she could not control her tears.

"Mom, you can stay here with me as long as you wish. You need to cool your head. School will soon be out and I plan to get a full-time job. Don't worry, we will manage somehow."

"Oh, dear Rosy, I never imagined your father would reduce his family to a situation like this."

Meanwhile, Boris continued to keep close company with his new friends, borrowing large sums more frequently to cover personal expenses and feed his growing gambling habit that was not being satisfied. He was now running a tab for over seven million dollars with the money lenders. Vincy was keeping careful records of every transaction. Recently Tommaso had instructed him to make sure a lean was registered against the Abrosky residence. Boris was becoming sicker by the hour with his new disease. He was insanely driven to win back all the moncy he was continually borrowing and losing.

He ran into Charley at the coffee shop. "Eh! Charley, you have abandoned me; I don't see you at the casino anymore."

"Boris, my friend, once you started with the big rollers, I could no longer keep up with you. I belong to a smaller league; I work hard for my money." Charley responded with a blank look and waved his friend goodbye. Watching his old friend exit, Boris thought sadly, *I will have to do something, and soon. I must put my house up for sale, pay off Tommaso, and live on the remainder, and my pension.* Valeria came to his mind.

He was going to call Valeria tonight and beg her to come home; he could not make it alone. Everything would soon be back in order. He missed having his wife around. He decided to stop by a realtor. He remembers one that had a good reputation. The Abrosky name was well known and one of the agents gladly offered to come over and work on an estimate before placing the house on the market. While the realtor prepared some papers, and after full checks came back, Boris was informed there was a lien on the property. After informing Boris, the realtor was puzzled by his reaction. In fact, he seemed totally oblivious of the matter.

"A lien! A lien? Who has put a lien on my property? Who *could* do that?"

"It is for you to find out, Mr. Abrosky. Unfortunately, my office is not at liberty to pursue the matter further."

After a sleepless night and pacing every inch of the floor space, Boris called his lawyer to inform him about the realtor's discovery. Either he was too scared to face the truth or in denial. When the lawyer called back to inform him that one Tommaso Ancone was the lien holder, Boris almost fainted. He grabbed a chair, sat and stared into space for a good while. Then suddenly he caught himself. *Those crooks have baited me!*

"Sons of a bitch!" He shouted. "Tommaso and Vincy, those sons of a gun, they set me up! They bragged and flaunted their cash. They shoved it in my face and had me eating out of their hands, and when the time was right they put a lien on my property? Oh, what a fool I've been!"

He was going to call Tommaso and give him a piece of his mind and order him to remove the lien. He dialled the number; he knew Tommaso answered and passed the phone to Vincy.

"Boris! How are you? Of course! We would be happy to remove the lien! No problem there; just give back my money!"

Boris' tone dropped, "Vincy, this is why I want to place the property for sale, to repay you."

"No problem, once we have the money the lien would be removed."

"I am not denying you the money; but the lien makes the sale difficult. You know that, Vincy!"

"Boris, what other security could you offer against your loan? I did the research; you have nothing!" Boris felt he was stabbed in his gut by that statement.

"What security? You guys were anxious to give me your money!"

"Yes, we were, but as a loan bearing interest, Boris. Are you pretending to be naive? What is the matter with you? No one gives away money for free!"

Boris slammed the phone down; he brought his hands up to squeeze his head. Jogging his memory, he could barely recall details of one evening the three of them were drinking at the casino bar, and he signed some papers that Vincy thrusted under his nose. He was desperate for more cash when that was done. With a foggy brain he remembered scribbling his signature as instructed. Actually, he was given a copy that night; maybe he shoved it in his filing cabinet and forgot about it.

His whole body trembled. Boris was scared. His stroke did not scare him this badly. *How am I going to repay those goons? Jesus! Tommaso did rub me the wrong way when I first laid eyes on him. How did I get sucked in? How could I?* With this awareness fully kicked in, he wished he could drop dead. His troubles were snowballing by the minute. One good thing was that he had no more money left to continue with his gambling addiction; the casino was now beyond his boundaries.

Tommaso and Vincy missed having him around. Tommaso said to his associate, "Eh! Pal, we cannot be fools here, you better check on our buddy, Boris, and see what his intentions are. He needs to repay our money at twenty-four percent interest; the total loan increases with each day. We cannot let it ride much longer."

"I will pay him a visit and see what he has to say. He hasn't been showing his face around here anymore."

"What does that tell you? He is totally broke, and he cannot borrow from us any longer! Vincy, he is yours; handle it right, *capisci*, you understand?"

"I understand, boss. We need to get our money back!"

Boris, in the meantime had become a recluse in his own house. He moped about. He was terribly disturbed. Occasionally he would take the dog for a walk, and when people wanted to pet or talk to Chico, he was curt, preferring to be in his own world of despair. Mrs. Jennings noticed his disturbed mood, Susan invited him for coffee, but he wasn't interested. They thought maybe he had a relapse as his head now hung low as he walked. To add to his mood, when he called Valeria last night, she bluntly refused to talk to him. Rosy gave him the message: "Mom said she will return when the finances are back in order." He thought, *God help me! I might end up thrown out of this house sometime soon if something doesn't give. She tells me when the finances are in order. How am I going to get it in order with all this entanglement?*

He arrived home one day after a walk to find a car in his driveway. Once he got closer he spotted Vincy stepping out.

"Good morning, Boris! How have you been? You have not been coming to the casino anymore, so I thought I should pay you a visit."

"Good morning, Vincy. How can I come to the casino? I have no money to gamble."

"That is exactly what we figured, Boris. Tommaso wants his money back! When do you plan on repaying?"

"Vincy, how can I repay you! You have blocked my property from being sold! I have no money!"

"Boris, that is your problem. You asked for loans and you were granted the loans. It's time to pay back. If I were you, I wouldn't fool around with Tommaso."

"Eh! Vincy, say what you like. I have no cash; what can I do!"

"Don't ask me what to do; find the money and pay back! I will be kind to you. You have a couple of days, and you better have the money for Tommaso; for your sake, my friend. I am just here to warn you." He got in his car, slammed the door, and drove away.

Boris didn't feel like going into the house. He felt the sky was crushing down on him. Now that his wife wasn't here by his side, the place felt haunted and looked a wreck; his housekeeping left much to be desired. The place had become a pig sty. He walked around the house towards the back and walked straight to the ridge of the property. He stood there for a while staring into blankness, thinking of the words Vincy had just said to him; the threats he faced. Boris was now emotionally vulnerable. He took the escalator down to the river.

The tranquility down there felt like a world away. He knew the trails along the river well; he had walked them many times in the past. At certain spots where white caps were seen, the river roared violently. The loud sound sidetracked him. He stood there staring, thinking, *would it be considered cruel if I jump into that water and put an end to all my troubles?*

When he seemed not to be moving, Chico the dog sensed something was wrong and started barking aggressively, tugging at Boris' pants, startling him to get moving. Boris then turned around and looked up at the grandeur of his house, the beauty, the perfection in artistry. *How many would desire what my family owned! It is still a masterpiece!*

The rude awakening for him was how much longer he would be allowed to live in it. His bad debts had grown quickly and continued to mount with every passing day. His tunnel was dark, and he could see no light ahead. It was a discouraging picture for a man like Boris Abrosky

Chapter Fifty

The Countryside

At the old resort in Sardinia, Lucio was adjusting well to his new life. The daytime was splendid with pristine air rejuvenating him. But at night, once he entered his cabin and stepped into the living room, there he would see the box on his bookshelf, almost staring at him. It seemed to contain a magnet that would automatically pull his eyes towards it. He had sealed the flaps with tape to keep it shut. Tonight, an invisible force seemed to direct him towards it with no hesitation. His feet shuffled under a tired and aching body, exhausted from his new daily routine. He could no longer ignore the pending scut work. During the day his mind would occasionally float towards memories of Chiara. A mystery voice buzzed in his ears.

"You must look at those records; it is your duty." Lucio thought, *am I going crazy, or is it Chiara's ghost after me?* "Look into those papers." The cloud of darkness would again obscure his brain, disturbing his peace.

"Ok," he said as he grabbed a letter opener and tugged at the tape. "Let's get it over with it!" He placed the open box on the small coffee table in front of the TV. He flopped onto the love seat and began the dreaded chore. His hands started to shake as he pulled the first paper from a tattered cream coloured envelope, *this must have been handled many times over. By who?* He asked himself. *Who else, other than Chiara?* Wide eyed he stared while reading a death certificate. From the hospital, Casa de Saulde Grande Rio, Rio de Janeiro, Brazil: Maria Fernandez, expired from natural causes at 2: 30 p.m., March 30, 1986. Certified by: Dr.

Emanuel Campos.

Lucio's hands shook; she was only five years old. He picked up the album to again examine the pictures; it must be this little girl that died. "How sad," he murmured. She had sparkling big eyes; her features were like Chiara's. He placed it aside and continued to go through some bank draft receipts; payees he never heard of. Some were sent to Chiara's mother. She had mentioned to him in the past that occasionally she would send money to her mother. He liked Chiara for sharing and caring about her mother, therefore he never objected. More digging. A name popped up that he recognized: General Charran Mihar. A shiver ran up and down his spine. "Dear Lord were does he come in?" A letter of few lines:

Chiara my dear lady,

I am in receipt of the DNA test results, as you must have also. It attests to my negative paternity of your young son. I wish you success in tracing the biological father. I have enjoyed your company in the past and I would be honoured if you could still consider accompanying me occasionally on my foreign engagements. I disclosed to you originally that I am a married man; our discreet relationship holds no ties or promises. Of course, I would reimburse you as usual for your services.

Regards,

Charran Mihar.

Lucio felt sick to his stomach. *The young boy is Chiara's son and I suspect, so was the little girl. She died, but where is the boy? Who is looking after him? Wait a minute, how old would he now be? Did she ever find out who fathered him?* His head felt light; he couldn't think anymore. It was enough shock for one night. He placed his findings back in their place. He would now try to digest the whole situation; why Valeria never revealed her past or fully confided in him. He was totally infatuated by her; her past probably wouldn't have mattered. A pang of sorrow pinched at his heart. *She must have suffered a lot, alone with those secrets. In looking back, at times she did seem preoccupied.* Sometimes he noticed her eyes red from crying and when he would question her, she always brushed it off and distracted him with her kisses and love making, and bliss would soon overcome them.

Valeria surfaced his mind. *Does she think of me? I wish I could see her. I miss her smile, her touch, her company. God, is it my destiny to get involved with women that belong to other men?* He shook himself to reality and the bleak night continued for him, tossing and turning, sleepless in bed.

The next day he was quiet around Attilio. Lucio had a lot on his mind. The young boy's image kept flashing in his vision. *How old was he now? Where was he? Rodrigo was born in 1978, it was now 2001. For Chiara's soul to rest in peace, should he look for him? Maybe he should contact the General. He may be able to shed some light on the entire matter.* The next evening at supper, his taciturnity persisted. Assunta and Attilio eyed one another. Assunta nudged her husband under the table; a signal to speak up.

"Lucio, is anything wrong?" asked Attilio. Assunta followed up, "Yes Lucio, you seem distant, as if in a world of your own. Are you not feeling well?"

Lucio hesitated; he wasn't sure if his discovery would shock them. They had kept away from Chiara in the past, for their own peace. *Can you imagine Assunta finding out there were children involved?*

"No, nothing is wrong; I am fine. I was contemplating taking a short trip to La Maddalena; there is someone there I have not seen for a while and it is time I paid him a visit."

"You sound serious; is he not well?" asked Assunta.

He loved Assunta like a sister, but sometimes she was too nosy. Patiently he replied, "I am sure he is fine. Since it has been a while, it's time I checked in on him." He swallowed hard and thought, *Charran Mihar was no friend of mine. He could never be!*

A Don Juan, cheating on his wife; selecting beautiful women like my Chiara for hire.

At the same time Valeria entered his mind. She was also married, he thought. That made him a perpetrator. No! He was a widower. The chemistry between them was irresistible, and she was starving for love. He lifted his head and spoke, "Attilio, if you can spare it, I would like to go away for few days. While on the coast, I plan to look in on my friends, the Mayor, Enzo, and old mother-hen, Vittoria."

Attilio placed a hand on his shoulder, "Lucio, my dear cousin, since when do you have to ask permission? I can manage here. I encourage you to go ahead and do what is important to you."

"Thanks Attilio, I will leave mid-week."

On Wednesday morning, Lucio left the countryside with many unanswered questions on his mind. He headed for the marvellous coast of La Maddalena where the General's splendid palazzo was located, and which was also a tourist attraction. Good cheerful Enzo had arranged the meeting. By afternoon, Lucio was on his *traghetto*, a small boat, and then a short walk to the front of the building. Lucio was well known from the City Hall; his visit would be honoured. There he was standing on a high cliff overlooking the bay, knocking on the door of one of his wife's former lover.

Chapter Fifty One

The Meeting

A well-dressed maid wearing a grey and white uniform greeted him. *"Buon pomeriggio,* good afternoon. I am Lucio Alvani. I am here for a meeting with General Charran Mihar?"

"Come in please." She led him to a waiting room.

"Si accomodi, make yourself comfortable," she nodded. A few minutes later, Mr. Mihar entered wearing his impressive uniform; a tall fellow with good features, looking impressive as ever. He was definitely a distinguished gentleman with his Austrian accent. They had met briefly before but never engaged in conversation. They shook hands and the General was cordial.

"Can I offer you a drink; an aperitif or espresso?" He gestured for him to sit on the plush leather sofa. He took a seat facing Lucio while he spoke.

"Consigliere, welcome to my home. What brings you here may I ask?"

"I think we have something in common, Mr. Mihar; a woman called Chiara?" Lucio spoke as he concentrated to maintain his composure.

"I see. Chiara Fernandez! A very lovely woman from South America. But that was years ago, when I needed an escort. I have not seen her for many years."

"I was told she got married. I have never looked for her nor have I seen her since."

"In case you didn't know, she became my wife. She got ill, was bed-ridden for many years, then she died not too long ago."

"I am so sorry, Consigliere." The general seemed sincerely touched.

"What brings me here Mr. Mihar could be seem as the skeletons in my wife's closet. I am unsure, but I believe she had two children. I found a letter from you in her collection. I also found bank draft receipts for payments from you. One letter mentions a DNA test. I gather she must have been searching for the biological father of her son. Can you please tell me what you know about Chiara's past? I need to know, General. Did she confide in you? What do you know about the identity of her children? From my findings, the little girl is dead, but there is a young boy. Do you know anything about him? I found a picture of him; I think it is him. He could have been about seven years old. His name is Rodrigo Fernandez. This was all kept a secret from me. Now I am left tormented by these findings. If you know anything, or can help me, I would appreciate it. After all, you and Chiara were friends." Lucio blurted out everything in one huge breath. He leaned back on his seat, emotionally exhausted but trying to hide it.

Charran Mihar got up from his seat and paced, holding his chin as if in recollection. "Mr. Alvani, your wife had a very sad past. Did you know her mother was her pimp? I respected her, and yes, you are right, she did confide in me. I liked and loved her for what she was. Poor girl, from the age of fourteen she was forced into prostitution. They needed the money to survive. Her father was an alcoholic, and they had been abandoned in the slums of Rio De Janiero, homeless. I will not go into more details. I cared for her; she was my companion and friend. I had to attend functions and conventions; my wife often didn't wish to travel. She also had other clients.

"Yes, she became pregnant twice, and her mother took over and looked after the children, I was told. I will be honest with you: Chiara's company was highly requested by many including myself, when I travelled. She loved her children immensely. Then, when her mother died, they ended up with babysitters that were not so reliable; again, so I was told. The little girl contracted pneumonia and died. As for the little boy, I am not aware of what happened to him. Later in life, as I didn't require her service, I lost touch with her. When I gave her money, it was because I felt sorry for her."

Lucio got up and thanked the General. After talking to him, he didn't resent the man as much as he had before their meeting. He looked older, his hair totally grey, but there was kindness in his eyes. He was sure he meant what he said about Chiara, that he had wanted to help her.

Lucio extended his arm for a hand shake, "Thank you for your time, General Mihar. Should anything resurface in your memory, I would appreciate if you could somehow let me know. It would help me gain closure. I think is my duty to now find the boy, or young man by now. I owe it to my wife."

Lucio went on his way. His assumptions had been confirmed. It was painful to hear another man speak of his relationship with Chiara. The truth always hurts. He appreciated the General's sincerity. He vowed to move forward and try and find Rodrigo Fernandez.

Chapter Fifty Two

Revelation

Once back in his cabin at the countryside, the urgency to dig further into the secret box tormented Lucio. He felt he needed to deeper explore Chiara's past. *How mysterious had Chiara's secret life been! How could she have abandoned her children? I only knew the sweet side of her.* He made a firm decision to find the young man at all cost. Rodrigo Fernandez had now become his one main goal. The papers in the box offered no new clues. *Where do I start?*

In the following days Lucio experienced many conflicting thoughts. Should he let it all go? Would that give him closure? Should he appease the love of his life and find her child? Then an idea popped up to banish any doubts he held. The caretaker of the cabins. Chiara had offered him her services, maybe he knew something, or she may have confided some little thing in him. He needed to talk to Attilio privately first. Then he thought, revealing the information on the two children would be embarrassing, so he abandoned the idea. He was being consumed by all the indecisions. As a result, his days were spent experiencing more confusing than ever.

Yes, my cousin and the caretaker could shed some light on my search.

A week had gone by since Lucio's return to his cousin's country resort. Attilio noticed his distracted mood; he was not focusing on the tasks at hand. Some of the animals had been left out of the barn at night, risking the danger of being killed by wild animals roaming. He didn't want to reprimand him, after all he was helping from his own kindness. For Lucio, sleepless nights had resumed, and he knew he looked like a basket case.

The sooner I could confront and gather more real information, the better for me.

When Attilio pulled up that morning, Lucio sheepishly called out to him, "Cousin, why don't you come in, I wish to show you something! I need to talk to you before I lose my mind. I desperately need your advice."

"Lucio, you are the *consigliere*, the council for the city of Alghero, and you seek my advice? I am honoured!" He said with a smile as he got out of his truck.

"I have noticed you moping about since your return. Don't tell me you wish to move back to the city?"

"No, not at all, Attilio; I love it here, but I am in a serious predicament and desperately need your input."

Attilio gently placed a hand on his shoulder, "Cousin, I am at your service for whatever bothers you, once I can help." Lucio also put an arm on his cousin's shoulder and led him up the few steps to the cabin. Lucio took a deep breath and headed to where the box sat. The first thing he pulled out was the picture of the boy. Slowly and meticulously, he recounted his findings, fighting back his emotions.

"You see Attilio, I have been blind. Chiara's past included two innocent souls. Here is the death certificate for the little girl. I am sorry for her. But the boy; I feel compelled to find him. I figured he is probably a young man by now. I need your support in this." Lucio felt a huge sense of relief by sharing his discovery with his cousin. He figured with Attilio's support he would be brave to face his future.

***

As Lucio planned his moves in Sardinia, Valeria in Ottawa was battling with her own feelings. Should she return to the chaos in Niagara that Boris had created? Rosy knew more and feared for the outcome but kept it light for her mother. Valeria didn't realize how bad their situation really was since she had chosen to remove herself from the chaos. Boris had lamented sorrowfully to his daughter the night before when he called, but careful not to disclose the worst of the news. He couldn't speak about his fear of one day not being able to use his own key to enter their home. His banker had tried communicating with the bank's head office to temporarily relax Boris' late payments and penalties.

He realized how much money he had borrowed against his home to feed his out of control gambling addiction and the disease grew out of hand in the race to regain the losses. When he had turned to Charley to borrow money, his friend's response was stern. *No, Boris! I refuse to see you bury yourself deeper into that hole you are digging. I tried to pull you out, but you wouldn't listen.*

Later, when Boris kept calling his one friend, he would no longer pick up the phone. Now Boris felt totally abandoned. He owed Tommaso and Vincy a lot of money and he was way behind on mortgage instalments. Now it had become impossible to sell the house with the lien on it. This is why, when he called for Valeria and she refuses to talk to him, he would end up burdening his poor daughter with so many distortions of the truth. Now he sat at home alone, night after night, with his dog, Chico, his only companion. *How much longer can I keep on going this way! I am in way too much debt; money is scarce. God! How could I have gone from riches to rags? I never saw this happening. Life stinks!*

While all these thoughts were going through his mind, a sudden heavy knocking on the front door startled him. The dog began barking like crazy.

"How the heck did they get through my gate?" he muttered under his breath. With his recent preoccupation, he must have neglected to close the gate. He peeped through the window; a black car with head lights on and engine running was parked in the driveway. He was afraid to open the front door. Chico continued barking wildly, when a loud noise was heard, and broken glass scattered on the floor next to Boris' feet. Chico reacted ferociously, ready to attack and protect his master. Boris, now electrified with fear, backed away. He felt a lump in his throat and his hand reached down to touch his dog.

A black gloved hand with metal knuckles reached in to find the door knob. Chico moved in on the attack. Boris scampered to find anything he could to defend himself. He grabbed a baseball bat and as he turned around, he saw a masked man struggling with the dog. The man held a gun with an attachment; it must have been a silencer. Chico fell to the floor; one shot to his head silenced the faithful animal. The intruder skillfully grabbed Boris in a choke hold and pressed the gun to his forehead. Boris was now extremely terrified; not a word could be heard coming from him.

A deep threatening voice said, "I got a message for you, Abrosky! This is only a warning! I am not going to pull the trigger yet, Mr. Bigshot! You have got two days to come up with the money you owe the boss, you know his name! You had better deliver! He needs cash! No brick or mortar! And you know to keep this confidential, my friend." He pressed the silencer harder against Boris' forehead. "Should you try anything funny, that beautiful wife of yours, your daughter, and your sons, would be next."

The attacker shoved him aside and Boris hit the floor with a heavy thud. Kicks were dealt about his body. Boris then passed out after a few minutes. He didn't know how long he lay there in the darkness. The sky was dark, no moon was visible. It began to rain and the draft coming through the open door made him shiver as he came to. He couldn't recollect anything that happened, or why he was lying there. Squinting to adjust his eyesight, he caught a glimpse of Chico. The dog lay motionless in a pool of blood. He began screaming, pulling at his hair. He fell to his knees wishing he was also dead. That is when the drama began to replay in his mind. The heavy-set masked intruder, heavy footsteps, the deep voice he had heard, and the screeching of tires as he sped away. His body ached and he had a splitting headache. He was disheartened. Boris shook in fear and couldn't stop crying. With a broken heart he threw himself over Chico's body; the grief was too much for him. His true buddy lay lifeless before him; he was gone, leaving his master alone.

"Oh! My God! I have really messed up my life. What have I done to my wife and my children!" He was sobbing and talking loudly. Boris had reached an abyss. He could not imagine how to begin to get out of the horrendous mess he found himself in, if at all.

***

In Ottawa, Valeria and Rosy, totally unaware of what had taken place at their home in Niagara, were sitting, sipping coffee the next morning. Valeria brushed a hand across her forehead and reluctantly declared, "Rosy, I have no intention of returning home to your father. I will find myself a job and look for a place to live here, not far from you."

Rosy looked at her mother cross-eyed, "Mom, I cannot believe what you are saying. How could you talk about leaving dad at this stage in his life?"

"Rosy, I have had it with him! We used to be on top of the world, financially speaking, of course. Now he has driven us into a skid row with his addiction. Lately he has been hanging out with some shady characters; they are the wrong people for him. His infatuation with casinos has him totally consumed."

"Mom, you will see, Dad will soon come to his senses." She was hopeful.

"Rosy, he has remortgaged our house that was clear of debt, and who knows what else he has gotten himself into!"

"Mom, please don't be pessimistic, and don't read into things that may not exist. Dad has always been wise with his family's security."

"Yeah! Wise and foolish too, especially when you choose to chase rainbows! He kept saying every day that he was going to re-win his money. I am sure he got deeper and deeper into debt. I don't want to think about it, Rosy. He has turned my life into pure hell, and now at this stage there's a mortgage on our house?" She became worked up all over.

"This is totally absurd, I tell you Rosy! We both came from backgrounds where good financial sense was taught as of utmost importance in life. He has gotten totally out of control on me. First, the retirement that he couldn't cope with, then the stroke. For a while there, things were going well and I was relieved, then the gambling started. At first it was fun, just a short pastime, but then there was no stopping him. And worst of all, I didn't see it coming."

"Mom, at least dad is alive. I have parents. Look at poor Pablo; he has no one. He tells me all the time that he is a pebble washed ashore on the beach. The waves of the ocean have been the force behind him." Then Rosy walked away; she didn't want to talk about Pablo anymore. She was stressed from listening to all the complaining.

She had to admit that her mother had gone through plenty with her father. She had her own reservations towards him, especially when it came to Pablo. Boris made him feel inferior the first time Rosy brought him home. He openly scorned Pablo with his questioning. Then he cornered Rosy in the next room.

"Rosy, he is not for you! What do you know about him? Who are his parents?" He questioned her with his loud strong voice that Pablo overheard it all from another room. Maybe it was intended. Wounded like a bird with broken feathers, Pablo had said to her, "I will never come here again, Rosy."

"Pablo, why; what's with you?"

"I am not good enough for you. I guess I don't measure up to your dad. My love for you doesn't count, by to his standards at least." She recollected the conversation. As far as Rosy was concerned, she thought her boyfriend was kind, compassionate, and attentive, in total contrast to her father's personality and behaviour. The most important thing to her was, she loved him and he was madly in love with her. Pablo had taken Boris' comments to heart and he had alienated himself from her for some time. Rosy didn't want to dwell on the unpleasantness of that experience. She walked away from her mother wondering what was in store for her father in his old age. As for her mother, Rosy knew she wasn't wrong about her claims. The phone rang and startled her.

"Hello."

"Rosy, how are you? It's me, Dad; can I talk to your mother? Please put her on."

"Dad, mom will not pick up the phone. She refuses to talk to you." Boris burst out crying, begging, "Rosy, I must talk to her. I am in real trouble, Chico is dead and I wish I was too."

Rosy left the phone hanging from the wall and went to fetch her mother. "Mom! Mom, you must talk to dad, he is crying and sounds desperate. He says Chico is dead!"

"Oh no!" she ran to grab the phone, almost tripping on a chair on her way. "Boris, Boris!" All she could hear was his uncontrollable sobbing; he couldn't speak. "Boris, calm down, get a hold of yourself. What's wrong?

In unclear words Boris finally responded. "Everything is wrong, Valeria. I need you; please come home," he pleaded.

"I will catch the first bus to Toronto and should be there by late afternoon. Ok Boris, bye now." She took a deep breath and shook her head from side to side. Rosy was standing close by, watching her mother. She was relieved.

Thank God! She is going back to him!

Chapter Fifty Three

Loan Sharks

An agitated Vincy walked up and down the promenade outside the casino, waiting for Torpido, the hit man. He was late in reporting to Vincy on his assignment, which big Tommaso impatiently awaited. Then Vincy's cell phone rang.

"Eh! Shmuck, I am waiting up here in the penthouse. What's keeping you? I have opened a bottle of bourbon and it's evaporating. When are you joining me?" Who else could it be other than Tommaso. He was a privileged casino club member with VIP access, exquisite delicacies, and services of all types. Tonight, Tommaso had requested a deluxe room with the marvellous view of the Falls. The bunnies would arrive much later when they are summoned. The two of them alone would celebrate another winning, and another loan contract. Vincy had no inclination that Tommaso, the fox, didn't fully trust him or anyone else with his affairs. He secretly kept another confidant within reach; Dardo Guerriera, from El Salvador. Dardo roamed around carrying a pistol in his waist band and wasn't allowed to drink any alcohol.

Finally, Vincy arrived. The waiting had irritated Tommaso. "Sorry, I was delayed," lamented Vincy, striking Tommaso's shoulder apologetically. Tommaso didn't want to hear excuses. He gave him a dirty look while pouring him a drink. "This is the most expensive brandy in the house." Holding up his glass with an air of superiority, he approached the spread on the table and filled his

317

plate. Then he glanced at his watch, tilted his head and turned to Vincy. "When did you say that Torpido guy was going to report to you? Have you heard from him? It's getting late and no sign of him."

"Not to worry; he will soon check in with me. You don't know Torpido. After a messy job, he likes to spruce himself up. He needs to smell good for the blonds waiting for him. He usually needs a good lay afterwards." He chuckled, smiling at Tommaso. "A nerve relaxer! Don't we all need that!" Vincy continued, trying to make light of the situation.

"Look, Vincy! I don't know this fellow and I don't want to know him. As long as nothing has backfired! With a job like that, you never know!" Tommaso, the boss man, was a big man who liked to dictate orders to the goons, especially Vincy. But for himself, he wasn't getting his hands dirty. Vincy called him "chicken shit" behind his back.

"Nothing to worry about that! Torpido has a silencer, and he knows his moves. He is precise and does the hit with three sparks; one right on the forehead, and one on each eye," bragged Vincy reassuringly. "He told me how he operates. This is why he nicknamed himself Torpido; silent and on target. Yeah! Alonza Gutzman is his real name; a Columbian."

"I don't want to know his name and I don't care where he is from. I never want to meet your guys; they are yours. *Capisci!* Do you understand! As long as he does the job right. You are in charge of hiring and firing, Vincy." He looked him straight in the eyes, squinting and holding the stare.

"All I care about is loaning money at high returns, and we don't lose any. You are getting a good percentage of it, right? Otherwise, you will be replaced, Vincy. I don't have to tell you that!"

Vincy knew only too well how Tommaso operated and he walked on eggshells most of the time. But the money was good and he enjoyed the high life.

***

Valeria had made it home to find Boris shivering with fright, like a cornered animal. With the dog gone, the house in shambles, the front panels boarded up, broken glass at their front entrance, she couldn't believe the derelict condition of their place. Boris had also aged immensely in a short time.

"Please God, give me the strength. Where should I begin?" She implored in despair while looking at her husband. There he lay on the lazy-boy, motionless. Disheartened, she approached him. "Can you wash up and make yourself decent? The first thing to do is get you to a doctor. You have to be checked out." She took both his hands and helped him out of his chair.

From the doctor's office, he was taken by ambulance to the cardiac department of the hospital; his blood pressure was way out of control. He was hospitalized to stabilize the pressure. Valeria returned home to find papers served to her. The bank was going to foreclose on the property. She had never before dealt with the serious aspect of their finances. She was in total shock by her discovery and didn't know where to turn. Boris wasn't well enough. She had to take the matter into her hands. She called the manager of the main branch to arrange a meeting. She needed to stop them at all cost, until her husband was better. In the meantime, she also reported the break-in to the police. Boris had told her it was a break in, a failed robbery attempt. The dog on the defense was shot while defending his master and home, which was not totally untrue. Valeria had no idea of the threat her husband received, or what they were in for. The police came to investigate and take finger prints. But Torpido was gloved, so there were none to be found.

Alonza Gutzman was alert and vigilant; he arranged a meeting with Vincy. "There is a turn of events here. I warned the man not to try anything funny otherwise his family would be next. Now his wife has gotten the police involved."

"Torpido, you are the man to take care of the job! It's up to you, man!"

"Eh! I have no trouble taking care of him, but now I have his wife on my hands. Should I teach him a lesson? I need more money, partner! I am warning you ahead of time."

"I don't think she knows how deep her husband is involved!"

"Yeah! These kept women never do."

The bank had given a few days grace after Valeria's pleading and due to Boris' hospitalization. A few days later, Boris was discharged. When Valeria questioned him about the house and the bank, he burst out sobbing like a baby in pain, as he knew there was no way out this time around. She called the lawyer and arranged a meeting with all the children. They dutifully arrived, were informed of the situation, but there wasn't much any of them could do for their parents. After consultation with the lawyer, Valeria was informed the matter was beyond repair. They needed to immediately file for bankruptcy.

Boris alone knew his fate. He had taken himself into the hands of dangerous loan sharks. They had sweet-talked him into easily accepting their money, fuelling his gambling while it escalated out of control.

"Eh buddy, you need cash? No problem; we got plenty of cash for you. How much you need? Here!" Some hundred-dollar bills would be thrown on the table by Tommaso, while winking at Vincy. "On the House!"

Now he was living on borrowed time. He could not repay their loan. He was waking up during the night drenched with sweat from nightmares. The rope around his neck was slowly tightening. *Charley had warned me, but did I listen?* He had a few dollars in his pocket. He walked to the plaza up the street and bought a big bottle of Vodka. Valeria was spending a lot of time in church these days. Tonight, she had gone to the novena, to participate in a prayer group. He returned home, walked to the end of his property, the bottle clutched tightly under his arm. It was dusk, a quarter moon appeared in a semi cloudy sky. He took the escalator down the steep gorge to the lower level of the Niagara river. It was peaceful out there; not a soul in sight. His reality seemed transported to another planet altogether. He lifted his eyes to the sky; it appeared much further.

Another world up there. I wish I could turn myself into nothingness and be there forever, safe from the cruel world here.

The river boats had finished their tours for the day. He had explored the riverside many times before, throughout all the seasons. He knew all the hiking paths. He sat on a stone, opened his bottle, and gulped Vodka until his brain numbed. He staggered towards the river's edge, his vision was blurred with drunkenness; the river flowed placidly. The calmness soothed him. A couple of crows flew low above him screeching. Boris, in his euphoric drunken state didn't take notice. He stood there for a while staring at the greenish looking water. He stepped further to the edge. Greenery extended itself over the edge into the river. He inched in some more, mesmerized, feeling strangely calm and contented. As he took another step forward, suddenly there was no ground under his feet. His body descended slowly into the depth of the river. The sharp bend was deep and hidden by shrubberies. There, Boris accidentally fell and let go of his body, to find peace.

When Valeria returned home much later, Boris was nowhere to be found. When he had still not returned home by late into the night, she feared the worse and called the police to report him missing.

Chapter Fifty Four

The Discovery

The once opulent Abrosky property that everyone admired had now become a house of suspicion with Boris' disappearance. The neighbourhood had suddenly become overrun with police cars with their flashing lights. A police man wearing an orange and yellow striped safety vest was directing traffic as curious motorists were contributing to the congestion. Yellow police tape cordoned off areas of the property. Inside, Valeria was being bombarded with questions for which she had no answers. Mrs. Jennings had come over on seeing the commotion and was allowed to enter and visit her friend. She hugged Valeria, silently offering her support. She placed a motherly arm around her shoulders trying to alleviate her out of control emotions.

Mr. Glen Dondulan, the officer in charge of the investigation was eager to make headway. Valeria was overwhelmed by the sudden turn of events. She tried to cooperate the best she could with the authorities though she was in shock about her husband's disappearance and had as many questions as anyone else. From their experience, the officers expected the worse but didn't say. One of the assistant officers, Mike Sorzas, had run a quick check and soon discovered that Boris had declared bankruptcy. The Abroskys were given a grace period before foreclosure by the bank; there was a registered lien against their property for a huge sum. A gambling addiction had taken Mr. Abrosky and his wife to the poor house. The assistant officer called his superior on the side and said, "Glen, I think we are dealing with either a homicide or a suicide," and handed the report to him.

"I am not yet done; I'll have the investigation department look into it some more."

***

Vincy was being investigated by the cops. As an old expert, he kept his responses prompt and precise. He knew better to remain cool as a cucumber; he was confident the registered papers were in proper order. Tommaso had warned him about the investigators getting anywhere near him, "You Vincy, will be history! As you know, I am incognito, and I choose to keep it that way!"

Vincy relaxed. He knew Torpido's work was untraceable; no finger prints, no anything! The break-in was viewed as an attempted robbery. Lately there had been a few on River Road and none were solved.

Valeria's children returned to be at their mother's side. The boys took over her position of communicating with the police because they could easily see she was in no condition to continue. Rosy was kind and caring as always, and Pablo had also made the trip to offer support. She was not sure if to celebrate or not, as she told him, "Dad has vanished, now you have no reason to stay away. No more worry of him putting you down," with tears of sadness streaming down her cheeks. "I still wish we could find him; he's my father! I am sure he meant you no harm; that's just his rotten personality." Pablo reached out and gave her a tight hug while he wiped away her tears with the back of his hand.

It was the end of October; the leaves were turning into their fall shades. The white fluffy clouds of the day had suddenly turned into nebulous balloons set for a downpour. A scattered shower came down fast and furious. The northern wind had picked up from the lake. The Niagara river flowed in a vigorous turbulent motion. Boris' body had been caught under the thick shrubberies that hung over the sides. The river had gained momentum and with that the body was easily set afloat. The next day the river had calmed and jet boats came out to conduct tours. One tour guide was pointing out the beauty of the Falls to his passengers when his eyes fell some distance away on what seemed to be a body floating on the caps of the white foam; this was nothing new to him. Immediately the discovery was radioed to the authorities. They took the appropriate measures and removed the body from the water. It was later identified at the morgue as that of Boris Abrosky, of Niagara Falls.

***

Rosy and her brothers took over and handled the funeral arrangements. The dailies and obituary reported his death as an accident. This suited Vincy well; no ties to him so no dirty work became necessary. The final service at the church was well attended; the mass was followed by kind words and praises for Boris who was a community patron. They mourned the loss of a good parishioner. His colleagues and associates from near and far, all came to pay their respects. There was a police presence due to the large congregation. Boris had a respectable and decent send off.

Charley cried for his friend's misfortune. Vincy and Tommaso dressed in their black suits, played their parts well, by sending flowers, condolence and mass cards. They lined up and greeted the family like two respectable businessmen. Valeria's co-workers and boss, Mr. Patty, were all present offering sympathy for her loss. Mrs. Nora Jennings offered true love and support to her dear friend. Susan and Florence, the nurses, became close to Boris during his illness, so they were also in mourning. Valeria was going through the motion of the funeral, in shock, not truly realizing what was really happening in her life.

After the funeral and the sponsored reception by the church, when everyone had left, the realization finally set in for Valeria. *Boris was now gone forever.* All life's trials and tribulation had come to an abrupt end. Through her grief, she didn't seem to care anymore about anything, not even her faith. She refused to move to Ottawa with her daughter. "Rosy, I am a Niagara girl; here is where I will remain. I don't want to become a burden to you or your brothers." She stood her ground, insisting to be left alone.

They helped her to find a two-bedroom condo which she took up occupancy with a heavy heart, wallowing in self-pity. She felt she had lost everything. All her new found hopes and dreams were stolen from her, and Boris had taken them all with him.

Christmas rolled along. Niagara is known for its festivities. The art work in the glamorous and attractive lighting along the Falls is a winter wonderland that attracts thousands of tourists. Valeria had no desire to take a tour of the art work which had been a family tradition every year. She hibernated in her two-bedroom condo, only going out for necessities, and unwillingly at times, to church. Mrs. Jennings usually called to check on her well-being. Susan felt somewhat responsible for having encouraged Boris in gambling. After the funeral she avoided Valeria.

Valeria felt lonely and bored and cried a lot with useless time on her hands. *Oh My God, how my life has drastically changed!* She would silently moan. The cold winter had set in. The sun hardly appeared on those January days, the sky remained usually cloudy, and the days were dark and gloomy. Valeria brooded; she was not happy with herself. She was slowly slipping into a depression. She often thought of Boris, and even with all his craziness she missed and grieved for him. Days slowly passed, and soon it was well into the New Year. Church had become a task, and this Sunday was no different; same seat, same place, and alone. She remembered how Boris would sing loudly in his baritone voice and echo through the church.

The priest stood at the podium delivering the liturgy. "New resolutions…, good deeds…, we are into a New Year…" Valeria could not concentrate on the message. Her brain was playing tricks on her; thoughts swayed in every direction. *If the good Lord would only take me too, I would be happier.* She arrived home in the lowest of moods. She walked in and made her way to the kitchen.

There on the counter, her phone was blinking with messages. She checked, and Mr. Patty's voice came on, "Mrs. Abrosky, forgive me for calling you on a Sunday, but I was wondering if you could possibly come to our office tomorrow morning, Monday. We are in a bind else I wouldn't be bothering you. I desperately need to have a chat with you. I would be pleased if you oblige."

Driven by a force beyond her control, she immediately picked up the phone and dialled the number.

He was working on the Lord's day?

"Hello!" He was really working on a Sunday.

"Mr. Patty, Valeria here. You called?"

"Valeria, how are you? I am so glad you called back."

"I am fine, I guess; as best as can be expected. One day at a time…"

"Valeria, would you be able to come to the office tomorrow morning? I would really like to have a talk with you." She brought a hand up to massage her aching forehead to help her think clearer, then spontaneously replied, "Ok! What time?"

"Say, ten? Would that be too early for you?"

"No, I can be there." She slowly placed the phone down. *What else have I got to do!*

Mr. Patty was delighted. If he could only get Valeria back on his payroll, half of his problems would be solved.

Valeria walked around the apartment for a while, then she sat down and stared at the four walls. Her stomach was growling but she had no appetite. The past trauma she suffered had placed such a darkness on her horizon; all her hopes were destroyed.

No, Valeria; I do not think you are looking forward to tomorrow!

***

While Valeria was brooding about her sad life, her forgotten friend at the other side of the ocean was also in despair. Months had passed since his inspection of Chiara's personal effects, and his decision to look for the lost son. Day and night, he felt tormented and anxious. He had sent out many letters, made dozens of calls, asked many favours from old acquaintances, but got no leads on the whereabouts of the mysterious Rodrigo Fernandez. Chiara was appearing in his dreams; she seemed restless and he felt haunted. When in an awakened state, he dared himself to think of Valeria; this would leave him more broken hearted. In his dream, there were huge iron gates preventing him from reaching her.

Valeria has to be considered a closed case for me. Chiara had gone, Valeria left, and Rodrigo was elusive! But I would not give up.

Chapter Fifty Five

Lucio's Voyage

The flow of tourists at the resort had been constant until October. It was now a slow period at the resort so Attilio's need for assistance was reduced. Lucio needed his cousin's help. He had spent the evening before going over the papers again and again, hoping to discover something new; maybe he had overlooked something. He couldn't stop looking at the picture of the young boy. His eyes spoke silent words and that touched Lucio's heart.

The next morning, he made his way to the barn where Attilio was busying himself constructing new shelves to accommodate the chickens and roosters, also attending to other animals that were within the compound.

"Good morning Attilio," he greeted loudly as he made his way to him.

"Eh! Good morning! How are you, cousin?" He lifted his head to acknowledge him then continued with his task.

"I could be better! Attilio, please, I need your full attention. I am afraid that until my search sheds some light on this Rodrigo boy, I will have no peace. Can you help me?"

"A private investigator would find all the leads in no time. Can you afford to hire one?"

"Attilio, you know I only worked at the City Hall. I was well paid but we lived from pay check to pay check. Then Chiara's sickness came and it took away a lot of my savings. I don't have a lot of money; I cannot afford a private investigator."

"Lucio, if I can help you in any way, I will. Let's go over all the possibilities again. If we don't want to invest money on a private investigator, we will have to do it ourselves. What is wrong with us that we can't try, eh?"

"Attilio, you sound encouraging. I like that! Let's see where we should start."

"Simple! He lived in Rio De Janeiro; start from there! City Hall, registry office, schools; you know all this, I don't have to tell you!"

"Attilio, I have already done all that, up to a certain point, and still no leads. It would seem he has disappeared off the face of the earth."

"Didn't you say someone suggested that it was possible he was taken by a house of charity?"

Lucio had been skeptical in trying to cover up for Chiara and had left out the details of the General. Although Attilio had heard a bit of gossip on the compound in the past, he was a man focused on his own affairs and didn't dwell on the clients that put bread on his table.

"Lucio, check deeper. You might have to take a trip down there. You have to be your own private investigator. Check things out; where they lived, the neighbourhood; get to the source. There is nothing better than to do it for yourself, cousin! You are a smart man! Come on Lucio; it's time to move forward!"

"I have considered that. I will need a translator as I speak neither Portuguese nor Spanish. This could make my search difficult."

"Lucio, you have Italian and English under your belt; that should help you! There is a heavy population of Italians in Rio, and Spanish should not be all that difficult to understand."

Attilio was a positive thinker and a good man. Then he continued, "Did you think of my son, Ugo? He lives in Rio; you forgot! Maybe he can help. Did you think of her siblings; her older brothers, and older sister?"

"Forget about them, they were totally estranged from Chiara. They had disowned Chiara and her mother. As for your Ugo, yes; I believe he would be able to help me if he could."

"Then Lucio, the next step is book tickets to Brazil! I will go with you. Assunta will not mind my absence, for a couple of weeks that is. Let's see what we can dig up. It will also give me a chance to see my son. I shall call Ugo and inform him of our plans. The South Americans I know are incredibly obliging."

"Attilio, you tell me? You forgot that I was married to one! She was the sweetest person you could meet; unfortunately, with a secret life." He mumbled the last part of his sentence. Attilio offered him a handshake and smiled compassionately at his cousin.

"Attilio my dear cousin, you and I have a mission to accomplish. And the sooner the better. I feel more hopeful now that you have decided to accompany me."

By the following week, they were on a flight to Rio De Janeiro.

Chapter Fifty Six

Brazil

Lucio's expectations of Rio were not high. When he used to be inquisitive and would question Chiara, she would usually be evasive, never caring to elaborate on anything relating to her native country. Her lack of enthusiasm would discourage him from wanting to know more, or travel to the southern part of the globe. He had encountered some wonderfully interesting people from Venezuela, Argentina, and Brazil, not omitting his sweet wife.

Once they arrived at the airport and were picked up by Ugo and his wife, greeting them pleasantly, they headed towards Copacabana. The scenery that extended in front of their eyes was marvellous. Lucio didn't know where to look first; Christ the redeemer was one sight that could not be avoided. What a landmark it was; majestically situated atop the Corcovado mountain, seeming not just to welcome but to offer salvation within the outstretched arms. It was a phenomenally impacting sight to anyone arriving into the country. Ugo was driving along the miles of sandy golden beaches; another fantastic stretch to admire. The sun was shining, and the clear blue sky seemed in total harmony with the huge expanse of the Atlantic Ocean. The air felt pleasantly warm, and the lightly cool breeze from the ocean was an interesting first experience for the new visitor. Rio was no surprise for Attilio since he had been there many times before. He enjoyed watching his cousin's eyes widen with amazement. His son and family lived in a middle-class district as they were both professionals, lawyers, therefore could afford a better standard of

333

life than most of the population. There were many very deprived areas in Rio. To not waste time, Attilio had already discussed with his son, the main reason for their visit. After breakfast, he reminded Ugo, "Son, you have to excuse us as you know Lucio and I are here on a mission. We are hoping to dig up as much as we could, to come up with the best approaches. Any input from you would be appreciated."

"Papa, I had a discussion with my senior law partner after you first told me of your trip. He is a local, and he has much experience working with the people from the different communities in Rio. There was a period of time when corruption, crime, drug trafficking, famine, disease, and pollution, were most rampant in the deprived areas. The conditions were so bad that there was a record high adult and infant mortality. My friend has advised that you check out the area by the port, the favelas or slums in the urban outskirts. A lot of people ended up in the urban northern area where there is no electricity or sanitation, and the poorest of conditions. I was told under military rule hordes of residents were displaced."

"Ok, son, we would be on our way. We should start from the areas you suggest." Attilio had heard a rumour that Chiara had come from the slums, he could not say it to his cousin, but he was planning to skillfully structure the search to lean in that direction. He was hopeful if they were to discover something of importance, there is where it could be.

Lucio and Attilio, partly from Ugo's advice and partly Attilio's intuition, began the search in Rio De Janeiro. They explored all the relevant places that they felt could provide leads, to steer them closer to locating Rodrigo Fernandez. When Lucio visited the squalid areas, he found that he couldn't bear to stay there for long. It was disturbing to him when he pictured his dear Chiara ever coming from such levels of poverty. There were collapsed buildings and homeless people to be seen everywhere. It was such a pitiful site. Suffering and hunger could not hide; the empty eyes and soiled faces were almost unbearable to see. He saw one young child sleeping on the street; he seemed all alone, abandoned. The squares were crowded with many young people; no doubt there was trouble brewing there. Lucio didn't feel safe. Days had passed and there was still no light on the whereabouts of the young man.

An idea came to his mind. *They must have been Catholics, then he must have been baptized, confirmed, or has some connection with the Church. The poorest of the poor Catholics would never abandon the Church.* He asked Attilio and Ugo, "I say we visit some of the churches in the poor areas. Let's talk to some of the old priests and staff that have been there for a long time. Maybe it's just a hunch but I feel one of them would be able to shed some light on our search."

"Eh! At this point, we are desperate! There are millions of people in Rio De Janeiro. It's like looking for a needle in a haystack. Lucio, I am at your service!" Attilio responded.

Ugo gave them a list of the old churches in the derelict areas and off they went. On every rectory door they knocked and asked questions, but nothing came up. No one knew or heard of the family. They were at the end of an avenue when they noticed what looked like an old abandoned church. Lucio insisted they go in. Attilio pushed open the large squeaky side door when a musty smell threw him back a few steps. Lucio followed behind. Attilio turned to him and said, "Cousin, are you sure you want to walk into this building? Look, the plaster is peeling off, the saints are smothered with dirt; this place looks as if it would collapse at any time. I certainly don't want to get crushed under the rubble and no one finds us."

"Attilio, we've already come this far; let's check it out." Lucio courageously stepped forward. As they entered they noticed a balcony to the left with a rail above their heads suggesting an upper level; whispers came from the direction. He grabbed Attilio's arm and whispered, "Listen, some voices are coming from up there; do you think they are praying?"

They proceeded further towards the front, treading carefully in the dilapidated church. They reached the altar. From habit, Lucio kneeled down in reverence; to him it was still a church. Attilio hesitated, left with no choice but to follow suite, he placed his aching knees on the cold dusty marble. They remained there quietly for a short time. The murmuring had stopped. A squeaky door to their right opened. An old nun appeared with five more behind her, some were younger. They were all dressed in the traditional black floor length gowns and white habits.

Forming a bee line, the old nun was followed by the others as they approached Lucio and Attilio. She inclined her head with a half-smile. "I am Mother Theresa," she said, her hands hidden under her scapular. She then proceeded to introduce the rest of the nuns. With a warm smile, the Mother asked, "May I ask you gentlemen if we could be of any help? The good Lord has sent you our way!"

The other nuns also smiled warmly and kindly as if waiting to follow orders. Lucio spoke up and introduced himself. "Sister, my cousin and I are looking for a young man, rather I should say, he was a little boy. This is his picture, he would be older now. His name is Rodrigo Fernandez; I believe the picture was taken when he was about seven."

Mother Theresa studied the picture then passed it on to the other nuns. She asked, "How is he related to you? May I enquire why you are looking for him?"

"You see, he is my deceased wife's son. I am from Europe. I have reason to believe he was left here in Rio as a young boy. I believe my wife wants me to find him. So far, we have had no luck. We have checked every possible lead. This is our last attempt before we return to our country, just a last-minute idea. Sorry to have troubled you, Mother Theresa." Lucio anxiously blurted it all out.

She took the picture again in her hands, delicately examining it as if reading a scripture, then passed it back to the bunch. They all shook their heads, no recognition. Attilio's eyes caught a very old nun, much older than mother Theresa, standing half behind the door the nuns had come through. Mother Theresa followed his eyes and smiled and nodded for the nun to come forward. She approached, with her hands also hidden under her scapula; her age was reflected in the manner she leaned forward as she walked.

"This is Mother Superior."

"Mother Superior, could you please take a look at this picture. These gentlemen are searching for this young boy," she said loudly as she handed the picture over.

The Mother held it with both hands, focusing intently, then revealed, "Mother Theresa, it's been a long time now, I am not sure. He reminds me of a little boy that used to come here years ago with his grandmother, old Mrs. Fernandez; she worked occasionally in our kitchen. Do you remember her?"

"I'm sorry, I do not recall," said Mother Theresa.

"Poor soul, I can now remember. She had said to me the little boy was her daughter's child, left in her care. She worried about him a lot as he was exposed to social displacement among the many other children. She believed her grandson was special and had much potential. She wanted the best for him. Poor woman! She was not well at all health-wise, worked hard, but was eventually killed in one of the violent riots. I remember the boy wandering in the streets, dirty, hungry, alone, and crying; he came here looking for his mamma. That is what he called her, Mamma! He was too young to relate to death. He was teased and chased by other boys at times. They would make fun of him saying, "Your grand-mamma is dead, gone forever, don't you get it?" That was the harsh reality of street life for the orphans.

Lucio shivered on hearing of the cruelty the child suffered, tears welled up, just to listen was painful. Now he was more determined than ever to find Rodrigo. He asked, "Mother Superior, please tell me, is there anything more you can recollect? You see, his mother was my wife. She was also critically ill and has passed on. It is now more important than ever that I find him!"

"Sorry, I do not; I am old and not as sharp as I wish to be. All I can say is, he was pretty much left on the streets to fend for himself. Homelessness among the street children is a huge problem, a crisis. We would do our best to help as much as we could, but all we did was feed a handful; there were too many."

They thanked the nuns and left the dilapidated church in a sorrowful mood.

No wonder Chiara buried her past and never talked about it or wanted to share it with anyone, even me. I understand now, dear Chiara.

Lucio looked up to the heavens.

Attilio noticed Lucio was extremely pensive and broke the silence by saying, "Lucio we are going to have a chat with the senior partner at Ugo's firm. He should be knowledgeable on what took place at the time of civil unrest, and the surge of street children during the time we are exploring. We will conduct further research. Don't worry. The Mother Superior has given us something to work with. Can you imagine, of all the places we have covered?"

The next day, with Ugo's influence, Lucio and Attilio were sitting across the desk of Nardo Mendosa. He was a huge man, well groomed, with a strong voice that pierced your ears when he spoke. He was direct, precise, and knowledgeable. Lucio related to him the nun's words, which he admitted didn't offer much to work with.

Nardo Mendosa scratched his head with his pen, and said, "The country was in a real predicament then; homeless children were losing their lives every day. If I recollect correctly, there were missionaries here from the House of Charity, a famous organization that do missionary work in poor countries all over the world. They had taken in a lot of children. I wonder if by chance your Rodrigo Fernandez was fortunate enough to have been among them."

Lucio's ears perked up. "How can we find out, Senhor Mendosa?"

"Who knows! With so much corruption, it could be difficult. I would all my resources to research the chapter of The Houses of Charity that worked in Rio at the time. I am told they take in the most deserving children that no one else wants. They rehabilitate them, school them, making them as functional as possible for when they grow up. Give me a few days, and I would get back to you."

Chapter Fifty Seven

The Ongoing Investigation

While anxiously waiting to hear from Nardo Mendosa, Lucio was silently and desperately praying for good news. Attilio kept asking Ugo to join in on the search as time was a crucial factor for him. Assunta was alone back home, and he was concerned the days were quickly passing by with no bright light at the end of the tunnel.

"Dad, Nardo Mendosa opens doors; be patient and have faith in him, trust him. He is well connected." A couple of days later, they were summoned to Mendosa's office.

"Buonas Dias, Amicos che passa?" He greeted them with a big smile. Waving a sheet of paper, he said, "This information just arrived this morning. I wasted no time calling you."

Lucio was holding his breath; from Mendosa's good humor, he felt optimistic.

"Gentlemen, please take a seat. You need to listen to what I have to say. We could be heading somewhere."

Lucio and Attilio listened attentively, ready to take in whatever news had come. Attilio was attuned to the culture of some lawyers and sensed that this information could cost them more than they had catered for. "Ok, tell us, we are listening." He said in a stern voice.

"Attilio, and signor Lucio, you know nothing comes from nothing. I had to disburse some money to get this information, but I must say it was well worth it."

Lucio glanced at Attilio who took over. "Nardo, by all means, we are not here to play games or take advantage of anyone. Of course, we are prepared to pay for your time and whatever expenditures this has cost you, as long as it's within reason." He said it thinking: *Sure! You can't live in Copacabana, have an office in an area as this, and just operate on favours!*

"You are not going to believe how many people I had to question, and how many phone calls I had to place. The end result is I found a lead. I believe there may be better luck if you make another trip. May I ask where you are heading after Rio?"

"Back to Sardinia, connecting in Rome," Lucio promptly responded.

"Well I suggest you change your route. You need to fly to New York if you are anxious to find your boy and talk with one Father Gregorio Caldarelli. He is originally from Rome, with past connections to the Vatican and the old pope. A priest dedicated fully to missionary work, he is renowned for his kindness and accomplishments; from England to Boston, India, Buenos Aires, and Rio De Janiero, just to mention a few. My dear gentlemen, I am told he is an eighty-nine-year-old sick man, now confined to a wheelchair, diabetic, recuperating from a stroke, and hard of hearing.

The good news is, he is still at the House of Charity, also called Hospice, in a deprived area in New York. He has taken in and recruited people from all over the world to help them through the Charity. He has successfully rehabilitated many children, including finding sponsors for some. The house is sustained by donations, and some support from the poor parishioners of the attached church. Father Gregorio was the missionary that visited our city many years ago, and at that time he recruited mostly homeless children. I have a hunch that your boy might have been among them. What you need to do is go visit this priest as soon as you can. Use that picture you have, take it to him. I wish you luck in stirring Father's memory. You should go as soon as possible because time is against you, even as we speak. Maybe if you are lucky, someone at that Hospice might be a long-time employee and would be able to help you. Don't waste any more time here. I have documented all the information you will need! I don't want to get your hopes up too much, but I will tell you this, an informant here has assured me that Rodrigo Fernandez's name was on the list of names of the homeless and taken away by the missionary."

Lucio and Attilio looked at each other, spellbound, with new hope. Attilio took out his wallet and asked, "Nando, thank you for your time. This means a lot to my cousin here. What do we owe you for your trouble? We do appreciate all you have done for us."

"Attilio, give me whatever you think this information is worth to Signor Lucio. I also suggest you donate generously to the House of Charity once you get there."

Attilio handed him two hundred-dollar bills, US currency, as everyone craves. He thanked him, and they shook hands then left the lawyer's office. They had the information they needed. Their task now was to re-route their flight to New York.

"Lucio, no use to go back to Europe now then travel to the US. Besides, you heard Nardo! The priest is aged and ailing."

"Yes, Attilio, I agree, we are on a mission, let's complete it."

"We will get Ugo's secretary to make the arrangements. With our lack of knowledge of Portuguese and Spanish, that would be quicker."

Two days later they were bound for New York on a United Airlines flight. Once they stepped out at JFK airport, they flagged down a yellow cab and gave the driver the address to the House of Charity. While driving through Manhattan, Lucio felt encouraged. The skyscrapers, the fancy shops, the traffic; this was a thriving city, alive and promising. As the driver continued, they drove further and deeper into a dilapidated area, but not as bad as the slums of Rio. Lucio took a deep breath and tried to calm his anxieties. It was late afternoon when they were let off at the door to the address. They rang the doorbell and a plump elderly lady wearing a white apron opened the door. She wore a white net on her head to keep her hair out of her face. With no reservations, she let them right in.

Attilio did the talking as he sensed Lucio's nervousness. "I am Attilio, and this is my cousin, Lucio; we are from Italy. We came a long way to meet Father Gregorio. Would he be able to receive us today?"

"Oh! Welcome to New York. I am Lisa, the assistant manager to Father Gregorio. He is sitting in the recreation room having his afternoon tea with the residents. Let me tell him he has visitors."

In no time she was back and pleasantly announced, "Please follow me."

As they were being led into the large recreation room, they noticed a gentleman in priestly attire sitting on a wheelchair in the far corner, sipping tea next to a large window. Other residents were seen about the room, occupied with visitors or nurses, or engaged in recreational conversation. In another corner stood a large antique Steinway piano; Lucio thought it looked like the oldest resident there. Father Gregorio's assistant manager introduced the two men, and they were received in a cordial and pleasant manner. He shook hands with them, and in a weak voice asked, "My brothers, what brings you two gentlemen all the way here, to the House of Charity?"

"Father Gregorio, we are here on a mission. A friend of ours has sent us to you. We have flown here from Rio De Janeiro. We are originally from Italy."

The priest listened attentively. As a man of God, he never refused to listen to anyone with a problem. Without pretense, he kindly asked, "How can I be of help to you, my friends. My poor health is not allowing me to function as efficiently, but I would certainly help you if I can. My faithful assistant, Lisa, is also competent. May we offer you some tea?"

"Thanks, Father, we are fine," replied Attilio.

Lucio looked around and asked, "Father is there somewhere private where we can talk. We are here on a delicate matter. I have a picture I need to show you. I am looking for someone and we have reason to believe you either know him, or once knew him."

Father Gregorio signalled Lisa who was standing a short distance away and asked to be taken to his room. The gentlemen followed as instructed. They walked through a long corridor, and at the end Lisa opened the door to a fair size bedroom, with blueish walls covered with pictures, a modest bed, and a desk and chair. Lucio's eyes scanned the room, checking for anything that could be of interest. He turned to Father and asked, "Father, who are all these people? You seem to have a gallery here."

"They are the people God guided us to save, placing us on their path, and they all have better lives now."

Lucio pulled the picture out of his wallet and held it in his hands. "Father, I am desperately looking for this young boy. We were told that maybe he was one of the fortunate ones saved by you, years ago from the slums of Rio De Janeiro," and he passed him the picture.

"There is a collage on one of the walls with the children we recruited from Rio some years back. My vision is poor, I wear a hearing aid and most times it doesn't work. You must forgive me. Lisa, please get me the magnifier; I want to take a good look at the young boy's face. I certainly want to help these people."

Lucio agitatedly looked around the room. What seemed to be so difficult for him was the many faces he saw in the pictures. He turned to Father and said, "His name was Rodrigo Fernandez. He was around seven years old here. I was told he was homeless and lived on the streets."

Father struggled with his magnifier and tried hard to

concentrate. "There had been countless children over the years, who were all brought here from horrendous situations in their birth countries."

Lisa spoke, "Father, do you remember that shy young boy? He used to be a loner and cried for his mamma all the time. He didn't want to be called by his name, he used to say he was a pebble. Father put a hand to his forehead while Lucio held his breath, waiting for his miracle. *After all, these people are holy!*

Father Gregory responded in a weak but loving voice, "Don't tell me it's who I think it is! Lisa, you refreshed my memory; thank you. I can picture him now, always in the corner of the dining room, always with a sorrowful look and tears in his eyes. He never responded when called him by his name. I used to pray extra for him to come around. Then, when he turned twelve, he was attending school and it came time for confirmation. Studying the Catechism was doing him good. He came home after school one day; I remember clearly, and he searched for me in the old church. I had just finished confessions. And there he was by the confessional, 'Father, I have a big request of you.' 'What is that, my son,' I had asked. 'Father, my teacher said I need a sponsor for my confirmation. Will you accept to be my sponsor, Father?' "

"I answered, 'You need two sponsors, my dear son.' He innocently replied, 'Yes, you and Lisa. I don't know or want anybody else. I have already picked my name too.' "

Father Gregory closed his eyes and gently rubbed one side of his wrinkled face as he recollected. Pleasant thoughts came through. "Dear God, how could I ever forget him! I had found the child totally abandoned, living in squalor. He was a bag of bones but smiled sweetly; it melted my heart. At that moment I vowed to myself, I would not leave that place until the little boy was part of my salvation."

"So, you do know who we are talking about! Do you know where he is now,

Father? He must be grown up by now."

"Indeed, he is a brilliant young man. We here are mighty proud of him. Lisa, please get the latest picture from the wall of our Pablo De Santos." She removed and carefully placed the framed picture into Father's frail hands.

"Here it is. This was taken the last time I visited him."

Lucio and Attilio were handed a picture of a young man and Father Gregory standing in front of a University building. The young, handsome man towered over Father. He was of a slim stature, dark hair, an infectious smile, and sportily dressed.

Lucio's heart leapt. "Father, we must meet him! When can we? Where is he? You see, Father, it's a long and complicated story. He had a mother and I knew her. She was my wife. I know she cared a lot for him and his mamma. Unfortunately, she became seriously ill and has passed on. Only after my wife's death did I learn more about her family in Rio. From whatever little I had to go on, I have been driven to find him. Call it the will of God, or my dead wife's spirit pushing me to search, but I will have no rest until he is told the truth about his mother."

"I am assuming you are not his father?" The priest politely enquired.

"No, Father, unfortunately not. But with his permission, I can be his step-father."

"My dear fellow, I can call him right now and let you talk with him. I prefer to arrange a meeting for you to meet him. I can assure you, it will be the best gift from God, for both of you."

Chapter Fifty Eight

To Canada

Father Gregory placed his call. In no time he was connected to the young man, and the priest beamed with pride as he spoke. "Pablo, my son, how are you? This is Father." Lucio and Attilio could actually hear a happy male voice on the other end. Lucio felt a shiver run up and down his spine. His impossible dream was finally turning into reality.

"My dear Pablo, remember I would always say to you, you must never lose faith? And at the right time good things will come your way?" There was silence. "Pablo, are you listening to me? I have a surprise for you. I have two gentlemen in front of me right now. They have come a long way looking for you. One of them would be of high interest to you. I am giving them your phone number and address. They would fly to Ottawa to meet you. My prayers have been answered for you in every way, my son. They will be furnished with all the information necessary including your updated picture. They are Signori Lucio and Attilio Alvani, cousins from the island of Sardinia in Italy." Pablo always trusted Father Caldarelli implicitly; he was his role model and saviour and he was honoured to have him as his Godfather.

Attilio and Lucio wasted no time. They thanked Father immensely, and Father blessed them in return. On their way out both men reached into their wallets and slid generous amounts into the donation box, reflecting their gratitude. With renewed hope they headed back to the airport to catch the first flight for Toronto, then to Ottawa.

***

349

Valeria had just disappeared through the check in and was waiting at the gate to board her plane. She was flying Air Canada to Ottawa. After meeting Mr. Patty, a decision was made. It had not taken much convincing from him for her to return to work at World Travel. Since Valeria's world had turned upside down, with unbearable dark gloomy days, she decided the best thing for her was to go back to work and keep occupied before she loses her mind. Besides, she enjoyed her work and she now needed the money. Mr. Patty offered her an excellent position. She was going to be in charge of bus tours for group travellers to various countries, chaperone and tour guide at large. Valeria had gladly accepted.

She was now at the airport in Toronto, on her way to spend a few days with her daughter before totally committing her time to her work. Her heart was still healing from deep wounds. She sat there aloof. Two men passed by looking for seats, one of them almost tripping over her carry on. Gate nine was full. "Sorry," one of the men apologized and continued moving on. She didn't even look up or respond as she was deeply absorbed in her personal thoughts. Soon it was time to board.

As she stood in line, she caught a glimpse of two gentlemen a little further up. Excitement immediately flooded her heart. *My God that looks like Lucio from Sardinia, or someone that resembles him! It cannot be! What would he be doing here!* She took a closer look; the other face didn't register. They were deeply absorbed in conversation. She couldn't hear what they were saying. Her curiosity got the best of her. She never again got in touch with her Lucio, as promised, and same for him. She didn't dare allow herself to think of him too much once she was back home and focusing on family commitments. She was left guilt ridden by their private relationship before she had returned to her home. Her past behaviour was not acceptable by the church. She had accepted that her actions then were due to temporary insanity.

She boarded the plane. As she made her way to find her seat, she stopped cold. She found herself face to face with the one person she could not dream of meeting at that point in her life. Lucio Alvani sat right there in front of her, occupying an aisle seat. She froze; her heart strings struck a glorious symphony. Lucio casually looked up, he swallowed hard, dumbstruck. She was holding up the passengers. Robotically she moved forward, dazed. Lucio loudly said, "Valeria! Am I hallucinating?" Attilio looked confused. "Valeria, I will come to you after takeoff."

Attilio asked, "Who is she? What's going on? How do you know her?" Lucio was beside himself. How could these turns of events take place in such a short time? Attilio was waiting for his answer but Lucio was on cloud nine; he forgot his cousin was sitting beside him. He kept looking back to locate where she sat, beaming like a school boy, and couldn't wait to talk with his lost love again. Adrenalin suddenly kicked him into high gear. Finally, the plane took off and as soon as it levelled off he was standing beside her seat. He wanted to take her in his arms and never let her go, now that he had found her again. *The obstacles.* Since they had not communicated he didn't know that Valeria was now widowed. They talked briefly.

"Lucio what a shocking surprise! What brings you here to Canada, to Ottawa?"

"A long story; we must talk. And you?"

"My daughter; I am going to visit for a few days." He wasn't moving one bit, he stood there as if his shoes were nailed tightly to the spot.

"So good to see you! How have you been? Has life been kind to you?" he asked.

Valeria swallowed; she couldn't respond right away. Then she said, "Like yours, a long story here too."

Attilio sat waiting, wondering. *Has my cousin turned into a Romeo? He does not behave like this in public, no matter who he meets!* He sensed his cousin's reaction to the woman did not come across as innocent. Lucio finally returned to his seat just before landing. His main concern was to make sure he got an address or phone number to reach Valeria. It was a must, apart from finding Pablo De Santos. Attilio asked again. "How do you know this lady, cousin?"

"Attilio, we worked together for a few months. She was involved in promoting our island for a Canadian Agency. She is magnificent at her work. We must show her your resort if she ever comes again..."

Attilio interrupted, also in an unusual manner, but with an amused smile, "Eh! Cousin, you are attracted to her! You lost your head as soon as you spotted her! I wish you could have seen yourself!"

"No, no, she is just a good friend! She is married too," Lucio said unconvincingly.

"Too bad! You are a widower, available, but she is not. So, don't go getting any ideas now."

Lucio changed the subject. "Well, it sure has been exciting, hasn't it! What a whirlwind! I can't wait to meet Pablo!"

Attilio thought to himself, *a whirlwind you said, cousin?*

Soon the plane landed. Lucio had a burning desire to talk to Valeria and arrange to meet.

Attilio was not missing a beat, carefully observing his cousin's agitation since he saw the lady. *Sorry, cousin, your enthusiasm is not only about Pablo! You are up to something but I will wait to find out.*

They all met as they headed for the baggage claim area. Lucio gently placed a hand on her arm and said, "Valeria, I want you to meet my cousin, Attilio."

After the short introduction, Lucio continued, "Valeria, I am not sure how long we will be here…"

Attilio cut in again with, "Not too long!"

"Where can I reach you? Can we meet? Attilio and I would like to take you out," he was stumbling on his words, glancing from his cousin to his distraction, "Maybe dinner?"

Valeria offered a big smile. "Yes, of course, we should! I need to check with my daughter first."

"Valeria, it goes without saying; she can join us too." Lucio wished to have her to himself. After spotting Valeria, the anxiety of meeting Pablo had temporarily reduced. He was thrilled to the bones. She scribbled her phone number and address and handed it to him. She shook hands with Attilio, they exchanged pleasantries, a quick kiss on both cheeks for Lucio, and then she headed for the exit.

"Attilio collected the suitcases, turned to Lucio and said, "Nice lady, your friend." Lucio smiled and thought, *but obviously out of reach*. They were making their way to the exit when they got a glance of Valeria disappearing around the corner through the exit doors. She was met by a young lady and a young man.

It was dusk and there was a chill in the air. The sky was overcast, and a fine drizzle was coming down. Attilio said, "It's been quite a day. I suggest we check in the hotel, get something to eat, have a stiff drink of brandy, and call it a night! Tomorrow morning, we will get in touch with Pablo and set up a rendezvous."

"Good idea, cousin! Enough excitement and travel for one day."

Chapter Fifty Nine

Awaited Encounters

Lucio slept deeply but couldn't wait for daylight. He got up early, hit the gym, showered and got dressed, then patiently waited for his watch to reach nine o'clock. He had to call Pablo. He needed to meet him first, Valeria would be next. He had noted Attilio's scrutiny so he thought he had better keep matters simple. As soon as he dialled Pablo's number, he answered. "Pablo, I am so looking forward to meeting you. We are not sure about your schedule, but we would like to meet with you as soon as possible as we need to fly back to Italy soon."

"I understand; I cannot wait to meet you too. We are in luck. My class today is not until three in the afternoon. Then I go to the library to study until late. Since you are in town for a short time, it's best you come to my place, so you can see where I live."

"Great! Let's say ten thirty, if that is fine with you, Pablo?"

Pablo was easy and accommodating especially since they had been sent by the loving and respectable Father Gregorio. The cab dropped them off at the address he was given; it was close to the university. A smiling, courteous young man opened the door and greeted them. Lucio had the picture in his hand which he didn't need. He immediately recognized Chiara's sparkling eyes looking back at him. They walked into a modest living room furnished with the bare essentials, and tidy for student quarters. They all sat down. Lucio didn't know where to begin. Pablo felt bashful but his kind demeanour filled the room with pleasantness.

Attilio broke the ice by saying, "My cousin here has been

355

relentlessly searching for you, Pablo."

"Yes," continued Lucio. "I would have had no peace until I found you. We have so much to talk about. I must tell you that your mother's love has driven me here or, call it a combination of circumstances and fate."

He pulled a picture from his wallet and handed it to Pablo. "My dear young man, this is your mother, my deceased wife." Pablo scrutinized the picture carefully. He was stunned.

"My Mother? Mama always said I had an older sister; I barely remember her as she was hardly around; she was always coming and going. I also had a younger little sister, but she died. My mama loved us a lot, but she also vanished, and my older sister never returned."

"Pablo, we have somewhat retraced your footsteps. I am glad how things have turned out for you. We met Father Gregorio; he is a holy man and he not only saved you, but he led us to you. I have searched for you high and low, to the point of despair until Father opened the door."

Pablo listened attentively. Other than keeping Father dear in his soul, and the vague memory of his mama, he wished to erase the rest of his childhood from his memory forever; even the little he remembered. The nightmares still haunted him from time to time.

"Pablo, now that I have found you, we have so much to talk about. I personally will make it up to you, should you accept me as your stepfather. From what I gather, your 'mama' you refer to was your grandmother. Your real mother was my wife, who silently endured her suffering. I have proof for you of what she secretly left behind. I have to tell you, she loved you secretly placed, within her heart, Pablo. She did whatever she could to provide for you, your mama, and your younger sister. She never returned because she couldn't return. Sickness robbed her of her life. She was diagnosed early with MS, followed by dementia, and after some time, she died."

Pablo looked and took it all in wide eyed, remembering himself, lost and alone in the slums of Rio, and then his new life in New York. Then he said, "At least when I got to NY, Father made sure I was safe in a bed at night. He called us his flock, and he was our pastor."

"Now Pablo, please tell us about yourself. What are your goals? I am told you are a brilliant student."

He smiled shyly, "I am studying Architecture; this is my fourth year. I would graduate soon then apply for my masters. I always loved buildings; skyscrapers are amazing. Before I came to Ottawa, I used to wander the streets of New York looking up and counting the floors of buildings; they intrigued me. There was a magnet within me that continually led me to observe the sky scrapers. I would envision the creation of structures, erected from scratch on empty land, constructed in the finest material, zapped with luster Carrera marble, the best imported windows and impressive glass, and special ornate steel doors. The front courtyard, welcoming with water falls, immense lush gardens, and lustrous blue signs illuminating the signatures: PEBLO 1, PEBLO 2, and so on. They will be distinguished, and recognizable, since they are the realistic dreams originated from the mind of the architect. This is how I will pursue my passion. It's hard work but I love it. I guess coming from poverty, it's not about money, but more about creation, art."

Lucio and Attilio admired how proudly Pablo spoke of his area of work, yet he was graciously humble about it. Lucio felt a bit saddened when he reflected on the young man's unfortunate childhood; no one would guess from his appearance. His sick wife that once sold her body to provide for her loved ones never had a chance to enjoy the benefits of her sacrifice. She would have been so proud of her son, he thought. *But according to their religious belief system, she would know.*

"Pablo, this is our first encounter. I want to be there for you, if you permit me, and I would like you to come and visit me some time in the future. I have no doubt you would love our island. Now that I have found you, I hope to keep in touch regularly. You are a grown, independent young man; I can see that. Just know, I am proud of you."

There was so much to talk about, Lucio thought, but this was enough for now. There would be other visits from now on. What a loving son Pablo would make. They got up to leave, Lucio handed Pablo one of his calling cards, hopeful for happier times ahead. Everyone was happy in their unique way.

Now it was time for Lucio to place a call to Valeria, to plan a friendly dinner meeting. Back at the hotel, Attilio busied himself making notes for his business as spring was soon approaching and much planning was important for his return. Lucio had stepped out to get a snack, and when he returned he said to Attilio, "Tonight I will make dinner reservations for us, and my friend, Valeria. What type of food would you prefer?"

"Lucio, I will stay behind if you don't mind. You go and meet your friend; enjoy your visit with her."

Lucio was more than happy to go alone. He wasted no time to go place his call. On the second ring Rosy picked up the line. "Hello, Rosy Abrosky's residence." She was such a character and liked to answer her phone with an impressive tone. Lucio asked for Valeria, and Rosy quickly called her mother. Covering the phone, she whispered, "Mom I think it is your friend you had met on the plane."

"Hello, Lucio, how are you?"

"I am great, how about you?"

"Fine, enjoying a chat with my daughter."

"Valeria, as I suggested at the airport, can we meet for dinner tonight? My cousin is checking flights for our return. It would be nice to get updates on each other before I leave."

"Yes, Lucio, that would be nice. My Rosy has late classes; that leaves me free. I would love to have dinner with you."

"Great! Any preference?"

"Lucio, whatever suits you, I am fine with anything."

"You are easy to please, Valeria. I forgot. Would I be picking you up at your daughter's place?"

"Lucio, just a suggestion, there is a small bistro by the market square called, Luxe Bistro; a lovely place. Why don't I meet you there?"

"This is fine. See you there at seven." He considered himself lucky that she had accepted his invitation and he didn't have to insist. After all, she has her own family.

Valeria walked into the restaurant and Lucio was already there waiting for her. He immediately stood up to greet her in his well-mannered way which Valeria greatly admired. He had ordered champagne to celebrate this fortunate and timely encounter. They stared at each other for a moment. It was Valeria who broke the spell.

"So good to see you, Lucio. I never expected to meet you in Ottawa. Tell me how have you been? How is Enzo? The Mayor? And your gorgeous island?"

He gently took her hand, brought it up to his face, and inhaled deeply as if he held a freshly plucked flower. She allowed him. After taking his fill, he spoke, "Valeria, never mind about me, Enzo, or the Mayor. I would like to hear about you! How have you been? You forbade me from thinking about you, and you wanted me to try and erase my memory of you. Is it possible to dictate to a bleeding heart?"

Lucio caught himself being philosophical, and emotionally overwhelmed by the chance of his present company. As if jolted from a dream, he declared, "Valeria, my apologies, I have no right…"

"Lucio, we have not talked or been in touch for quite some time. A lot has happened since my Sardinia trip that you could never imagine. I consider myself fortunate to be here; my daughter Rosy, her love gives me strength. Lucio, I don't want to bore you; it's not all pleasant. I recently became a widow. I lost Boris, our savings, our mansion, all due to my husband's huge ego. I will not go into details because it's all still too painful. I now live by myself. The good news is I promised Mr. Patty of World Travel that I would return to work full time. I am the head tour guide of international travel. Who knows, you may be seeing me sometime in Sardinia, should I choose to."

Lucio's ears perked up. He expressed his condolences to her for the misfortune she suffered, but at the same time, silently it offered him hope.

He grabbed hold of both her hands, "Valeria, I am so sorry you went through all of this without me by your side. I understand your pain. I wish you had made contact with me. Thinking about it now, maybe you couldn't. My life has also changed. After you left, I felt as if I was losing my mind. I missed you so much. The walls of my apartment seemed as if they were closing in on me. Vittoria gave me a secret box that belonged to Chiara. It opened a can of worms that almost drove me insane! I discovered things about her past that I never knew. The information took me down! But something good always comes out from something bad, not so?"

"Yes, when one door closes, another opens. This is what gives us hope in life," responded Valeria in a low voice.

"I have also moved. I no longer live in Alghero; I am now retired. I took refuge at my cousin's resort, with a variety of animals, nature's greenery, rocky soil, creeks, lakes, and all the amazing colours and shapes of nature. It is soothingly therapeutic after living in the city for a long time. I help Attilio and his wife, Assunta, who prepares the most delicious meals. We have bus tours stopping by and we cater to overnight tourists. Life at the resort improved my general wellbeing. Then with my cousin's help, I made the decision to look for the young man from my wife's secret past. Every now and then I thought of you and indulged in memories of our own affair. I have missed you so; you could never imagine, Valeria. You were real, but forbidden to me, out of reach. I have been one miserable old man. Attilio has been kind and supportive. I could not have made it to here, if not for him and his family. And now here I am in Ottawa to complete the mission of finding Chiara's son, and the bonus I received was to find you again!"

Valeria felt his sincerity; he spoke with true feelings. They reached for each other and their lips sealed in a lingering kiss.

Lucio said, "Valeria, no more guilt, you are a widow and I am a widower; we are entitled to love each other freely, with no hang ups, agreed?"

"Lucio, we can talk about it more. My marriage has been loveless and my heart empty, until I met you. I am now fifty-nine and my life is passing by. Maybe I would still be able to enjoy some happiness in my remaining years."

Chapter Sixty

Life's Surprises

Lucio's evening in Valeria's company had surpassed his expectations. The sad but incredible updates on her life had brought him renewed hope. With much relief, he felt the shadows from the dark clouds that hovered over him for the longest time, finally lifted and converted to bright rainbows. He felt encouraged to freely ask if they could meet for lunch the next day.

"Valeria, my dear, we are on a time restraint. I would like you and your daughter to meet me for lunch, and that would also give you a chance to meet my wife's son. He's a fine young man; I have no doubt you are going to like him. I must also see him again before we depart. My cousin needs to get back home, and I must not take advantage of his kindness, therefore I would return with him. But I shall return soon! You must show me Niagara as I have never before visited that part of the world." He was fishing for an invite but Valeria seemed distracted. Then after a long pause she finally spoke.

"Signor Lucio, do you request the privilege of my expertise as your private tour guide? I am not sure if I can measure up to the charm and hospitality of the Sardinians."

He responded with a big hug and after letting her go she said, "How can I deny you that, Lucio, after how graciously you have treated me. You had restored my faith in the male gender. The days spent on your island were of great splendour."

"It's a promise; on my return to Sardinia I shall check to see how soon I can return to Canada."

363

Lucio returned to his hotel feeling like a teenager in love. Attilio had dozed off in front of the TV. He slapped Attilio's shoulder and said, "Cousin, our journey sure has been worthwhile; blessings from the heavens have come our way."

"I do say. Maybe I am wrong, Lucio, but you seem head over heels with that Valeria lady. I warn you, Assunta does not condone relationships with married women."

"Attilio, I got news for you; she is a widow. I invited her and her daughter to lunch tomorrow. I also invited Pablo to join us, and you will too!"

He had left a message on Pablo's phone to meet him and his cousin for lunch. He was sure, as kind as he was he wouldn't mind the two added guests. They were going to meet at Rideau Centre at an Italian restaurant. Later, they would be heading for the airport where Attilio had booked them on Alitalia for Rome.

The plan was to meet at the restaurant. Lucio always believed in being early. A table for five had been reserved. He anxiously awaited the arrival of Valeria and her daughter at the front lobby. Pablo had responded and left a message also that he would be able to join them. This was to be their temporary goodbye. Valeria arrived on time, accompanied by a lovely young lady with long blond hair and as attractive as her mother; they both smiled gracefully. Valeria had spotted Lucio in the distance, standing and waiting, just as he did in Sardinia. He gave her a sense of security; his caring manner was reassuring.

"Hello Lucio, how are you? This is my daughter, Rosy."

"My pleasure, Signor Lucio," she said as she extended her hand.

"Nice to meet you, Rosy. I must say you look a lot like your mother."

They walked to the table, and just as they finished the introduction with Attilio, Pablo arrived. Rosy immediately turned to him and gave him a gentle hug. Lucio and Attilio looked at each other speechlessly, then back to the young couple. Lucio broke the temporary silence, "Oh! You two know each other?"

"Yes, he is my boyfriend," answered Rosy.

Lucio could not believe what was happening. *How on earth could all these turns of events be taking place at one time! Was it a dream, or really happening right in front of my eyes?*

Valeria's voice brought him back to reality. "Lucio, Attilio, our young Pablo here is a student at Carleton University, and he's a friend of my daughter. They are both studying Architecture. They met in the first year while doing a project together."

Lucio said, "I don't believe this! Call it fate, call it the will of God, call it whatever you want, Valeria; Pablo is my wife's son; the young man I have been desperately searching for. Now I find out he is connected to your daughter and has brought me right back on your path!"

Pablo also looked confused as he asked, "Do you two know each other?"

"Yes, Pablo. Valeria and I worked together in Sardinia when she was promoting our island for a Canadian agency. As you know, I have never been to Canada. We ran into each other when we boarded the plane to Ottawa. Valeria was coming here to visit her daughter, and I was flying in to meet you. This is great! Let's drink to this happy reunion. It sure is worth celebrating!"

They all took their seats as Lucio ordered a bottle of Merlot and they toasted to unions and reunions. They gregariously engaged in conversation; there was so much to say and share among them all.

Lucio called out, "Pablo, I must say one thing to you, my young man, you sure have good taste in women."

Pablo smiled pleasingly as he admired his lovely Rosy. His cell phone rang and he excused himself to take a call, distancing himself a short way.

When he returned his face was solemn. They all sensed something was terribly wrong. Lucio reacted promptly and stood close to Pablo to offer support. "Bad news, Pablo?"

Pablo could hardly speak and lost his composure. Rosy hugged him, "What's wrong, my darling?"

Tears were flowing down his cheeks. "Father Gregory is no more." He lowered his chin in grief.

Attilio and Lucio looked at each other. "My God, we had just made it on time," said Attilio.

Chapter Sixty One

Love Conquers All

Although the meeting with father Gregory had been brief, Lucio would be forever grateful to him for the great work he did for unfortunate children, but especially for keeping Chiara's son safe and guiding him well. He put his arm lovingly around Pablo's shoulder to comfort him as he said, "My dear, Pablo, it's always painful to lose a dear one and I feel your pain. Father Gregory will no doubt be greatly missed. But he would certainly live on forever in the lives of the many people he has touched, including you, and us. Personally, I would always be indebted to him for leading me to you. I know I would never be able to replace your dear Godfather, Pablo, but please don't forget, I pledge to be here for you from now on, my long-lost son. In my inexperienced way, I promise to try and make up for the unfortunate experiences you have endured."

Attilio added, "By having you connect with Lucio and myself, is the last legacy your great Father has left you."

They were all trying to console Pablo. He was hurting at the moment. They all felt badly about his sad news among their happy ones. They offered him their love, support, and sympathy. He received much love, and they all promised their support for him. Eventually though, everyone needs to move on with their lives and pursue their own dreams.

Lucio's heart ached to leave Pablo; he wished he could stay behind with him. When he saw Rosy walk hand in hand with him, he felt relieved knowing that someone loved and cared for him. He pained about Valeria also. He hugged her and whispered in her ear,

"I love you." Holding her gaze, he promised, "And I promise to return to you soon."

After they parted, Valeria headed back to Niagara, her work was soon resumed at World Travel. The long hours of hard work she put in paid off handsomely; she had managed to make record bookings. Mr. Patty was all smiles and well pleased with her achievement.

Lucio would call her regularly, encouraging her in every way, and profusely professing his love and admiration for her. She was now living for his phone calls and longed to hear his voice every day; he missed her immensely from across the ocean. His utmost desire and plan was to convince her to bridge the distance between them.

He also kept in touch regularly with Pablo. They would discuss his studies, assignments, and exams. Lucio showed total interest in him. In his heart, he wished he could give back to Pablo all that he had missed out in life. Pablo never questioned about his biological father and Lucio often wondered if it would ever surface. Given the circumstances he thought the topic was better left alone. Lucio's moderate savings were limited but he was prepared to share whatever little he possessed with Pablo; he felt this was the son he never had. He hoped Valeria would feel the same too.

Since returning to Sardinia, Lucio found his focus had shifted. What before was simple acceptance was now no more. He admired how his cousin worked hard to realize his dream. It all made sense. He was rewarded by the love and affection of his family; Assunta's devotion, their children, and grandchildren, all made the home harmonious. No wonder he had felt good in this refuge. But now that he had found Pablo, and Valeria was now free and available, he swore to himself it was time he made things happen. He felt downright cheated by life. Both himself and Pablo had been robbed and affected by the ugliness of misfortune. But now, by the will of God, there was Pablo; a gift to him from Chiara, Pablo's mother. He figured if Chiara didn't fall sick so early in her life, the child would not have been abandoned. Maybe one day she would have confessed her past to him and revealed the boy's identity. Now Valeria was widowed, and with her children if she was willing, they could all be one big family. With an earnest heart, he wanted to believe the universe still had some happiness in store for him. He thought to himself, *what I wished to achieve has materialized by a series of lucky events, not by will alone.* Once again, he talked to his confidant.

"Attilio, can you manage without me for a short time?"

"What's on your mind, cousin?"

"I want to go back to Canada, to Pablo and Valeria; I need to see them again."

"Lucio, your happiness is our happiness. Never mind about the resort or worry about if I can manage; there is plenty of help around here. You go and visit Pablo and Valeria. Her Rosy strikes me as a fine young lady. Yes, I think you should go."

In no time Lucio was back in Canada, happily accepted by his newly found son in Ottawa. But his old soul came alive when embraced by Valeria's warmth and gracefulness. Spring had rolled around, and as previously requested, Lucio wanted to tour and educate himself about the splendour of Niagara. Nature had sprung alive and renewed, in May.

Wide eyed he admired the amazing Niagara Falls. "What an unbelievable creation," he exclaimed while holding Valeria close to him. She smiled at him, feverishly in love.

"Yes, the Falls experience never fails to leave people in awe, Lucio." He noted the well designed and manicured gardens around the Falls. The magic of the lights at night were spectacular. The sculptured array of greenery and flowers were artfully designed. Cascading fountains soothed the mind like gentle music. Valeria detested the sight of the casino but still did the tour with Lucio.

The magnificent Niagara wineries with wine tasting events

intrigued Lucio. At the world-famous Shaw theatre, they enjoyed a couple of popular plays. The marvellous town of Niagara-On-The-Lake offered a lifetime's worth of pleasurable sightseeing, with its magnificent array of flowers skillfully arranged in every colour, shape and form. Its quaint coffee shops which served Canadian and English desserts, the ice cream shops, and restaurants were all delightful. Lucio and Valeria walked hand in hand, truly enjoying each other's company. Niagara looked unusual to her; she was admiring her own town with different eyes. After some days in Niagara, Lucio took the train to Ottawa, and there he spent some quality time with Pablo. With Lucio's genuine kindness, Pablo's shyness slowly vanished. He asked Lucio, "Tell me about Sardinia, Mrs. Abrosky has peaked my curiosity since she returned from her business trip. Now I can't wait to see it. She says it is the most beautiful island she has ever visited."

"Pablo, it is my wish that you visit soon and meet the rest of Attilio's family, my relatives; they would be your family too."

"Yes, I would love to, Lucio, thank you. But right now, I work two jobs. That is how I support myself. My school has highly recommended me for a job opportunity in my field this summer. Maybe I can visit before I start working?"

"Should we set a date? I would take care of your airfare, and I also want to discuss helping you with some of your school fees."

"Lucio, thank you for the thought, but you don't have to! You hardly know me!"

"Pablo!" He gave him a stern look. "You forget I was married to your mother? I do know you; you are family!"

Pablo had warmed up to Lucio from their many long-distance phone chats. Lucio had gladly filled him in on things about his mother that a son should know, like the lively, loving, and charitable person she was. He was careful to conceal any unpleasantness of her past; he felt Pablo had suffered enough and didn't need to hear anything distressing about his mother's difficult past, nor her horrendous illness which led to her death at a young age. They got along quite well, and they were happy with one another.

They were both heading to Niagara for the weekend and Rosy would join them later. Pablo was hesitant, then said, "Lucio, I apologize for bringing this up. I must confide in you that Rosy's father rubbed me the wrong way. I stopped visiting the house with Rosy. He was arrogant and had a way of putting people down, especially me. He referred to me as "that foreigner boy," maybe due to my Latino skin. I truly love Rosy and she is not to blame for her father's behaviour. She felt badly for me. She understands me."

"I never met him so I cannot comment, but I am sorry to hear that he was not amiable to you."

"I am sorry how he died, and that he is dead. He was the main cause of arguments between myself and Rosy."

"How odd, Pablo. I felt attracted to Mrs. Abrosky, and I am a widower, so in a different way he was an obstacle for me too."

"Is that so? She is a pleasant lady, and I think she went through plenty with him."

The two confided in each other like two old friends. They bonded and their friendship genuinely grew. Each thrived on the other's company.

Lucio's intentions to visit Canada again was not only to see Pablo, but also to have a serious discussion with Valeria. He felt they were both getting on with age and time was too precious to waste. Since they were both free, he thought the sooner they could get together the better. He had done a lot of thinking and planning. He wanted to share his ideas with Valeria, hoping she would feel the same about their future together.

Valeria affectionately embraced him on his return from Ottawa. They lingered together comfortable in each other's arms. "Valeria, my darling, I have missed you so." He took her hand and placed it on his heart. "Do you feel how fast it's beating? I cannot bear to be without you, my dear. We have a lot to discuss." Valeria missed him just as much. She felt safe now that he was there with her. She kept silent, ridden with guilt of being recently widowed.

Once at her home, he sat her down, took both her hands and held them together in his. Valeria's heart fluttered like a disoriented butterfly; she tried to get up to serve drinks. Lucio held her firmly, "No, just sit here with me; no drinks. I want to stay totally sober. Valeria, I want you to come back with me to Sardinia. Or, I will remain here until you kick me out. We belong together, Valeria!"

"Lucio, I understand how you feel, but I have connections and obligations here; my children, my job. I cannot just pick up and go! Besides, I am financially broke."

"Valeria, I have a proposition to make to you. I don't want to take away your freedom or jeopardize your job. Your obligation as a mother towards your children is important; I understand how you feel. I am not a rich man, whatever I have I wish to share with you and Pablo, and your family. I want us all to be a family and no more distance between us. We need to be together, my dear. I want us to get married. To be fair to you, I am prepared to make our homes on both sides of the Atlantic. I can go back and buy a villa in one of your favourite spots in Sardinia. Here in Canada we can have a condo or whatever you choose. Valeria, it would not be fair to you to take you away for my own selfish need to spend my life with you. So, you can have the best of both worlds, if you would accept me as your companion, your husband. Yes, me, this miserable old man. I am at your mercy, Valeria, my love."

Valeria sat there feeling numb. Slowly she took his face in her hands and looked at him as happy tears rolled down her face. She had never known such kindness, such sincerity, such love from a man, in her entire life. Here she was now, with this man begging her to accept his unselfish love. He was willing to go to any extent to make her happy and comfortable.

"Lucio, some God up there must have saved you for me, for Pablo, and for my family. How privileged I would be to have you as part of my family." She kissed him and hugged him affectionately, sobbing softly into his shoulder. He held on to her tightly. "How can I refuse you," she mumbled.

With the blessing of the combination of their children, Valeria and Lucio got married at St. Anna's church in Niagara. Mrs. Nora Jennings, Susan Butler, and Florence, were among the guests. They congratulated the happy couple. Mrs. Jennings was truly happy for her beloved friend. The smart old fox thought, *good for you Valeria!*

Lucio returned to Sardinia and showed Assunta and Attilio his marriage certificate, to prove to them that his union with Valeria was legal. He knew they scorned any relationship not within the ten commandments. He had a big project on his hands; to shop for a villa on the island that Valeria would love. He needed a large place to accommodate the children when they visited, and maybe grandchildren one day. Valeria had promised to fly in as soon as he was ready for her.

After two weeks of high searching he found a marvelous place sitting on the hilly side of La Costa Smeralda; a two storey building in white stucco, with impressive roman pillars stately holding up a square overlay to the double front entrance. The traditionally designed home contained a terrace overlooking the golden sandy beach at the indented coastline, with its hues from emerald green to the deeper blues of the sea. It was a paradise on earth with the perfect climate. All Lucio needed was Valeria's approval. Valeria soon flew to Sardinia. When her husband took her on the tour of the new place, she turned to him and said, "You couldn't have picked a better place."

"All for your liking, Valeria."

She admired the spectacular residence wide eyed, while asking, "Darling! Can we afford it?" After all, she had been left broke.

"My gift to you, to share with our family."

The magnificent new home became Lucio and Valeria's new residence, with open invitations to their combined families. Valeria moved to Sardinia; she was open to enjoying both worlds. Lucio had welcomed her with red roses and champagne. Vittoria, Lucio's past helper had set up a table on the terrace with exquisite appetizers. He poured two glasses of champagne and handed one to Valeria. He toasted, "To us, my dearest."

He placed an arm around her waist and led her towards the edge of the terrace. The sun was disappearing behind the horizon. "Valeria, my darling, look up at the sky, do you know that means a beautiful day awaits us tomorrow?" The view was breathtaking. Valeria was overjoyed. In disbelief she pulled Lucio closer, "Lucio, I can honestly say, I have been bestowed by love and splendour, and all because of you, my darling."

La Costa Smeralda became their favourite place where they hoped to host many family celebrations in the future. Valeria continued with her tour guiding career, catering to tourists from Europe and the rest of the globe. She fully enjoyed her job at this later stage in her life. Her knowledge, eloquence, and self-confidence were well received by most travellers; their generous tips reflected their appreciation of her work. She would return home and empty her purse and pockets on the bed. The denominations of the tips were in U.S., Euros, and other currencies. She would call Lucio to come and see her good fortune. "Darling, we must be grateful for our blessings." Smiling, she would freely hug him and enjoy the warmth of his body against hers.

"We were meant to be together, my darling. With you by my side, Valeria, I am the happiest man on earth."

Her life felt blessed and fulfilled with his devotion to her. She would sometimes take him by his hand and lead him away. "Lucio, let's go run bare feet on the sand. We are still in time to catch the splendour of a Sardinian's sunset before the sun goes down." Like two young teens, they would race on the beach, coming together later, energized, in love.

"Oh! Canada! Lucio, we can't forget Canada!"

When their heart desired, they would fly to Canada. There again, Valeria would continue with her work with the agency, pursuing her passion while Lucio waited for her at home in Niagara with a Sardinian dinner. "Are you tired, my darling," he would ask.

"How can I be tired, my dear? My work isn't work, but an expression of love."

Their lives continued with many family celebrations, and whatever bounty life presented. Pablo was right in there as part of the clan. With his newly adopted family, and Rosy, he felt special; life now had deeper meaning for him.

For Valeria and Lucio, their hearts had found fulfillment and their souls became one. With the air in their splendid island ever so pure, their preferred choice of home was Sardinia, and their children agreed on that. They would sit on their terrace holding hands, until they reached a ripe old age, like so many of the centenarians on their island, all blessed in one way or another, by love and splendour.

About The Author

Gina Iafrate is bilingual. She writes in both Italian and English. Originally from Italy, Gina Iafrate now divides her time between Hollywood, Florida; Niagara, Ontario; and Europe. Gina's works have been exhibited at The Pier 21 Museum in Halifax, and in Phoenix Magazine, The Horizon, and Author's Voice.

She is a 2016 Book Excellence Award Finalist.

She lives with her husband in Hollywood, Florida, and Niagara, Ontario, Canada.

Other books by Gina Iafrate:

The English Professor

The Girl From The Cornfield

Soon to be published:

Releases From my Soul: A Collection of Anthologies.

More information is available at her website at
www.GinaIafrate.com.